LORD DEMON

LORD DEMON

Roger Zelazny
and
Jane Lindskold

AVON · EOS

AVON BOOKS, INC.

1350 Avenue of the Americas
New York, New York 10019

Copyright © 1999 by The Amber Corporation and Jane Lindskold
Interior design by Kellan Peck
ISBN: 0-380-97333-2

Library of Congress Cataloging in Publication Data:
Zelazny, Roger.
Lord demon / Roger Zelazny and Jane Lindskold.
p. cm.
I. Lindskold, Jane M. II. Title.

PS3576.E43L66 1999
813'.54—dc21

99-20950
CIP

First Avon Eos Printing: August 1999

AVON EOS TRADEMARK REG. U.S. PAT. OFF. AND IN OTHER COUNTRIES, MARCA REGISTRADA, HECHO EN U.S.A.

Printed in the U.S.A.

FIRST EDITION

QPM 10 9 8 7 6 5 4 3 2 1

www.avonbooks.com/eos

For Jim, with much love.
And for Paul Dellinger—thanks for all the letters.

LORD DEMON

I

IT WAS ORANGE. It was green. It was one of my best. I had decided against a pot or a vase and had created a bottle for the first time in ages. The crafting had taken me the better part of one hundred and twenty years, on and off. Depending on their intended use, bottles have taken me far longer and also far shorter periods of time than other items.

I explored the interior of this one to my satisfaction, manifested myself outside of it, and clenched my left fist until the ring I wore upon that hand began to glow. When it had reached a sufficient level, I pressed it against the bottom of the bottle, marking it with the sign of Kai Wren, master bottlemaker, my sign.

I stepped back and regarded it there on the tabletop, allowing myself a faint smile. Then I seated myself cross-legged upon a heap of cushions and relaxed into the moment.

Kai Wren bottles are of course priceless—going back over fourteen centuries. I don't know how many of them I've made over all that time. Virtually indestructible, they will keep any

1

wine decanted into them fresh for a span greater than two normal human lifetimes. They will do the same with cut flowers. And even if nothing is placed within them, they are said to bring their owners considerable good luck—by way of wealth, good health, happiness, long life. And this, too, is true. I place a certain measure of my particular *chi* within their structure, and my will is made manifest within my work.

A few knowledgeable private collectors have gone to inordinate lengths to obtain Kai Wren specimens for their collections. Sorcerers have sought for them and conjured with them, for they do lend themselves to magical usage. A few Oriental art experts in museums and galleries know of them—and there are full-time scouts who make a living searching out my pieces for their wealthy employers.

Oliver O'Keefe entered the room with a catlike silence, realizing that I had finally completed this one and that possibly— in ways incomprehensible to him—I was happy. I have made a study of emotions and I think it may be that I was.

After placing the bottle on the table once more, I rose. O'Keefe grinned at me. He was a short man, solid though not stocky, with fair skin that bore a host of freckles, and close-cropped, sandy hair.

We made quite a contrast, he and I, no matter what shape I took.

" 'Tis a pretty one, boss," he said. "Even better than that green one you did back in the 1700s, I think, and that's always been my favorite."

"Why, thank you, Ollie. I've a special fondness for this one myself."

" 'Tis a Saturday night, and Tony's on duty at Pizza Heaven. Feel like a celebration?"

I smiled. "What shall we get on it?"

"Well, you always like your pepperoni," he said.

"That's true. And perhaps a few mushrooms—be they very fresh."

"I would check on this, of course."

"Of course. Sausage? If it smells fresh?"

"Excellent idea."

"You suggest something."

"Some sliced bell pepper?"

"Very good. Might as well pick up a few bottles of Mexican beer."

"Certainly."

"There's still plenty of money in the barrel?"

"Oh, yes."

I smiled again. It was virtually the same order time after time. But we enjoyed our little ritual in arriving at it.

I watched him zip into his jacket and go. The man served me. He'd been with me for over three hundred years, what with four first-class spells that kept him in good repair. But he was unlike any servant I'd employed before.

I'd met him in a pub in Dublin, where he'd gone to sell his fiddle. In my ignorance, I asked him what a fiddle was, to which he proceeded to play his for me. Instead of buying it, I offered him a job, and we'd been together ever since.

I am not overfond of going out into the world of humans, and Ollie was an excellent go-between for me on such excursions. He was glib, personable, and he always seemed to know his way around. This is no small talent, given how quickly the world of humans has changed these recent centuries.

I left my glassblowing lab and strolled, admiring my wall hangings, my collection of rugs. I could have gone on forever. My personal bottle—which this was—is an entire world unto itself, its interior noncontinuous with human time and space. Any of those bottles of which I had spoken contained their worlds. You could fill them with water and put flowers in without disturbing one. Or, if you could figure out how to enter, you could make your way inside without getting your feet wet.

Mine has its own strange flora and fauna, including a troupe of insubstantial milkweed fairies who dwell in a curtained-off section where a light, misty rainstorm has been going on for about thirteen centuries now. There are ogres, too, and dragons, and other creatures even stranger.

The temperature within my bottle is gently clement, though I allow snow in the mountains. I maintain a vast forest, complete with hidden grottos, ruins, and mossy granite boulders on which strange shadows dance despite the arguments of light.

There is an ocean as well, for when I feel like swimming or sailing.

Despite the bottle's enclosed environment, we will not suffocate within it. Once, long ago, my bottle dwelled for some centuries at the bottom of the East China Sea following a shipwreck. Not a trace of the waters without disturbed our comforts, although we did have a bit of trouble receiving guests.

Our bottle-owners have these treasures at their fingertips all their lives, though most of them know it not. Even in ignorance, ownership of a Kai Wren bottle always benefits one. Those who know its secrets may lengthen their lives for centuries by taking a big vacation within—this is what has become of a lot of the old sages, many of whom I still visit.

Giving way to a small desire to celebrate, I found my way— "outward" I guess you'd call it—through a small, perpetually misty and twilit region of mountains calculated to resemble a Taoist painting. For me, this is a kind of Faerie, where a man could hide himself and beautifully sleep the sleep of a Rip Van Winkle, where a lady could become a Sleeping Beauty in a rose-tangled castle and cave grown into a jade mountainside.

I heard a hearty howl from my left and another from my right. I walked on. Always good to let the boss know you're on the job.

After a time, an orange fu dog the size of a Shetland pony appeared to the left, a green one to the right. They seated themselves close to me, their great, fluffy tails curved over their backs.

"Hello," I said softly. "How's the frontier?"

"Nothing unnatural," growled Shiriki, the green one. "We passed the O'Keefe recently on his way out, but that is all."

Chamballa merely studied me with those great round eyes set in a flat face above a wide mouth. I have said that she was orange in color, but her coat was no garish citrus hue. It was closer to the ruddy glow of a coal that has not yet become fringed with ash.

I nodded.

"Good."

I had found them some nine and three-quarter centuries ago, half-starved, dying of thirst—for even some more and less than natural creatures have their needs. Their forgotten temple had fallen apart, and they were a pair of unemployed temple dogs nobody wanted, roaming the Gobi. I gave them water and food and permitted them to come back to my bottle with me, though I was a creature such as they had been cautioned about. I had always avoided contact with temple dogs if I possibly could. Me and my like, they'd been trained to rend into tiny pieces, to be carried off to a variety of uncomfortable places, with a mess of dog-magic for company and security.

So we never talked employment. I just told them that if they cared to live in the abandoned dragon's cave in my Twilight Lands, there was fresh water nearby, and I would see that there was food. And I would like if they would keep an eye on things for me. And if there was anybody nearby that they needed simply to howl.

After a few centuries details were forgotten and only the fact of their residency remains. They call me Lord Kai and I call them Shiriki and Chamballa.

I walked on. Where I'd no need whatsoever to go outside what with O'Keefe tending to everything, there was that small desire to celebrate, to walk and to breathe the night air.

Coming to the edge of the worlds, I considered my appearance. Within my bottle I wore my natural shape: humanlike in that it possessed two arms, two legs, a recognizable torso and head, the usual number of eyes and suchlike. However, I stood eight feet tall on my taloned feet (these possessed of five toes) and my skin was a deep blue with a trace of purple. Around my eyes were angular segments of black. Some have supposed these are cosmetic (indeed, at one point a thousand years ago there was a fashion for such), but they are natural. They make my pupil-less dark eyes seem to glow and give my countenance a forbidding cast, even when I might not wish it.

Yes, this would not do for the world of humans. Quickly, I slipped into the human guise I use for my infrequent journeys without: a Chinese male of mature years, glossy black hair untouched by gray, average tall, but with an aura of command. I shaped my clothes into the dull fashions of the American city in which we now dwelled, sighing inwardly for the elegant robes of bygone China.

These preparations a matter of desire, I manifested outside the bottle with barely a pause in my stride. As I had wished, I was in a garage belonging to the son of the late lady who'd formerly kept the bottle on a parlor table. Either location was an easy one for our comings and goings. The son has not yet decided whether to give the bottle to his wife or to keep it on the table, where he enjoys looking at it. I had no opinion at the moment, and so stayed out of the matter.

Letting myself out of the garage's side door, I strolled off in the direction—several blocks away—of Tony's Pizza Heaven.

It was a starry but moonless night, crisp and breezy. I knew that something was wrong when, as I passed one of the town's small parks, I scented blood and pizza on the air. And demon.

I faded. I moved with absolute silence. All of the ways I have learned to inflict death and pain over the years rose up and came with me. At that moment, I was one of the most dangerous things on the planet.

. . . And I saw the tree and them.

They had hung him from it, upside down, from a lower branch and punctured him in many places, whence they drank. With their nasty little teeth, they tore off pieces on which they dined.

I drew nearer. There were six altogether around poor O'Keefe's dead and dangling carcass. They were two feet tall, yellow-eyed, portly, and solid. Their complexions ran from green through gray to yellowish. Their claws were short and sharp. A discarded pizza box lay on the grass nearby.

"How do you like your human?" one asked, talking around some slobbersome gobbet.

"Better than pizza," replied another.

"Hey, try a slice with some pepperoni before you knock it," said a third.

I raised my hands, appearing within the circle of fire which now rose about us. From their waists down, all six of them were turned to stone. They squeaked like guinea pigs and, one by one, their gazes were drawn to my blazing countenance.

"Uh-oh. It's one of the big guys," said the nearest.

"Hey, boss," ventured another. "We can't pay the proper

obsequies with our legs all stiff like this. Good joke, though. Ha-ha. Turn back now?"

I reached out and picked up the one who had just spoken, his voice going silent as the rest of him stiffened. Then I squeezed, enlarging my hands until I held but fistfuls of gravel. These I tossed into the air, watching them burst into flame and fall as a small firestorm, the ashes burning away in a small wind that rose as they neared the earth. I gave the creature no possibility for any sort of regeneration.

"Hey, we sorry," cried one.

"Yeah. What we do?" said another.

I reached out and pulverized the second one, making the world a richer place by its absence. The others squealed again.

"Silence! I want stupid demon talk I ask for talk!" I ordered. "You be shit-brained spoilers of everything you touch. Not worth nothing most of the time."

"Right, we not important at all," agreed another. "Little shits, like you say. You one of the big bosses. We no mean get in your way. Let us go. We be your slaves forever and ever. You say 'shit,' we eat shit, you laugh—just like that. Want us hit enemies, rub feet, bring wine—whatever you want."

I blackened him to ash, and the others cowered.

The fourth finally turned his head toward O'Keefe.

"The man," he said at last. "You do this because we kill the man—no?"

"At last," I said, "someone asks why."

"Yes, sir," said the fourth. "He your human?"

"That's right."

"Maybe your servant many years?"

"You begin to understand."

"We no know. We just little shit-brains, like you say. If you be little dickheads like us, you still wouldn't destroy great lord's property. May be shithead, but not fools. We sorry."

"Yeah," said the fifth. "We sorry big bunch now we know. Let us go and—"

I turned him to dust and watched the tiny fire tornado he became burn itself to nothing. I looked back at the fourth one, who looked quickly away, saying nothing.

"You are smarter and more polished than the others. As

Confucius said, the form is more important than the content. You knew O'Keefe not and can feel nothing for him, yet you know what is right to say of this man."

"Me too!" said the sixth (and remaining) demon. I ignored him.

"You cannot completely help being what you are," I said. "Yet you have dwelled in palaces," I said to the fourth, "and you in the gutters," to the sixth, "and something of both has stuck."

They hung their heads. I left a long silence. Finally, the fourth one spoke:

"It was Tuvoon, the Smoke Ghost," he said.

I looked at him.

"I know that you would know our sort does not do this kind of thing much these days. You would want to know who gave us the *shen* coin and told us when and where to do the man," he went on.

I nodded.

"This is a very grave charge," I said.

He, too, nodded.

"One I not make lightly," he proceeded, "without solid proof for you, and knowing it will probably cost my life."

At that, the sixth one howled.

"Shouldn't've said nothing!" it told the other. "Now he do flash-burn and we die."

The other shuffled and struck his fellow's head. "Sometimes lie is bad," he said, "and sometimes silence. This time only truth maybe save us. Use head. Learn to think."

Rocking on his stony base, the sixth demon prostrated himself at my feet and lay still.

"See? He learn a little," said his companion, and I realized that in his odd way he was slipping in a word for his buddy's life.

"Stay on your belly," I told the one who was kowtowing, and, releasing some of the stiffness from the fourth demon's legs, I motioned him a little off to the side.

"Did Tuvoon give you any indication why he did what he did?" I whispered.

It was about then, I saw that the little demon realized that they might live if his buddy didn't learn any more of what we were saying. He withdrew even farther away, lowered his voice even more.

"No, sir," he said, gesturing across the park toward an alley. "Another demon found us scrounging over there, and he sounded us out on the job. That was yesterday. Said the man might be by tonight because he often passes this way on Saturdays. The demon offered *shen* coin, and, when we agreed, gave us a few then. Told us Tuvoon would be in town two days off. We supposed to get the rest tomorrow."

"Did he say anything—anything at all—indicating why he might have wanted this thing done?"

"No, sir. He did not."

"Are you supposed to see Tuvoon tomorrow?"

"That's right."

I glared at the stars.

"Eve?"

"Yes."

"Tell him that I will be waiting tomorrow night at this time, and at this place's analog on our own plane, and that I will bring a piece of his soul with me, for I demand full satisfaction."

I heard the little demon swallow, then, "Yes, sir," having heard of—but I'm sure never seen—a duel of this sort.

After freeing him and the other demon, I gently took Ollie down from his tree and turned away.

"Uh, we can do that for you, boss," said the demon with whom I'd held the most converse.

"No. You've touched him enough. You're free. I'm letting you and the other worthless one go. Stay out of my way, and you'll go on living. What's your name, anyhow?"

"Ba Wa," he replied.

"Ba Wa," I repeated. "I will remember you."

To his credit, he did not blanch more than a little.

"I just want to say that I'm sorry, again, though, Lord Demon."

I did not respond, and then he was gone.

II

AS I ENTERED the bottle, I could hear Shiriki's and Chamballa's great, long, mournful cries. They knew.

I bathed Ollie in his bathroom, dressed him in one of his best suits, and laid a preservation spell upon his entire room. I closed its door as I departed. I ought to make funeral arrangements. He was nominally Christian and might appreciate one of their rites. Perhaps I should try to get something in that area arranged tomorrow, before the duel. Yes, probably.

I located a Christian temple called Holy Cross the next day. I entered there and wandered until I found the man in charge.

"I want to give my friend a Christian burial," I said.

"Well, you've come to the right place. What funeral home is he in?"

"None. I laid him out in his bedroom."

"I see. Traditional. Would you like him buried in our cemetery?"

I nodded.

"Yes. Let's do that."

"As I see it, the only thing that you need is a death certificate."

"What's that?"

"A piece of paper going from the Coroner's Office to the Office of Vital Statistics saying that this man is indeed dead."

"Well, of course he's dead. I wouldn't be here if he weren't dead. How do I get this paper?"

"Go to see the coroner."

"Who is he?"

"I'll draw you a— Never mind. I'll drive you over. Uh, about the funeral itself, what were you planning to spend on it?"

"What is customary?'

"Uh, a few thousand."

I had about twenty thousand in large bills in my pocket. I withdrew them and placed them on his desk.

He counted. He seemed for a moment to be choking, before he swept it all away and conveyed it to a wall safe.

"Yes. I'll be glad to help you. We shouldn't have any problems. Your friend will have the best funeral I ever gave."

A bit of very minor hypnosis left the coroner with a much smaller bill on his desk and me with a death certificate in my hand. I'd had him alter a few dates from what I knew them to be.

I passed the certificate to the minister, who asked whether I needed any help with the body. I told him no, I'd bring it over myself later.

The following evening, I arrived at the proper time and place bearing Tuvoon's spirit sword. To have a spirit sword created for you is something of a backhanded compliment. It means that demonkind views you as dangerous enough to have one of these special weapons forged against you. I bet that Tuvoon—like me—could have lived without the compliment, but I wasn't thinking about the pain a spirit sword causes. I was engulfed in fury.

Tuvoon and his mother—Viss of the Terrible Tongue—were waiting in the park. Viss wore the appearance of a plump Chinese woman of middle years, but her skin was brick red and her eyes were unreadable.

Tuvoon the Smoke Ghost was a more spectacular sight. Like some others of our kind, he is only partially substantial, no matter upon which plane he dwells. Today he was solid from the waist up, to all appearances a handsome Oriental youth of pleasing mien. From the waist down, he seemed to be made of gray-and-white smoke. Where his bare feet should have been, there was nothing.

I laid my burden on the ground at the feet of Viss (for she had been my teacher), stepped back three paces, and kowtowed.

She stooped, raised Tuvoon's bane. From above, I heard her say, "Seven Fingers's blades have not lost their cunning."

"True."

"Excuse me for staring, but it is not often one holds one's son's life."

Seven Fingers had been our master swordmaker, but even he feared Viss, who had been teacher to many of our kind. It was rumored that Viss had tutored a god or two along the way. She'd been my teacher; also, Tuvoon's.

"You know, of course," she said, "that if you kill my son, you will die in the next instant."

"Unfortunately, yes," I said.

I heard a sound near my left hand. I moved quite slowly to regard its source. The blade had been driven into the ground between my first and second fingers, leaving the webbing intact by about one sixteenth of an inch.

I heard a small chittering as Tuvoon came to stand beside his mother.

"Your friends?" he asked.

I looked toward the source of the chittering. Ba Wa's companion, the stupid demon, was selling tickets and seating people.

"Excuse me," I said to Tuvoon and Viss.

Making my way through the crowd, I found Ba Wa in due time. When he saw me coming, he began to tremble.

"What you doin'?" I asked.

"Thought I'd make a little on the side. The old American way. Like truth."

I shook my head.

"No," I said.

"No?"

"No. You got it. Give back tickets. Clear the field. I need you for this, or I would kill you. You disgrace!"

"Right, boss. Sorry about that, boss. I take care of right now."

I retreated to the others.

"One of the little shit demons was getting uppity," I said. "Everything's okay now. Give them a few minutes to clear the field."

"No," Tuvoon said. "That was your responsibility. We fight now."

"Very well," I said, taking the spirit sword from where Viss had set it and raising the blade in its particular attitude, divided by its spirit. "Let us begin."

I came on in a rapid attack mode, swung twice, connected once, doing only superficial injury. Tuvoon moved about me, found an opening, tried a second tack, failed.

"Your honor has been satisfied. Blood has been drawn," Viss remarked.

"They're stalling!" I heard someone call. I tripled my pace and cut again. For the first time metal touched metal with a sound like a glassy bell.

Tuvoon moved like a whirlwind, practically invisible even in his solid parts. I barely managed to avoid the next blow. Above my increased breathing I could hear the shrieks of the rabble.

Then I was disarmed, as was Tuvoon. Someone had thrown a blanket over our weapons, tangling them.

"Enough! This is a farce," Viss said. She held the blanket. "Sheathe both blades."

We did, though they remained close at hand.

"Come over here. I want to talk while the alley trash departs."

We followed her.

"Kindly tell me the cause," she said, fastening me with a gaze that took me back to centuries before when I had quailed before my teacher, "for this duel."

I answered, "Last night, a dear servant of mine was murdered in the human-world analog to this park by some of the scruffy little scrub demons who hang out there. Under questioning, they told me that Tuvoon was their boss and that he was delivering payment in *shen* coins for the job.

"Son!" she said. "What is the truth of this?"

"Well, I guess I was going to bring them some money," he said. "Devor gave me it last night, when he heard I'd be passing this way. Said it was to cover his gambling losses."

"With them?" Viss asked.

"Yes."

"Some people have no self-respect. Who would gamble with street shit?"

"Devor apparently." Tuvoon chuckled. He did not seem too unhappy to have our duel ended. Two fingers pressed closed the thin slash in his upper arm where I had cut him.

I reached out across a great distance and snagged the fleeing Ba Wa. I drew him to us.

"No! No!" Ba Wa cried, covering his head with his hands. "I stop bets. Even now Wong Pang give money back!!"

"I want to know," I said, "whether anyone was gambling with Devor the night before my servant was killed."

"Oh, yeah. Pitt, One-Eye, Bat's Laughter, and Roaming Nose played coins for a time with Devor."

"Who won?"

"Pitt, mainly. I think."

"Could that have been what Tuvoon was to drop off the following night—Devor's gaming debt?" Viss asked.

"I suppose it could have."

"Anybody got any other questions?" I asked. "No? In that case, depart!" I told Ba Wa.

He was gone in an instant.

"You were going to fight Tuvoon to the death on that scant evidence!" Viss said angrily.

"Well, I was mad," I said.

"Put up your blades!" she commanded, and such was the force of her personality that neither of us considered not obeying.

We both stowed our weapons extradimensionally, only the

hilts remained, reduced to the size of tie tacks. The one I fastened to the edge of my trouser pocket was a polished piece of smoky quartz.

"Well, which of you guys is going to buy me coffee?" Viss said, her tone softening only slightly.

The brick red faded from her complexion so she now wore the appearance of a stocky, middle-aged woman about five and a half feet tall, hair slightly unkempt. Tuvoon rearranged himself so that his less solid parts were hidden by his clothing.

"I think it's my turn," I said.

We slipped into the human world, using one of the established Gates. After so many centuries of converse with the Earth plane, demonkind has established several of these to various points around the globe. If one wants to go to somewhere there isn't a public Gate—like when I went to Ireland—the best way is to enter one of the unihabited planes shunted off from our own. These planes, commonly known as traveling planes, have been stocked with mapping spheres. Of course, there are private Gates, like mine into San Francisco, but using one of those without the permission of the owner is considered very bad form.

After we arrived on the Earth plane, Viss walked us a good part of the way across town, to the diner she claimed had the best coffee. I have to admit, it wasn't bad.

Seated in a booth, staring out into the night, she said, "We have to learn what is going on. Suddenly, there is more to it than simply the killing of your servant. It was either a challenge to you or an attempt to make my son look guilty. I know Devor from a long time ago. He had a reputation as spendthrift gambler and an indulger in *imbue*."

"Sounds as if he hasn't changed much," I said.

While most of us enjoy gambling, demons don't seem to have a whole lot of vices—foibles and egocentricities, yes; vices, no—and *imbue* is about the only drug that can affect us. Devor had always seemed to have something of a hankering for it. It is expensive, too, and getting more and more so every day, I understand—as the supply shrinks.

"Is he an enemy of yours?" she asked.

"No," I replied. "Don't much care for him—but not to the point of death."

"Does he have any close friends?"

"Passion Flower, Snow Goon, Night Bride, the Walker," Tuvoon answered. "Hard to say how close they are."

"Any of them particularly after you, Kai Wren?"

"No reason I can think of."

She glanced at her son, who shook his head.

"So much for the obvious," she said. "Though none of them is precluded, of course."

I nodded. "Of course. Strange, though, thinking of having real, dyed-in-the-wool enemies after centuries of peace."

"Relatives?" she asked.

"No, lost the last of mine in the wars."

The wars were about a thousand years ago, on another plane, and pretty much finished off the High and the Mighty: i.e., us Good Guys won. Some of the real old evils passed at that time, some of the worst things from the oldest times finally bought it in the Demon Wars. We took our losses, too, as is the way of those things.

"Our bottle," she said, "the one you paid me with for your martial training . . ."

"Yes? Got any problems and I'll fix them. Promise. That, or make you a new one."

"No problems," she said, "in the whole twelve centuries we've had it. Snuggest place I ever lived. I really got to think of it as home. Felt I ought to tell you, that's all. I appreciate someone who knows what he's doing."

I laughed.

"Coming from you—" I began. "Thanks."

We sipped our coffee.

After a time, she said, "You know, I sometimes think our kind is too solitary. Loners sometimes get a tendency to magnify everything that happens to them. Then we might brood on it and one day just blow up, or go into total depravity."

"I've heard this notion before," I said, "and I think you're probably right. Trouble is, I don't make friends easily."

Tuvoon laughed.

"I know what you mean," he said. "Mom and I do have a few friends, though, and I frequently make it to the Conventicle."

Viss snorted.

"They only meet once every fifty years," she observed.

"Gives you something to look forward to," Tuvoon said.

We all laughed, and when the time came we had a second cup of coffee. We discussed again an age-old speculation as to how our feelings compared with humans'. Hate we could understand, but we all wondered about love. Was there really such a thing, or did humans the world over lie to each other every time they said it? I didn't believe that. I knew I could become very fond of things over a period of time. Was that love? A strong fondness? There was no way of knowing, was there? Unless one could figure out how to be human for a long enough period of time, I didn't know, and I didn't know anyone who did.

"One of life's little mysteries," said Tuvoon.

"Nonsense," said Viss. "Kai Wren loved that old Irishman like a brother."

"You think what I felt was really love?"

"I do."

"Never thought of it that way."

She shrugged.

"I've miles to go," she said.

"Me too," I responded.

We rose. I paid the tab, we stepped outside and faded into the night.

I stopped by my bottle to clean and rack Tuvoon's spirit blade and to pick up a few items.

I swirled my cloak the gray of all my other garments, finishing the lot with a dusting of starlight. The boots I wore came to mid-thigh, and I wore a standard blade at my side. I permitted myself one touch of color—a red feather in my cap. Then I pushed the cap back on my head at a rakish angle.

Pleased with the effect, I made my way out into the world of humans, slipped over to a traveling plane, and commenced flying through the sparkling twilight, past ghostly dolmens and ruined castles. No one lived in them. They were by way of mirages, created by the life force of this place in mimicry of the Earth.

After a time, I came to the ground, found a small sphere in

a hollow tree by a crossroads. I withdrew it, opened it, and studied its contents. It was a representation of the Earth, and a twinkling line across the Atlantic showed that I was nearing Ireland. I replaced the sphere and sped on. Shortly, I had a feeling that I was over land. I climbed higher into the air and spread my senses wide.

There. Ahead. A nonhuman mind hovered above a hilltop.

"Hello," I greeted, and adjusted my course to meet it.

It said nothing, but simply regarded my approach.

When I was at a respectful distance, I halted.

"And what might you be up to?" it asked.

"I've a story to tell and a need of the right man to tell it to."

"Well, Ireland is full of stories. One more won't hurt. Come join me. Where did you learn to speak the Irish?"

"From my servant, Oliver O'Keefe."

"Lots of O'Keefes in Ireland."

"This one was born in 1611 and he was murdered last night in San Francisco."

"Here. Come sit by me and tell me more."

I did, and he uncorked a small jug of poteen and passed it to me.

"Have a swig of this," he said, and I did, and it was wonderful.

"Thanks."

"Now, I know you for one of the Chinese sidhe, and we have never had much to do with each other one way or the other. So, as I see it, we don't have anything against each other."

"That's how I see it, too."

"Might I be askin' your name?"

"I'm Kai Wren, the bottlemaker," I said.

"Holy shit! Lord Demon himself!" he said. "Call me Angus of the Hills."

"Very well." I withdrew a copy of Ollie's death certificate and passed it to him. "Everything on it's right except for the date of birth," I said, "since humans don't understand these things. I filled it out from what Ollie told me over the years. He was born in your jurisdiction, I believe. Little village, back of beyond."

Angus nodded.

"Then you can take me there and is it proper if you wish to?"

"Oh, yes."

"There is no higher authority that I must go through if I wish to meddle in the humans' affairs? You are the ruling spirit?"

"Yes . . . But what exactly do you have in mind?"

I dug into my pouch and retrieved three cut emeralds the size of thumbnails.

"A gift to thee, mighty Sidhe," I said, "for hearing my petition."

He accepted them, raised them to the moon one by one, and stared through them.

"Damn!" he said. "They're perfect!"

"Of course. Now, let me tell you of O'Keefe."

Angus of the Hills unstoppered the bottle, took a drink, and passed it to me. It was still a fine brew.

"All right. Now," he said.

"Well, Ollie'd married and his wife bore him twins—a boy and a girl," I explained. "But she died in childbirth."

"Sad."

I nodded.

"He left the children with his sister-in-law and went off to sell his family fiddle in Dublin to raise passage to someplace where he could find work to support his family, there being no job in the village.

"But I heard him play, and I asked what else he did, and he told me he was a good handyman.

"So I offered him a job, the kids were taken care of, and we stayed together down the years. Sunday off and any other day he really wanted. I'd even bring him back on occasion to see his family."

Angus nodded. "His descendants are likely scattered all over the world," he said.

"I know. That's why I'd rather give something to an honorable person from his village, to keep a nest egg against somebody's need for a sudden operation or a tractor breaking down—not to mention starvation, lapsing mortgages, and sick children."

"You're a good-hearted one, for a Chinese sidhe," he said. "I'll bet you think I'll say the priest or the mayor would know everyone's needs, but that's not true. The George O'Keefe, keeper of O'Keefe's Public House, hears everyone's troubles— plus he's a direct relation of your friend. Come and meet him. I think you'd better tell him the whole story and be ready with a small miracle or two, to make it convincing."

Angus proved correct on all counts, and the cost of my charity was an arthritis cure and one for a cataract. I'd a feeling Angus might be coming in for a couple of generations' worth of stout.

Finally, I stood, nodded to both of them, and said, "I must be going now."

I stepped around the corner to a private stretch of alleyway.

Angus followed, his beer mug still in his hand. "Good night to you, Lord Demon."

"And to yourself, Angus," said I, and I sped upward.

Later, at home, I decided to sleep. And I did.

III

AND SO.

And so we made inquiries through third parties—Lord Swizzlediz, who can be quite charming—concerning Passion Flower, Snow Goon, Night Bride, and the Walker, as well as Devor himself.

It seemed that Devor was living at the very edge of his means, heavy with gambling debt, hounded by creditors. Passion Flower had lived with him for years, until his luck turned. Snow Goon still hung around with him—for old time's sake, apparently—and Night Bride was seeing him more and more frequently. I don't know what, if any, role the Walker had in all this, but he did seem to pass through Devor's life with some regularity.

I continued to keep an eye on all of them, but nothing new transpired in the months that followed. I recorded the entire matter and registered it at the Board of Duels. Hardly a necessity, but something that could serve to smooth things out later on.

I began seeing more of Tuvoon and Viss socially. Tuvoon and I started fencing together, with Viss coaching. I got out into the world of humans a little bit more. I resolved to attend this year's Conventicle. I did not start work on any new art projects.

It came like a sudden warm wind. If you feel it and recognize it, you have a chance of living. A thousand years is a long time, but never would I forget the tingle as *chi* itself is broken into shards of nothing.

I swirled through sideways spaces and projected myself upward from Earth as far as I was able. A moment more and I would know.

A moment more and I was still alive. It was okay.

I waited for a time, then pushed my way back tentatively toward the plane on which I had been attacked. After a certain point, I could still feel the rumbles, so I waited for them to subside. I moved nearer as they did, easing myself through the spaces. Before I cracked into the plane I made myself invisible. There was still a frightening feeling in the air and Horsehead Mountain—from which I had been watching but minutes ago—no longer existed.

Eagle's Head Mountain stood intact about thirty miles to the north, Hawksview about thirty-five to the northwest. I studied them as I flew eastward and home. One more blast like that could do me, no matter what.

Changing into a red outfit, red-booted, with the red feather in my cap, I headed for the cemetery where Tuvoon and Viss kept their bottle in an old mausoleum.

"Knock! Knock!" I went—or its equivalent—stepping over and through. A familiar servant admitted me, and Viss met me in the form of a young Chinese girl of about eight. Her hair was loose and her golden brown skin bore the blush of innocence.

"Kai Wren," she said, her voice light and reminiscent of small bells. "What a pleasant surprise! Would you care for some tea?"

"Yes, please."

I sank into a stack of cushions. She studied me.

"What is it?" she asked. "You seem distraught."

"I've been shot at with a theronic rifle," I told her.

"Theronics have been illegal since the Demon Wars," she said. "It is a capital offense to own a theronic weapon. You could blast a god with one of those things."

I nodded.

"And it's one sure way to get a god or demon," I added.

"You'd better tell me what happened," she said.

"I got word from one of the little scrub demons that there was going to be a big mah-jongg game on Barefoot Mountain last night, that Devor, who is actually a good player, was hoping to take the Twister for a bundle to clear up his debts."

The tea arrived. I accepted and sipped.

"You know, Devor is actually a good gambler when he's not taking *imbue*."

She nodded.

"I've spent some pleasant times long ago, gaming with him," she said. "So what happened?"

"I wanted to watch this game, see what happened, see if anything pertaining to O'Keefe came up. At first, I was simply going to sit among them, invisible, and do this. But some of us are very good at detecting a concealed presence, so I decided to remove myself about thirty miles to Horsehead and watch and hear the proceedings through a magic tube."

She nodded.

"And . . . ?"

"I went and set myself up on Horsehead and began observing. Somebody who wished me permanently out of the way must have spotted me and gone over to Hawksview with that theronic rifle. I felt it coming and fled, but he blasted the whole top half off Horsehead Mountain."

She shuddered.

"When I got back, the players had cleared out from Barefoot Mountain. I collapsed against a boulder and looked back at ruined Horsehead. Someone brushed by me then—I think it was the Walker. He was only visible for a moment. His elbow brushed mine and then he was gone. He chuckled as he passed."

"Showed you how he saved your life," she said.

"What?"

"Obviously, that's what he did to the one who fired at you.

Those weapons are deadly accurate—as you know if you've ever used one."

I nodded.

"Why, though?" I asked. "The Walker owes me nothing."

She shrugged. I finished my tea. She poured more, the pot seeming enormous in her tiny, delicate hands.

Of course the Walker did not have to owe me, I decided. He could simply want me in his debt. If Viss was right, then the Walker must know who had pulled the trigger.

"I wonder what I know that someone wished removed from common knowledge?"

"Anyone who's been around as long as you have must know a hell of a lot."

I shrugged. "Not sufficiently specific," I said.

"I know. But I've a feeling you've accidentally found your way into something big, and someone wants to keep the fight close and tidy."

"Shouldn't have brought in a theronic, then. Word's around our plane by now."

"Someone got scared."

"What will happen?"

"Nothing," she said. "Unless it reminds someone of something connected to what's going on and they come forth."

But the matter passed and nothing special happened, either in the world of humans or in the realm of demons.

I undertook the teaching of a course at the local community college, a course involving the construction and use of "acrobatic kites" and "fighting kites." An old man named Li Piao had taught it for many years, and I used to watch the hillside when his classes met. He was very good. Then, that fall, when I looked in the catalog for the course, it was not listed. I phoned the office and learned that Li Piao had suffered a stroke. I obtained his phone number and address. After a phone call confirming that he would receive me the next morning, I drove around to see him.

The house before which I parked my car was small but neatly kept. Still, as I came up the flagstone walk, I saw small signs of the owner's recent illness: the heavy head of a dark pink peony brushed the earth; bits of windblown detritus clustered in corners; a glazed porcelain flowerpot was knocked onto one side. I righted it as I passed, enjoying the cool feel of its smooth glaze, then I rang the bell.

The old man who answered it was a little tall for a Chinese and vaguely Mandarin-like in his bearing despite the fact that he leaned on a crutch. The longest wisps of his snowy beard touched his chest, but that same beard's thickness could not hide a mouth that bore the twisting of paralysis. Still, he smiled in greeting. Clearly, life had not completely borne him down.

"Do I have the honor of addressing Li Piao?" I asked politely.

"I am Li Piao," he answered, "and you must be Mr. Kai. Come in."

I did as he bid me, following him through a wide hallway and into a living room overlooking a fine garden. A fat, somehow jolly, little terra-cotta teapot rested upon a tray set on a low table. There were two cups and a plate of wafer-thin almond cookies as well.

After directing me to a seat on a comfortable sofa, Li Piao maneuvered himself into a wooden chair with a high back and arms. Clearly the chair had been chosen because it enabled him to push himself onto his feet and reach the crutches he carefully leaned against a second chair.

As I watched him, I found myself admiring his spirit. Here was a man who had once enjoyed the vicarious flight of kites, now bound firmly to earth by his crippled body, but refusing even to consider defeat.

"I must ask you to pour the tea," Li Piao said. "It is very fine green tea, imported from Taiwan. The cookies are of my daughter-in-law's making. They are very good—not overly sweet."

I poured, making a small ceremony of the action. Li Piao accepted his cup with a nod of thanks. He rested it, along with two cookies his strong left hand plucked from the plate I held out to him, on the arm of his chair.

"How?" I asked, gesturing at the neatly laid tea tray. "How did you manage this?"

He chuckled, a sound as warm as his smile. "I did not,

except for adding the hot water to the teapot and removing the plastic wrap from the plate. My grandson set it up for me last night when he came for a few hours to help me."

"Ah." I nodded, sipped. The tea was indeed good, the cookies excellent. "I have long enjoyed watching your classes fly their kites each spring."

"So have I," he said, with the first trace of sadness I had seen in him.

"I was wondering," I continued, "if you would consider permitting me the honor of continuing your class for you. We would necessarily need to begin a few weeks late, but the registrar at the community college has said that adaptations could be made."

I did not think it necessary to tell Li Piao that my offering to teach the course for nothing had helped to sway that doubtful lady.

"I would have no objections," Li Piao said, surprised. "How could I? Knowledge of kites, of their crafting and flying, is not mine alone."

"True," I said. "I was hoping that you would consider coming and sharing your wisdom with the class. I can be your hands, but I do not have your knowledge."

That might be a small lie (though I was to learn later that it was not), but I did not see how flattery could hurt. Simply and immediately, I wanted to see the skies above the park alive with kites once more.

For a moment, Li Piao's old eyes lit with pleasure at the prospect. Then he shook his head ruefully.

"I would, but I cannot. The doctors tell me a long time may pass before I am able to walk unassisted once more. I do not trust myself to drive, even if they would permit me."

Sipping tea, I smiled. "I can collect you before each class and bring you home again. I would even toss in a meal or some share of the teacher's salary to sweeten the deal."

I knew from my talk with the registrar that Li Piao had been well paid for his efforts but that otherwise he was retired. He might welcome some cash.

"I could not take money for such!" he protested.

"You would be teaching the course," I reminded.

"Still!"

He looked indignant.

"There is no reason you should not be paid for your time," I said, speaking as if the matter was settled between us.

We bargained then, over tea and cookies, setting our terms. I think we both enjoyed it. When he looked as if he might refuse, I said:

"You have not asked what I did when I was employed in the world. I was a great healer—one who followed the traditional methods. I may be able to speed along your healing."

I had him then, I could see it. Even if he did not desire himself whole for himself alone, he could not have refused me without feeling he was being selfish toward those who were taking time from their own daily duties to assist him.

"You know acupuncture?" he asked.

"Yes, and something of herbs and something, too, of more esoteric arts."

I reached out then and seized the bent, paralyzed index finger of his right hand. Taking a deep breath, I ran a portion of my demon *chi* down it. I could feel the paths within revitalizing, then he moved it.

"I accept your offer," he said, firmly, his tones those of someone who is awed, though not too awed to be thoughtful. We made our arrangements, and I said that I would have the registrar call him soon.

I left quickly after that. I did not feel like playing games with the man. Neither did I feel like letting him die. From our brief talk, I suspected that he still knew a lot more about kites than I did.

I picked him up for my Saturday and Sunday afternoon classes, and he would sit on the sunny hillside and watch the kites. I gave him his treatment afterward and took him to dinner.

"Some of your kites are very, very old," he said.

"I come from an isolated part of the old country."

"Some of them I've only heard of, never seen."

"Soon you will be making them."

"I believe you. You must have been a good healer before

27

you retired. All the sensation is back on that side, and I can limp around now."

"Next month you will throw the crutch away."

One day the following month, we all had our various kites in the air, a colorful blossoming of squares and rectangles (for today was devoted to assorted traditional types), when a fine Thai Pakpao refused to fly as it should. I gave my green-and-blue Chinese butterfly to the student and stepped aside with Li Piao to see what could be done to mend the Pakpao.

The problem was with the string bridle. Li Piao made subtle adjustments to the length of the string, then I raised the Pakpao aloft once more. Not wanting to risk becoming entangled with any of those kites already flying, I had moved us a distance away from where the rest of my class was clustered.

"She looks good," I said. (A Pakpao is a female kite; the larger, male kite is called a Chula.)

"She does indeed," Li Piao answered, but I could tell from his tone that his attention was elsewhere.

I turned my attention from the Pakpao and glanced to the east, where an errant wind was blowing a small cloud near. A bit of rain fell upon me. I sensed what was happening, but by then it was too late.

There came a clap of thunder just as Li Piao cried out, "Kai!"

The lightning chased me down the Pakpao's string and filled my body. I sent it back into the sky, released the string, and clapped my hands. The lightning returned whence it had come and the cloud blew apart.

"Kai Wren! I did not do it, my friend," Li Piao cried, limping near.

"I know that," I said, rather puzzled by his words.

"It was a magician hidden in the cloud who tried to slay you."

"You know something of these matters?" I asked.

"I studied the Art in my youth. I did not know such a stroke could be returned."

"Was it a human or a demon sorcerer?" I asked him.

"Human," he said. "I'm sorry you have such an enemy."

I shrugged.

"It will make life interesting," I said.

"You are not afraid?"

I laughed.

"May I ask," he said after a moment, "whether you are related to the potter and bottlemaker?"

"Yes," I said softly.

"Years ago, in Canton, I saw such a bottle," he said. "I have never forgotten its hue and its beauty. Do you think it possible I might see another one day, before I die?"

"Yes," I said. "You may."

He lowered himself to the ground before me. Fortunately, most of our students were at such a distance that they could not see this humble display—and those who did surely dismissed it as the old man stretching his crippled limbs.

"Kai Wren is also known as Lord Demon," he said.

"How do you know this?"

"As I told you, in my youth I studied the Art."

"Rise up," I said, oddly miffed that my quiet venture into the world of humans should now be colored by demon things. "I have asked nothing of you but the friendship of kites. I will treat you now, and then we will go to eat."

After a few words on the wisdom of watching the weather, I dismissed the class. Then I completed Li Piao's cure and took him home with me. It was times like this when I really missed O'Keefe. My first new friend in years, and he had to settle for less than the best hospitality. . . .

Entering my bottle did not upset Li Piao; neither did an encounter with Shiriki and Chamballa. He patted them both, stroking the curls of their manes.

"This one," he said of Shiriki, "is the color of Imperial jade. The other might be made out of dark amber or perhaps carnelian. I had always thought the carvings of fu dogs fanciful rather than representative."

"Live and learn," I answered, but I was pleased. The dogs wagged their tails.

After we left the dogs, we walked to my palace. Unlike a Western edifice, the structure did not dominate the landscape, but rather complemented it. I had lavished a great deal of care on its construction, curling each pagoda roof by hand in wet clay before setting my magic to work.

Seeing it sprawled in the rise and fall of the land, catching rainbows and waterfalls in its curves, Li Piao said nothing, but his eyes shone among their wrinkled folds. I escorted him up broad stairs shaped from polished water agate and through an intricately carved door leafed in gold.

Once we were situated in a comfortable parlor, I let some of the bottle's better servitors prepare a meal.

Afterward, we sipped tea and listened to music.

"Li Piao," I said, "you seem a happy man."

"I am, Lord Demon," he stated. "My family is grown, and they have turned out well enough. I was a sufficiently successful food merchant to support them so that they did not want. I had a little time for studies, some good friends in their day, and I had the kites. It has not been a bad life. This is why I did not fear visiting with a demon."

"Yet you feel that your life was somewhat incomplete?"

"All men do," he said, "that is part of being . . . human. Sorry."

"Do not apologize for being human. No. I could not help noticing that while your family loves you, they do not have enough time even for their own families. I wondered whether you were sometimes lonely."

"Oh, of course. But that is all right. It makes our times together that much sweeter."

"I see. I was going to offer you a home here with me. I would even complete your training as a sorcerer."

He laughed.

"I am too old," he stated.

"I will make you young."

Li Piao shook his head.

"I do not think you understand, Lord Demon. I appreciate your kind offer more than any I have ever received. But the later years are good, too, and I would spend them with those I have known and loved."

I reached out and squeezed his arm.

"Perhaps the offer was not a kindness on my part," I said, "so much as a matter of selfishness. But I like you, human—

even more—for your honesty. I will always be your friend. I will not even touch your memories of this discussion, for I would like you to come and go as you would, for a visit."

"This humble one is honored."

"Come. Rise and join me," I said. "There is a thing I would show you."

He joined me. I took him on a long, timeless route through realms of wonder—and as we went, I ran my *chi* through him. One day he would learn that though I had never trained him, I had enormously enhanced what his old teacher must have seen in him, making him perhaps the greatest natural magician in the world.

Coming to my showroom, I gestured. Plates, pots, and bottles were displayed everywhere. I took down my favorite bowl. It was green, and dragons guarded whatever it might bear. Like all of the items, it was enhanced and virtually indestructible.

"A present, then," I said, handing it to him. "Eat from it regularly. It will improve your health. And think of me then—human who can plain-talk with a demon. Come! I will show you more now before I take you home."

Timidly, he took the arm I offered, the bowl in his other hand, and we walked and flew through places of light and twilight.

Autumn came on, and I packed a small bag and slid it into sidewise space. I had let Tuvoon and Viss talk me into attending the Great Conventicle in both the human and ghost mountains of northern China. The journey was easy, save for the mazelike tunnels of the entryway and these were almost fun, we knew them so well. As we went, I felt something small slide into my jacket pocket. As Viss was on that side of me, I said, "What are you doing?" as I put my hand in after it.

"Don't remove it on pain of rotten luck, unless your straits are quite dire. It is my small blessing. Promise?"

"Very well. I bear a lady's favor."

"Exactly."

We entered the palace beneath the mountains. I passed several congregations of my peers in gardens and on walkways. Three times I heard a whispered "Godslayer!" from the crowds.

"I'd forgotten," I said, "and I was hoping they had, too."

"You know it's not something easily forgotten," Tuvoon told me. "Everybody wants to be part of a legend or two."

"That guy would have taken me apart if I hadn't been damn lucky," I told him.

"I was there, too," he replied, "and it wasn't all luck."

"Shit!" I said. "He was a demigod, and I was a brash young demon who probably surprised him more than anything."

"Nevertheless, your victory was a turning point in the battle, and the battle proved a crucial one. It's certainly not bad being known as the only demon in memory to have single-handedly killed a god."

I shrugged. "These kids don't know what it was like."

"So let them have their hero."

I growled, and we made our way to our quarters.

There were numerous messages awaiting me—mostly invitations to dine and a few to appear on panels dealing with obscure thaumaturgical concepts the organizers must have thought my generation enjoyed more than theirs. They were wrong.

That day I had drinks with Stormmiller, Pigeon Eyes, Icecap, and Spider Queen—lunch with Dragon Gore and He of the Towers of Light; dinner with Seven Fingers and Spilling Moonbeams. I had hopes of finding the Walker and speaking with him, but he was nowhere to be found. Neither was Devor—in fact, his entire group was conspicuously absent.

Cocktails are a European and American import, one of those things that became popular when some of the more trendsetting demons emigrated along with various waves of Chinese expatriates. Perpetual exiles that we are, a change of physical anchor point doesn't trouble us overly much. Cultural shifts, though, those touch us more deeply. Even after my own emigration, I have always entertained second thoughts about American cultural values.

Seven Fingers knew this. If anything, he is more conservative than I am. When I met him and Spilling Moonbeams for an early dinner immediately following the one panel in which I deigned participate, I found the restaurant's decor purely and elegantly Chinese. The dominant motif was the T'ang Dynasty, but there were just enough touches from later days to keep it from seeming static. The maître d' escorted me to a private chamber, separated from the main dining area by a teak screen beautifully carved with the phoenix and the dragon.

In keeping with the spirit of the Conventicle neither of my hosts wore human shape. Seven Fingers rose to his full seven and a half feet in height to greet me. For the occasion, he had polished his green scales a handsome emerald and highlighted the deep red of his three large eyes (the odd one set neatly in the center of his forehead) with an expensive rouge made from crushed rubies mixed with minute diamonds. He wore a floor-length robe in black silk embroidered with chrysanthemums.

His daughter (though some say she is his niece and others that she is neither of these things), resembled the moonbeams of her name. Unlike Seven Fingers, who is a solid figure of a demon, her natural form is partially ethereal. Imagine an ink stroke across a page that suggests a woman, a curve, an undulation, a hint of fine-boned features. Shade it in with silvery hair falling to the floor in massy abundance that is only partially on any one plane, bring out the features in hints of moonlight and stardust and you have Spilling Moonbeams.

She is lovely and unapproachable. No wonder the jealous suggest that her father is also her lover.

She is also comparatively young, born at the close of the Demon Wars even as her mother, the fearsome Krys of the Unknowable Rage, expired from wounds inflicted by the curve-bladed axe of the god Rr'grr. The midwife who brought forth Spilling Moonbeams was Viss of the Terrible Tongue, sister to Raging Krys. Some say that Viss wished to keep the baby and raise her in company with her cousin, Tuvoon the Smoke Ghost. Seven Fingers, grieving for his mate, would have nothing of that. He reared Spilling Moonbeams himself, nursing her on intrigue and enigma, permitting no one else near.

All of this and more awoke in my memory as I greeted my hosts. When I saw that the properly and formally reared Spilling Moonbeams was prepared to greet me with the three obeisances and the nine kowtows, I reached out and raised her. My hands partially passed through her, but I had almost expected this and schooled myself to show no surprise.

"Do not bow to me, child," I said firmly. "I am here as a guest, not as anything else."

She lowered dark lashes over two bright eyes that glittered with an emotion I could not quite place.

"You are the Godslayer," she said in a whispery voice. "Without you, I would not live. I seek only to honor you as my father has taught."

It's true enough that if I hadn't gotten in my lucky shot at Chaholdrudan when I did, Spilling Moonbeams wouldn't have made it. Krys of the Unknowable Rage had gone down a few minutes before and her need had distracted both Viss and Seven Fingers from the battlefield.

We weren't doing very well that day. Many of our best were wounded; morale wasn't just low, it was nonexistent. Only the right crisis was needed to create a general rout. When Chaholdrudan crashed in death, his ichor baptized demonkind with new hope.

Lying is not in me, but I could not accept this lovely child offering me respect that should be reserved for an emperor. I continued to raise her until she stood.

"My victory was only one of many that day," I said firmly. "Rise. If I'm not mistaken, I scent thousand-year eggs with ginger."

Seven Fingers was watching his daughter with unmistakable pride. At his subtle signal, she obeyed my request. When we were all seated, Seven Fingers removed the cover from the serving dish on the table. There within were indeed thousand-year eggs, nestled attractively in a bed of thin sliced ginger and pickled scallions. He helped me to a choice portion with the host's long ivory chopsticks.

Course followed course, each elegantly prepared. At first the conversation was general: discussion of the Conventicle, comparison of the current Organization Committee with those past, anecdotes about old friends present and absent. When we reached the fourth course, Seven Fingers commented:

"So, Kai Wren, you have been brought from your solitude by Viss and Tuvoon."

Although the words were neutral enough, there was an undertone of acid to them. Remembering old rivalries, I decided to ignore the undertone and speak only to the words.

"Yes, that is so. Recent events have carried me once again into my old teacher's orbit. We spoke of the isolation within which many of demonkind dwell. She and the Smoke Ghost reminded me that a Conventicle was coming up. I thought to come and see some old friends."

Seven Fingers smiled. "And we are glad that you did. It is too long since we visited in this easy fashion."

Spilling Moonbeams murmured words that seemed to echo her father's sentiments. I said something courtly in return, but it seemed that an exchange of mutual admiration was not going to be sufficient to finish this subject.

"Viss often has motivations so obscure that perhaps not even she understands their full implications," Seven Fingers said.

Remembering an aunt who desired to adopt a motherless niece against her father's wishes, I reminded myself that these were hardly the words of a neutral party. Long lives mean longer grudges. Therefore, I merely made a small encouraging noise within my throat and plucked a delicate black mushroom from the dish before me.

"When Viss is interested in some course," Seven Fingers persisted stubbornly, "it is unlikely that her desire is disinterested."

I nodded, sipped my tea, patted my fangs with a fine linen napkin, and considered my next words.

"Viss was not the one who renewed our acquaintance," I said, wondering how many present at this Conventicle knew of the abortive duel between Tuvoon and me. Ba Wa, the scrub demon, must have advertised it to some extent to have sold tickets at such short notice. "It was renewed by accident. I initially continued it out of a desire to emphasize that I held no malice toward Viss or her house. Later, I found I enjoyed the opportunity to visit with her and Tuvoon."

Spilling Moonbeams went and fetched forth dishes for the next course: duck and abalone, beautifully arranged. Without speaking, Seven Fingers helped me to choice portions while carefully framing his next statement.

"There was a duel," he said, "between you and Tuvoon."

"A misunderstanding," I answered, "since corrected."

"But if it had not been, you might have killed the Smoke Ghost."

I had little doubt that I would have been the victor, but deciding that humility would be the best course, I merely nodded.

"And then Viss would have been forced to avenge her son," Seven Fingers continued.

"She as much as said that she would," I answered.

"She has your spirit sword, you know," Seven Fingers said. His tone was gentle, but his gaze was as sharp as one of his own blades.

I hadn't known, and the knowledge was an icy wind across my heart. Then the chill went away. Viss had not given it to Tuvoon when we dueled, even though I had brought his spirit sword with me. Surely there was nothing to this.

"I believed my spirit sword was broken beyond repair in the Demon War," I said.

"It was broken," Seven Fingers answered, "but not beyond repair. I repaired it."

I bit back the "Why?" that was my first response. None of us like the spirit swords, but all of us agree that they promote good manners. They remind each of us that there is at least one weapon that can do us mortal harm and against which we have no perfect armor. Seven Fingers forged many of them in the First Interlude of Exile, during which all demons needed to be allies. Then they were stored in the great Armory of Truce.

Over the years, some spirit swords have been broken, but others have come to various custodians. I obtained Tuvoon's, for example, in a deal with Pigeon Eyes for a certain vase. Until Ollie's death, I had no thought of ever using it. If anything, I viewed it as a favor to Viss that the sword was in my possession rather than in anyone else's.

"So Viss has my spirit sword," I said. "If you warn me against her, why did you repair it for her?"

Seven Fingers frowned. "I did not. I repaired it at the request of Night Bride, who indicated that it would then be returned to the Armory of Truce. I know, too, that it resided in

Truce for some time, but somehow, sometime, it came into Viss's possession."

Wheels within wheels turned in my head. Did whoever had arranged for Ollie to be slain know this? Had Viss known I had Tuvoon's sword? If so, why hadn't she arranged for an exchange? Was there anything to Seven Fingers's veiled hints? And why was he making them now? Did he have a reason for making me distrust Viss?

"This duck," I said, placing a portion on Spilling Moonbeam's plate, "is possessed of the crisp and delicate flavor of ginger; the sauce is kissed with fragrant oils."

Father and daughter took my hint. From that point until just before we adjourned late in the Hour of the Dog, conversation remained general.

Then, when the last course was finished, Seven Fingers sent his daughter from the room.

"Lord Demon," he said with an awkwardness that had not been present some moments before, "what do you think of my daughter?"

I answered honestly. "She is among the most beautiful demonesses I have ever seen. She is also well-spoken, intelligent, and obedient. I think she is a credit to your parenting."

"Since Krys died, I have had to be both mother and father to her," he said. "I am proud of my daughter."

I nodded, waiting for him to continue.

"Would you consider Spilling Moonbeams as a possible wife?"

I started. What gossip I had heard these past months indicated that all believed that Seven Fingers would never relinquish his daughter.

"I had not looked for that honor," I answered carefully.

"And now that you know to look?"

"I am honored," I said honestly, "but I could not consider contracting a marriage until I learn the truth about both Oliver O'Keefe's death and the most recent attempt on my life."

Seven Fingers looked unhappy. I hastened to add:

"I would be a foul creature indeed if I brought blood vendetta upon a new wife and her family."

His features cleared. "A noble thought. After?"

"I would consider your offer seriously."

"We will talk of dowry then," he said, pleased. "She is heir to treasures that I have laid by for a thousand years."

"And worth," I said in my most courtly tones, "every gem and *shen* coin."

We parted then, mutually satisfied with the outcome. As I considered the benefits of both acceptance and refusal, I took a long walk to and among the catacombs. Here the river ran over polished cobbles and through caverns that sparkled like belts and diadems of frozen bubbles. It is one of the lovelier sights I know.

"Hey, Godslayer! Wait up!" came a call.

I should have been slightly alarmed as I had not noted that anyone was following me. . . .

I halted and waited for the lithe figure of many-armed Fire's Fever to approach. I had only just met him in one of the bars in passing.

"Yes?" I asked, as he came on like a ghost. Was there really someone there?

He closed, and we exchanged greetings.

"I hear you're the best there is," he said then.

"Hardly," I replied, and began to turn away. I felt a rude, hard hand on my shoulder, holding me, turning me.

Angered, I shrank to the size of a pebble, rolled to a position behind him, and grew again even as his hands spouted a strange green fire through the area I had just occupied. I cupped my hands and blasted both of his ears, chopped both sides of his neck, gave him the illusion of snakes, shrank myself again, and returned to the dark shore.

The green fires sprang up on his every surface, and he began to rake the cavern with them. A droplet of it struck my right forearm, and I felt an agony such as I had never known.

"Is that the best you can do, Godslayer?" he called. "Shortly, then, I will eat your soul."

Something clicked as I retreated beneath the attack. "Eat your soul" had been among the old gods' favorite curses, because they could actually do it.

I marshaled my forces and attacked with the first thunderstorm that underground realm had probably ever felt. Fire's Fever laughed loudly, maniacally.

"Is that really your best shot, Godslayer?" he asked. "Your reputation seems unearned to me."

I fell upon him then, and we wrestled. His many arms did not offer him the great advantage they might have, but I was aware of a certain weakness flooding me, emanating from where the green fire still burned my forearm.

Feeling my *chi* ebbing, I threw a spell at him of the sort I had used to transform the scrub demons into stone. With incredible fluidity, my opponent bowed back out of range so that only stone turned into stone—the cavern's mica-flecked surface becoming dull gray granite.

"Nice trick," he admitted. "I think I'll crush you now, burn you, then eat you."

He was upon me with grips like iron manacles. Then my left hand brushed against my pocket. I recalled the present of Viss, one of the deadliest of our kind.

My hand dipped, emerged holding a derringer.

I shoved it against him and pulled the trigger. He grew transparent, and the frantic lines ran through him.

"No!" he cried.

The entire cavern rang, bellowed, crashed, twinkled. I held the derringer to his brow and fired the final charge. The wall behind him fell over as he melted in my arms. I digested some of his energies as they swirled about me. This was no demon . . .

"Godslayer! You've done it again!" cried a voice from the direction of the nearest tunnel.

Suddenly, many demons were rushing down the quiet ways.

"Congratulations!" I heard Viss saying loudly. "Your second demigod, and he'd even brought a theronic to use against you!"

"No!—Yes!" I corrected. "I don't know. His energies confuse me! I must rest."

"Come this way."

Although for a moment I was troubled by the thread of Seven Fingers's warning, I let her lead me back to my quarters.

"I am going to calm you to sleep," she said, "and warn anyone against disturbing you."

"Thanks."

At first there were my victim's dreams, full of omens and portents. Then there were troubled ones. But at last I slept long, slept deep.

IV

THE FOLLOWING DAY, I did not want to stay for the banquet they planned in my honor—no telling who might show up—but Viss insisted it was owed, so I attended. I, in turn, insisted that she be my date, and she agreed.

"You know a lot more than you're saying," I said the first time we were alone together and could speak of such matters.

She gave me a lovely smile.

"I'd like more than a grin," I said.

"I suspected there has been a vengeful god on your trail," she said.

"Why?"

"There are still a few crazy young ones who could be stirred up along those lines."

"But what for? Who'd do it?"

"You have a human magician and some demons on your case also. I've never heard anything like it before."

"That's why you slipped me the derringer and wished me well?"

"Don't be crazy. You're better equipped than anyone I know to stop a god. You may even be the last of us with a track record."

"All right. I trust you. But I'm wondering how much you really know."

"Nothing much," she said, "but a combination like that really frightens me. We have to learn everything we can. You do see that, don't you?"

I nodded. "Of course. Just because I'm a solitary individual doesn't mean I don't care about the others."

"Then you'll help?"

"I guess so."

Nothing much that I could help with turned up, though, in the months that followed. Then, one day, Li Piao came by with Shiriki and Chamballa at his side. They seem to enjoy escorting people in, even when they know they're welcome.

"Your friend is intact, Lord Kai," said Shiriki.

"As always, you do an exemplary job," I said. "One day you must have puppies to carry on the family tradition."

"Really?"

"Well, I meant—if you wish. There aren't that many of your wonderful kind left."

Shiriki and Chamballa looked at each other, then looked away. What had I done? The poor things weren't all that imaginative, and I was hardly giving them an order to go and breed.

"Go to the kitchen for a fine meal," I said. "I would reward my friends."

They bowed and departed.

"Amazing," said Li Piao, "that this pair has survived at all. They are so large and must eat a great deal."

"Yes."

"I've found something of interest. You may already be aware of it. I do not know."

I clapped my hands for service.

"Some sorbet, some tea, some music. Be seated, my friend, and we will discuss it as we refresh ourselves."

He nodded. "Gladly. You did not tell me that the wondrous dragon bowl you gave me might be used for divination."

I smiled.

"I prefer to have people discover such things for themselves," I said.

"Well, as I developed more and more aptitudes along those lines it seemed more and more likely, and I decided to try."

"I see. And . . . ?"

"The dragon told me strange things."

"Yes?"

"Rabla-yu was the name of the god you slew a few months back. He came to Earth by way of the Mongolian Gate—invoked and assisted by a magician named Fu Xian—originally from northern China, now residing in Atlanta."

"Oh?"

"Fu Xian was the one in the cloud. He tested you with the lightning. Had it seemed especially debilitating he would have passed the advice to Rabla-yu to employ against you."

"You make it sound as if Rabla-yu had feared me!"

"He was an ignorant young demigod asked to prove himself against someone known as 'Godslayer.' Fu Xian had reached across the planes, seeking a brash patriot among his kind. There is a cabal which would like to see the demons completely crushed. Rabla-yu was perfect for testing the water."

We spooned rose sorbet.

"Rabla-yu forced the Mongolian Gate, eh? That's one of the first created by demonkind to give access to Earth. Interesting that he wasn't using god Gates."

"That's the Gate the dragon said he used."

"I think the higher-ups among the gods should be notified. We have a treaty which this violates."

"There are channels for reaching the elders?"

"Oh, yes. I'll see that it gets done."

The servitors brought in our tea.

"Would you care to play a game of Go with me? I had a friend I used to—"

"Of course. I miss it myself. In these fast-paced days, my relatives do not have the time to humor me with a long game. I'd be delighted."

I had a servant fetch the board and the stones. We commenced playing.

*   *   *

It was good, luring Li Piao into an occasional game of Go. These games took large enough chunks of time that I sometimes had company for long stretches. It also gave me an idea.

Devor was a good player when he wasn't on drugs. I asked Lord Swizzlediz to let it be known that I sometimes liked a small game for high stakes and didn't mind losing if the play was good. I wanted to discover whether Devor was sufficiently hard up to cheat—and perhaps ascertain how much money he needed.

Nothing much happened for a couple of weeks, and then one night Devor turned up at a coffee shop when I was having a cup with Viss. He looked good. His skin shone lambent gold, wings like those of a swan but feathered in the palest green fell like a cloak down his back. The slanting eyes that met mine were silver and impossible to read.

"Good evening. May I join you?" he asked.

"Of course. Have a seat."

We sipped for a while and exchanged pleasantries. I had forgotten how charming he could be.

"I heard recently," Devor said, smiling coyly, "that you like a nice game of mah-jongg or Go or human cards every now and then when the stakes are high and the play is fast and clever."

I nodded.

"That's true," I said. "You may well be out of my league, though, from what I've heard. I am a pleasure player."

"Aren't we all?"

"True. But I've always understood you to be something of a professional as well."

He shrugged.

"It's so hard to draw the line," he finally said, "when you've enjoyed it so much and played it so long . . ."

I nodded.

"We must get together for a game sometime," he continued.

"Yes."

"Say next Thursday evening? I'm not doing much of anything then."

"Sure. Your place or mine?"

"Yours. I love that bottle."

"You've a pretty nice one yourself."

"Had to sell it," he said a bit gruffly. "Ran into some problems a while back."

"Oh. I'm sorry."

He shrugged.

"It teaches you to value property. I'll be all right again. Recover. Get another."

Gods! He would have gotten a fortune for that bottle, even highly discounted.

"Who'd you sell it to?"

"A museum, behind what used to be the Iron Curtain. They have a hip curator, and they came into some money. He'll take good care of it."

"Sounds like you had some rough times."

He shrugged.

"Everybody does, I guess, if you wait long enough. Next Thursday, then?"

"How about the early side of the Hour of the Dog?" I said.

"Sounds good."

Viss and I watched him go. We sipped our coffee. I'd a feeling the game would be interesting.

Devor started out letting me win more often than not. Then he began beating me slowly, consistently. There was nothing untoward that I could detect. If he were pulling a fast one, he was evidently careful about the entire affair. I watched him like a hawk.

We played every Thursday for a month. On the fourth night he won a lot, but if he were cheating it was beautifully done and it could easily have been a normal run of the game. I clapped him on the shoulder at its end, after I had paid him.

"I must say that you gave me my money's worth in entertainment. I hope you'll be by next week. I'm coming to enjoy this."

He smiled.

"I'd be a liar if I said I didn't enjoy winning tonight," he said. "But I did enjoy playing with you. Might I ask a favor?"

"Please do."

"I have always wanted to see your private collection of

glassware, but I have never felt I knew you well enough just to ask. If you've the time and inclination, though, I'd love to."

I nodded.

"Come on," I said.

When we stood among brilliance he was silent for many minutes as he stared. Then, "I'd no idea," he said. "It's seldom that one sees such wealth—and this is what wealth is all about, isn't it? No matter what, you could always sell one and be back on your feet."

"I guess so," I said.

"How long did that perfume bottle take to make?"

"Seventy-eight years."

"You have to wait for just the right astrological configuration and perform each step in its required sequence?"

"That's right. Of course, I often work on several projects simultaneously."

"Amazing."

We strolled through mist and music.

"I gather you heard a rumor at first that I might be implicated in your servant's death."

I nodded.

"Only a rumor, and I was quick to dismiss it. I apologize for even that, though."

"I need no apologies. I am sure I would feel the same had I such a good and loyal retainer for as long as you and the O'Keefe were together. No. It is I who owe you an apology, for I never told you that I was sorry to hear the news and I was."

"I understand," I said. "You and I were never all that close."

The magic mountains towered about us, their mists drifting. Then came a succession of howls.

"Greetings, Lord Kai," Shiriki said. "All's quiet."

"Everything under control," Chamballa added.

"Can you render yourselves invisible?" Devor asked them. They glanced at me, and I nodded.

"If we need to," they responded in unison.

Walking on, Devor nodded. "You may have the only pair left in the world—or out of it. Why don't you breed them? A lot of traditionalists would love to have a pair. You could make a fortune."

"Well, they're sentient beings—if not too imaginative—and the decision is theirs."

"I'll bet they'd be proud to be the parents of a new race of their kind and see their pups carrying on their ancient tradition in many courts."

"Perhaps I should discuss it with them sometime."

"I'd love to buy a pair myself."

I frowned. "Why? Traditionally, fu dogs were created to attack and mutilate our sort."

"These don't," Devor countered reasonably. "I don't figure that their pups would either. So much of that kind of thing must be in the training."

"Hm."

"Remember my offer."

"I don't own them," I reminded. "They just work for me."

"I understand. But keep me in mind if they ever come around to that way of thinking. Of course, I'd charge a fee, but I could place the pups in distinguished palaces."

"We'll see. Let it be," I said.

I saw Devor out of my world and into his, not knowing whether to be angry about his presumption or oddly sympathetic toward him.

"Thursday," he said.

"Thursday," I repeated.

The next evening, Li Piao and I shared an excellent meal at my place. Following it, before I could lure him into a game, he smiled, and said, "I've been watching Fu Xian. While you may consider a human sorcerer below your notice, he's just right for mine."

"I have done some small investigating," I said. "What did you learn?"

"He has friends in the same line of work."

"Yes?"

"There is a short, heavy man named Ken Zhao—a water magician, I believe—and Po Shiang, taller, thinner. I'm not sure of his persuasion. They have been hanging out together a lot, and doing some workings involving all of them."

"I knew that Fu Xian had some allies," I said. "Though I did not know the participants. Now I must ask you a large favor. Playing with new powers is always a treat—and you are very good. But I want you to leave those three alone, for my sake. They could easily become alerted, through you, that I am watching and aware. I do not want them to know this yet."

He bent his head.

"Thy will be done."

"There may be a need later on, and I thank you for what you have done so far."

"It is dangerous, I see, and I do not wish to interrupt your strategy."

"Thank you," I said, meaning it.

"Shall we play?"

"A pleasant game, dear friend, rather than one where I must always watch the Devourer."

"The Devourer?"

"A little joke."

"Tell me of it?"

"Surely."

Somehow, I relaxed and told him the entire story behind my recent involvement with Devor. Li Piao wound up knowing everything important that had happened to me for the past few years.

I was a little startled how much he had already deduced based on his previous education and his scrying. His teachers back in old Canton must have been very wise.

Then for a long while, we just sat in silence.

Finally, "I treasure your trust," he said.

"It just came out," I answered, almost defensively, although I wasn't sure whether this was because I knew how much I was still not telling him or because I felt weak for confiding in a human.

"Sometimes it must."

"I am not normally that talkative."

"I know. But I'll bet you told more than you realize to the

O'Keefe. You probably got so that you did it without even knowing."

I smiled. "I do believe that you have a point."

"Let us play Go," he said.

And so we did.

That night there was a commotion. I'd sent Li Piao home with a particularly tough ogre. There was that in the air which made me uneasy. I would not risk him as I had the O'Keefe, but when the ogre returned he reported no difficulties.

I had a servitor bring me a plateful of lobster-stuffed spring rolls and some jasmine tea.

After a time, I called for a blanket. I drowsed.

Then came the howls.

I turned myself into a wind, blowing down canyons, through mountains. I awakened the Lung Shan, the venerable dragon of the mountains, as I passed.

"Lord Demon, what is it?" he asked.

"Someone is after the dogs," I said.

I heard him stir. The dogs were his neighbors and resided in one of his abandoned caves. There was something of a family feeling between them.

"Lead on," he said, emerging in a tangle of coils part silver, part moss-in-snow jade, his curving fangs and talons all ivory.

I did. We swirled and raced. And I heard a final howl.

"Stay here," I told the Lung Shan as I departed the bottle.

I sniffed chloroform as I passed. Outside, I heard the sound of a pickup truck departing the area, but I could not track it. What could I do?

Li Piao. It was just coming into the Hour of the Snake, a decent hour of the morning. Perhaps I could get him to do a little divining before I went after Devor's guts.

I located my car, which I kept in a garage not far from the house holding my bottle, and drove across town. When I pulled up in front of his place, Li Piao came out grinning. "You are the most social Chinese demon I've ever seen," he said. Then he saw it wasn't really funny.

"Sorry," he added. "What's wrong?"

"Someone has stolen Shiriki and Chamballa. I want you to

do me a divination and find out who. I will keep my suspicions to myself so as not to prejudice the reading."

He nodded.

"Come this way, please."

I followed him into the house. This time we went through the living room and into the kitchen. The cozy room smelled of rice and ginger. A picture of the Kitchen God was hung prominently on one wall. A small shelf beneath it held a brass incense burner.

Li Piao removed the dragon bowl from many silken wrappings and placed it in the center of a circular table of dark wood. He gestured for me to be seated. After filling the bowl halfway with water, he added a few drops of clear oil. Locating a pendulum, he swung it above the bowl.

Five minutes passed, then several more. Finally, I could bear it no longer.

"It was Devor, wasn't it?" I said. "The other night after our card game he was talking of how much money one could make breeding fu dogs."

He shook his head.

"It was not Devor. Please let me continue the reading."

Puzzled, I nodded and watched.

"Fu Xian took them into the east," he finally said. "Ken Zhao and Po Shiang assisted him."

"Are you certain?"

"I'm getting very good at this. I'm certain," he said.

"Knowing is better than falsely accusing someone," I said, frowning, "but I was so sure. Get me that address in Atlanta, please."

He obtained a pad of paper and wrote the address out, tore off the top sheet, and passed it to me.

"I don't like the idea of your going after a magician," he said.

"He's only human."

"But he has allies. So do you. You told me of some of them."

"All right. We'll try Viss. Maybe Tuvoon, too." I grinned. "Why am I letting a human push me around this way?"

"Because I have good sense."

"Can you come with me?"

"Yes."

Viss and Tuvoon stared when I gained us entry to their bottle.

"Lord Demon," Viss said formally. "This gentleman looks vaguely human."

"Can't deny it," I said. "He just saved me from rushing into a possibly dangerous situation by insisting I come and tell you about the dogs."

"Then I think that you should. In the meantime, we've just received some blocks of the most wondrous tea. Pray join us."

I told them what had happened.

"I will accompany you to the abode of this sorcerer. Tuvoon?" she asked.

"And I."

Li Piao nodded. The expression in the agèd eyes beneath his long white brows was still enigmatic.

We stepped outside. There was no one about. We joined with the winds and moved up several planes. Soaring, I took us east. After a time, I landed us in the countryside, where I moved some small rocks. I withdrew a sphere then, on the order of the one I had located on my way to Ireland. I looked at the map and felt I could negotiate the rest of the way.

I tucked the map back into its cubby and got us there.

We approached Fu Xian's side door and hammered on it.

"A moment please," came a voice from within.

I gave the others a signal. Viss and Tuvoon melted into the shadows, guarding my back. Li Piao remained at my side, leaning more heavily on his walking stick than was precisely necessary.

The door was flung open by a short, heavy man. His skin was more brown than golden, the almond shape of his eyes less pronounced than in a pure ethnic Chinese.

"Ken Zhao?" I queried politely, knowing that I was correct. "I have come to speak with you and your associates about a small matter of business."

"Business?" he said haughtily. "This is a philosophical and educational school. We do not interest ourselves in business."

"It is a matter of misplaced property," I persisted. "Let me speak with your master, Fu Xian, if you truly know so little."

I could see that I'd gotten to him. For a moment he warred among conflicting impulses to slam the door in my face, to call for Fu Xian, and to assert his own importance. Something like a compromise won out.

"Wait here," he said stiffly.

I disliked being left like a tradesman on the doorstep, but before I could act a voice spoke in my ear.

"The building is warded quite strongly," Viss said softly. Her voice was clearly audible, but when I glanced to where she should stand I saw nothing. "It's a good job—for human magic. If you go inside and we remain out, we will not be able to assist."

"Then you must come in with us," I said simply. "Can you keep them from knowing you are with us?"

"We can try," Viss said.

Ken Zhao returned at that moment. He gestured for us to follow him and, despite his rudeness, we did this thing. Two visible and two invisible, we followed Zhao into a room designed to intimidate. The colors were bold. Creatures from legend and myth glowered from the carved panels and silk tapestries.

Two other men waited for us here. I knew them from my own research and from Li Piao's descriptions. Tall, thin Po Shiang stood clad in a mandarin's cap and robes. I doubted that he was eligible for the many buttons that ornamented the front of the cap, but this was not the time to taunt.

Fu Xian did not rise as we entered, but kept his seat like an emperor receiving his most humble vassals. He was not a handsome man. Indeed, there was something toadlike about his fleshy lips. The dark eyes almost hidden within their folds held malice.

This was the one who had sent lightning at me from the cloud. He, at least, knew exactly who I was; thus, his arrogance was inexcusable. Still, if I wanted the dogs back, I needed to restrain myself. Silently, I promised that Fu Xian would learn humility.

"We have things to discuss," I said, looking over Fu Xian's head to where his henchmen stood. "Do not irritate me, and you both may live."

They laughed.

"You really mean that," Po Shiang said.

"I most sincerely do," I told him. "As of now, neither of you has wronged me more than I can forgive. My quarrel is with Fu Xian."

"You'd better let him get to the point," interrupted Fu Xian, impatient of being ignored.

They both turned and regarded him. My thought was that neither of them liked his peremptory tone.

"I want my fu dogs back," I said, "instantly. And if they have been harmed . . ."

"I assure you that even if I were the sort of person who would harm them, I would not do it in this instance," Fu Xian said. "They're worth a fortune."

Impatient with his arrogance, I clapped my hands together and touched his shoulders.

Sliding from his chair, he collapsed into a quivering mass on the floor.

"As you did unto me from the cloud," I remarked.

"I . . ." Fu Xian gasped something that might have been an insult, but I forbore from treating him and his as I had the scrub demons who had slain Ollie. Here there were only three, and I did not wish to remove a source of knowledge before I had learned what I desired.

"I want my dogs," I repeated.

Po Shiang raised Fu Xian back into his chair and studied me through narrow, slitted eyes.

"They are not your dogs, demon. How can they be when they were created by the gods to guard against you and yours?"

"Still," I said, keeping from rebuking him as I had Fu Xian until I knew more, "they have resided peaceably with me for a long while. I wish them returned."

"Forget it," Ken Zhao retorted, emboldened that I had not called the lightnings on Po Shiang. "They're a long way from here. You'll see them again someday, but you won't like it when you do."

My temper flared now, and I gave in to an impulse to revert to my demon form. When I stood before them, head brushing the room's eight-foot ceiling, skin the cerulean of a summer sky, eyes dark as the bottom of a pit, they trembled—and this was before I spoke and they caught the glint of my fangs.

"I weary of this game. Killing you would be contrary to my needs, but I have nothing against a bit of mutilation."

I raised Ken Zhao by one leg and let the short, stocky man dangle upside down in the air, his garments all awry. Popping my index-finger claw, I drew the ideograph for Truth in the bared skin of Zhao's belly. The seven strokes were neatly done, though the blood that ran from them marred the elegance of my calligraphy.

"I want my dogs," I repeated patiently, hissing through my fangs. "Now."

Fu Xian was still shuddering from the force of the lightning stroke, but Po Shiang retained his poise.

"They are not here, and nothing that you do to that fool will make me tell you where they are."

"How about," I asked, dropping Zhao on his head on the carpeted floor, "what I might do to you?"

Po Shiang gestured broadly and fire sprang up in a circle around him. Normally that would have stayed me not at all, but beneath the red-and-orange glow, I recognized the lambent green of the flames Fire's Fever had used to attack me. Even at this distance, I could feel them trying to feed on my *chi*.

I sketched a quick ward to protect both myself and Li Piao. It sprang into being in the form of a cooling mist that quelled the fire's heat.

"You are not a human magician, Po Shiang."

He chuckled. "I hadn't figured on giving myself away so soon, but you would have found out once you started tracking me. Better to give myself away a bit too soon than risk the Godslayer's power."

For once I was glad of that reputation. I'd never admit it, but that green fire *scared* me. The gods hadn't had anything like it during the Demon War. If they had, we would have lost. Now it seemed to be common currency.

Viss came visible then.

"Unless you would like your souls melted with a theronic weapon," Viss said, and reaching into her pocket she produced a fat-barreled weapon quite a bit more powerful than the derringer she had slipped me, "you will return the dogs instantly."

Po Shiang studied her thoughtfully. To appearances she was still the round-faced little girl, but her gaze was steady. To one who could read auras her true nature would be revealed for what it was.

"A wise old fellow—Sun-Tzu—was fond of saying that when the last trick fails, the fox goes to earth, grants concessions to the enemy, and lives to return another day," said Po Shiang.

"I'm not certain that Sun-Tzu put it quite that way," Viss said pleasantly.

"Still, the sense is there," Po Shiang replied. He brought elegant hands together (surely I had seen long nails like that somewhere before?) and clapped them sharply twice. The perfume of roses filled the air, and a pink light seared my eyes.

When my vision cleared again, Po Shiang had vanished, leaving behind only a shower of rose petals.

Li Piao bent and scooped up a handful of the petals. "Wild roses are symbolic of dissension, Kai. I don't think you've seen the last of Po Shiang."

"Good," I answered shortly. Then I turned my attention to the two who remained.

Ken Zhao was sitting up now, rubbing his head though I had kindly dropped him on the carpet rather than on the tiled portions of the floor. He looked upon my alien majesty with a poise I found admirable.

"We're screwed, aren't we?" he said to Fu Xian.

"I think so," the other replied.

"Not you two," I said. "I think that you might yet negotiate the waters of the righteous."

"How is that?" said Fu Xian.

"Your master served you only to mock. You helped in his plans unknowingly."

"He is not our master," Fu Xian said stubbornly. Perhaps he was more stupid than I had thought. Ken Zhao was quicker on the uptake.

"I allied myself with Fu Xian," he said smoothly. "My association with Po Shiang was incidental. As Confucius said: 'The oak does not choose to harbor the mistletoe.'"

Tuvoon snorted. "I don't think Confucius ever said such a thing."

"So sue me," Ken Zhao shot back.

"Peace," I growled. I crossed to the chair which Fu Xian had recently occupied and slouched in it. The fit was bad, but I was tired of hitting my head against the ceiling.

Viss came and sat by my feet. Tuvoon prudently guarded the door. Li Piao had discovered a pile of documents in a carved chest at the back of the room and was inspecting them with every appearance of interest.

"Now," I said to the two human wizards, "if you cooperate with me, I am inclined to spare you."

"That's hardly fair," protested Fu Xian. "We were duped by Po Shiang, too! We took risks to get the dogs and then he hies out of here and leaves us. No doubt he's taken the dogs, too."

"Nevertheless. I can forgive if you will serve me."

"We're in a hurry," said Tuvoon, "Viss and I. So there you are—you have Lord Demon's offer. You two had better decide quickly if you're working with us or if you're barbecue."

He licked his lips, a theatrical gesture that seemed overdone to me, but appeared to convince Fu Xian that we were quite serious. With a quick glance at Ken Zhao, who nodded rapidly, he began talking.

The dogs, apparently, had been taken by purely human agency, but Devor had been bribed to show them how to get in and out of the bottle. An offering of *imbue* large enough to keep him stoned for a month—or longer if he rationed himself—had apparently undone whatever fragile friendship we had built over our games of Go.

"And who gave you the *imbue*?" Viss asked, leaning forward.

"Po Shiang brewed it in his alchemical lab," Ken Zhao volunteered. "At least he said that he did. We had no reason to disbelieve him."

"He showed us the ancient scroll," Fu Xian added, "from which he claimed to take the formula. The script was archaic, but the sense appeared to be there."

I frowned. "Do you have this scroll?"

"No, Lord Demon," Fu Xian said. "It was his property."

"Who," asked Viss, "told you that *imbue* would be the perfect lure for Devor?"

"We cast the I-Ching coins and followed the portents," Fu Xian answered.

Ken Zhao cut in, "But as I recall it now, Po Shiang steered our conclusions."

The hurt and angry look that passed over Fu Xian's toadlike features confirmed Zhao's deduction.

"So Po Shiang set the entire theft up," I mused aloud. "If he knew so much and was so powerful, why did he need you two?"

Ken Zhao barked hoarse laughter. "Because he never entered your bottle, Lord Demon. Master Xian insisted on the honor for himself, and, of course, someone had to stay behind and guard our backs. Since my specialized knowledge of water magic would do us little good outside, I went into the bottle while Po Shiang stayed safely without."

Viss nodded. "It does seem that he did not want us looking too closely at him, Kai Wren."

"But he blew it here," Tuvoon said.

"Or did he?" I wondered aloud. "He has gotten away, and I am no closer to finding my fu dogs."

I made a few decisions.

"Tuvoon," I said, "might I ask you to take these two fools to some place where they are unlikely to be found?"

"Alive or dead?" he asked.

"Alive," I answered. "We may have more questions for them, but I do not want Po Shiang to rescue them—or to kill them himself when he learns that we have not impulsively slain them and destroyed what knowledge they may have."

"Good thinking," Tuvoon said. "I know where to take them."

He gathered them up and was gone.

"Viss," I continued, "I believe we need to speak with Devor. Can you find him?"

"I can try," she said. "Where should I bring him?"

"My bottle," I said. "I will be changing the locks as soon as I leave here, but I will tell the Lung Shan to admit you."

"Very good." She stood then and looked up at me, little girl impish with a woman's wisdom in those twinkling black eyes. "Later, Kai."

She vanished.

"And me, Lord Demon?" Li Piao asked.

I turned to him. "What have you found there?"

"Some papers, perhaps some spells. The calligraphy is terrible, but I believe I can read them in time."

"Would you like to have them?"

"Yes."

"Then first we will gather them and take them to your house. Then I would ask you to come to my bottle. There is something I am forgetting—something I am overlooking. I wish to review everything that has happened since the night of Ollie's death. Perhaps between us we can discover what, in my fury, I have overlooked."

The old man smiled. "I would be honored, my lord."

And then, a teak chest of scrolls slung between us, we also departed. Apparently, we did not make our escape too soon. When we dropped the papers off at Li Piao's house, the old man turned on the television news and we learned that Fu Xian's school had been destroyed when weird green lightning from a clear sky set fire to the entire block.

V

AND WITH THIS news to light our way, we retired to my bottle. The misted mountains seemed lonely without the howls of the fu dogs calling the "all clear." The Lung Shan swam upon the currents of air to give us his report.

"Lord Kai," he said, and his undulations were in the way of a kowtow of deep respect, "nothing has happened in your absence."

"Thank you . . ." I began, but the dragon was continuing.

". . . Because I prevented it from happening."

"Oh?"

I caused Li Piao and myself to hover in the air. The human showed no fear, either of our peculiar position or of the enormous serpentine being in the air in front of us. Indeed, I fancied that he was studying the fashion in which the dragon moved upon the thermals.

"Tell me more, Lung Shan."

"Some hours ago, there came at the entry of the bottle a great hammering sound, as if one knocked upon the door. I knew that you possessed a key, so I did not answer it. I also told the ogres and other denizens not to answer."

"Good."

"Then the hammering ceased. It was followed by a noise like unto the hissing of a blowtorch."

"Indeed?"

"This puzzled me, so I went to one of the translucent sections and took a peep without."

"And?"

"And there without was a man-formed creature, but I do not think that it was a man, for from one long fingernail he spurted a jet of fire so hot that it was white. He was endeavoring to cut his way into the bottle. His efforts were for naught. Eventually, he departed."

"Was that the last you saw of him?"

"No. He returned shortly and bore with him a cluster of theronic grenades."

"What!"

"I swear, my lord. Knowing that these could break the interface or at the least destroy the bottle, I emerged via the back door and engaged the man-formed creature."

"Did you destroy him?"

"Alas, I failed, but I did force him to flee. His departure was somewhat hasty, so he left the bandolier of grenades where he had positioned them about the neck of the bottle. I retrieved them and brought them within."

With a flick of his long tail, the Lung Shan presented me with a braided lanyard on which were slung five fat, lead-cased, theronic grenades. I accepted these with the caution they were due.

"You have done well, great dragon. Do you have anything else to report?"

"That is all, Lord Kai."

"I thank you for your aid. Do you need to be relieved at your post?"

"No, Lord." The dragon showed fangs like ivory scimitars. "This is the most fun I have had in many centuries. I have posted ogres at the back door and set the Effervescent Celestial

Tigers to prowling all areas. Your palace servitors have been issued weapons from the armory."

"Again, you have done well."

"I am honored, Lord. I do miss the fu dogs, though."

"So do I." I indicated Li Piao. "This man has my permission to enter here. Taste his aura so that you may not mistake for him another who wears his form."

A long tongue flickered out and licked the air about Li Piao. The old man flinched, but only once.

"I will know him, Lord Kai."

"Two others may be admitted, Lung Shen: Viss of the Terrible Tongue and her son, Tuvoon the Smoke Ghost. Still, since we cannot be too careful, send me a message first, and I will confirm that they are who they say."

"Yes, Lord."

"Permit no others to enter, no matter if they had permission before this time. If any seek entrance, do not acknowledge them, but send me an image of their likeness and aura."

"I shall, Lord Kai."

Li Piao cleared his throat, and when I glanced inquiringly at him, he said:

"Mighty Lung Shan, did you perchance take an image of the man-formed one who tried to gain entrance before?"

The Lung Shan sighed. "I did not. I was too concerned with watching him. I could describe him, however."

"Pray, do so."

"The man-form he wore was tall and slim. He was clad in the robes of a mandarin and arrogance."

"Po Shiang?" Li Piao queried me.

"It certainly sounds like him," I agreed. "Come, we will go to my palace and be refreshed. Then we'll think about how to best approach this problem."

We bid the Lung Shan farewell and descended through the air to my palace. As we flew, I pointed out to Li Piao the nearly invisible forms of the Effervescent Tigers, the flitting shapes of the milkweed fairies. He had already met some of the ogres, but had never seen them in force.

"You really built this place with a back door?" he asked, chuckling slightly as we ascended the stair to the front entrance.

"Even a mouse knows the wisdom of having an escape prepared," I answered, a touch indignantly.

"True," he agreed.

We went to my favorite parlor, and the servitors took my orders for food and hot tea. Li Piao watched them depart—unless one looks for form, they are little more than heat shimmers in the air.

"You have many of those here?"

"As many as I have need," I replied. "It was part of my initial design specifications. Saves trouble with servants."

"What are they?"

"Call them emanations of my will given a somewhat permanent form. They are capable of a variety of tasks and when they are not needed they retire into the essence of the bottle."

"So they don't get bored."

"Yes."

"But they can fight."

"If so ordered," I agreed. "As I have been somewhat martial in the past, it seemed like a good idea to shape my servitors so that they could defend my home."

"Wise." There was a pause, then Li Piao asked, "But where does all the food come from?"

"Food?"

"Such as that your servitors have gone to prepare."

"Ah. When I constructed this bottle, I set in place a certain amount of undifferentiated matter. This is what the servitors draw upon to make meals. I use it as well for my projects, although often I bring in materials from without. Natural materials have a certain ambience that one does not find in the created twins."

"I wonder why this is so?"

"I can't really say, but if you want a good example look at laboratory-created gemstones. They lack the subtle properties of their natural kin even if they are chemically identical."

"True."

Li Piao looked thoughtful and, since I was reviewing events since Ollie's death, I let silence rise and flow over us. Tea came, then noodles spiced with sesame oil and topped with thinly sliced chicken and slivers of vegetables. We ate in silence, each occupied with his own thoughts.

When the noodles were finished and a platter of crisp eggplant fritters accompanied by a dish of sweet and pungent pork arrived, Li Piao spoke:

"Kai, have you remembered anything?"

"No. It continues to escape me."

"I have learned that if one stops trying, often the subconscious mind finds the answer."

"I have found that also."

"Would you be willing to permit me to distract you?"

"How? I don't think I could relax enough to play mah-jongg or Go."

Li Piao met my gaze. I still wore my demon-form so that what he saw was inky darkness surrounded by a slim crescent of white.

"Lord Demon, I have many questions about the nature of demonkind. If I am to help you, I think I need to know more."

I considered. What he said was true enough. If there was anything I didn't want to tell him, I could simply refuse.

"Very well. Ask your questions."

Li Piao licked his lips nervously. "Demons are not really demons, are they? They're something else."

I cocked an eyebrow at him. "Why do you say this?"

"Too many things don't fit. You've told me of these theronic weapons, for example. At first I thought that they were modern inventions—imitations or coevolutions with human technologies. The more I hear and overhear, the more I believe that your people have possessed them for far longer than humans have had guns and grenades."

I made a sound to encourage him, but gave nothing away.

"Then there are the names and manners of your people—those few whom I have met. They don't match with Chinese lore, neither do the wars I have heard mentioned . . . this 'Demon War,' these 'gods' who are your enemies."

"Perhaps," I suggested mildly, "we merely use different names for things and events of which you already know. Perhaps humans know little of the real events of supernatural realms."

"Perhaps," Li Piao said stubbornly, "but I don't think so."

I studied him, this long-bearded, tenacious human. How much did I owe him? How much should he know about the reality of things?

"The knife," Li Piao hinted, "is more useful for the sharpening."

"And the laborer is worthy of his hire," I responded dryly. "Very well. I will tell you what you wish to know. You are clever enough to have figured some out on your own."

I clapped my hands and more tea was brought, along with some almond cookies. I poured, then began my tale.

"Somewhat over five thousand years ago, in a cosmic plane not too different from this one, a war broke out between two factions. For ease of telling, let me call them the gods and the demons.

"The precise reasons for this war have been lost in the mists of Time and Rationalization. Suffice to say that in the end the gods won. They banished the remaining demons to another plane. Call it Kong Shyh Jieh."

Li Piao frowned. "The Empty World?"

"Close enough. The demons found themselves dumped on a gray, featureless plain. The sky above was light gray, the surface on which they stood was a darker gray. At first they pooled the resources of their own natural *chi* to survive, but without sustenance of any sort, they would have been doomed. As things were becoming quite grim, the demon who is today called He of the Towers of Light found a conduit to another plane—the plane within which is your own world."

"Ah!"

"The conduit was tangential with your own world—in fact, it was in the wilds of Outer Mongolia. Through this conduit, the demons brought back *chi* upon which to sustain themselves. They brought back trees, animals, and, over time, they began to import cultural touches."

"Ah. I begin to understand."

"Moreover, some of our number began to interact with humans. Thus, we have contributed to your culture, even as you contributed to ours."

"I never doubted that." Li Piao had on his thoughtful frown

again. "Still, why China when you had all the world from which to choose?"

"Partly it was proximity to the original conduit. Partly it was because the Chinese civilization, even in the reign of the Mythological Sovereigns, was far more sophisticated than anything else in the world at that time. The tendency toward long-reigning dynasties created an order of which we approved."

I paused to remember and sip tea.

"Pray, continue," Li Piao prompted. "This is fascinating."

"Over the next thousand years, the Empty World became far less empty. The living things we imported and our own abilities generated a wellspring of native *chi*. This, in turn, we employed to sculpt our environment for maximum generation of *chi*."

Li Piao smiled. "It sounds rather like *feng shui*."

I sipped my tea. "Where do you think the early Chinese got the idea? Finally, after a thousand years of residence, the demons learned to tap the inherent *chi* of the Empty World.

"By this time, the Empty World was empty no more. Generations of demons had been born there. Still, the elder ones longed for revenge against the gods. Thus came the first of the post-Exile wars."

I fell silent and, after a moment, Li Piao leaned forward.

"And?"

"And the demons lost."

"Oh."

"But this did not start a reign of pacifism. Instead, a trend was established. The demons would build up *chi* and resources. Then they would bridge the chasm to our original plane; they would attack and be driven back. Demons are nothing if not persistent. Meanwhile, internal rivalries developed. Feuds between demon clans kept the atmosphere martial between wars with the gods. Then, about a thousand years ago, came the Demon War."

Li Piao gestured for permission to speak. I nodded and took the opportunity to refill my teacup.

"Lord Kai, I admit to being a bit confused. How old are you?"

I had to think about it for a moment. Like the older Chinese cultures, demons do not tend to celebrate birthdays after the first until the person celebrated becomes venerable.

"About fifteen hundred years, give or take a few," I said, at last.

Li Piao hid his astonishment well enough.

"So you were born in Kong Shyh Jieh."

"Yes, but it has never been an empty world for me. The days of colonization and most wars were long over. The only major war in which I fought was the Demon War."

"When you earned the title 'Lord Demon.' "

"Even so."

I spoke on then, telling him something of my childhood, of my early interest in the arts of pottery and glassblowing, of my training in arts magical and martial, of the death of my parents and one sister in the Demon War. I told him of the armistice that followed the Demon War when the Armory of Truce was built and the weapons of power housed within it.

"Kai, I don't understand why you and the other 'demons' restricted yourselves to Kong Shyh Jieh and our Earth. Didn't you have access to any other planes?"

I nodded. "Several, but none as fruitful. You have seen the plane through which I have taken us for swift travel?"

"Yes."

"Most are like that: featureless. Others are dangerous or just plain strange. The labor needed to develop them would be extensive. We are not a prolific people. The No-Longer Empty World and Earth are sufficient for the needs of all but those few who still hold old grudges."

"But why haven't your people gone beyond the Earth? Surely there must be other places where the planes touch. Think of the resources that are out in the solar system—the galaxy— even the entire universe!"

I shook my head. "Sadly, this is not the way of it. The only conduits we have found on that plane take us to the Earth. Our created conduits require someone on both sides."

"A summoning spell."

"Precisely. So, unless the human race finds its way to other planets and summons us to join it, we are restricted."

"Which makes the lure of the original plane all the stronger, I suppose."

"Yes. The lure is not very strong for me, I must admit. This is my home. I can create demi-planes within my bottles for variety. Then there is the ever-changing Earth for amusement. The last few centuries have revealed *amazing* things. I subscribe to all the popular science magazines."

"But . . ."

Whatever Li Piao would have asked next was interrupted by a ringing of bells. Then a servitor bore in a polished crystal sphere within which an image of the Lung Shan was coiled.

"Lord Kai," he said, "one of those of whom you have spoken has come seeking entry."

"Who?"

"Viss of the Terrible Tongue."

"Show me her image."

The dragon did it and I inspected it on both a visual and essential level. She checked out.

"That's Viss."

The dragon said, "There is another with her, one I have seen before, the one called Devor."

I recalled that I had asked Viss to find him for me.

"Show me his image."

Lung Shan did, and this image, too, checked out.

"Let them both through, Mighty Dragon," I commanded, "but do not let Devor depart or enter again without my express command."

"I understand."

The image in the sphere winked out, and I handed the crystal to the servitor. Then I turned to Li Piao.

"It appears that we are about to have visitors. Now that you know what you do, do you care to remain?"

"More than ever, Lord Kai."

The servitors escorted Viss and Devor. He looked terrible—the fourteenth day of a thirteen-day drunk. She had put on the guise she had worn when she had been my teacher: ageless, feminine, elegant, but powerful. Something in me quickened at the sight.

I rose, and Li Piao did also.

"Lady," I said. "Thank you for coming and for your help in finding this . . . creature."

"What else are friends for, Kai Wren?" she replied with the smile I had longed to elicit when I had first been her student.

I clapped my hands, and the servitors brought tea. Pointedly, I did not pour any for Devor. Viss cradled her teacup in her hand and studied the translucent golden brew as she spoke.

"Our problems are akin to viewing the painting on this cup through the tea. We believe that we see clearly, but in reality what we know is distorted."

I nodded. Li Piao nodded. Viss continued:

"So what have we learned?"

"That the gods have grown ambitious," I offered. "Po Shiang is apparently willing to break the treaty, as was the demigod I slew at the Conventicle."

Li Piao cleared his throat. "Lord Kai, in all the history that you recounted to me, the battles between the demons and the gods were instigated by the demons. Is that true?"

I thought. "Yes."

"I disagree," Viss said. "I am somewhat older than you, Kai Wren. From my memories of history and from what was recounted to me by my elders, I would say that for as long as the demons had nothing of value, we did indeed seek to regain the way to our plane of origin. However, once we made our place of exile into a lovely and fruitful place, then the gods were all too willing to fight."

Li Piao glanced at me. I shrugged.

"Perhaps this is true. I do not claim to be a historian—I am a potter and glassblower."

Viss smiled. "And a fine swordsman and warrior."

"As need demands," I replied.

Li Piao made a soft sound that might have been a chuckle, but when I looked at him, he was staring into his tea.

"We have also learned," Viss continued, "that those fu dogs which you have housed since after the Demon War are of value to someone."

I directed a kick into Devor's side. He was so far gone that he didn't even flinch. Viss must have seen the look of disgust that flickered across my features.

"You should have seen him before I got him this sober. Do any of your magical bowls or bottles contain an antidote for *imbue*?"

"Not specifically," I said, thinking, "but I may have something that will serve. Wait here while I go look."

I departed and came back bearing a bowl the size of my fist that appeared to have been carved from a single pearl. Viss exclaimed in delight. Li Piao smiled. I was less pleased.

"I have never worried overmuch about addiction," I said, "but this bowl purifies anything that is placed within it."

Standing over Devor's slumped form, I spoke a few words. His inherent magic resisted me for a moment, but I was the more powerful. In a moment, he was washed from head to foot in a pale silvery light. Then he began to diminish in size until he was a doll-like figure I could place within the pearl bowl.

I did this, first removing his garments with an impatient gesture. Careful to position him so that his head would remain above the surface, I filled the bowl about halfway with warm water. Then I set the lot on a shelf and commanded a servitor to keep Devor from drowning.

"There," I said. "Let us see what that will do. In the meantime, we can continue our discussion. Let me begin by stating my goals. First, I want my dogs back. Next, I want to punish those who have dared act against me—both in this and in Oliver O'Keefe's death. Finally, I wish to learn if the theft of the dogs and Ollie's murder are in any way connected—both to each other and to any larger plot."

Viss nodded. "Neatly stated. My goals are less personal. Needless to say, I am interested in knowing who framed Tuvoon as the one who ordered your servant's death. As to the rest—I am worried about this undue interest that the gods are showing in our affairs. If after a thousand years of peace they have decided to become aggressors, we must know. Otherwise, demonkind will be caught unawares. We have become lazy in peace."

"But not powerless," I reminded her.

"No," she said, "not that."

Li Piao said, "Lord Kai, you told me that there was a council of the gods which dealt with the demons in matters of treaties and such. You were going to speak with them after you were attacked by Rabla-yu. What reply did you receive?"

"Unsatisfactory," I admitted.

"That is hardly surprising," Viss said quickly, "given that an admission of knowledge on their part would be akin to admitting that they knew that there was intent to break the treaties between us."

"True," Li Piao said. "Still, perhaps further inquiries can be made on that front."

I agreed. We continued talking well into the Hour of the Horse, when the skies over my mountains were dark as polished jet.

Devor seemed to be less in a stupor than asleep, but I decided to leave him in his healing bath. After a time, I offered Viss a place to rest, but she declined, saying that she wished to check on Tuvoon and his prisoners. Li Piao agreed to stay, having phoned his family sometime in the Hour of the Hare to explain that he was visiting some friends for a few days.

Given that the ogres were busy guarding the frontiers of my bottle, I escorted Viss to the exit myself. She was all business and efficiency, but I was left with the thought that she was a remarkable figure of a demoness.

I returned to my own chambers to sleep and to dream. In the latter part of the Hour of the Monkey, when the fingers of false dawn were threading into the sky, I awoke from a dream in which I had been speaking to Ba Wa. I had just asked him if he knew why Tuvoon would arrange for Ollie's death. The scrub demon's voice was soft, but I distinctly heard him telling me:

Another demon found us scrounging over there and he sounded us out on the job. That was yesterday. Said the man might be by tonight because he often passes this way on Saturdays. The demon offered shen coin, and, when we agreed, gave us a few then. Told us Tuvoon would be in town two days off. We supposed to get the rest tomorrow.

Another demon! I sat up in bed, nearly crowing my pleasure. That was what I had been seeking to remember! Ba Wa had never said that Tuvoon had arranged the assassination himself. Nor had Devor—Tuvoon had been the first to introduce

Devor into the picture. Who, then, was this demon who had offered the job to the scrub demons?

Rising, I went to my writing table and dampened my inkstone. In a few concise brushstrokes, I ordered Ba Wa to come to me and to bring with him Wong Pang, the other demon whose life I had spared that night in the park. Then I notified the Lung Shan to expect visitors and to notify me when they arrived.

Pleased with myself, I donned robes of death's white embroidered with owls. Best to look as intimidating as possible.

When the servitors informed me that Li Piao was awake, I had them bid him to join me for breakfast on a pleasant terrace overlooking gardens of cherry blossoms and magnolias.

He raised an eyebrow at my attire. Still cheered, I explained:

"Last night a dream revealed to me what I have been forgetting. Ba Wa mentioned another demon who may be connected to this mess. I have summoned him to me."

"And you want to terrify him."

"Essentially. I would prefer not to resort to torture, since Ba Wa may be of further use to me. Just in case, I've told him to bring one whom he regards as a friend."

Li Piao kept any unease carefully schooled from his features, merely tasting a slice of ripe peach.

"Wise."

A message from the Lung Shan informed us that the two scrub demons had arrived. I inspected their auras via the crystal, then ordered the remnants of breakfast cleared away. With a few fingerstrokes, I cast a glamour that gave gentle Li Piao the appearance of a massive demon with muddy green skin, curving horns, and the faceted eyes of a housefly. I finished just as the servitors wafted Ba Wa and Wong Pang into my presence.

Both scrub demons looked terrified. Ba Wa's yellowish skin was pale; Wong Pang was positively gray. As soon as they perceived me standing before them in my robes of deathly white, they flung themselves onto the floor in front of me, kowtowing and banging their misshapen foreheads on the floor.

"Cease, you miserable wretches!" I thundered.

They stopped so fast you would think I had turned them into stone.

"Rise and face me!"

They did, looking as if they would rather not.

Ba Wa had learned the virtue of silence from our previous meetings. He must have shared some of his wisdom with Wong Pang, for even that fool kept his tongue behind his pointed teeth.

I stared at them, narrowing my eyes into dark slits. My only movement was the slow caress of my fingers along the length of my sheathed sword. When at last I spoke, my voice was almost friendly.

"I have a question for you, crawlers in the dust. Answer me and I may let you live."

Ba Wa nodded vigorously. Wong Pang hazarded a squeak that just might have been: "I hear, great, mighty one."

I pitched my voice as low as thunder. "When Ba Wa recounted to me the events leading up to your murder of my servant, he mentioned that a demon came to you and told you of Ollie's habits so that you might slay him."

Ba Wa saw I wished confirmation.

"Yes, Lord Demon, that what I say and what I say is true."

"This demon is the same who promised you payment in *shen* coins."

They both bobbed in agreement.

"Who was he?"

Ba Wa and Wong Pang spoke as one: "It was He of the Towers of Light, Lord Demon."

I frowned, and they took my frown as disbelief.

"It was!" Ba Wa assured me.

"Was! Honest!" Wong Pang squealed. "He of the Towers of Light—great demon ruler. Have seen at many festivals and at Conventicle. No mistaking."

"Silence!" I bellowed, and I did not protest when they flung themselves trembling to the floor.

While they groveled, I considered. He of the Towers of Light was indeed a demon of great reputation. One of the original Exiles, he had discovered the conduit to Earth. Later, during the Shang Dynasty, he had made his reputation first as a war-leader and then as a trader with humanity.

During his first reign, demons had resided in China, using

their powers to masquerade as some of the less savory elements from Chinese mythology. (It's amazing how quickly the peasantry and the lower orders of the aristocracy—China was essentially a feudal state at this time—will obey orders when the king commands demon henchmen.)

Later, such direct intervention in human politics had been viewed as gauche, but at the time it had been the best means for demons to harvest the *chi* that was so essential to building a livable superstructure in the Kong Shyh Jieh.

Would He of the Towers of Light stoop to treating with scrub demons?

When we had lunched together at the Conventicle, I learned that HE had become something of a monk after the Buddhist pattern. He resided in a territory in the Demon Realm sculpted after his own image. It was a beautiful but stark place that many said bore more of a resemblance to the Origin Plane than it did to our new homeland.

"You shits certain that it was He of the Towers of Light who came to you?" I asked sternly.

Wong Pang chittered, "Yes! Sure as shit, Lord Demon!"

Ba Wa was more careful. "He sure look like He of the Towers of Light, boss. Still, demons can look like other demons, right?"

I nodded, thought of another question.

"You told me that this demon gave you *shen* coin as a down payment for your services. Do you still have any of those coins?"

Wong Pang wailed in despair. Ba Wa shook his head sorrowfully.

"I spend mine, boss. Cost of living keep going up."

"True. Many months have passed. Perhaps it was too much for which to hope," I said, and Wong Pang stopped gibbering. "Still, I would like to see one of those coins. If you have a chance to reclaim one, bring it to me."

They began bobbing, eager to please.

"But," I cautioned, "I only want to see a coin if you can assure me beyond any doubt that it is one of those you or your allies were given by He of the Towers of Light."

"Yes, boss!" they assured me.

"And do not speak of this charge, or of our conversation to anyone!"

They groveled.

"To anyone!" I growled. "You little shits understand?"

Their abasement was a disgrace to see. I softened my tones slightly from the ringing thunders I had been using.

"And if you succeed, I may have a reward for you."

Ba Wa grinned, then hastened to appear humble. "The joy of serving great lord is all reward us little crawlers in the mud need. We look for *shen* coin."

"We keep mouth shut," Wong Pang added, "tight as a frog's butt."

"Good."

I sent them away. Li Piao looked at me.

"What is a *shen* coin exactly?"

The incongruity of those gentlemanly tones coming from the grotesque visage I had given him was unsettling to me. I wiped the illusion away with a gesture.

"A *shen* coin is . . . Do you recall what I told you earlier about how the first exiled demons worked to enhance both their own *chi* and the *chi* of the land?"

"Certainly."

"*Shen* coin came into use then. They are shaped rather like Chinese cash—round with a hole in the middle."

Li Piao smiled. "I wonder who borrowed the form from whom?"

"I don't know," I answered, "but I suspect that the humans borrowed from us, since the earliest Chinese coins resembled tools or shells. In any case, a *shen* coin bears within it an amount of *chi*. Sometimes it is the issuer's personal *chi*, other times it has been harvested from some resource. Whatever the case, the *chi* can be drained from the *shen* coin and used in a variety of ways."

"Or," Li Piao reasoned, "hoarded against need. So if you can examine one of the *shen* coins with which the little demons were paid, you might be able to find who issued it."

"It's a long shot," I agreed, "but I have difficulty believing that He of the Towers of Light would do business with one of those creatures."

"Who is this He of the Towers of Light, anyhow?" Li Piao asked.

I told him, and I was just finishing the tale when Viss of the Terrible Tongue arrived. Again she wore the guise of the lovely but fierce swordswoman. Idly I found myself hoping that she would maintain her current preference.

"Hi, fellows," she said. "How's Devor?"

Then she did a double take as she noticed my costume.

"Whose funeral is it? Or maybe I should ask whose is it going to be?"

"No one, yet," I assured her. "I was interviewing the scrub demons again. I recalled something I wished clarified."

"And?"

"They say that the demon who paid them *shen* coin to go after Ollie and told them that Tuvoon would pay the balance was He of the Towers of Light."

"No! I can't believe that old stick would stir from his meditations long enough to develop such a level of intrigue."

"My thoughts precisely," I said. "It seems far more likely that some fool adopted his appearance. Tricking scrub demons isn't hard."

"No." Viss looked thoughtful. "Still, unless what the scrub saw was just an illusion, that body-of-light form HE's been favoring since the Ch'in Dynasty isn't easy to imitate."

"I hadn't considered that," I said.

"It's the lack of solid matter," she explained. "I've made something of a study of the question since Tuvoon is partially ethereal. Essentially, it's harder for a solid body to assume an ethereal form and vice versa."

I cocked an eyebrow. "I've never had any problem."

"Wren, my dear student, I don't think you realize how very talented you are. You're really more like one of the demons from the earliest days of Exile than you are like your own generation—and certainly you are more powerful than those born these past five hundred years. Why do you think they were so eager to honor the Godslayer?"

"I hadn't thought about it," I said honestly.

Viss honored Li Piao with a friendly smile. I swear the old man colored like an adolescent boy.

"Our Kai Wren," she told him, laughing, "has become far too much the artist. It's almost a pity he wasn't born in more warlike times. His potential for the combat arts is being wasted."

Remembering how easily I had summoned up my powers when my fury at Ollie's murder filled me, I wondered about that, but I kept my silence on the matter.

"You asked after Devor," I said, directing the conversation elsewhere.

"Yes, how is the sot?"

"When I checked on him earlier, most of the effects of the *imbue* seemed to have worn off. Whatever hangover remains should merely make him amenable to answering questions in the most direct fashion possible."

"Good." She examined my attire. "Are you going to maintain the 'Deathlord' garb?"

"Why not?"

"Then perhaps I should alter my appearance to something more fearsome as well."

Her complexion started turning from the healthy golden brown of a Chinese maiden to brick red.

"No!" I protested.

She looked at me, startled. "No?"

"I mean," I said hastily, "perhaps you should retain that more winsome form. We could work a good demon/bad demon routine on him."

"Isn't that rather stale?" she asked, but her coloring began to lighten.

"The desire to find an ally never grows old," I assured her.

"And your human friend?"

"I had thought to have him sit by where he could see and hear but not be perceived himself." I looked at Li Piao. "If Devor mentions any places or people, perhaps you could scry his accuracy and signal me."

"A sort of lie detector?" he asked.

"Oh, we have spells that could force truth from him," I said idly, "but they are painful and an old liar like Devor probably has much skill in manipulating his answers. You would provide information far more valuable than mere truth."

"Very well, Lord Kai," he said. "Tell me where to go and how to send you messages."

And I did this thing. We retired to a stark room with walls of scarlet glass. They were painted with cryptic trigrams in gold, and the floor was textured like the shell of the sacred tortoise. I had servitors bring chairs draped in white silk for Viss and me. Devor would stand.

I cast him from the pearl bowl with a single gesture. He collapsed in a dripping heap on the floor and grew to full size.

"Stand!" I commanded.

Devor endeavored to do so. Naked and wet he was a pathetic figure. His native demon-form had been warped by excessive indulgence in *imbue*. Once he had been the proud golden figure with the green wings and cresting horns who had come to play Go with me. But now his coloring was tarnished to a dull hue like worn brass plate over rusted iron. His wings were thin with molt, their green faded to the muddy shade of algae. Even his horns appeared bent and weak.

I made a quick gesture to assure that he had not constructed this pathetic illusion to gain our pity, but what stood before us was in truth Devor.

"Devor, you have abused my hospitality."

He stared at me, a blank expression in eyes that should have sparkled like emeralds. Pathetic.

"Devor, why did you let those human sorcerers into my bottle?"

He muttered, *"Imbue*. More than I'd seen in centuries."

"For that!" I spat, and my spittle turned into fire that guttered out against the floor, marking out one of the trigrams concealed within the tortoiseshell. It was the combination of the trigrams for fire and lake which indicates great disharmony.

Viss spoke. "Devor, how did the human wizards know to contact you?"

He shrugged. "Dunno."

I snarled. Viss hastened to speak again.

"Devor, that is not enough. Lord Demon has every right to slay you."

"So do it!" he muttered. "My head aches."

I said with soft menace, "I could insist that you live, Devor, and more than your head would ache."

"Tell us what you can, Devor," Viss urged.

"They summoned me," he said.

"Through what Gate?" Viss asked.

"A new one, in Atlanta," he answered. "Never been through before. Had a funny taste."

"Taste?" Viss prompted.

"Aura. Not all demon magic."

"Whose then?"

"Human?" He shrugged. "I wasn't analyzing. I was pissed. I'd been winning a handful of *shen* off of Night Bride. First time in a long while."

"Try to remember," I suggested.

He shot a look at me and did. The effort was obvious. Tufts of fluff drifted from his wings to eddy around his ankles.

"Maybe god magic?" he offered. "Haven't tasted a god Gate for a long time, but some of the rash ones slip across now and then for a game."

That was news to me, though I wondered why I was surprised.

"You play with them?" I asked.

"Yeah."

"What are the stakes?"

"*Shen* coin, *imbue*." Devor shrugged. "*Imbue* comes from Origin. Harder to make here."

I tried to remember just how old Devor was. It occurred to me that he might well be one of the first Exiles. Over six thousand years old, survivor of who knows how many battles, now reduced to addiction and gambling with ancestral enemies for a hit. I almost pitied him. Almost.

"Did you tell any of the gods you gamble with about my fu dogs?"

"Might have." He bit his lip in an effort to remember and blood like molten gold dripped out. "Yes. I did to several. Checking out the market in case you decided to sell 'em."

Viss tossed him a linen handkerchief to blot the drip from his lip.

"Tell us the names of the gods you gamble with, Devor."

"What if I don't know?" he asked, a crafty look in his eyes. "My head aches something fierce."

"I could make it hurt worse," I offered, "so that how it feels now would be feeling better."

Devor winced at that. He drooped there for a few moments. Just as I was considering prompting him with an earthquake inside his skull, he said:

"Kaupaetis."

"Very good," Viss said, glancing at me.

Inside my head, I heard Li Piao murmur, *"I've an image."* I nodded.

"Abesteyne."

"Go on," Viss said after getting the go-ahead from me.

A stream of names followed: Teekahaire, Wenobee, Zvichy, Montocryxe, Hayati, Thet-Bibo, Moxabanshy, Skywamish. After each name, Li Piao informed me that he had an image, confirming that Devor was not just making up nonsense.

At last the stream dried up to a trickle, and for a few of these names Li Piao could not summon an image. Whether this was evidence that Devor was trying to fool us or that his *imbue*-fuddled head couldn't remember any better, I didn't know, so I kept the sting of the acid lashes I applied to his slumped shoulders at a merely torturous level.

"I think," Viss suggested after we had three misses in a row, "we should let Devor rest."

"Reward him for failure?" I snarled.

"Give him a chance to think some more."

"Very well," I agreed as if reluctantly. In reality, I was tired of torture and anger. Also, I was troubled by the implications of this long list of names.

With a wave of my hand, I miniaturized Devor once more. Then I set him in the pearl bowl and again gave him over to a servitor with orders to keep him from drowning. As an afterthought, I instructed that Devor be given a cup of something to sip and a light meal while he soaked. If he had *imbue* enough, he might well not have eaten for some time.

Then I escorted Viss from the chamber and to my favorite parlor. As we strolled down the corridors, I said to her:

"I had not thought there would be so many."

She frowned. "Yes. I dislike that myself. Yet, given the numbers of gods who dwell in Origin and other planes, a dozen or so is not too many."

"Yes, I see what you mean. I wonder if Po Shiang's real name is among those Devor gave to us. Yet, I noted that Rabla-yu was not among the gamblers."

"A troubling thought," she agreed. "There may be many arrayed against us."

We went into my favorite parlor where Li Piao joined us. I had the servitors bring us pear wine and prepare a banquet. It had been long since the breakfast peaches, and I was starving.

VI

AND SO DAYS passed, turning into weeks which passed, and yet we learned nothing useful. Beyond that first list of names, Devor had nothing to tell us about the gods and their intrigues. He swore that his interest in the fu dogs had been entirely based upon their potential resale value. At last I set him free, for too many of demonkind knew that he had been taken by Viss on my behalf. Godslayer or no, the customs and rituals that govern our kind frown on keeping one of our own prisoner indefinitely.

I thought about magically enhancing Devor's craving for *imbue* and then implanting a physical inability to tolerate the stuff so that every time he had a snort he'd collapse retching just as the high got good. I didn't though.

During his sojourn in my bottle Devor's system had been washed clean of the stuff. Withdrawal hadn't been pretty, but it had been absolute. If he decided to let the crap ruin his life again, well, that would be punishment enough.

And the two human sorcerers, Fu Xian and Ken Zhao, knew little enough about Po Shiang. Their own talent for magic was considerable enough to show that they'd had a bit of enhancing along the lines of what I'd done to Li Piao (although not as intensive). Clearly Po Shiang had wanted his human henchmen to be useful.

These two we could keep prisoner and did, for they were missing and presumed dead in the fire that had demolished their place in Atlanta. Viss offered to stow them in her bottle, and I accepted her kindness. Po Shiang obviously had something against me. I didn't really want two of his lackeys within my fortifications.

So fruitless weeks passed, and, when I observed they were in danger of becoming fruitless months, I decided that we could no longer avoid checking out even the most minor leads.

Before this point, in strict observance of protocol, we had made our inquiries through decorous third parties like Lord Swizzlediz. Now, I started looking up Devor's associates myself. Perhaps *imbue* had dulled him to the significance of something or other, but certainly all the others would not have been so far gone.

It was a slim hope, but it was something to do. Once or twice I had tried to start a new project—a bowl, perhaps, to replace the one I had given to Li Piao. I rarely got further than blending and kneading the clay body before a sense of urgency would ruin my concentration. Images of Ollie hanging from a tree or of the sundered crest of Horsehead Mountain or the green flames with which Fire's Fever had sapped my *chi* would intrude. I could not ignore an urgent awareness that beneath the quiet sense of "everything as usual," a storm front was brewing.

I started with Passion Flower, but she was nothing like I had hoped. Apparently, her association with Devor had been purely good times and good fun. When he was forced to sell his bottle, she moved on. As I left her company (having easily resisted her not-so-subtle attempts to make me her next supporter), I reflected how different she was from Viss, who had, if anything, drawn closer to me as my troubles and frustrations mounted.

Night Bride was no better. She was one of those dark-souled young ones who believe the propaganda that demons are intrinsically evil. I found her company unsettling, for her speech was laden with references to those passages in human holy books that paint us in the worst possible light.

I asked after the Walker, but he was apparently off on one of those long sojourns which had earned him his name. I was forced to settle for Snow Goon and the Twister. These two, at least, had paid some attention to the godly gamblers who occasionally joined their games, but, beyond being able to confirm some of the names that Devor had given us, I learned nothing new.

These failures did nothing to improve my temper. The skies within my bottle raged with storms, and the servitors grew adept at catching the things I flung about in my anger. Needless to say, I didn't get very many visitors. Only Li Piao continued with imperturbable calm to make his weekly visits for games and conversation. Even Viss and Tuvoon took to calling ahead.

"Why," Li Piao asked, as he set a shining black stone onto one of the intersections of the Go board, "don't you speak with He of the Towers of Light?"

"What good would that do?" I replied. "His only connection to this is that someone borrowed his appearance to speak with a couple of stupid shit demons."

"True," Li Piao said. "I thought he might know something. You say he is very old, even for your kind."

"And nearly a complete recluse," I countered.

"Indeed."

Nearly an hour passed before either of us spoke. It was again Li Piao who braved the storm: "How about the sword-smith Seven Fingers?"

"Why?"

Li Piao shrugged. "If a war is brewing, perhaps someone has asked him to make new weapons."

"Hm."

More silence.

"There are other ways to track a war," Li Piao persisted, "than just interrogating frivolous people about what they might have observed."

I stared at him for a long moment. Not only was he making some sense, he was royally beating me this game. As a strategy game, Go makes chess seem easy—partly because the moves are so deceptively simple.

"Why do you care?" I asked.

"You are my friend."

"I am a demon. You are a human."

"So?"

"Our wars will have no effect on you. They never have."

"Does that change the fact of our friendship?"

I sighed. Human emotion. Yet . . . I had cared about Ollie, a caring that was as real as the smooth stone I cupped in the palm of my hand.

"No," I said, "it does not change the fact of our friendship. Tell me what I should do."

Li Piao nodded. "Speak with Seven Fingers. Do you have bankers—especially ones who pay interest on *shen* coins?"

"After a fashion."

"Find out if anyone is hoarding a large amount of *chi*."

"That might be difficult."

"Still."

"Very well."

"And talk to He of the Towers of Light."

"Anything else?"

"I shall think on it."

We played on in silence. I couldn't quite make myself resign, so he beat me soundly. After he had left, I called for a glass of pear wine and sipped it, plotting out my strategy for the morning. Li Piao was right. I'd been thick.

I finished my wine and retired to my bedchamber. Outside, the storm clouds had cleared, stars glittered against the velvet night. I slept deeply and well.

So the next day I went and looked up Seven Fingers. I could hear him out at his forge, banging away, so I didn't bother with the front door. Seven Fingers doesn't live in one of my bottles. Most demons don't, just in case I've given the wrong impression.

Seven Fingers and his lovely daughter live on an estate situated on the lower slopes of Hawksview Mountain. Hawksview is rich in minerals and metal ore. Seven Fingers's parents had made certain it would be when sculpting the area. It also has a tribe of cheerful little dwarves who like mining.

No kidding. They mine and sing and sell their ore to Seven Fingers. He turns the raw stuff into weapons. Sometimes he pays them in his work, but most of the time they get *shen* coin.

Know what they spend the *chi* on? Replenishing the ore in the mountain. It's a tidy system.

I'd been to the estate from time to time over the centuries. Ceramics and glasswork don't have a lot in common with metal-working, but some of my tints and glazes use materials best found on Hawksview. I could have created a lode for myself, but it wouldn't have been worth the effort, so I bought what I wanted. Seven Fingers has always been welcoming—that bit with my slaying Chaholdrudan has paid off there, too.

Leaning back against a bit of twisted metal that might have been sculpture, but might have been slag, I watched Seven Fingers hammering away. His form was not unlike the one he had worn when hosting dinner at the Conventicle, but was longer in the torso to accommodate two extra sets of arms. His hands, I realized after a bit, had five fingers but two thumbs. Tidy.

After about a quarter of an hour Seven Fingers noticed I was there. He grunted, put his work to quench, and lumbered over to me.

"Lord Demon."

"Seven Fingers."

We shook hands. That extra thumb felt rather odd.

"I don't want to take you from your work," I said.

"No problem. I would have been taking a break soon anyhow. It's hot work."

"What are you making?"

"A *jen chiang* for Stormmiller."

"He having trouble?"

"Apparently. Said that some capricious wind sprites are causing all sorts of havoc out his way. He's going hunting."

"With a *jen chiang*?"

Seven Fingers shrugged. "He also ordered some steel arrow-heads."

I tried not to seem too interested.

"Anyone else having troubles like his?"

"A few people," Seven Fingers said. "I don't get all the weapons business—I charge too much and won't rush an order. Pigeon Eyes was my apprentice once, you know. Her work is good, and she's set up her own shop. Apparently, she's been really busy."

"That's what I get for living in a bottle," I said. "I miss all the excitement."

"Oh, I don't know." Seven Fingers wiped all thirty of his fingers (and twelve thumbs) clean on an already sooty rag. Then he shrugged away his extra arms. "I heard you tangled with Devor and some human sorcerers."

"That's true."

"Heard your fu dogs were stolen."

I marveled at the amount of gossip among our supposedly isolated people. I'd need to tease Viss about this.

"That's true, too."

"Found them?"

"No."

"But you let Devor loose."

"He didn't take them. The humans did."

"Humans?"

"That's where the trail leads." I considered how much to say, decided to hold back a bit. "To the humans and possibly an ally."

"A demon?"

"I don't think I'd better say just now."

"Suit yourself." The smith checked the fire, seemed satisfied with its condition. "Come inside, have a cup of tea and a word with my daughter."

"I don't wish to inconvenience you."

"Oh, come along!"

So I went. It wouldn't do to offend him; besides, tea would taste nice.

Seven Fingers brought me into a room decorated with elegant, almost abstract carvings in highly polished wood. They were unpainted except for a touch of color—usually metallic—almost hidden within a curve or shadow.

"My daughter's work," he said with gruff pride. "She calls it *Next*—apparently they're all tied into a theme. No idea what she means by that, of course. That girl's way beyond her old man. Let me see if she's free to join us."

When he left I strolled from carving to carving, studying the smooth, twisting forms she had brought out of the wood. The more I looked, the more I was certain that they were not as abstract as I had first believed, but what they were meant to represent escaped me. The licks of color reminded me of masks or shrouding veils. I had to fight down an impulse to scrape the color away to see what lay beneath.

Illusion, misdirection . . . I heard a soft footfall, almost inaudible on the thick carpet, and lowered a hand I had not realized was raised, retracted an extended claw.

"Impressive," I said to my host and hostess by way of greeting.

Seven Fingers beamed. Spilling Moonbeams looked shyly embarrassed. I could tell that because today she wore a figure more closely human. Her hair was still a fall of gossamer and her skin blue-black night, but she had shaped a woman's form and donned silk pantaloons and jacket that concealed her less solid elements.

The entry of several of the mining dwarves pushing a tea cart saved us from finding a way out of that awkward moment. Seven Fingers gestured me to a table made of highly polished cherry wood—a prosaic thing in such a setting, but nonetheless a tribute to the woodworker's art.

"Why don't you sit on that side?" he said. "I took the liberty of ordering more than tea. I'm famished."

"I didn't know that your little people did anything but mining," I said as I seated myself.

Spilling Moonbeams smiled. "Of late—perhaps these last two hundred years—some have requested a break from the mines. We have accommodated them in the household staff. Their fondness for meticulous detail makes them easy to train."

"I wonder if it's the influence of the human plane?" I said. "People there no longer know their place."

"Perhaps," she said, pouring tea. "Perhaps it is merely curiosity."

We talked of such things over cups of excellent tea and some marvelous pickled melon and noodles. Carefully, I steered the conversation to those things that were coming to obsess me: gods, weapons, war, sorcery.

Father and daughter proved quite helpful. Seven Fingers loved talking of his profession—his art. From him I learned that many more weapons of power were in circulation than I had realized.

"Ever since the theft from Truce . . ." he began.

"What?"

"Didn't you know?"

"I didn't get out much until recently."

Seven Fingers frowned. "I guess it happened about twenty years ago. There was an earthquake in the vicinity of the Armory. No one was ever able to prove decisively whether it was caused by magic or merely an act of nature."

Spilling Moonbeams snorted delicately. "I will never believe it was an accident."

"I said it was never *proven*, daughter," he said. "The quake cracked the exterior wall of the Armory sufficiently to violate the magical barriers. There was a fire, too. Various artisans were called in to effect the repair. When it was completed, an inventory was taken, and it became apparent that several items were missing."

"What?"

Seven Fingers looked uncomfortable. "A couple of cases of theronic weapons, some personally tailored weapons."

"Like my spirit sword?"

"Quite possibly."

"What do you mean by that?"

"The area where the spirit swords and their ilk were kept was reduced to slag. Even I could not tell precisely what had been taken and what had been destroyed."

"And no one was told?"

Seven Fingers sighed. "I am not a politician, but as I understand it, the feeling was that if the gods learned that so many of the old weapons were at large, they might decide we were in violation of the terms of the treaty that ended the Demon War."

Spilling Moonbeams muttered something that sounded like: "Which is precisely what I think someone wanted."

"You told me once," I said carefully, "that you had repaired my spirit sword."

"Yes, I did, at the request of Night Bride."

"And you said that she returned it to Truce."

"I said that it was *stored* in Truce. My assumption was that she had it placed there. Night Bride is a strange creature. She fears demonkind although a demon herself. I believe she wanted all checks and balances in place."

Recalling my interview with that one, I could believe Seven Fingers.

"But you said," I continued carefully, "that Viss now possesses my spirit sword."

"Yes."

"How do you know this?"

"Some scrying was done at the time to try to locate the missing weapons. I selected yours because I had worked on it comparatively recently."

"Did you do the scrying yourself?"

"No. It was done by Icecap at the request of the current governing council."

"You realize that this implies that Viss was one of those who engineered the violation of Truce."

"Yes."

"Then why . . ."

"Because she denied it and said that she had found the sword half-buried in the dirt a few miles from Truce. She passed all tests against her veracity—as did Tuvoon."

Again there was a gentle sound of disbelief from Spilling Moonbeams. I ignored it.

"Did you ask her to return it to Truce?"

"The council did. She refused."

"Oh?"

"She said that if it had been lost once, then it could be lost again. She pointed out that over the centuries since Truce was established a fair number of spirit swords had come back into circulation. The council had no real grounds to insist, not if they wanted to keep things quiet."

"And they had ample reason for wanting that," I agreed, remembering the Demon Wars, remembering the vendettas that had arisen between demon and demon before the war. "Yes. I understand their motives."

I wondered, though, if I understood hers.

We drank more tea then, ate other dainties that the former miners brought to us. At last, the time came for me to depart.

"Where do you go now, Lord Demon?" said Spilling Moon-beams, for perhaps she read something in the darkness that is my eyes.

"I'm going to follow the advice of a friend," I replied, "and visit He of the Towers of Light."

Departing, I shaped myself a shape equal parts wind and speed. Taking to skies now glimmering rose and gold with the first brushstrokes of the setting sun, I composed myself for a long flight. He of the Towers of Light was in possession of some prime real estate at the undeveloped fringes of the Empty Land.

He wasn't much for modern conveniences—the phones and faxes that many of the demons had borrowed from the human plane—and these days he answered communications spells pretty much on whim, but when we'd visited at the Conventicle he had made it clear that I was welcome to visit.

I flew through the night and into the next day. Beneath me the landscape changed from the sculpted, realistic terrain that thousands of years of demon labor and demon magic had brought out of the emptiness to something that must be closer to the original plane: flat and gray, the surface coarse, like window screen, and with the same distorting effect on vision.

Darkness was gathering once again when I first perceived the glow of the Towers, stark and majestic, beckoning to me across the stark plane.

Chi does not accumulate quickly, especially not when it is needed to generate the basic necessities of life. Had not demonkind been able to shift shape (with the use of *chi*) into forms able to subsist on the thin resources of Kong Shyh Jieh they would have died.

The Exiles didn't die, but many centuries passed before they were able to do much about remodeling their new place of residence. By the time they could, much of what made Kong Shyh Jieh survivable had been imported from the Earth—much of that from China for the simple reason of convenience.

When terrain sculpting became a real possibility, debate arose. If, as had been originally intended, Kong Shyh Jieh was reshaped to resemble Origin, the imported materials would not fit in. True, they could be rendered into raw matter (at great cost) and reworked to suit the new theme, but not everyone was happy with the idea. Demons, like humans, grow attached to things, and the "furnishings" of Kong Shyh Jieh represented a triumph against nearly impossible odds.

So a compromise was reached. Kong Shyh Jieh's "public areas" would be sculpted to incorporate the imported matter. A large park would be constructed along the lines of Origin so that the Exiles' offspring would not forget their heritage. Additional land grants were given as rewards to those who had been of great service to demonkind. These could be sculpted in whatever fashion the owners wished.

What I was approaching was one of those grants. He of the Towers of Light had chosen to sculpt his property after one of the more showy regions in Origin. His current sobriquet was a tribute to the artistry he had demonstrated in furnishing his grant. It also served to remind just about anyone who had a sense of history that he was one of the few remaining Exiles, one who had seen Origin and dwelled there. And, as an added kick, it reminded those who judge worth by wealth that he possessed *chi* enough to sculpt a terrain that owed nothing to imported furnishings.

I understand that some of his contemporaries thought that he was crazy when he started pouring a fortune in accumulated *chi* into the work. I doubt that any of them would question his sanity or his wisdom now.

Weary as I was from my long flight, I felt invigorated by what arose before me. Slender needles of pure white light rose from billowing crystal dunes that captured the light in their minute facets and scattered it into tiny rainbows.

Closer in I could see that the curtain of light did not stand in solid ranks, but undulated in arcane patterns that trapped *chi*, fed it back into itself and then, when the current became too strong, let it flow over barriers toward the interior.

I'd seen the setup before and admired it. I did so now, thinking that if this was what Origin was really like, no wonder some wild-eyed fanatics were willing to start a crusade to regain the home plane for demonkind. And that no wonder the gods were so powerful, since they had this to draw upon from birth.

I penetrated the curtain of light, feeling much of my exhaustion drain from me. A bit of fear I hadn't known was there also drained away. If HE hadn't wanted me to visit no doubt I'd be lending my spare *chi* to the system and starting a long trudge back home on foot. It's a good way to discourage salesmen.

Once I had passed through the curtain, I saw the Towers: hard, somehow cold bars of white light, solid slabs of varying heights standing like some futuristic cityscape against a lime-green sky. There was nothing to detract from their austere beauty: no plants, no birds, no vehicles. A fat succulent of some sort, rather like a ruddy, wild portulaca, threaded itself between rocks that continued to channel the *chi* toward the Towers. There were no flowers.

Now that I had arrived, I transformed my body back into my favored demon-form, clad in garments of red and gold, complete with feathered cap. Then I started making my way toward the Towers, walking lightly so as not to disturb the rocks.

He of the Towers of Light located me before I had crossed more than a few hundred yards.

"Hello, Kai Wren," said a voice from the air. I looked about and saw no one.

"Hello," I said. "I thought that I might take you up on your invitation to visit."

"So I see."

"If this is a bad time . . ."

"Not at all. Indeed, it is a most auspicious time—for you."

I forbore from saying something inelegant like: "Huh?"

"I'm glad you think so."

"I don't just think, Wren. I know. Come to the first Tower you encounter. I will meet you there."

"Thank you, Lord."

I gave myself wings not unlike those of Devor, although these were deep blue, not green. Then I lofted into the air. I made no real attempt to choose a Tower. The correct one, I was certain, would intercept me.

As I closed, the Towers ceased being white. Instead, they cycled through the colors of an alien rainbow: mauve, umber, citrine, turquoise, amber, jet. The Tower that loomed over me shifted into a shimmering copper as I landed before it. The rubbery plants here were white, making for an eye-searing combination.

Even up close, the Tower did not resemble any human building. There were no stones, no mortar, no concrete, just a living, faintly pulsing unit of *chi*. HE must be frightfully wealthy by any standards, even those of Origin. I wondered if the gods ever grew envious.

Then there was motion within the interior and I remembered my manners and flung myself facedown on the ground. We had dined as equals at the Conventicle, but here we were within HIS own domain, a realm that was more absolutely his than any earthly king has a kingdom. A few words drew me to my feet.

"Rise, Kai Wren, Lord Demon, Godslayer. Know yourself welcome here."

I did as I was bid.

A few feet in front of me, wearing the light from the Tower about his shoulders like a cape, stood a figure so ordinary, so mundane that I felt vaguely disappointed. Rather than the flamboyant body of light which he had worn at the Conventicle, He of the Towers of Light wore the form of a small, Oriental man, bent with age and leaning upon a slender staff of polished wood. His attire was a simple robe of white silk; his worn feet were bare. I battled an obscure impulse to shift into a simpler form myself and won.

"You have been stirring things up, Kai Wren."

"I have? I thought that things had been stirring me up."

"Perhaps. Perhaps it is all one and the same. Illusion binds us to the Wheel."

I blinked. Were the rumors true that the ancient demon had turned Buddhist in his dotage? Stranger things were known to have happened. Look at Night Bride and those like her who choose to overlook that we had created the legend of our wickedness.

Silence was my best reply, and so silence was what I offered. After a time, HE shuffled his feet and tapped his staff, perhaps impatient.

"Sir, I have been making inquiries into the death of my servant, Oliver O'Keefe."

"As I said, stirring things up."

"And I . . ." Rapidly, I summarized for him the chain of associations that had led me to someone who had worn his form. The venerable demon studied me from those mild human eyes.

"My form? How do you know it was not I?"

I didn't know what to say. I had simply assumed that some-one of his power and prestige would never treat with alley trash. While I fumbled for an answer, He of the Towers of Light continued:

"Although, it was not I."

"I didn't think you would have anything to do with those foul creatures," I said.

"Your reasoning is faulty, Kai Wren. You wear ignorance and arrogance in equal parts. These make you useful to others."

I was angry now, but the throbbing *chi* around me kept me prudent. Reflexively, I had already tried to tap it and had learned that not one-tenth of one percent of that which surged about me was available to my use. I had no doubt that HE could tap all of it.

"Kai Wren, you are an artificer, a warrior, a dreamer, but you have never been a politician."

"Well, no."

"Given your talents and reputation, that may not have been a wise decision on your part."

"Demons are by nature solitary!"

"I think not. I think you prefer to believe this. Consider the evidence of your own experiences these past months. You have encountered groups of friends, allies, teachers, and students. We may not live in mobs as do humans in their cities, but we are a social folk."

"As you say."

"I do, and I am correct."

I had learned what I had come for. There was no need for me to stand here and be taunted by this crazy old coot. Yet, I remained. There was too much I didn't know.

"Come into a more comfortable place, Kai Wren. I believe that we must talk."

This was in the way of an order, so I did so, but without

any grace. Later, I would have reason to be embarrassed at my lack of courtesy.

He of the Towers of Light took me to a chamber that resembled the interior of an icicle, as much as it resembled anything on Earth. He motioned me to take my ease upon a divan covered with the bluish white fabric that is called falyss in the ur-language of the demons. I wonder if it were true falyss, which is made of the fibrous pod-lining of a small shrub on Origin, or if it were synthetic.

It did not seem polite to inquire, given what that might imply about HIS continuing commerce with a place held by our enemies. Instead, I made appreciative noises, waiting for HIM to bring up whatever it was he felt we must talk about.

"Tranquillity," HE said when we had both been supplied with beakers of saffron liqueur, "is highly overrated. Have you discovered that yet, Kai Wren?"

I considered my answer carefully.

"I have enjoyed my tranquillity, Venerable One. It has given me time for art, for leisure, for the contemplation of great mysteries. I believe I prefer it to war, for example."

"Not all of your associates would agree, Kai Wren. War is the quickest means of disrupting the status quo."

I frowned. "My associates, Venerable One? Who do you mean?"

HE made a small sound indicative of displeasure. The gaze HE cast upon me made me feel rather like a small child who has been found wanting. It was not a feeling for which I particularly cared.

"Kai Wren, why have you come here?"

"To make inquiries, sir."

"And are you satisfied with the answer you have received?"

"Yes, sir."

"Why? I could have lied to you."

Oddly, that possibility had never occurred to me.

"Did you, sir?"

"No. Do you believe me?"

I tapped a small amount of my personal *chi* and essayed a truth sensing. HE made no effort to block it and so for a moment I saw his aura outlined in fractal patterns that meant he spoke truth.

"Yes, sir."

"But this time you made an effort to test my veracity."

"Yes."

"Have you been so cautious in all of your inquiries?"

I colored a deeper blue.

"No, sir."

"And why not?"

I answered him honestly.

"I have been called Lord Demon, Venerable One. I know myself to be a dangerous creature—and those I have spoken with know this, too. The consequences for crossing me would be such that none would do so lightly."

"Yet what if they did not do it lightly?"

"Sir?"

"What if that which could be gained was so great that a certain amount of risk—regarding, say, your response—was viewed as reasonable?"

I didn't like the direction this conversation was going, but I was eager for him to continue.

"You mean like the attempt to have me assassinated by Rabla-yu?"

"Yes. Though even that may not have been quite as you believed." He set down his drink with a certain deliberation. "Or were led to believe."

"Led?"

"Who did you speak with after the death of Rabla-yu?"

"Many demons, sir. I believe I even spoke briefly with you."

"Yes, but who did you speak with first?"

"Viss of the Terrible Tongue. I was somewhat in shock from my battle with Rabla-yu . . . and perhaps from the firing of a theronic weapon so close to me."

HE smiled without humor. "Yes, that theronic weapon. For an outlawed weapon type they have suddenly become quite prevalent. Tell me honestly, Kai Wren: the word that was bruited about the Conventicle was that Rabla-yu brought the weapon and that you turned it on him. Was that the truth?"

I studied the old demon. Theronics were illegal. To admit

that I had carried one would open me to censure if HE so wished. The admission would also open Viss to questioning, a thing I was not certain I liked at all.

HE waited patiently for my reply, and perhaps he worked some small magic on me, for I answered honestly.

"No, Venerable One. I had the weapon in my pocket. I didn't know it was there, however."

"Oh?"

Again I found myself answering truthfully.

"It was put into my pocket by Viss of the Terrible Tongue. She knew there had been attempts on my life and sought to give me an edge. When I was hard-pressed, I recalled her gift and used it to good effect."

"Tell me, Kai Wren, why did you attend the Conventicle? You had not attended for hundreds of years."

"Well, Viss and Tuvoon thought I should get out more."

"Curious, isn't it, that Viss should convince you to go to such a public gathering when—by her own apparent admission—she believed you would be in danger there."

"Surely she did not become worried until after our plans were already made."

"Yet she made no effort to stay close to you or otherwise protect you?"

I considered this.

"No, sir, but I am Kai Wren, Lord Demon. I do not need a baby-sitter!"

"But apparently you did need a highly illegal concealed weapon."

I could give no answer to this. The situation *was* peculiar when I looked at it from his point of view.

"And tell me, Kai Wren," HE continued, "this was not the first recent attempt on your life by means of a theronic weapon, was it?"

"No, sir." I felt as if the words were being dragged from me.

"Yes, I thought not. There was some concern about the truncation of Horsehead. You did not report the incident, but one who was on the periphery did so."

"Who?"

"My nephew, the Walker."

"The Walker! I have been trying to locate him. Did he say who fired the rifle?"

"Yes."

"Who?"

"Do you really want to know?"

"Of course!"

"Then you must promise not to storm off in a fury after I tell you. We will need to speak further."

"Very well." I could always kill the bastard an hour or so later.

"The Walker swears that the one who fired the rifle was Viss of the Terrible Tongue."

I gaped in shock; the desire for vengeance drained from me like wine from a gashed skin.

"Viss? The Walker must have lied."

"He did not. It was Viss."

"Viss wouldn't have missed," I protested sullenly. "She is one of the most dangerous of our kind."

"Yes, she is," HE agreed, "a fact you seem to have overlooked in your dealings with her."

"But she was my teacher!"

"Viss has been the teacher of many demons—and even of a few gods."

"But she has been helping me!"

"Has she? How much have you learned with her 'help'?"

I considered. Had I really learned much for all my investigations? I was no closer to learning who had slain Ollie, my fu dogs were gone, and there had been at least two attempts on my life. All I had done was flown some kites, asked some questions, and played games with Devor.

"Not a great deal," I admitted. "But Viss would not have missed!"

"The Walker interfered," HE said, "when he jogged her arm. He tried to warn you before he fled into hiding."

I remembered Viss telling me something similar. What a clever way to divert my attention from her! And why had she not suggested we ask the Walker who had fired the rifle? Could it be because she didn't want me to know—or because she had already sought the Walker and knew he was not to be found?

"How did the Walker happen to be on the spot?" I asked. "Isn't that a bit too convenient?"

"Not really. The Walker had dropped in to watch the mahjongg game Devor was playing with Night Bride, Pigeon Eyes, and Snow Goon. He got bored and decided to explore the mountain—his obsessive desire is to find other conduits from this plane to others."

I had heard something of this. Several of the more recent conduits to other planes (most as useless as could be) had been found by the Walker.

"He came upon Viss in time to spoil her aim."

"Why didn't he tell me about this?"

"Would you have believed him?"

"I could have tested his truthfulness."

"And in that time Viss could have killed you both. He fled, after letting you know as best he could that he had played a role in your salvation. He hoped that would leave you receptive to believing him when the time came for him to tell you more."

"But he hasn't come to me!"

"Viss has been much in your company of late. He feared her."

"With good reason," I replied sharply. "Tell me then, Venerable One, if Viss wanted me dead, why hasn't she simply slain me? As you have noted, we have been much in company."

"Viss," HE answered, "does not really want you dead. She wants a political uproar. The death of Lord Demon via a theronic rifle shot would cause such—she would have made certain of that. Your desire to do your own investigating robbed her of that opportunity. Thus, she set up the second attack."

"But she gave me the theronic!"

"Yes, she did. I believe that Rabla-yu was to have taken it from you and slain you. She, then, would have slain him in revenge—derringers are only two-shot weapons, you know."

"If she wanted Rabla-yu to kill me with the theronic, why give it to me?"

"I believe she planned to frame you as the one who engineered the theft from the Armory of Truce. She would 'find' most of the missing weapons in your bottle and return them to great fanfare. She would be a hero without question."

"Are you saying that *she* engineered the theft from Truce?"

"Yes. It enabled her to lay hands on some spirit swords as well as on quantities of theronics. Even if she returned ninety percent, the ten percent she would have kept would make her quite well armed, and if she damaged what was returned . . ."

"Why?"

"So we would not rearm, believing ourselves fully stocked?" HE shrugged. "We move into the realms of speculation, here."

"I think we've been there for quite a while."

"Then you don't believe me?"

I tapped my claws lightly on the divan.

"You have given me much food for thought—but as you yourself have said—much of it is speculation. I would need to question Viss, myself."

He of the Towers of Light did not look pleased.

"I can tell you why your servant was killed."

"Why?"

"He had been approached to betray you. He refused. Since he knew too much, he had to die."

"If Ollie had been approached, he would have told me!"

"I believe you were in the midst of a delicate artistic operation at the time."

An image of a lovely bottle, all green and orange, flashed into my memory. I had been so pleased with it then. So much had happened since. Had I even removed it from my workshop?

"I suspect," HE went on, "that O'Keefe would have spoken to you the night he was killed, perhaps over dinner."

I nodded slowly. That would be like Ollie—he would have thought the matter settled and, as such, that there was no need to ruin my satisfaction in a job well-done.

"But why such a crazy murder plan? They could have made it look as if he was killed by a human mugger! Why frame Tuvoon? I might have killed him!"

"I think not. They were very careful. Didn't Viss interrupt the duel before it became too heated?"

"Yes," I admitted, "but what if I had simply gone after him instead of declaring a duel?"

"As you have said, Viss is quite dangerous. She would have

stopped you—perhaps slain you then. However, the circumstances of the duel made you a fine pawn."

"Why use me as a pawn?"

"You have many assets, Kai Wren. Among them, two of the last fu dogs."

"Not anymore," I said bitterly. "What do they have to do with this?"

"I don't know precisely, but I do know that they are creatures of power. In the early days of the Exile, demons feared them as they feared few things created by the gods."

"Yet the gods abandoned them," I mused, "once we were banished."

"So it seems."

I thought over all that He of the Towers of Light had told me. There was a certain pattern, but I was not certain that I believed him. I only had his word for what the Walker had said and . . .

"How do you know that Ollie had been approached to betray me?"

"The Walker heard something of it from Devor. I don't know where Devor heard it."

"I can ask him myself," I said, rising as if to make my departure. HE forestalled me with an autocratic gesture.

"Kai Wren, what do you plan to do next?"

"I plan to speak with Viss."

"To tell her what I have said?"

"Probably. Does that bother you?"

"Only in that it will bring harm to you."

I smiled. "I am not such a fool as you seem to think. I shall take precautions. Even if Viss is innocent of your accusations, she is quite likely to lose her temper when I tell her what you have said."

"Then you still believe her innocent?"

"I believe in keeping an open mind. All I have against her is your word for what the Walker heard and saw. That is slim evidence on which to condemn a friend."

"Use your magic to test my honesty, Kai Wren. I am telling you the truth."

"As you know it to be, Venerable One. I will learn it for myself."

HE seemed to fold into himself, and I knew the desire to argue further had gone from him. I stood politely until he addressed me again.

"Very well, Kai Wren. If you will do this thing, let me offer you two small gifts that will make you better able to resist what I fear is coming upon you."

I bowed stiffly. He continued:

"First, I shall use my powers to transport you back to more populated areas. I would not have you vulnerable during the long flight."

"Thank you, sir."

"And I will permit you to recharge your depleted *chi* from my stores. I would not have you return weakened."

This was a generous offer indeed.

"Thank you, sir. I am grateful."

He motioned with two hands, and a chunk of the wall detached itself from the main. As it drifted over to me, I saw that its shape was a spinning cylinder, slightly pointed at each end. Even without any special preparation, I could feel the *chi* that hummed from it. My skin prickled.

"Grasp that firmly," HE ordered, "and direct the flow inward. You must take care that you do not overburden yourself."

His warning was not an idle thing. A glut of *chi* could distort perceptions, ruin enchantments, and cause other, more subtle damage. Younger demons rarely faced the problem, but it was a real risk during the wars with the gods.

I touched the throbbing cylinder, first with the tips of my claws, then by holding it more firmly in my palms. The *chi* flowed into me, electric and warm. The sensation was rather like being immersed from the inside out in a perfect bath. I longed to submerge myself and be lost, but HIS warning was fresh in my mind. When I felt myself renewed, I released the cylinder. As it drifted back into the wall, I noted that it was hardly depleted and adjusted my estimate of HIS resources upward by several degrees.

I had cause to think more about this later.

"Go now," said He of the Towers of Light, and there was sadness in his voice.

And, sweeping off my hat in a deep bow, I did as he bid.

HIS transportation spell carried me to the Origin Park. From there I made my way to the mausoleum in which Viss and Tuvoon kept their bottle. They had given me an entry key, and I used it, knowing full well that knowledge of my coming would be carried to the owners.

I strolled down a path paved in river-rock cobbles and took delight in my artistry. Even after the passing of twelve hundred years, the work was holding up well. When the curving roofs of the house came into view, I heard the faint ringing of bells from strands strung in the trees. A nightingale burst into song; I glimpsed the white haunch of a chi'lin as it fled into a deep green grove. I felt curiously at peace.

Viss herself, wearing the beauteous form of the swordmistress, answered the door. She smiled at me.

"Hello, Kai Wren. To what do we owe the honor of this visit?"

"I've been doing a bit of investigating," I said, "and have come to share my conclusions with you and Tuvoon."

"Come into the Garden of Peonies and Gardenias," said she. "Tuvoon and I enjoy it particularly at this hour."

"What time is it, anyhow?" I asked, having lost track of time during my sojourn in HIS strange lands.

"Midway through the Hour of the Sheep," she replied. "Have you eaten?"

I had not, but supercharged with fine *chi* I did not need to do so.

"I am not hungry," I said, and followed her shapely form through the house, preparing myself to tell her of HIS suspicions in a way that would not hurt her too deeply, nor turn her enmity upon that ancient Exile.

In the garden, Tuvoon rose to greet me. Returning his salutations, I took a seat next to a white peony whose petals were stained with deep red.

"As I started to tell your mother," I began, "I have been doing some investigating. Matters are quite grave. The web of intrigue is more complex and intertwined than I had believed."

Tuvoon nodded, his features serious. "Pray, tell."

And so I did, beginning with my interview with He of the Towers of Light. I had learned little enough from Seven Fingers and, knowing the rivalry between their families, had no desire to intensify old animosities.

As I spoke, I saw Viss's lovely features grow pale, becoming as something made from alabaster or palest porcelain. Her fingers knotting and unknotting the long sash that nipped in the waist of her plum-colored tunic was the only reaction she permitted herself.

Tuvoon had less self-control. Two or three times, he leapt to his misty feet and drifted about the courtyard. I heard the rhythmic grating as his finger claws scraped into the stone of the walls.

I sincerely did not perceive my danger until Po Shiang came into the courtyard and, by then, it was far too late for me to do anything.

Seeing my enemy striding in with a conqueror's confidence, I sought to leap to my feet, to draw the blade I had concealed in the sidewise spaces. I could do nothing but move my head, and found myself struggling against invisible bonds. For a moment, I foolishly believed that all three of us had been captured, and then I saw Viss rise and look down at me. Truth was as bitter as pomegranate rind in my mouth.

"You are a great warrior, a great artist, and"—her smile was not kind—"a great idiot, Kai Wren. HE told you the truth, but you have associated too much with humans. Your emotions blinded you to the facts."

"Viss!" I protested. "Why?"

Po Shiang shook his head. "Tell him nothing. He is too dangerous!"

"Is he really?" Tuvoon drifted over and, for the first time, I recognized the danger inherent in what I had taken for a somewhat indolent young demon. Now, all too clearly, I saw that he was the son of Viss of the Terrible Tongue. I wondered that I could have been so easily deceived.

Tuvoon gave a casual wave of one hand, and I felt a great pain reverberate through my skull. Involuntarily, I cried out, and Tuvoon laughed.

"He does not seem so dangerous to me."

Po Shiang snarled, "He is the Godslayer. Now he knows

too much—and at least one Exile knows what he knows. We must slay him."

"Nay!" Viss spoke sharply. "If he was slain, there would certainly be an investigation. I could not swear ignorance—nor could Tuvoon. Unwittingly, by speaking with He of the Towers of Light, Kai Wren has guarded his life."

"We could make it seem an accident," Po Shiang said.

"I would know it was not," said Viss firmly, "and that, too, would come out."

"Can we keep him a prisoner?" Tuvoon asked doubtfully.

"For a time, perhaps," Viss answered, "but that, too, would turn against us. Our laws prevent us from imprisoning one of our own for any significant time period. I would certainly be questioned, as would Tuvoon."

Po Shiang frowned. "Well, I certainly am not going to take him into Origin. That would get me lynched."

Despite the paralysis that was trying to steal my voice, I managed to croak:

"Let me go and I will swear not to interfere in your business for a hundred years. By then, surely, what you plan will have met with success or failure. If you fail, what matters? If you succeed, I will be no threat to you."

Viss looked tempted. "You would swear not to interfere by either word or deed?"

"I would."

She nibbled the tip of a claw. Po Shiang huffed in anger—or perhaps in fear.

"Given time enough, Kai Wren," she said at last, "I believe I could convert you to our side. We are not merely ambitious. We have the best interests of demonkind in mind."

"We don't need to discuss our plans in front of him," Tuvoon snarled. "He is well restrained. Set a guard on him and let us go to a more private space."

Viss agreed, the thoughtful look still in her eyes. I waited, bound within my body, four ogres watching me from the four corners of the courtyard. When I sought to free myself by either magic or muscle, they guffawed. I wondered what Viss and the others were discussing.

One thing was certain. I didn't feel peaceful any longer.

VII

MY CAPTORS RETURNED several hours later wearing the expressions of people who have solved a difficult problem to their satisfaction. Tuvoon was even chuckling.

"Oh, you're going to love this, Godslayer," he said, and for the first time I realized that the Smoke Ghost envied me my reputation. "You're going on vacation."

Viss frowned at her son. Then she motioned to the ogres.

"Bear the prisoner to my alchemical laboratory," she said, "and take care that he does not get free, or I will have your skins for gloves."

As the ogres bore me with exaggerated care through the twisting corridors, Viss walked beside me.

"You've posed a pretty problem for us, Kai Wren, for either killing you or imprisoning you would pose problems. We could not take your parole . . ."

She must have seen the indignation in my eyes, for she gave a brittle smile.

"I might have trusted you, knowing you to be a creature of your word, but my allies would not."

"An oath given under duress and all that," muttered Po Shiang. "It simply isn't tactically sound."

"Our solution isn't perfect," Viss continued, "but it must do. It is not as if we need you to be out of circulation for anything like a hundred years."

Tuvoon cut in with a manic laugh. "How would you like to be a human, Lord Demon?"

I didn't like the idea at all, but I did not see how it could be done. Certainly I could be made human in appearance, but not in nature.

"Son, lording over a fallen foe, even if he is a fool, is not seemly," chid Viss with a shake of her head. "As I have said before, I still hope that Kai Wren may become our ally. He would be invaluable when the initial conquest is completed."

We had come now to a room with a vaulted ceiling and tiled floor. Light came from both skylights and clerestory windows, making it bright despite the four solid stone walls. Bottles and retorts were arrayed on shelves and counters. Interesting scents came from a variety of pots and cauldrons.

Viss sniffed the steam coming from a large iron kettle, looking for all the world like a young housewife checking her soup. Po Shiang crossed to where a test tube burbled over the blue flame of a Bunsen burner. Tuvoon only leaned against a doorframe and chortled to himself.

"Preparations seem just about done," said Viss. "Tuvoon, stop laughing like a jackass and bring the silver-bound chest."

"Yes, ma'am," he said, perhaps recalling what a dangerous creature was his mother.

What I could not understand was how I had come to forget that the power that was in her could be turned against me. Had I been drugged or enchanted? Was it merely that I was prey to emotions, as Viss had said? I did not know, and that not knowing made me feel even more vulnerable.

After sending the ogres to stand guard outside of the chamber, Viss opened the silver-bound chest and began to arrange the contents on a cleared counter. What I saw there made my heart pound like that of a frightened rabbit.

Bowls, bottles, flasks, vases, jars, and even a teapot: each was beautiful, each was a work of art—each was the work of my hand. I knew them all: one was Devor's bottle, another was a bowl I had made for the Twister's engagement, yet another I had believed resided in the Smithsonian in Washington, DC.

"Kai Wren's works," said Po Shiang mockingly, "are known to grant luck and health to the owners. Is it any wonder how well our plans are proceeding?"

Viss caressed an elegant fluted vase in rose-colored glass. I had believed it in a private collection in France, though, now that I thought of it, that information was at least fifty years old.

"I have been building this collection for nearly a century, Kai Wren," she said. "I believe it to be the largest in existence—except for your own, of course."

I managed a few words. "I am flattered, ma'am."

She ignored my compliment. "They are lovely, but another example of your foolishness. You told me once that you infuse each piece with a portion of your own *chi*. Not the *chi* we have all learned to generate and store via landscaping and suchlike, but of your own peculiar, personal *chi*."

Po Shiang poured the infusion from his test tube between two flasks, perhaps to cool it, for he kept checking the temperature against the inside of his wrist.

"Like calls to like," he said, "as even the most elementary practitioner of magic knows. We have here before us an assemblage of your personal *chi*. When we have finished our workings, your *chi* will drain from you."

Viss interrupted him, "All but what minimal amount is needed to sustain a human."

"And you will be, for all effects and purposes, human," Po Shiang finished.

"A funny-looking one," Tuvoon said. "That is, if we weren't kind enough to suggest that you take a human shape."

"If you do not, Wren," Viss said, "we will force your body to do so—Tuvoon has some very creative ideas in that line."

"Why make me human?" I spat out.

"When you go missing, those who choose to look for you will look for a demon, not a human," Po Shiang said. "You will not be in any of our custody, so we need not fear questioning."

"And," Viss said, "we are going to arrange for your lodging

on Earth so that you will not be able to contact anyone yourself."

Tuvoon laughed. "I thought of that—a mental hospital will be perfect. You can say whatever you like, and no one will listen to you." He rubbed his hands together briskly. "Now, are you going to take a human shape, or do I get to pick? I've been trying to decide whether a harelip or a clubfoot would be better. Maybe both."

He might just be taunting me, but I could not take the risk. That Viss and Po Shiang could work the magic they planned, I did not doubt. Like did call to like. That was one reason I found so much comfort in my gallery at home.

"I'll shape," I croaked.

"No tricks," Viss said, drawing a slim, deadly blade from sidewise space. "This is your spirit sword. I would hate to use it on you, but I will. I am good enough that I can weaken you considerably without having to kill you."

I nodded. "No tricks."

Still, they didn't take any chances. The paralysis was lifted only the bare amount necessary to enable me to channel *chi* for a shapeshift. Viss stood with the blade of the spirit sword against my throat, just in case.

When I wore the same human form in which I had gone calling on Li Piao, the paralysis was restored. Po Shiang drew the fluid from his test tube into a syringe and shot it into my arm. Dizziness descended upon me, bringing with it nausea and disorientation. Through a haze of distorted perception, I saw them doing things that I could almost understand. I felt myself becoming weaker and weaker.

Eventually, I sank into blackness and was glad, for it was a relief from misery.

My first awareness as I came to myself, such as I was, was of a medicinal scent, sharp and acrid. Next was the realization that I could not move. I was lying on my back, and straps of various sorts kept me there. After a time, it occurred to me to open my eyes.

The small, square room in which I found myself was painted white. An insipid landscape in pastels adorned one wall. From what I could see from my enforced relaxation, the bed in which I lay was also white. As far as I could tell, I was alone, but a monitor of some sort was attached to me with slim wires and beeped rhythmically.

I resolved then and there to remain still while my head cleared. If I alerted the staff of this place—surely the mental hospital that Tuvoon had mentioned—they were certain to come in. No doubt they had permission to give me drugs to make me sleep again.

Something like this had happened to a fellow in a novel I read once. His enemies stashed him in a private sanitorium and authorized its staff to dope him to the gills. *He*, however, turned out to have superhuman strength and recuperative powers, and had busted his way out. I wasn't so well equipped.

When I felt stronger, I tried taking on a body of air. No luck. Then, in rapid succession, I tried a fire spell, a thunderstorm, a transformation into stone, a simple shapeshift. Nothing. I ended up straining against the bonds, whining somewhere deep in my throat. Nothing. Nothing, that is, except that my efforts somehow alerted the orderly. Despite my protests, another needle was slid into my arm, and I slept.

My captivity stretched on for a week or more. I was permitted the freedom of my room—no more. The staff called me Harvey—a glance at my chart told me my full name was supposed to be Harvey Wang. I at least convinced them to call me Harv—otherwise I felt too much like a white rabbit who wasn't there.

Despair became my constant companion. I wondered what was happening in Kong Shyh Jieh. Why would Viss side with the gods? What was there for her to gain? Access to Origin? Couldn't she have bargained for that on her own?

Sometimes the despair lifted enough for me to feel hatred. That was no relief. I was accustomed to taking action as I felt appropriate. To feel such wrath and be bound in this human body, by these straps of cloth and drops of chemicals, was worse than despair.

I knew I was verging on madness the day that I saw an old man tapping on the pane of my window.

Evening was gathering without. Even if the window hadn't

been such an unpromising exit point, I would have avoided it, for all it showed was a large, asphalt-topped parking lot as seen from the twelfth floor.

I paced past the window, never looking out. I even ignored the tapping at first, thinking it wind-driven drops of rain. Only when the taps drummed out "shave and a haircut" did I stare.

A skinny old man floated there. His features were obscured by the milky glass, but I could see that he was smiling broadly. The white bar of his smile became a focal point from which I next recognized a flowing beard and eyebrows, then the features of Li Piao!

I gaped in amazement, wondering only a little that my madness should take this form.

"Li Piao!" I called out. "Hi!"

He motioned for me to be quiet. I did so, and the tapping started again. This time I realized that he was testing the glass. I grew excited and checked the clock. At least twenty minutes would pass before the guards made their next check—it might be as much as thirty if I did nothing to remind them of my existence.

I was still convinced that I was going insane, but this insanity was the most entertaining thing to happen to me since I had come to this place. From my daily trips to the showers, I knew that many patients simply stood in front of the windows, staring out. I did this now, more from passive curiosity than from a constructive desire to block the view of the window from the doorway.

Now Li Piao held something that glowed red in his hands. A small blowtorch, I thought. It was preternaturally hot, sufficient to cut through both the glass and the wire within. This high up, there were no alarms. He cut around a portion and, reaching awkwardly through the bars, pushed it free.

"How long until a nurse will be through?" he asked.

I glanced at a clock. "Fifteen minutes, maybe ten, maybe twenty-five."

"We can do it, if you help," he said. "Take the torch and cut a large enough hole for you to get out. The bars can be unlocked from out here—a fire safety feature."

I took the torch and began cutting, remembering the times

I had used similar tools in my fancy glasswork. Metal sounding against metal informed me that Li Piao was at work on the bars.

Now that the glass was parted, I could see that Li Piao was not hanging from a rope harness or standing on a ladder, as I had assumed. Insight cut through my clouded mind. He was flying!

My first reaction was, oddly, jealousy. I pushed that away. Li Piao was drenched. He was shivering despite his garments, which were close-fitting and made to repel water. His hands were shaking so much that he was having trouble with the rusty locks.

"How did you find me?"

"Tell you later," he promised. "Can you climb through that hole?"

I nodded. "I think so."

I handed him the torch and was clambering onto the windowsill when I suddenly recalled the drop. I could not fly, not now. Twelve stories was a considerable fall.

"How am I to get down?" I asked.

Li Piao tucked the torch into his clothing along with whatever he had used to undo the window bars.

"I am going to carry you," he said. "I cannot hope to fly supporting two, but I believe I can manage a controlled fall."

Courage has never been something I suspected myself of lacking. Even though my slaying of Chaholdrudan had been partially luck, I had not feared battle. Nor have I ever feared dealing with my enemies. Now, faced with trusting my life, pitiful as it had become, to the arms of a frail old man quaking with fatigue, I quailed.

Li Piao opened his arms. "Hurry. If anyone sees us, I don't know if we will escape from the grounds, and your enemies are not likely to be so merciful a second time."

I positioned myself so that my feet hung into the wet darkness below. My left hand was bleeding from where it had scraped against the sill. Li Piao pressed himself back against the wall so that he could get his hands and then his forearms under my armpits.

"Here we go," he muttered. I heard his feet push off from the wall, then we were falling.

All my vanity was needed to keep me from screaming in terror, but I pride myself that not even a whimper escaped. The ground was rushing up at us, then I felt our descent slow. The sensation was not like that of a parachute catching us from above, but rather of a pillar of hot air pushing against us from below. The pressure slowed us so that we hit the ground with jarring—not fatal—force.

Li Piao made a shrill sound somewhere between a cry of pain and a laugh. He motioned toward a minivan.

"My granddaughter waits." Then he crumpled as he tried to lead the way. "My ankle!"

I essayed to lift him, finding him not much of a burden, even to my reduced strength. The side door to the van was open. As I bundled us both inside, I heard the engine starting. Li Piao indicated that I should put him into the front passenger seat and I strapped him in as the van backed out. A slender hand thrust a towel back to me and another at Li Piao.

"Dry off, Grandfather. You, get into the area farthest back and hide yourself as best you can."

The voice was female, young, and very determined. I did not argue—her words made sense.

We drove over what felt like a gravel road for what had to be several miles. During that time, I contrived to make myself a hiding place among the bundles in the back of the van. I was just pulling the towel (neatly folded) over the top when I felt the van ease to a stop.

Through the muffling fabric, I heard Li Piao's granddaughter say, "Yes, it was, thank you." I guessed she was responding to a question.

The side door on the van slid open. I caught a flicker of light from a flashlight beam and held my breath, wondering if I had hidden myself well enough. The wait seemed interminable, then the side door rumbled shut. The girl said something I couldn't distinguish over the pounding of my heart, then I felt the van accelerate to highway speeds. Even so I waited until Li Piao gave the okay before coming out.

"We're going to a hotel," he explained. "Tomorrow we'll head back to San Francisco."

"Where are we, anyway?" I asked.

"Outside of Nashville, Tennessee. Pretty much the middle of nowhere. I'd have hidden you in the middle of a city."

"How did you find me?"

Li Piao's tones mixed wonder and a certain smugness.

"The dragon bowl told me. I couldn't contact you nor could I get to your bottle, so I did some scrying. It felt a bit like eavesdropping, but I was concerned."

"Thank you," I said. "I am eternally in your debt. And in the lady's."

"My granddaughter, Li Plum," Li Piao said, his pride evident in his voice. "She was the only member of the family I knew wouldn't think I had become senile."

"Pleased to meet you, Lord Demon," Plum said. I caught a glimpse of a fine profile as she turned toward the backseat before returning to her driving. "Grandfather has told me a great deal about you."

"He has told me little about you," I said, almost miffed. "You do not live nearby?"

"I do when I'm in the US," she said, "but I travel a great deal. I'm just back from an extended trip to Hong Kong and New Zealand."

"My granddaughter is a *feng shui* expert," Li Piao said. "She is in great demand."

I was impressed. The art of *feng shui* is similar to that which demonkind had used to bring *chi* into Kong Shyh Jieh. I wondered if Plum might be a sorceress.

We drove for over an hour until we came to a motel. Plum parked the van in front of a door numbered 1-1, a potentially auspicious number.

"Lord Demon," Plum said, "when I give the symbol that all is clear, I want you to get inside as quickly as possible. You are not dressed for public observation, and we don't know how long it will be until someone starts looking for you. It is better if you are not seen at all."

"Yes, ma'am," I said. She was right. My shredded hospital pajamas would excite comment.

"Grandfather, don't stress that ankle. I'll be right back to help you."

"Yes, Plum."

I thought I heard him sigh.

We made the transition into the room without any trouble. There I got my first look at my other rescuer. She was a pretty enough girl, clearly Chinese, but hardly traditional. Her ink-black hair was cut oddly, the bangs at a sharp angle, the long hair in back cut like a swallow's tail. I suspected that this was artistic, for she wore a black tee shirt trimmed with lace, jeans with round holes in the thighs, and an elaborately fringed jacket. Her jewelry was bright and modernistic.

I wondered what her clients thought of her. Probably they were pleased to have such a contemporary-looking advisor.

"Grandfather and I guessed that you would be short of luggage," she said, surveying my attire with disapproval. "We bought you some clothes. I hope they fit."

"Thank you," I said.

The tan trousers were a bit loose, but I had seen men wearing worse. There was a belt to keep them up and a selection of tee shirts. I chose a bright red one, hoping that luck would come with its color. For footwear, I had to make do with some cheap canvas tennis shoes. As I was lacing them on, I realized how deeply in debt I was to these people.

I came out, feeling self-conscious as Plum inspected me.

"Not too bad," she said. "Do you eat pizza?"

A sharp pang of memory touched me then, and I realized that I had not had any since before Ollie's death. I seemed to hear him saying that it was certainly time.

"There's a place that delivers," Plum said, pushing the menu toward me. "What do you like?"

"Sausage, perhaps," I said, determined to face the sadness I had not acknowledged until then, "and pepperoni are both fine."

Li Piao added a request for mushrooms and Plum placed the order. By the time we were seated around the room's small table with the box between us, and I had finished two slices, I was ready to think.

"Are we in danger of anyone tracing the van?"

Plum shook her head. "I altered the license number with some black paint before we went out. I've cleaned it off since.

I also have added a couple of magnetic racing stripes. We can lift them off before returning the van to the airport rental."

"We have plane tickets for three on an early flight tomorrow," Li Piao said. "Hopefully, no one will be looking for us there."

I found myself wishing for my powers. A few quick brushstrokes of illusion and we could look like anyone at all—or better yet, I could sweep us through the sidewise spaces and home. But I had no power and I was dependent on the charity of these humans.

Then I remembered. I was not completely without resources.

"I have several bank accounts in San Francisco," I said.

"Do you remember the numbers?" Plum asked.

"I do."

"You should draw on them quickly," she said, "before your enemies realize that you have escaped and will need money."

"I will," I said. "I wish that you had not needed to be seen by the guard at the mental hospital. Two Chinese will be remembered, especially if a third escapes."

"True," she said, "but we could not get you out without a van. The grounds were too extensive. It's a risk we had to take. Grandfather needed all his powers to get to you."

"Yes." I frowned, still worried.

"They may not look at the airport," she soothed me. "All they have to trace us is a vague description and an incorrect license number. Tomorrow we will do our best to look confident and stride through."

Li Piao added, "And I will not need to maintain magical flight, so I can do some small charms to assure that no one will be interested in us."

I nodded.

"When we get to San Francisco," I said, "I fear I will still need your help. If the usual way into my bottle is blocked as Li Piao says, then I will need to activate the back door."

I swallowed hard before admitting, "I have no magic."

Li Piao twinkled at me. "And I have more than I ever have had before. I suspect your 'healing' touch, Lord Demon. Don't worry, we will manage."

That night, I shared a room with Li Piao, while Plum adjourned demurely to an adjoining chamber. While the old man snored peacefully, I lay awake worrying. So much was beyond my control. I hadn't felt so helpless for at least a thousand years—probably the last time had been when Viss was teaching me swordplay.

Inevitably, my thoughts turned to her. Why had she betrayed me? I had thought we were friends—perhaps even something more. Was her ambition so dominant that nothing else mattered? Reluctantly, I recalled the warnings that Seven Fingers had tried to give me. Why hadn't I listened?

And who was Po Shiang?

At last, I drifted off to sleep. My dreams were vibrant, colorful, and completely useless.

The next morning, despite my worries, we departed Nashville on schedule. Evening found me installed in a guest room at Plum's house—staying at Li Piao's would have been too obvious. Indeed, the old man was going to shift residences himself the next day. His family was distrustful of strangers as a whole and would not give out Plum's address nor mention where he was staying.

Plum took me by several banks. I closed all three of my savings accounts, giving me a substantial amount of cash to draw upon. Fortunately, the banks did not trouble me for ID beyond the account numbers and a matching signature.

Once I had money, my first move was to reimburse Plum and Li Piao for the expenses entailed in my escape. My second was to purchase a small but versatile wardrobe. Plum sniffed a little at the conservative cut of my choices, but I had no desire to stand out. I wished I could show her my brocades and silks, my feathered hats, and high-topped boots. I found myself brooding that she should think me a stick in the mud.

Where was all this emotion coming from? Had Viss and Po Shiang truly made me human? I had thought that I was essentially a demon without powers, but I began to consider the possibility that the alteration had been more thorough. This troubled me in turn and it was a thoughtful and somewhat sullen Kai Wren who made his way to Plum's kitchen.

She sat at one end of the polished maple table going through a large stack of mail. Much ended up in the wastebasket positioned conveniently beneath her hand, but some she perused and put by for later consideration.

"Hi, Kai Wren," she said, glancing up from a handwritten missive. I had begged her not to call me "Lord Demon." "There's coffee made or, if you prefer, you can put on the kettle for tea."

"Coffee would be fine," I said, pouring myself a cup. As I stirred in cream and sugar, I found myself remembering the many times I had gone for coffee with Viss and Tuvoon. Had they been plotting against me even then? I shivered.

"Do you need a sweatshirt?" Plum asked.

"No, I'm fine."

I sat across from her, sipping my coffee and feeling useless. After about fifteen minutes, I rose, retrieved a pad of paper and a pen from my room, and started working out plans.

First of all, I must try to gain access to my bottle. There were two main entrances—one into Kong Shyh Jieh and one into the human plane—or there would be if the bottle remained where I had left it. If it had been moved, then things would become difficult indeed. However, there was a back entrance known only to me and specially prepared for such an emergency. With Li Piao's help, that could be opened.

What then? My best hope for regaining my powers was access to the possessions stored in my bottle. Try as I might, I had difficulty thinking beyond that point.

I was doodling and daydreaming about revenge when Li Piao arrived.

"I decided to come tonight," he said after greeting us both. "There have been strangers about, asking questions."

"Did they follow you here?" Plum asked.

"I don't believe so."

"Good." She smiled at me. "Using *feng shui* techniques, I have made this house easy to overlook."

"Not," I said, surprised, "because of this!"

"No," she replied. "I have some small fame in my profession. I was attracting groupies and imitators. There was also the problem of theft. Since I travel so much, I prefer that my residence not call attention to itself."

I considered what I had seen of the outside of the house and its exterior decoration. Now that I did this thing, I realized that she had done a fine job. Watching my expression, Li Piao chortled:

"As I said, *I* would have hidden you in a city." He glanced over at my sheet of paper. "Making plans?"

"Trying to," I said, "but I admit that I am at a loss. So much will depend on my getting access to my bottle."

"I wonder," said Li Piao, "if it is still there at all."

"So do I."

He rummaged in his luggage, coming up with a carefully wrapped parcel that proved to contain the dragon bowl.

"Let us attempt to scry your bottle's location," he said, "rather than running over there in the flesh. If your enemies have learned of your escape—as I suspect they have—they may have watchers there."

Plum put aside her mail and watched with an air of professional curiosity as Li Piao poured water and oil into the bowl. When it had settled, he studied the surface.

"There is the house," he said at length, "and there is the room in which the bottle was kept. I see the table. It stands empty. Now the dragon speaks."

He fell silent, listening. When he lifted his head, his expression was grave.

"It is not there. The young man sold it to a collector for a large sum—in cash."

"Damn!" I let my fist crash against the table. The news, though not unexpected, was unpleasant.

"Then," said Plum practically, "how do we gain access to this back door of which you have spoken?"

"Without the bottle," I explained, folding my hands about my coffee cup to warm them, "we—rather, your grandfather—will need to synchronize resonances with the *chi* of the back entrance. He will need some training, but once he gets the hang of it, I don't think he'll find it too different from what he does when he uses the bowl for scrying."

Li Piao looked dubious. I hastened to clarify.

"I don't know how your teachers explained it to you, but what you do when you scry is to open yourself to the *chi* resonating in your scrying device. That's why there are so many different scrying devices: I-Ching coins, crystal balls, tarot cards, rune stones, pools of water . . ."

The old man nodded.

"It is not the material of the device, but the intention that matters. Do you follow me?"

"Perhaps," he said. "Continue."

"When you have established this resonance and your intent is made known, then you receive your information."

"Why," Li Piao queried, "then, do things like the dragon bowl work so much better for the task?"

"Because the maker of the tool"—I bowed slightly—"has created a partial circuit for that intent. If you were to use a soup bowl and a bit of water from a puddle, you could still scry, but the *chi* inherent in the device would be unfocused, thus you would need to use more of your will to force it to do the required task.

"With the dragon bowl," I continued, warming to my subject, "any marginally talented individual could scry. A master like yourself not only sees images but the dragon also 'talks' to him—clarifying the message."

Plum was nodding as if she followed this—which, given her profession and her grandfather's opinion of her skills, I had every reason to believe she did.

"This door of yours, then," she asked, "is set to be opened by someone who is in resonance with the particular wavelength of its *chi*?"

"Precisely," I said. "Since I believed it would be needed only by me, I am the only one who knows the pattern."

"You didn't give it to Viss or her son?" Li Piao asked.

"No. I didn't even give it to Ollie. I felt that if there was trouble of that caliber, I would be with him."

Plum's expression told me that she thought me thoughtless.

"I did not intend for harm to come to him," I said firmly. "Oliver O'Keefe was a musician, a loyal servant, and a good friend, but he was not a sorcerer of any type. Even had I given him the resonance frequency, he could not have used it."

Her features softened. "I did not mean to criticize, Kai Wren. I only wondered."

Li Piao looked weary, and no wonder, given that we had spent hours on airplanes that day. I was impatient to get back into my bottle, but I did not see how letting him rest would hurt. Indeed, forcing him to do magic while he was tired could lead to disaster.

"Our best time for attempting the contact," I said, fibbing only slightly, "will be very early in the morning—as the Hour of the Tiger passes into the Hour of the Hare."

"Very well," Li Piao said, and he seemed relieved. "I will sleep until then."

Plum studied me quizzically. "What time should I set my alarm clock for?"

"We should make the attempt around five A.M.," I said. "So sometime before that."

She wrinkled her nose in mock protest of the early hour, but said nothing. After a bit more conversation, we each retired. This night, I actually managed to sleep dreamlessly.

I rose midway through the Hour of the Tiger, showered, then donned a comfortable, cotton robe—blue flowers printed on white fabric—that I had purchased the day before. When I went into the kitchen, Li Piao and Plum awaited me, fully dressed. The air was warm with the scent of green tea.

"Is that appropriate attire for retaking your home, Lord Demon?" Plum asked. "It is attractive and certainly comfortable, but . . ."

I colored at her words, but, to be honest, I had forgotten that I would not be able to shift shape and attire at whim. I temporized:

"I heard you two moving and thought that I should come and teach your grandfather the resonance pattern without delay. Thus, he can be practicing while I finish changing."

She did not question me further. With some relief, I sat next to Li Piao and began to explain to him the mental state which he should seek. My description took longer than I had thought it might, for although I had opened his magical potentials, I had not taught him the complex vocabulary to discuss his abilities. He was like a boy of five suddenly given a man's legal and social freedoms without any real idea of what they mean within the greater society.

When I had done the best I could, I hurried up to my room, donned jeans, hiking shoes, a light denim shirt, and—for lack of a sword—borrowed a stout walking stick from a stand by the front door.

This time, when Plum reviewed my attire, she smiled. Her slight nod of approval warmed me considerably.

Without further delay, Li Piao set about seeking contact with the secret entry to my bottle. I needed to concentrate to my utmost and laid my hands on him to perceive his manipulation of the *chi* forces—a thing that before I could have done without any effort at all. In this way I could feel that the old man was doing everything correctly. Yet, despite this, he could not quite come into sync with the portal.

The Hour of the Hare was merging with the Hour of the Dragon when we finally admitted defeat. Li Piao's wrinkled parchment skin was as white as death when he let himself slump forward onto the table. Plum rose and hurried to bring him a cup of something hot and sweet. I massaged various of his acupressure points, wishing I could rejuvenate him with a burst of demon *chi*, but glad to have at least this skill to offer him.

"I'm sorry, Wren," he said after the drink was finished. "I could see it in my mind's eye, sense its proximity, but it remained just out of reach."

I frowned. "I suspect that they have immersed the bottle in something with its own strong *chi*, perhaps running water. I ran into a phenomenon similar to what you describe when my bottle was lost overboard in the East China Sea. Another possibility is that they have taken it back into Kong Shyh Jieh."

Plum pushed a cup of tea toward me. "Drink this. You look almost as bad as Grandfather."

I sipped, horrified that even an elementary operation should have taken such a toll on me.

Sipping her own tea, Plum said diffidently, "I have wondered, Kai Wren, ever since Grandfather first told me about your bottle, why you keep it on Earth. It would seem more vulnerable here."

"It may seem so," I said, "but it is not. Earth has strong natural *chi* that I can tap to guard the bottle. Also, by keeping the bottle on Earth, I create my own private gate to this plane. If it were kept on Kong Shyh Jieh, I would need to use one of the public gates or slip sidewise to the traveling plane. Either way, my business might arouse someone else's curiosity."

She nodded. "So in addition to being their own demi-planes, the bottles create a gate between planes?"

"That is correct."

"And how many of these have you made?"

I shrugged. "In my younger years, I did not linger as long over a project. My last project occupied me on and off for one hundred and twenty years . . ."

One of her eyebrows shot up in surprise.

I continued, "I did do other projects while I worked on it. The final stages of glasswork do not take long in terms of hours, but preparing the rare material I needed took considerable time. As I was saying, unlike that project, I have finished bottles within a year."

"And how many have you made?"

"I have lost track," I admitted. "Two hundred, perhaps three. Although I enchant them against breakage, they are glass, and some have been broken."

"So you have potentially created hundreds of gates between Kong Shyh Jieh and Earth," said Plum. "Would the same trick work if one of the bottles were taken to Origin?"

I frowned. "The point is moot. Since we were exiled, no demon has returned to Origin. All our battles with the gods have been on Kong Shyh Jieh or in the sidewise planes about us."

"Humor me," Plum pressed. "Could the bottles be used to create gates between Kong Shyh Jieh and Origin?"

"I have no reason to think not," I said, startled.

"No wonder even the gods might fear you," she said. "If you ever considered the potential of your bottles as instruments of invasion . . ."

"They are fragile," I protested. "No wise person would trust himself to a gate that could be closed with a solid kick."

"But if the bottle were well hidden?" she continued musing. "Yes, Lord Demon. I can see why gods would fear you—and why Viss would not want to kill you out of hand. Do any other demons have this skill?"

Modesty is not a demon trait.

"No," I said. "It is a family art, and I am the last of my family. Moreover, even when I was first apprenticed, my teachers said that I was the culmination of many generations of talent."

Li Piao looked up from studying his folded hands.

"That I can believe. As interesting as Plum's theories are, they do not resolve our problem. How can we gain access to Kai Wren's bottle?"

We sat thinking for a time over tea and then, after Plum suggested we eat, over breakfast. I wished I had my servitors and my enchanted larder to offer my friends, but, lacking that, I turned my hand to helping with preparations. All my work with ceramic and glass has given me a fine sense for timing of heated things, and what I lacked in knowledge, I made up for in precision.

Meal finished, we were thoughtfully washing up when Plum turned to me:

"Kai Wren, what are these sidewise spaces that you've mentioned?"

"Each major plane," I answered, "creates about it a number of related spaces. We do not usually consider them separate planes since they rely on their relationship to another plane for stability."

"If we could get to one of the related planes of Kong Shyh Jieh, would Grandfather have a better chance at obtaining contact with your bottle?"

"If the bottle is on Kong Shyh Jieh, yes, he would."

"Ah."

She said nothing more, then, but she had started a train of thought that I could not abandon. Sometime in the early afternoon, I came to where she was working on some paperwork related to her business.

"Plum, how do we find out what time it is in Ireland?"

"Ireland?"

"That's right."

She pushed her paperwork aside. "A time-zone chart would show us, or a map. Would you like to know?"

"Please."

After consulting a chart she had stored in her computer, no doubt to facilitate her overseas business travel, Plum informed me: "There's about an eight-hour time difference."

"Later?"

"That's right."

"So it's between eight and nine there."

"Yes," she grinned, "in the latter half of the Hour of the Dog."

"May I use your phone to make an overseas call? I believe I may have thought of someone who can help us."

"Who do you want to call?"

"O'Keefe's Pub." I provided her with a location. In a few moments, she had a number, had placed the connection, and with an inquisitive look, turned the phone over to me.

The connection was remarkably good. I could even catch the hum of business in the background.

"Is this the proprietor?" I asked the man who answered.

"Just a moment."

I heard a voice call, "George! You're wanted!"

A few ticks later, George himself picked up the line.

"Yes?"

"Hello, George." I spoke to him in the Irish, as the O'Keefe had taught me. "I'm doubting that you'll be recalling my voice, but I was in your pub some months ago. I was giving you a sum of money to be used for the poor and the needy."

"You're the friend of Angus!" he said.

"Aye, that I am, and it's Angus of the Hills I am needing to speak w'. Does he come into your pub?"

"You're in luck, man, for he's here tonight. He comes maybe once a week for a dram and a bit of conversation."

"May I be speaking with him then?"

"Sure."

He called out, "Angus. Telephone for you. Trunk call!"

Angus was next on the line.

"Aye?"

"This is Kai Wren, Angus."

"Lord . . ."

I interrupted him. "Speak not my name, friend, for I am in a spot of trouble. I was hoping to beg your help."

"What might I be doing for you?"

"It's not such as I would discuss over the telephone," I said. "Can you come to the San Francisco?"

"Can you not come here?"

" 'Twould be a mite hard," said I. "That's a bit of my trouble."

He considered. "Aye. I can come. I'll need to be finishing off some business first. Can I have until the morning?"

"By your clock or mine?"

"Yours, unless the need be dire."

"It will wait some hours yet. Come to the Old Saint Mary's Church on the edge of Chinatown. I'll be sending someone to meet you if I canna come mysel'."

"I'll be there by eight in the morning, your time."

"Thank you, Angus. You won't be at a loss for your kindness."

He laughed, a warm, slightly drunken sound. "I have not been wanting for good ale and better company since your visit. I'll give you this one on credit."

"Thank you. Until tomorrow, then."

"Tomorrow."

I hung up the phone. Plum was studying me with lively curiosity.

"Was that Gaelic you were speaking?" she asked.

"It was," I said, "and an Irish friend of mine is coming to help us. He will arrive by eight tomorrow morning. I did not want to draw attention to your house, so I told him to meet us at Old Saint Mary's Church."

"Who is this friend?"

"His name is Angus of the Hills. He's a spirit native to this plane—what the Irish call a member of the sidhe folk."

Plum nodded, glanced at the clock. Only the energy with which she jumped to her feet showed her excitement.

"I'd better lay in some beer then. Will he drink it from a can?"

"That I cannot say," I said, "but a bottle would be nicer.

I'll let you in on a secret. Do you know what exotic brews are trendy now in English pubs?"

She shook her head. "I don't get to England often. Most of my business is in the East."

I grinned. "American beers."

"No!"

"On my word."

"It takes all types," she said, "and I suppose the glamour of an export follows the strangest things. I'll lay in beer and some good food to welcome this Angus. Will you tell Grandfather? I think he's taking this morning's failure hard."

"I will," I promised. "And I'll remind him that he has no reason to chide himself. My enemies are not fools. I was the fool not to listen to warnings against them. I made their task easier with my trust, but I see now that they were going to get me one way or another."

Plum turned back, halfway out the door. "I wonder why they didn't just ask for your help. You seemed inclined to favor Viss, at least."

"I've been asking myself the same question," I answered. "And all the answers I can come up with frighten me."

VIII

ANGUS OF THE Hills was found and retrieved the next morning as planned, one of the few things to go smoothly these past several days, although I had to admit, now that I was out of my funk, the rescue that Li Piao and Plum had effected for my humble self had been artistry in the extreme.

We gathered in the kitchen, which was rapidly becoming our command center. Angus had taken the form of an Irish peasant: barrel-chested, possessed of a bit of a paunch, fair skin liberally sprinkled with freckles. His ginger hair looked as if it had been cut with a blunt knife, and his clothing was simple, but there was no mistaking him for what he was, for he walked like a king.

I made introductions all around, and we seated ourselves at the table. We broke our fast on congee and green tea while I sketched out the situation for Angus. When I finished, he thudded his fist on the table in one-handed applause (the other being occupied with spooning a porkball from his congee into his mouth).

"A tale after my own heart, full of blood and thunder, tragedy and derring-do! So the O'Keefe would not betray his master and died for it, is that the way?"

"As I have learned," I said.

"Then tell me how I may give aid. I will not let such a valiant scion of my island die in vain."

"Can you take us to Kong Shyh Jieh?" Plum asked.

Angus shook his head. "That plane belongs to the Chinese sidhe. I could not do so without invitation. Even with that, my coming could well attract more attention than you'll be wanting."

Li Piao asked, "Can you take us into one of the sidewise planes, then? Perhaps I could pry open the secret way into Kai Wren's bottle if I were on a tangential plane."

"That," he considered for a moment, "I should be able to do. Kai Wren's bottle is his own realm, so I should be able to escort you there without comment."

"Good," said I. "Then this is what we shall do. Between your powers, Li Piao and Angus, you should be able to translate all four of us into the sidewise plane. That is, if the Lady Plum cares to accompany us."

"I wouldn't miss it," she said with a decisive shake of her swallowtailed hair.

Once the decision was made, there was little left to do but effect it. Li Piao insisted on carrying the dragon bowl with him, wrapping it carefully in cloth and stowing it in a small backpack. This, a walking stick, and his inherent powers were all he took.

Plum took a flat automatic pistol from a drawer, checked its chamber, and dropped a few spare clips into the pockets of her jacket. Catching my surprised expression, she grinned.

"These are dangerous times to be a woman who must travel alone."

"Of course," I said, heartened by her confidence. Without my demon *chi* I could not tell if she had her grandfather's potential for magic, but I promised myself that if she did, I would reward her by intensifying her powers.

I took up the sturdy walking stick I had borne the day before and turned to Angus.

"Are you ready, Great Sidhe?"

"Are you, Lord Demon?"

"As ready as I ever will be."

"Then all of you gather close," he said, seeming to grow in size and yet diminish in substance until he became once again the genderless, formless thing that I had first sensed hovering over that lonely hill in Ireland. "When the lifting of the Veil comes, you must slip through with me. I'm hoping to drop it as quickly as I may so that our enemies will not be setting eyes on us."

"Kai Wren," said Plum in a soft voice, "you support Grandfather and give him aid as he seeks to open the door. Let Angus and me cover your backs."

I nodded, though it felt strange to be one of those protected, rather than a guardian. Still, human she might be, but she had a calculating mind. I placed my hand on Li Piao's bony shoulder.

"Ready, sorcerer?"

He looked up at me, and his ancient eyes within their wrinkles were bright.

"I am, Lord Demon."

Angus of the Hills lifted the Veil and we passed through. After the pastry-scented warmth and yellow-lit brightness of Plum's kitchen, the sidewise plane was a forbidding place. In color it was blue-gray touched with silver. In form it was like unto being within the heart of a towering thunderhead. Beneath us, as of something far, far away, I heard the rushing of water and knew it to be the coursing of the river called Forgetfulness.

"I have hidden us as best I might," whispered Angus, his presence a cloak about us, "but hasten."

Li Piao glanced down and clearly did not care for how his lower extremities vanished into the mist. I steadied him.

"Let me recite the resonance correspondences with you," I said, keeping my lips close to his ear. "I have no *chi* to lend the effort, but I can steady your concentration."

I sensed rather than saw his smile. "As you do my trembling knees. Yes, recite with me, Wren, but keep your voice low."

Step by step, I essayed to guide Li Piao into the mental state that must be achieved to open the secret way. Again I was reminded of my weakness. Usually, I would go through this routine as easily as a banker spins open a combination lock on a vault. Now we were as two thieves who carefully listen to the tumblers falling into place, taking their clues from the sound.

Yet, despite the slowness of the process, I could feel that we were winning our way through. Whereas our attempt the morning before had been halted by Li Piao's inability to mesh his power with the lock, now he had a firm grasp, and the key was turning.

It snapped open as Angus was beginning to grow anxious and Plum was casting this way and that, seeking to pinpoint a menace she could sense but not see.

The blue-gray mist rippled as Li Piao completed the opening. I pushed him through and went in hard on his heels, knowing that Angus would gather Plum and follow.

I had dreamed of this homecoming, of calling upon my servitors and laying delicacies before my guests, but what met my horrified gaze was devastation.

My secret door had carried us through to what should have been a hidden grove at the foot of the mountains, but the grove was open to the sky and the mountains crumbled into ruin. Sprawled about us, my ogres lay in heaps, their bodies returning to the clay from which they had been shaped. I took an unsteady step forward, dreading what I would find, yet knowing that I must see.

My palace had collapsed into itself. Fire had eaten through some portions; others were reduced to dust. Gaping holes, as from bombardment, were visible in those walls that still stood.

I continued my progress forward, aware of the small procession trailing behind me. The beauty I had wrought was no more. Little *chi* remained, and what was still present was ebbing.

The remains of milkweed fairies crunched underfoot; other creatures no longer even identifiable moldered beneath shattered trees and splintered rock. I felt no surprise, only grief, when we walked up a rise and saw the Lung Shan fallen and death filling a vale where once a singing stream ran over polished river rock.

Even the air was stale and, when I looked up, I could glimpse the interior of the bottle through the decaying atmosphere.

"I thought," I said, and my voice was steady with the steadiness of absolute shock, "to find the place looted. I thought even to find some of my enemies in residence. Never in my darkest nightmares did I imagine this."

A hand rested on my shoulder and squeezed in a mute offer of comfort.

"I'm sorry, Wren," Li Piao said.

"Why?" whispered Plum. "Why all of this destruction?"

Angus silenced us with a commanding gesture. For the first time, I realized how exposed we were. My feet had wandered with neither thought, nor caution. A crumbling rock wall offered some shelter, and I hunkered behind it, the others taking my lead.

"What, Great Sidhe?"

"Motion in the ruined palace below, a flicker of silver and darkness," he answered. "Those who did this may have left a guard."

Silver and darkness. The words stirred an image within my troubled mind.

"We cannot hide here," I said. "I will go and investigate. Angus, be ready to take the others outward and home again if there is danger."

I silenced a flurry of protest with a weary motion of my hand.

"I had many servitors, many creatures. Perhaps a few have survived and taken refuge in the ruins. They might attack one of you. If it is an enemy . . . well, I welcome such an encounter."

I went then, feet finding firmness in renewed purpose, even if that purpose was nothing but suicide or Pyrrhic revenge. For those moments, though my demon powers were still gone from me, I was again Lord Demon, and even Viss in all her might could have feared me.

Neither Viss nor Tuvoon nor even Devor came forth to meet me before a tumbled arch that led into a garden once filled with miniature roses. Nor was it Po Shiang or his minions. Instead, what flitted out to me, clad in a strange armor, was the slim, not quite substantial form of Spilling Moonbeams.

"Lord Demon!" she cried, and I could not account for the joy in her voice. "You have come, even as my father and I had hoped!"

"I am not Lord Demon," I said, my tones so bitter I hardly knew my own voice. "I am barely certain that I am Kai Wren.

Looking about me, I can believe that I am naught but a human called Harvey Wang."

"You are Kai Wren," she said, "the Godslayer, and I, at least, will call you Lord Demon. Who lurks behind you on the hillside?"

"Those who brought me home," I said.

"Call them here," she said. "I have a shelter sealed against what is destroying this place. We can talk there, free from fear."

I wished I could test her truthfulness as once I might have, but that was not in me any longer. Instead, I studied her anxious posture, the imploring gesture of her slim hands, and I nodded.

"I will get them," I said.

"Hurry," she pleaded. "Without armor such as I wear, the danger is immense."

I did hurry then, for I would not bring harm to those who had helped me. As I ran up the slope, I considered sending them back to Earth, but knew that they would argue and, if the danger was as Spilling Moonbeams had said, they might be harmed.

"Come with me," I said, motioning them after. "I have found one who claims to be a friend."

They did, but Plum questioned, as I had known she would.

"Can you trust this 'friend'?"

"I know only three I can trust for certain," I replied, "but this one and her father tried to warn me against Viss. If she, too, is against me, I know of no allies I can call upon among demonkind."

"That's a bit hard," Li Piao said, picking his way down the slope. "Didn't He of the Towers of Light tell you how it really was with Viss?"

I colored as I recalled how impulsively I had discarded that venerable one's warnings.

"Yes, he did," I admitted, "but HE is difficult enough to contact for one who possesses his full powers. For me . . ."

Our arrival where Spilling Moonbeams waited saved me from the necessity of saying more. Without waiting for introductions, she hurried us off to where a geodesic dome made from some glittering substance was concealed beneath a partially collapsed room.

"This area is safe," she assured us, seeing how everyone glanced up at the leaning walls and ceiling. "My father and I reinforced it before we set up the shelter. Watch your step as you come inside. The floor is below ground level."

She pushed aside a panel and a hexagonal door slid open. We must needs stoop to enter, but once we had there was room enough to stand. The dome itself created a rounded hut about fifteen feet in diameter at the base, smaller, of course, at the apex.

A neatly made cot against one wall and a footlocker-sized chest showed that Spilling Moonbeams had been staying here for some time. As we filed in, she removed her helmet and the long coat of armor and racked them by the door.

When she turned to face us, I could see that Li Piao and Plum were only now realizing how very inhuman was our hostess's form. Quickly, lest fear or alienation arise, I made introductions.

"Spilling Moonbeams, these are my friends. Li Piao, a human sorcerer; his granddaughter, Li Plum, a mistress of *feng shui*; and Angus of the Hills, one of the Irish sidhe."

"I welcome you all to my temporary home," answered Spilling Moonbeams. "I have a few campstools," she continued, producing them from where they were folded against a wall, "but I fear I do not have enough for all."

"Give mine to Grandfather," Plum said, seating herself on the floor. "I'll be comfortable enough here."

"And I fear one of those won't hold a brawny boyo like me," said Angus, joining her.

Spilling Moonbeams offered a stool to Li Piao and then shyly extended one to me.

"Lord Demon?"

I accepted. Spilling Moonbeams employed the remaining stool as a low table on which she set a tray.

"Camp food," she said apologetically, "but it may sustain you. I have only water to drink, but enough of that for all."

Her hospitality exhausted, she rested on the floor, something about her posture suggesting there might not be legs beneath her robes.

"I suppose you are wondering why I am here," she said.

I had not yet moved far enough from my initial shock to

wonder much about anything. The demoness's presence seemed right in keeping with the other changes to my home.

"I wonder about many things," I said. "What has happened?"

"First," she said, "can you tell me what happened to you?"

"I was a fool," I answered bluntly, "and spoke too freely to ones whom I trusted when I should not have. Having some future use for me, they stripped me of my powers and bundled me off to Earth. I am as you see me, a mere human, and the weakest of those here gathered."

Any doubts I held about Spilling Moonbeam's loyalties vanished then. Horror and pity flooded her delicate features. Her cup of water dropped unnoticed from her hands, and she made no move to wipe up the liquid that soaked her garments.

"Lord Demon!"

"No more," I said. "Now, child, tell us what has happened."

She stared at me as if unable to believe that I could announce such a thing and remain calm. Then, wiping what might have been tears against her sleeve, she began her narrative:

"I suppose it must have been soon after you were sent to Earth that Viss launched her war."

"War?" I exclaimed. "Against the gods?"

"Against the gods and against the demons both. She gave us some understanding only when the first battles were over and parties met to negotiate.

"Viss wants to be absolute ruler of Kong Shyh Jieh. With the full power of all its resources—both material and mystical—to back her, she intends to launch a new attack on Origin."

I asked, "What makes her think she can win now? Demons have been trying to win their way back into Origin for five thousand years."

"She has several reasons," Spilling Moonbeams explained, enumerating them on her fingers. "One, she plans to spend all the energy that Kong Shyh Jieh has accumulated on the assault."

"But," I protested, "that would leave us no *chi* to fall back on!"

"True. She believes that the desire to maintain a refuge is one reason why demons have continually lost their wars. Her second reason for attacking is that she has made allies among the gods."

"Allies?" I queried, thinking of Po Shiang. "Yes, we have seen evidence of this."

"These deific allies," Spilling Moonbeams continued, "have developed a new weapon, a green fire that painfully drains the *chi* from the one attacked."

"I've felt it," I said grimly.

"Father tells me that there were similar weapons in other demon/god wars. What makes this green fire particularly dangerous is that instead of merely draining the *chi*, it transfers it to the one who has sent the fire."

I remembered how Fire's Fever—Rabla-yu—had appeared to grow stronger during our fight. Yes, this green fire could turn the battle against the demons.

Li Piao asked, "Do you know how many gods are allied with Viss?"

"I do not, but rumor says that there may be dozens. Most of them are young hotheads but a few hundred years old. They have never seen a great war, and, as the society of the gods is extremely static and stratified, they wish to earn some renown."

"Demons," Angus asked dryly, "are immune to ambition?"

Spilling Moonbeams smiled at him. "We do not have the same problem with our younger generations. That, too, is part of the story, but if you will let me finish my first explanation, I will return to that."

Angus grinned at her. "You're being well on the way to rivaling the bards for holding an audience, Lady. Tell on. I'll hold my tongue."

"Viss has a final tactic she plans to draw on, and this is where you come in, Lord Demon."

"Me? She's caused me nothing but pain and loss. That's an odd way to make an ally." I looked into my cup, for I had no desire to see their faces. "I might have done much for her, if she had only asked."

"Viss," said Spilling Moonbeams, and her tone was gentle, "had ascertained in many small ways that you were not likely to agree to the destruction of Kong Shyh Jieh."

"No, I would not have."

"And she felt that this was integral to her goals. Instead,

she set out to gain at least some of what she wanted from you without telling you her secrets."

"What did she want?"

"The fu dogs and your magical bottles. I don't know why, but Father has confirmed that her ally is the one who has the dogs, and we know that she has looted this place and cleared out your gallery."

Her words only confirmed what I had suspected.

"Go on," I said, my voice rasping angrily.

"You must be wondering why Viss felt that it is so important for us to regain Origin."

I shrugged. "Isn't it the same old patriotic fervor? Viss has lost almost all her family in such struggles—as have I. I've given the entire thing up as a bad investment. I assumed that she wants a return."

Spilling Moonbeams shook her head, her pale tresses tracing spiderwebs upon the floor.

"There is a greater reason than that. Viss believes that if we do not regain Origin within the next thousand years, then demonkind is doomed."

There should have been a thundering line of music to underscore such an announcement, but the only sound in the geodesic hut was a gurgle as Angus poured more water into his cup.

"Spilling Moonbeams, I beg you please to explain," Plum asked politely, seeing that no one else was going to speak. "And while you're doing so, could you explain something that has me greatly puzzled?"

"I can try."

"What exactly is the difference between a god and a demon? In most mythologies I know, the gods are the rulers of the cosmos and the demons are the underdogs. That seems to fit you folks up to a point, but I admit I'm puzzled."

Spilling Moonbeams nodded solemnly.

"The terms do fit, I suppose, and that is why we have used them for so long. However, let me give you the official line. Before the first Exile, Origin had two intelligent peoples. One of those peoples was naturally inclined to an organized development of resources and culture. The other was more chaotic, frivolous, and creative. The first were the gods, the second the demons."

"Like the ant and the grasshopper," Plum said. "Both are bugs, but one stores while the other fiddles."

"Yes, that is how the gods would tell it." Spilling Moonbeams smiled. "As my father has taught me, the gods, with their tendency to create immutable structures, are like beavers who will flood the surrounding area so that it no longer can support the very things they desire. Demons are like squirrels who store away food and build nests, but live in a wide variety of settings."

"As long as there are trees"—Plum nodded—"or, more precisely, *chi*."

"A tidy analogy," Spilling Moonbeams agreed. "Whatever the real difference, the gods eventually exiled the demons. What Viss believes, however, is different from both of these theories in a very crucial way. She thinks that gods and demons both are dependent on some undefined element in the plane of Origin. Her belief is that the later generations of demonkind have been degenerating because of their separation from the essential life force of Origin."

"What does she base this 'degeneration' theory upon?" I asked, rather angry. I, after all, had been born on Kong Shyh Jieh.

Spilling Moonbeams gestured down to her own ethereal form.

"Many of the younger demons have been born with bodies that are only partially solid. If I take on a body all of matter, for example to visit Earth, I am much smaller."

"What is size?" I protested. "I can shapeshift to many sizes!"

"You are not of the degenerate ones," she said sadly. "I cannot shift into many forms, nor can I maintain a shift into a form that masses greatly different from this one for very long. There are others like me—my cousin Tuvoon, for example."

Plum cleared her throat. "I don't suppose that something like having a smaller gene pool could account for this, could it? Kai Wren mentioned that his whole family was killed off in the wars. It seems that your family has been hard hit, too."

"Demon genetics," Spilling Moonbeams said, "do not work quite as those of humans do. In some cases, inbreeding is considered quite advantageous."

Although her coloration remained midnight and stardust, I could have sworn that she blushed. "That is why Viss of the Terrible Tongue wishes to breed me with Tuvoon the Smoke Ghost, my cousin."

Plum raised a wry eyebrow. "And you don't like the idea."

"Not one bit!"

"Does Viss have any support for her theory other than a few insubstantial demons?" Li Piao asked.

"There are the scrub demons," Spilling Moonbeams said. "It is not widely advertised, but they are not a separate subspecies. They are the all-too-frequent result of more usual matings. They breed true to themselves, however. 'True' being used carefully, here, for the scrub children are often stupider and smaller than their parents. They also frequently lack any magical abilities beyond the most basic."

I thought of Ba Wa and his friend Wong Pang. Would that be how my children would look? I could understand Viss's fanaticism then—if not agree with her methods for gaining her goals.

Plum had not concluded her cross-examination.

"How come you know so much about this when Kai Wren doesn't?"

"Viss," Spilling Moonbeams answered coolly, stung by Plum's suspicion, "wants me to wed her son. When my father would not agree—he thinks Tuvoon is cruel—and I could not be convinced, Viss shared her theories and conclusions with us and hinted that she knew a way to avoid the problem. Perhaps she believed that I would wed Tuvoon to avoid bearing damaged children."

"But that was not incentive enough," Li Piao said.

"No! I have no desire to act as broodmare for my aunt and her son. Let me bear 'damaged' children like myself," she tossed her head defiantly, "or even a scrub demon rather than be so used."

I admired the demoness's passion, even as she continued to storm.

"The scrub demons are the ones I pity the most. True, they are crass, stupid, rude, and disgusting, but so might I have been if I had been cast out to forage from garbage cans. My father treats his dwarves more kindly—and they are mere servants— than these demons have been treated by their kin!"

She stopped suddenly, and an awkward silence fell. Plum, perhaps feeling that it was her responsibility since she had initially angered the demon lass, asked:

"And so you came seeking Kai Wren. What happened here, anyway? Why is the place so devastated? If Viss wanted the bottles, why didn't she treat this one more carefully?"

Spilling Moonbeams glanced at me, as if she expected me to answer. When I only shrugged she said:

"I can only offer conjecture since I did not arrive until after the damage was done. However, I did overhear some of Viss's allies talking."

She paused to arrange her thoughts: "As best my father and I can tell, Lord Demon must have commanded the denizens of the bottle to protect it against invaders. They did so, and when the *chi* that they typically sustained themselves upon was exhausted, they began to draw upon the very infrastructure of the bottle."

I nodded, recalling my orders to the bottle servitors. I had never envisioned events progressing to such a state, but, even as I recalled the ruin that surrounded us, I felt a peculiar kind of joy. That joy turned to ashes with Spilling Moonbeams's next words.

"Unhappily, Viss herself must have been given permission to enter the bottle, for, as I heard the tale, only those creatures like the great Lung Shan, who could conceive of betrayal and adapt their actions accordingly, dared attack her. Viss slew the Lung Shan herself; Tuvoon accounted for many of the Effervescent Tigers. When that was done, all but Viss withdrew. She looted Kai Wren's gallery, meeting some resistance there, for the household servitors apparently decided that she had exceeded the bounds of hospitality."

Li Piao uttered a deep and mournful sigh. "But in the end, she won."

Spilling Moonbeams bowed her head, silver hair curtaining a face of shadow.

"I fear that is so. Even now, the denizens of the bottle seek to draw *chi* into them so that they can return to their duties, but there is little enough left."

"They destroy," Plum said, understanding, "the very things they are bound to protect. How sad!"

"And that is why," Angus added, "you were so eager to get us into cover."

"Yes. This dome is similar to Kai Wren's bottles in that its interior is isolated from the area without. I have a supply of *shen* coins with which to power it."

"Your father's making?" I asked.

"Mine," she said with a certain coolness. "He is not the only artificer in our family."

I decided an apology would only increase the awkwardness, so I merely said, "It is a fine bit of work. I am grateful you would employ it in my cause."

She lifted her face to me, and the darkness seemed to glow brighter than even the soft brilliance of her hair.

"I would not have a life if you had not slain Chaholdrudan. All I have I would willingly give into your service."

"You overvalue my deed," I answered uncomfortably. "But whatever your reason, I am grateful. Now, let us all consider what we might do next."

Plum nodded briskly. "Lord Demon, your own servitors would not attack you, would they?"

"I see that our thoughts run parallel. No, they would not. Therefore, I will go out into the ruins of my palace and see if there is anything I can salvage. I will also seek to countermand the servitors' order to protect this place."

"Seek to?" said Li Piao.

"The servitors are unlike the other denizens of my bottle," I explained. "Being more closely tied to the bottle's own essence, they have almost no individual identity. If they are as severely depleted as Spilling Moonbeams says, there may not be any intellect that I can contact. Therefore, 'tis best if you all would remain within until I can be certain."

Spilling Moonbeams glanced shyly at me. "I have the armor.

141

It protects in the same fashion as does the dome, although it is less comfortable for long residence. I could accompany you and protect you if need arises."

"My thanks, Lady, but I must decline. If I am attacked, I would not want my enemies to know of your involvement. Best for all concerned if we keep that secret as long as possible."

"But by your own account," she protested, sounding for the first time less than meek and mild, "you are but human!"

"True."

I studied the armor where it stood upon its stand near the door. The lines of it were loose, no doubt to permit it to adapt to a shapeshifting should one be needed.

"Could another wear this armor?"

Reluctantly, she nodded. "If the wearer is not overly large."

"Then let Li Piao come with me," I said. "His talent for natural magic is great, and the denizens of my bottle already know him for one who is welcome within this realm. Therefore, even if the armor does not work as effectively for him, he may be safe. The three of you can remain and continue to discuss tactics. Plum has shown a gift for perceiving implications that I overlook."

The two girls looked at each other. I could tell that they were trying to decide whether or not they cared for each other's company at all. Angus saw the glance as well, and chuckled heartily.

"Be it as you say, Lord Demon. I'll be waiting here and listening to these two colleens sort out the problems of battle between them."

He chuckled again. Plum, at least, flushed in embarrassment. It was difficult to tell with Spilling Moonbeams, for, as always, her face was dark.

With Spilling Moonbeams's grudging assistance, Li Piao donned the armor. Then we ventured out into the ruins.

"Spilling Moonbeams has explained to me," Li Piao said, "that if the need arises for me to work magic, I may draw upon some of the force that creates this armor's protective field."

"I hope that the need will not arise," I answered. "I also hope that Spilling Moonbeams and Plum don't tear into each other in our absence."

Li Piao chuckled. "Angus will stop them from doing serious harm."

"I don't believe that I will ever understand females," I sighed, thinking of Viss.

"The secret," Li Piao said, "as I have learned through my long life, is no secret at all. They differ as much from each other as do men. Trying to classify them as if they do not is to fall into folly."

I helped him over a heap of marble slabs that had once been an elegant staircase, then through a crevice where an archway had collapsed upon itself. Here much of the damage had been initiated by bombardments—probably by Viss's forces. However, the rock had a peculiar softness, a tendency to crumble into gravel beneath our feet, that told me at least some of the damage was being caused as the servitors sought to draw *chi* into themselves.

Oddly, then, the continued decay was a good sign.

As we worked our way into the interior of the palace there were fewer signs of external damage, but the walls bowed and curved, reminding me of a soft ice-cream cone just beginning to melt.

"If nothing is done to halt this," I said, "there will be nothing here but pebbles which will become sand and then not even the dust will remain. I wonder . . ."

"Yes?"

"Is your granddaughter, Plum, a serious practitioner of *feng shui*, or is she just an interior decorator with an Oriental twist?"

"You saw how she has hidden her house," Li Piao answered. "She is quite serious—and something of a sorceress as well."

"Kong Shyh Jieh developed in part through techniques very similar to those used in *feng shui*. I believe I shall consult her."

The gallery, when we reached it, proved as severely damaged as any exterior portion of the palace. Dark smoke marks on the walls and floor testified to how fervently the servitors had sought to defend my property. Equally, the vacant shelves and display niches showed their ultimate failure.

As we stood in the center of the room on burned remnants

of what had once been a fine Persian carpet I felt the touch of a contact.

"Lord Demon?"

The inquiry was zephyr-light against my mind.

"Yes?"

"How may we serve you?"

There was joy in that routine request, a sense of purpose returned.

"Do you know the man with me?"

"Li Piao, the human sorcerer. Lord Kai, you are changed!"

"Forget that for now. It is enough that you know me and know Li Piao. I remind you of my charge that you will do him no harm."

"It is recalled." The mental voice was slightly indignant.

"Very good. Now, first of all, I remove from you the charge to defend this place."

"Lord?" Then, again with that sense of indignation, *"As the great lord wishes."*

"Don't worry. I don't mean to give up the fight. I simply don't want you to destroy yourselves in the process."

"Lord, the person Viss of the Terrible Tongue was among those who made war here."

"So I have learned. My next charge to you is that you will no longer grant her, nor her son, nor any but two I shall name to you entry, unless they are in my company."

Li Piao—who apparently had been following the conversation although he could only hear one side of it—now turned to me, concern writ on his lined features.

"Kai Wren, are you forgetting? Our number is five, counting yourself."

"Yes." I smiled, albeit sadly. "But I have learned not to trust too quickly. Spilling Moonbeams appears to be our ally, but I have nothing but her own words to prove that she is. Therefore, I will only grant you and Plum admittance here without my escort."

"I am honored," Li Piao said, "but what of Angus?"

"The Irish sidhe have their own politics. I dare not trust him too far, although he has given me no reason to feel otherwise. If we survive all of this insanity, then I shall gladly give him the key to my kingdom. Until, then, however . . ."

"*Very wise, Lord Demon,*" spoke the servitor voice.

Li Piao also seemed to agree. "So that we remain politic in our dealings with the others, it is best they not know of this arrangement. I will tell Plum when we have a moment alone."

"Do so," I commanded. Then I returned my attention to the servitor. "Make yourself visible to me as a light, then guide us through the palace by the safest ways. I wish to see what has been left to me."

"*Yes, Lord Demon.*"

The servitor appeared to us in the guise of a tiny phoenix, so faint as to be transparent, but perfect in every detail. I approved of the hopeful symbolism of its choice and gestured for Li Piao to walk with me.

Ours was not a happy pilgrimage, for every corridor we traversed, every room we entered, bore evidence of the disaster. What Viss and her troops had not destroyed, the servitors' fierce quest for *chi* had often finished. Still, among the rubble, I found some things of value.

Much of it came from Earth, trinkets and treasures I had brought to decorate my estate. From a sandalwood box I withdrew a small velvet bag of cut gemstones. A crumbling niche within a porcelain pillar still held a collection of fine jade figurines. A Ming vase painted with tigers had miraculously survived the collapse of the cabinet that held its fellows. Other things might yet be retrievable if and when the battle was won.

Two things in particular gave me hope. Next to a side door that Ollie was wont to use when he ventured outward stood a slat-sided oak barrel bound with hoops of iron. It was filled nearly to the top with currency—mostly American, since that was the country wherein our bottle resided. By some small miracle, it had escaped the fire.

Li Piao hardly knew how to react when I reached in and handed him a fistful of crumpled bills.

"Here, some recompense for all the expense I have cost you."

"It has been small repayment for my new health," he protested. "You have already reimbursed us for the expenses entailed in your escape."

"Then," I said, my expression wry, "consider it recompense for the trouble I am certain to cause you before this is over."

He continued to protest, but I effectively silenced him by ignoring him. I delegated a servitor to sort, stack, and band the remainder of the bills so that I might take them with me to Earth.

"You can manage that?" I asked, recalling how weak had been the voice with whom I had spoken.

"We can," the servitor assured me, *"if you will permit us to continue rendering the corpses of the ogres and fairies into dust."*

"That seems best for all concerned," I said, "but leave the atmosphere and terrain alone. I hope to rebuild this place when I am myself again."

"May we have the Lung Shan?"

I felt sad, for the mighty dragon had been among the first of the denizens I had created for the bottle, the general of my hosts and a frequent companion in early exploratory ventures.

"Yes, but leave me his bones; perhaps someday I shall be able to revive him."

My second valuable discovery took place in my glassblowing studio. That section of the palace was in far better shape than I had dared hope, perhaps because my various studios were separate from the rest of the palace—a simple precaution given the heats involved in firing clay or blowing glass.

Following the faint phoenix, Li Piao and I stepped over the threshold. I was feeling melancholy—an emotion I recognized by reference rather than by prior experience—but the sensation fled my breast as I saw what still stood on the bench where I had set it after its completion.

It was orange. It was green. It was one of my best. It had taken me the better part of one hundred and twenty years, on and off. The bottle I had completed the evening of Oliver O'Keefe's death waited for me, perfect and unmarred. I could hardly believe my good fortune. If Viss had to leave me but one of my creations, this was the one I would have requested. With this and the dragon bowl I had gifted to Li Piao, we might just win our undeclared war.

"Kai Wren," asked Li Piao, "is that what I think it is?"

"Yes." I raised it and turned it in the light, admiring the subtle blending of hues and tints within the glass. "I did not like to look upon it after Ollie's death. It made me uncomfortable, as if somehow it had been the cause."

Li Piao wisely did not tell me that what I had felt was an emotion akin to sorrow. He knew that demons do not care to learn that we might be as vulnerable to emotion as humans. I had now learned the taste of grief and knew well that was what I had felt.

"It is lovely. Is it still . . ." he searched for a word and shrugged, "magical?"

"We did not touch it," said the servitor voice, *"for if your enemy wanted your bottles, then we wished that there would be some for you on your return."*

"Are there others?" I asked, feeling the dreadful pang of hope.

"No, Lord. There are not."

I shook away disappointment and let my fingers caress the smooth glass. Within there was no kingdom, no estate in minia-ture, but still, there were powers. Carefully, I wrapped it in silk and cotton and placed it within a sturdy ironwood box.

" 'Tis best we return to the others," I said. "We cannot have them worrying overmuch." To the servitor I added, "Come with us so that I may show you my companions. During this visit, they are not to be harmed."

"You are not staying?" the voice asked in dismay. Adversity had certainly given it a greater range of responses than before. Perhaps this was due to the *chi* it had siphoned from my more versatile creations. Perhaps, it had possessed thoughts and cares all along and this was simply the first time I had cared to talk to it other than to issue a quick order.

"I dare not," I answered, the words bitter in my mouth. That I, Lord Demon, must dare not was as gall and wormwood. "I will return and reclaim this place. Those who have harmed you will pay for their trespass. Take this as my promise and be comforted."

"Yes, Lord Demon," and had I been given to imagination, I would have said that there were tears in the servitor's voice.

*   *   *

One task remained before we could depart my bottle.

"We can discuss tactics when we are in a less vulnerable place," I said, waving down various demands for my attention as soon as I ducked inside the geodesic dome. "If Viss decides to break this bottle, there is nothing I can do for any of us. However, before I leave, there is something I can do that will markedly improve our chances in the future."

Quickly, I explained the essential details of how the servitors had sought to protect the bottle and how, in the process, they had damaged the very thing they sought to defend.

"Their idea wasn't all bad," I said. "In fact, I have given them permission to draw *chi* from anyone who enters the bottle without my direct escort."

Li Piao already knew the exceptions to this rule. I could trust him to find a tactful way to inform Plum.

"However, even though I have permitted them to continue drawing what *chi* remains in the corpses of the slain, that will not be enough to replenish them nor to permit a reservoir to be built against possible need."

I turned to Plum. "I want to hire you on a professional basis."

"For *feng shui*?"

"Yes. I would compensate you, of course. The raiders were not interested in my money, only in more valuable things."

Plum looked angry. "I won't take any money from you!"

"But I am asking you to do your job!"

"You saved my grandfather's life. I'm not certain how long he would have kept living after the stroke paralyzed him. You not only gave him back use of his body, you gave him a sense of purpose."

"But . . ."

"Enough!"

I allowed myself to be silenced, but I thought once again that I never would understand humans. Observe their societies from the outside and you would assume that all that rules them is money or its equivalent. Then they display these strange upwellings of idealism. I guess that's what happens in societies created by emotional beings.

I returned to the issue.

"Is there anything we can do with the resources we have among us to intensify the generation of positive *chi*?"

"I'd need to look around outside," she said. "Is it safe now?"

"Safe from my servitors," I responded, "but I can make no promises for anything else."

She exited Spilling Moonbeams's dome, now wearing an absent, studious look that went oddly with her attire. Stroking her chin, she strolled about, checking the position of the mountains, examining the withered remains of various trees and shrubs.

"How far is it to the nearest major body of water?"

"About three-quarters of a mile that way is a small ocean," I said, pointing.

"Salt water?"

"Yes. Brackish, really."

"And rivers?"

"There are two major ones," I answered.

"Straight?"

"When I designed them they had a tendency to ramble," I said, "but I don't know what the battle may have done to them."

Spilling Moonbeams spoke, "The body of the Lung Shan has dammed one almost completely."

Plum frowned. "That's not good. We should free the waters so they can continue to flow; otherwise, the *chi* will stagnate."

"I have given the servitors permission to desiccate the flesh," I said, "but that will certainly take time."

"Can the corpse be moved before it is too fragile?" Plum asked, glancing at each of us, welcoming suggestions.

"I can do that," Angus said. "I'm not without some resources, not bein' dependent on quite the same things as these Chinese sidhe."

"Good," Plum said. "Be about it."

She turned her attention to Spilling Moonbeams.

"Can you fly?"

Spilling Moonbeams tossed silver hair. "Of course."

"Can you carry me?"

"Possibly. Why?"

"I think I can do a better job after an overview of the terrain. Lord Demon has told us we need to move quickly."

Spilling Moonbeams considered. "I will employ one of the *shen* coins from my armor since I no longer need it. That way I won't need to draw on the land for *chi*."

"Wonderful!"

Before they soared away, Plum turned to Li Piao and me.

"Walk around to the back of the palace. Shift anything that is blocking a path so that the *chi* flow down from the mountains won't be interrupted."

"And if something is too large for two mere humans?" said Li Piao, a twinkle in his eyes.

"Then use your Art, Grandfather. I'm certain that Spilling Moonbeams would give you one of her coins."

When the request was phrased that way, Spilling Moonbeams could not refuse. I wondered what the elegant demoness thought of this forthright human girl. It seemed inevitable that they would either end up close friends or bitter rivals. However, that situation was still too early to call.

When we had reconvened, Plum reported: "It looks hopeful. You used a rather classic construction—didn't you?"

I admitted that this was the case, although whose "classic" might be left open to discussion.

Plum continued: "The mountain slope on which the palace was constructed and the flanking slopes remain, although they could use some restructuring. Essentially, the dragon-protecting-pearl conformation is still in place. Were you able to remove any obstructions to the *chi*'s flow?"

Li Piao nodded. "Yes, although I fear that Miss Moonbeams's coin is exhausted."

"Please," said Spilling Moonbeams with her first truly relaxed smile, "call me Spilling Moonbeams. The construction is one name. If it were not, then I must needs resign myself to sometimes being called 'Spilling.'"

Li Piao chuckled. "As you wish. In any case, thank you."

"Kai Wren, tell the servitors," Plum said, "to encourage any evergreens. They will promote the development of beneficial *chi*.

With the obstructions gone . . . well, I can't say that you will see any sort of rapid improvement, but the region will stop deteriorating."

"Wonderful!" I said. "Angus and Li Piao, can you return us to Earth?"

Spilling Moonbeams interrupted, "May I come along? I have several suggestions to make."

"You may," I said. "Will Seven Fingers worry?"

"Lord Demon, I am a thousand years old!"

"Yes, I know, but there is a war trying to get started. Your father will be concerned."

"You're right," she conceded. "I'll tell him what is happening. Where can I find you?"

Caution continued to rule me, even though I was almost certain of her *bona fides*.

"Do you and your father have a private Gate to Earth?"

"Yes."

"Then come to the Old St. Mary's Church in San Francisco."

"That's in North America—California?"

"Yes. Do you need a map?"

"That's all right. I can get one. What do I do when I get to the church?"

I handed her a couple of quarters and wrote down Plum's unlisted phone number.

"Call this. Someone will come to get you."

She accepted them, studying my face.

"Don't you trust me?"

"I do," I said, wishing that were completely so, "but these are bad times. I would not make my friends vulnerable to harm. If we meet you, then we can make certain that no one followed."

"True," she said, accepting my explanation and, if she had perceived it, my lie with grace. "I will call in a few hours."

Placing my palm flat against the ground, I bid my land farewell. I wondered, as I accepted Li Piao's guiding hand, if I would ever see it again.

IX

I LEARNED A bit more about the frailties of the flesh when we returned to Plum's house. After a hearty dinner ordered from a convenient takeout place, I could hardly keep my eyes open. Reluctantly, we all concluded that sleep was necessary if we were to successfully plan our next step.

"In any case," managed Li Piao between yawns, "we should wait until Spilling Moonbeams can join us. Otherwise, we will end up repeating our efforts."

"True," said I, and we let the matter—and ourselves—rest.

Angus of the Hills departed as soon as we arrived, promising that he would check in daily at O'Keefe's Pub in case we needed him. Before he left, I made him a gift of the cut gemstones I had found in the ruins of my palace. Unlike the humans, he graciously accepted them as his due.

I slept long, slept well, and was awakened by the ringing of the telephone. It was answered only after the third ring, leaving me to conclude that I was not the only one who had slept late. A tap came at my door a few moments later.

"That was Spilling Moonbeams," said Plum, her voice faintly muffled by the wood. "I told her to wait, and I'd be there in about a half hour. She didn't seem to mind—apparently she had never been to Chinatown before."

"She wouldn't have," I answered, swinging my legs out from under the covers and marveling at aching muscles in calves and thighs. "Her father is a traditionalist. Their Gate probably opens into mainland China."

"Do you need anything before I go?"

"No. I'm fine."

I showered, shaved, and donned some of my new clothes, thinking that I'd need to learn how one did laundry if I stayed here much longer. The venture into my bottle—depressing as it had been in many ways—had left me feeling uplifted. I was growing somewhat accustomed to the limitations of my human form, if not resigned to remaining in that state. Now at least I had money, as well as the green-and-orange bottle.

It stood on my bedside table, the blown glass threaded with tiny bubbles. I amused myself with the fancy that I could feel its beneficial emanations working for me. Then I sobered. If the possession of Kai Wren bottles did indeed grant any benefits to the owner, then whatever I had, Viss had many, many times more. I dared not become too hopeful.

For a moment, I contemplated hiding it, then shrugged. If anyone could trace me here, they had power enough to take whatever they wanted. Let the bottle stay there in the sunshine, absorbing the light and casting its ambience on the house and all within it.

"Good morning, Lord Demon," greeted Li Piao as I came into the kitchen. "Can I get you anything to eat?"

"After last night's dinner," I said, "I thought I would never be hungry again. Amazing how wrong I am. However, don't disturb yourself. Tell me where things are."

He did this thing. I fetched myself some pastries and fresh fruit. There was coffee as well, so I finished the pot and then— following Li Piao's instructions—set up a fresh one.

"We should make tea as well," I said. "I think that Spilling Moonbeams will prefer that to coffee."

"Tea is best made fresh," Li Piao replied. "We'll ask her when she arrives."

I was eating my second pastry when the telephone rang. Li Piao answered it, spoke a few words, then handed me the receiver.

"It's Angus. He wants to speak with you."

"Top o' th' mornin' to you, Lord Demon," said the familiar voice, his brogue as thick as a stage Pat and Mike show. "I fear I'm callin' with some news that won't be makin' you smile."

"Has something happened to you?"

"No, not that, but you're kind to be asking." The accent suddenly diminished. "I've been told by the lords and ladies above me that they'll not have me messing around with the affairs of foreign devils. They dread that it will bring repercussions down upon our heads."

"I see," I said, for I did indeed. "Well, that can't be helped. Now that I think of it, I was bold to involve you."

"Oh, they're not after having my hide for that," Angus assured me. "I'm simply to stay out of it hereafter."

"I'm pleased you aren't in any trouble," I said, "and I am very grateful for what you have done thus far. With Spilling Moonbeams and perhaps her father on our side, we are not as lacking for magical support as we were a few days ago."

"Good. I was after that way of thinking myself. Still," his voice dropped, "if you're needing me for a matter of life and death, call. The George O'Keefe will know how to contact me. I'll help you and answer to the High Ones after."

"Thank you," I said, deeply touched. "I am grateful, but I hope that when I next call upon you it will be to invite you to my home for an evening of heavy drinking and tale-telling."

"I'll come for that, too," he said with a throaty chuckle. "Kick the bastards' asses for me!"

"For you and for me, both," I promised. "Now stop running up George O'Keefe's phone bill."

"With the pretties you're after giving me," he said, "I can pay that wee bill and more. Luck o' the Irish with you!"

"Thanks again," I said, "and good-bye."

Li Piao studied my face as I set the receiver back into its cradle.

"Angus is not coming back?"

"He can't," I explained, sipping my cooling coffee. "His hierarchical bosses don't want the equivalent of an international incident."

"Wise of them."

Soon after, we heard the garage door open and Plum and Spilling Moonbeams came in. True to her description the day before, as a solid figure of a human, Spilling Moonbeams was much smaller. If one overlooked her curvaceous figure—which I could not—one might have mistaken her for a child.

She was dressed in a red, embroidered Chinese silk pantsuit after the style worn by Chinese women for centuries. The snug jacket was high-necked and ostensibly modest; the knee-length trousers showed off a set of very shapely calves.

"I knew her at once," Plum said, "despite all the changes. Honey, that outfit is lovely, but you really stand out in a crowd."

Spilling Moonbeams glanced at Plum. (I couldn't help noticing how lush were her dark lashes.)

"Thank you."

Plum clearly did not know how to respond to this.

"Shall we get to planning?" I said desperately. The Chinese ideogram for trouble originated as the sign for two women under one roof. I was beginning to understand why.

To my relief, everyone settled around the kitchen table, preferred drinks at hand. A plate heaped with pastries and a bowl of fresh fruit was set in the center of the table. Li Piao shared out notebooks and pens.

"While you and Grandfather were searching the ruins of the palace," Plum began, "I explained to Angus and Spilling Moonbeams my theory that Viss and Company hope to use the bottles they have stolen from Kai Wren to facilitate invasion of Origin."

"It's a good idea," Spilling Moonbeams admitted. "I took the liberty of presenting it to my father. He said he wondered why we hadn't thought of it sooner."

Plum looked understandably smug. She had only to learn of the bottles to grasp their implications, but then humans adapt more rapidly than do demons. Just look at the technological leaps they've taken in the last few centuries.

"Before we go on," I said, "I had a phone call from Angus of the Hills."

Briefly, I summarized Angus's message. I saw disappointment but not defeat on the faces of my allies and was greatly heartened.

"Angus's help would have been greatly appreciated," said Spilling Moonbeams, "but we are not without allies. My father . . ."

She was interrupted by a rapid knocking at the front door. Plum rose, concern creasing her face.

"Should I answer it?"

"Let's take a look first," I suggested, taking up my walking stick and heading to the door. Once there, I applied my eye to the little peephole.

I could see nothing. A muted noise rather like an argument in progress convinced me that someone—or someones—were there.

Perhaps I recognized the voices on some subconscious level. Perhaps I foolishly forgot my recent loss of power. For whatever reason, before Plum could stop me, I flung open the door. The two who had been crouched against it spilled forward and onto the Chinese carpet. I slammed the door shut and pressed my stick to the throat of the nearest.

"What you shits doin' here? Spyin' on me?"

I spoke the language of the demons, but Plum did not need words to see that these were dangerous. I heard a click and saw from the corner of my eye that she had produced her gun from somewhere and was aiming it at the scrub demon I had not pinned.

Looking back, I wonder at my actions and know them born not of courage but of overconfidence. Even at two feet tall, stocky and squat, ugly as sin and reeking of garbage, one of the scrub demons could have accounted for anyone in that house— Spilling Moonbeams excepted. Even Li Piao required time to focus his newly acquired powers. He might have accounted for one, given that time, but then again, he might not have.

Yet I stood there, a piece of gnarled wood in my fist, my

foot resting on the scrub demon's chest, acting as if I were still Lord Demon. I was lucky that they weren't assassins, for my story would have ended there.

"What do you want?" I demanded arrogantly. "Speak or . . ."

I paused, for the first time realizing my weakness, but Spilling Moonbeams sauntered in, her teacup still held in one tiny hand. She spoke before the scrub demons could perceive the pause in my speech.

"Or I burn you to ashes."

"My carpet!" Plum muttered ruefully, but her gun remained steady.

I saw now that my foot rested upon Ba Wa, the more intelligent of the two demons who had survived on the night of Ollie's death. Seeing my gaze rest upon him, he began to babble in the demon tongue.

"Use English," I interrupted, "or Chinese so that all may understand."

He switched to English in mid-phrase.

". . . Not to hurt great Lord Demon, but to serve him! We are but little shits, but we want to live! Viss kill us all! Has already killed Pitt and One-Eye and Roaming Nose. Made example she said . . . terrible!"

Through the sole of my shoe, I could feel his shudder.

"So she killed a few shit demons," I said, being deliberately obtuse. "Did you fuck with her? Steal her goods?"

"No, no, no, no, no!" Ba Wa assured me, while Wong Pang whimpered assurances. "She make a big meeting, all the demons who will listen, come to Origin Park. Tell them how demons need to go back to Origin before they become dirt like us."

He wailed pathetically. "Then she make great flash bang and kill others, just like I say. Says creatures so weak, so ugly, disgrace to demons everywhere. Many applaud. Pang and I run away. Lord Demon always so good to us, so kind."

"Kind, kind, Lord Demon," groveled Wong Pang, drooling on Plum's carpet.

"So we look for you. You not at your bottle, but Spilling Moonbeams is. We watch her."

Spilling Moonbeams cut in, "You stayed in the bottle?"

"No, no." Ba Wa looked proud of himself for a moment. "We have broken bit of scrying mirror. We watch in that. Bottle makes us sick."

"How did you get into my bottle in the first place?" I asked. "How do I know that you are not in league with Viss?"

"Know where bottle door in Kong Shyh Jieh is!" wailed Ba Wa. "Door still there. Maybe Viss not know, not care."

Spilling Moonbeams nodded. "That, at least, is true. I slipped in the same way after Viss's troops had retired. It was sealed later, but for several days it remained available. With the guardians so weakened, it was simple enough to force."

"Probably left it in place until she could figure out how to reposition it," I reasoned.

"Lord Demon not kill us?" Ba Wa begged. "We afraid. We terrified. Viss say some young demons worth saving—make strong again with *chi* of Origin. Us just dirt."

"I wondered," Spilling Moonbeams said dryly, "how she was going to get around the fact that she herself had borne less than perfect children. I wouldn't be surprised if one or more of those scrub demons she slew were her own failures. She wouldn't want her crusade tarnished by late revelations. Now, if it comes out, she can brag that she cares enough for demonkind that she wouldn't even spare her own children."

"Her own children!" Plum repeated, horrified. "Maybe demons *are* evil."

Li Piao rested a hand on her arm.

"In modern China, parents have killed infant daughters because the law permits them only one child and they want a son. Viss's action is no more evil than that."

"I'm sorry," Plum whispered.

Where he lay on the floor, not even trying to escape, too inarticulate to plead, Wong Pang had begun to weep. He was still an ugly, yellowish gray creature. Red rims did not improve his yellow eyes nor sobs the shape of his needle-fanged mouth, but perhaps my own experiences had softened me. I gently kicked him.

"Stop crying, stupid idiot," I said. "I'm not going to kill you—not yet at least. And I won't let Viss kill you either."

"No?"

"No." I glanced at the others. "Do any of you object?"

The humans shook their heads. Spilling Moonbeams looked vaguely repulsed, but then that expression became one of pity.

"Unless they betray us by word or deed or even by inaction," she said, rolling Wong Pang over with the toe of her slipper, "they are safe. Viss's enemy is my friend. Kai Wren's friend is my friend."

We will pass over the slobbering howls of thanksgiving, the oaths of loyalty and service, the tears and shrieks of relief, that followed. Plum insisted that the scrub demons shower before joining us at the kitchen table, a thing they did with such great enthusiasm that the next item on the agenda had to be mopping up the bathroom.

It was well into the Hour of the Horse when we reconvened our meeting around the kitchen table. I had quietly warned Plum that the scrub demons' table manners were not likely to be good, so the food had been set out of sight.

Two more pads of paper had been set on the table and chairs with telephone directories had been supplied so that the scrub demons could see over the tabletop. Ba Wa was placed near Spilling Moonbeams, Wong Pang between Li Piao and me, so that we were ready for any late treachery.

"Ba Wa," I said, "tell us what else Viss said at this meeting."

Ba Wa would never be a pretty sight, but he had cleaned up fairly well. Plum had lent him a tee shirt and shorts belonging to one of her nephews. So attired, he might pass for a very ugly boy—if the viewer were terribly nearsighted.

"Viss say is time for demons to go to Origin home. Some say 'Why? Kong Shyh Jieh is demon home now. Is nice place and we not have to share it with stupid, bully gods.'

"Viss say if demons stay in Kong Shyh Jieh, all demon children become at best like Tuvoon the Smoke Ghost—not all there. At worst they become like One-Eye and Pitt. She do flash-boom then. Many frightened, but no one try to stop her. They listen sharp."

Spilling Moonbeams nodded. "They would. Any sane

demon fears Viss. Even my father. That's why he listened when she would rail on along the same themes.''

Waiting respectfully until he was certain that Spilling Moonbeams had finished, Ba Wa continued:

"She talk a lot about magnetic fields and magical resonances and things I don't know shit about. Then someone say 'This pretty talk, maybe even true, but what good do it do us? Gods beat demons war after war. Demons tired of fighting. So what we have ugly kids? Maybe now we know problem, we fix in Kong Shyh Jieh.'

"Viss say then she knows now she can win war. She have things she not have before. One, she have secret way to make gates into Origin so all fighting not be in sideways spaces or in Kong Shyh Jieh. This time gods get the flash-bang and burning and shit.''

I gave Plum a thumbs-up gesture. "Sounds like one to the lady.''

She smiled. Ba Wa looked puzzled, but, after draining an entire glass of cream soda, he went on with his report.

"Viss say, two, this time she have gods as demon ally. Some protest, 'We have god ally before. Never do us shit.' Viss say, 'But my god ally have new spell. You who were at Conventicle see it there. It get used on Kai Wren when he get attacked. Make him weak as kitten.' There was much unhappy talk then. After, people listen to Viss even more.

"Then Viss say, three, anybody who not fight with her is going to get fucked in the ass when the battle is all over and she is queen of all the demons and all the gods. She is going to win really good, then she have all the *chi* of Origin to back her up. Who want to be her enemy then?''

"Whew!'' Li Piao said when Ba Wa signaled his narration was concluded by jumping off of his chair and fetching more cream soda. "Viss has a good tactical sense—I'll give her that. Those who won't be swayed by idealism may be by ambition, and any left hanging back may be convinced to go along with her out of fear.''

"That sums it up,'' I agreed. "Spilling Moonbeams, who do you think will *not* go with Viss?''

Seriousness added years to that pretty, doll-like face.

"Well, I certainly won't be. I don't believe that stuff about her wanting to save demonkind from degeneration is what really motivates her. I think what moves her is more likely her new allies and the green-fire spell. She's just giving her ambitions the veneer of idealism."

"True enough," I said. "So she won't get you, and she won't get me. Anyone else?"

She blushed. "Well, I don't think my father will side with her. He's not going to want to bend knee to Viss as queen."

"That's all we can count on?"

"Us won't go to Viss!" burst in Ba Wa. "Not any of us little guys. She don't want us, not even if we crawl in the dirt and eat shit."

"Okay. So we get the scrub demons. Who else?"

"I'd like to believe that some of the oldest ones won't side with her," said Spilling Moonbeams, chewing lightly on her lower lip, "but that's probably an idle hope. They may not like the idea of Queen Viss, but they've lost a lot of wars. This is their chance to win."

"I wonder," I said, "if perhaps He of the Towers of Light might work with us? HE didn't sound thrilled with Viss. On the other hand, HIS personal grant is structured after the patterns of Origin. HE may be homesick. We'd better take care when approaching HIM."

Spilling Moonbeams sighed. "So we have two humans, three demons, a handful of scrub, one Kai Wren bottle, and whatever tricks my father has hidden away. Opposing us will be the rest of demonkind, an unknown number of gods, all of Kai Wren's gallery, and the contents of the Armory of Truce."

"Three humans and two demons," I corrected firmly. "You forget. As things stand, I am naught but a human with an interesting education."

"We can try to correct that," Spilling Moonbeams said defiantly.

"I hope so, most sincerely, but we cannot count on it," I said. "We need to know whether or not your father is working with us. Ditto for He of the Towers of Light. His nephew, the Walker, doesn't seem overly fond of Viss. Or—to look at it another way—he was at least willing to jog her elbow and so save me from a theronic. Maybe we can add him to our ranks."

Li Piao nodded. He'd been making notes on his pad while we spoke, and now he consulted them.

"We must also take care of your problem, Kai Wren." He waved me down when I tried to protest that there were more serious issues at hand. "No, listen to me. You are the God-slayer—a rallying point in your own right. Moreover, Viss is relying on two things she has taken from you."

"The bottles," I said, and, with slowly dawning realization, "and the dogs."

"Correct. We still don't know what role those dogs will play, but they are loyal to you. If you were not so restricted, you might be capable of dissuading them from helping her."

"They are creatures of the gods," I reminded him. "They are back with their masters at last."

"Their masters," the old man said, "abandoned them to die when they were no longer useful—abandoned them and who knows how many others. Shiriki and Chamballa may not be eager to return to the gods' service."

"True, but how can I regain my powers? I'm not just low on *chi*. I've been reshaped. I am as human as you, not just a powerless demon."

Li Piao nodded patiently. "I have been studying that as well. From what you told me of how the spell worked, your creations were used to draw your peculiar demon *chi* from you."

"Yes."

"The process must be reversible. You told me that Viss left you alive because you might one day be persuaded to serve her cause. Is Viss known for her capacity for the magical arts?"

"Not really. Her specializations have always been more martial."

"So whatever she did was probably not highly complex."

"We can't count on that," I reminded. "Po Shiang, whoever he really is, was a deific wizard."

"But, by his own admission, restricted in his knowledge of demon lore," Li Piao said. "He sent the lightning from the cloud to test your vulnerabilities. For the sake of planning, let us assume that whatever spell was used to convert you into a human is both not highly complex and fairly easy to reverse."

"Two big assumptions," I commented.

"Still"—Li Piao wagged a finger at me—"let us so assume. To reverse it, all we need to do is find the bottles and reverse the process."

Ba Wa clapped. "Then Kai Wren be big bad Lord Demon again?"

"That is my hope," said Li Piao.

"The bottles could be anywhere!" I said, feeling it was my place to protest since no one else seemed so inclined.

"I doubt it. They are crucial to Viss's plan. She would not let them go lightly. Where might she keep them?"

Plum got into the spirit of the game. "In her own bottle, of course. Which reminds me of a question I've been meaning to ask . . ."

Spilling Moonbeams interrupted. "Viss could have entrusted the bottles to one of her deific allies. If they are going to be used to send troops into Origin, wouldn't that be easiest?"

"Easiest, yes," Li Piao said, "but not necessarily best. Viss would not wish to give her ally that much power until she herself has established a power base among the demons. Otherwise, what is to keep her ally from turning on her and using the bottles for a reverse invasion?"

"True. Might she leave them somewhere on Earth?"

"I don't think so," I said. "She would be taking a terrible risk if she stored both me and the stockpile of my power in the same place."

"What if"—Spilling Moonbeams clearly did not like this new thought at all—"she has already drained the *chi* away?"

"That would be more difficult than it might seem," I said. "If she is not careful, she could overdo and ruin the bottles. Still, it is a possibility we must face."

And one, I realized, that generated a cool, prickling fear along my spine. Until that moment, I had not seriously considered that I might remain human forever.

Li Piao must have seen my fear, for he spoke rapidly:

"Viss may have removed the *chi* from the bottles, but she will not have spent it. If she did, she would make it quite difficult to reconvert Kai Wren, and we know that was a possibility she considered."

Wong Pang spoke for the first time. He'd been so quiet that I had thought he wasn't even listening, that our plans were too much for his little mind.

"Her"—he jerked a thumb toward Plum—"have question still."

Surprise at his contribution made us all turn to Plum. She smiled at Wong Pang, and he turned bright yellow.

"What I wanted to know," she said, "is how many bottles can be put inside other bottles? Is it an infinite number or is there a limit to how many mini-universes can be stored within each other?"

I considered. "That's an interesting point. There is a limit unless the bottle is specially prepared. I prepared my own, of course, since I knew the type of work I wanted to do there and because I wanted to be able to keep a gallery. In its current state, however, I doubt it could contain any more than a dozen pieces or so."

"Then Viss is in trouble?" Plum's brown eyes shone.

"Not quite, not yet," I said, sorry to disappoint her. "I won't go into the spacial physics involved, but she could store quite a large number of bottles within her own for at least a decade without complications."

I raised a finger to forestall comment.

"However, bottles stored within bottles within a single bottle would cause some very interesting complications. Look."

I drew a bottle, then sketched something like a cartoonist's word balloon next to it. I added several more.

"Currently, the bottles within Viss's bottle are able to shunt their need for space off into sidewise space. However, if all of them were shoved within another bottle—or even better—if a bottle was placed within a bottle, then placed within another bottle and so on, after the fashion of a Russian *matreshka* doll . . ."

"*Matreshka?*" asked Spilling Moonbeams.

"One of those wooden dolls that have a bunch of other dolls stacked inside it," Plum said. "I have one upstairs I can show you later."

"Then," I went on, "the spatial demands would be so constricted that there would certainly be problems."

"Problems?" asked Li Piao.

"Breakdown of internal integrity, warping of space and time." I shrugged. "I don't know for certain—I've never tried."

"But," Plum said eagerly, "it would certainly make it difficult for Viss to use them as she had planned."

"It might also destroy them completely," I agreed, "which would be a pity."

"It also might win us the war," Plum said firmly. "If we can get you back to normal, then stuff the bottles inside each other, and hide the remaining bottle inside of Viss's bottle but somewhere she can't find it, then get out of there fast."

Her words tumbled out in a rapid string, as if her mouth could not match the envisioned plan.

"Viss would lose the bottles," Spilling Moonbeams agreed happily, "and perhaps be forced to forgo the rest of her plan—especially with Lord Demon to oppose her!"

"There is one difficulty," Li Piao said. "This same intricacy means that we must either go prepared to bear all of the bottles and such away—a near-impossible task—or be prepared to work the spell to release Lord Demon's powers on the spot."

I let them work out the details. The solution couldn't be so simple. Indeed, I was certain it wouldn't be. However, it was the best plan we had, and it might win me back my powers.

I cleared my throat and tried to feel confident.

"Very well," I said. "Let's give it a shot."

X

VISS STILL KEPT her bottle in the mausoleum. I was pleased, for I had checked the Earthside locus first. No need to cross into Kong Shyh Jieh if we could enter the bottle from Earth—especially since not one of my small band of allies would agree to stay at home.

We entered the apparently locked structure well after dark. Only when the door was tightly shut did we dare a light.

Li Piao shoned a flashlight beam about cautiously until the light rested on a slender, white form set back in a niche.

"Is that it?" he asked.

"It is," I said.

Unlike my home bottle, which is cobalt blue blown glass, sleek and long-necked after the fashion of a wine bottle, I had modeled Viss's bottle from the finest kaolin white porcelain clay. Porcelain is the most difficult clay to work. The trade-off for its white purity and fine grain is a certain brittleness and the need for a very hot temperature during firing.

Yet porcelain had seemed to me the only material suitable

for Viss as I saw her then—opaque yet stainless, strong yet fragile, smooth beneath the fingers so that one might expect softness, yet unyielding. I wonder how I could have failed to realize then that I was in love with her!

Before glazing and firing, I had painted the bottle with stark, elegant renditions of the four guardian creatures. They watched now, the chi'lin (what some Westerners call a unicorn), the tortoise, the dragon, and the phoenix, as we manifested within the entry foyer.

To my wonder of wonders, I realized that I must remain on the list of those given free admittance. Otherwise, the guardians would have attacked without warning. I always include myself on the guest list during the design sequence to facilitate things, but, being a nice guy, I show the owners how to take me off once they take full possession of the bottle.

Few do so, but then I'd never given a bottle to an enemy before.

As we departed the entryway, Spilling Moonbeams gestured as if she were throwing a net. I saw something glittering faintly in the air, then she nodded, satisfied.

"There. Now all of you are invisible."

"Don't get cocky," I cautioned, striking Wong Pang sharply on the head when he strayed toward a grove containing ripe fruit trees. "We don't know how much time we have before we are discovered."

"Yes, boss," he whimpered.

"Did you design the interior landscaping here, too?" Plum asked, hurrying at my side.

"The gross details," I said. "That's why I'm gambling I can get us to the house unseen."

"I thought I recognized your touch," she said, panting slightly, for I was setting a good pace. "You like the traditional in your *feng shui*. I see you've used the dragon-protecting-pearl again here."

"You'll see some differences," I answered amiably, knowing the girl must be nervous. "Viss wanted several ponds rather than an ocean. They, of course, had to be balanced by various land structures, as well as being kept from stagnation. Tricky at times."

"Water attracts money," Plum mused. "I wonder how old are Viss's ambitions?"

I couldn't answer that, nor did I have much attention to spare for conjecture. My plan was to avoid completely the front ways toward the house, find a quiet place, then let Li Piao scry where in the house my stolen property was being kept.

He had tried doing so before our departure, but scrying across planes into a place he had never before seen proved difficult. All he could do was confirm our guess that what we sought was within Viss's bottle.

I located a sheltered glade I half-remembered creating with a press of the ball of my thumb into the damp materia. Like Plum's house, the glade was designed to be discreet and hidden, the sort of spot one would tend to overlook—a place for trysts and *tête-à-têtes*. For a fearful moment I imagined that we would find it in use, but the long-needled branches of the bowing pines hid only silence.

"Here," I said, "we should be relatively safe. Ba Wa and Wong Pang, go to the edges of the grove and keep watch. I'll be watching you—so no fuck-ups!"

Muttering "Yes, boss!" the two scrub demons scuttled off.

Plum frowned. "I'll watch, too."

Spilling Moonbeams nodded agreement and drifted off, presumably to do the same.

Li Piao had already unwrapped the dragon bowl when I turned back to him. He set it in a hollow of soft moss and filled it with water from a flask he had prepared beforehand. As the oil and water separated into layers, he said:

"It is fortunate that you had let me inspect your collection, Wren. My hope is that if I concentrate on a few of the more memorable items, they will be among the rest."

"Go to it," I whispered.

I stood over him, listening to him muttering softly in Cantonese. Almost, almost, I thought I saw the picture forming within the bowl, but it was only wishful thinking shaping the long pine shadows.

"Ah!" Li Piao gasped. "I have them. Many pieces, all together. A curved series of shelves like a tiered cake."

"Is there anyone with them?"

"Room is empty."

My heart leapt with hope.

"One door. Outside stand two guards. Ugly. Mean."

"Can you find us the safest route in?"

"Dragon is looking." Then, "Small door in magnolia garden. Side door into house through azalea alley. Locked. In house . . ."

He lifted his gaze from the oiled water.

"Yes, I know the route. The magnolia garden—can you get us there?"

"I can. I even remember which gate opens into it."

Gathering in the others, we crept down toward the house. Ba Wa could fly in short hops and offered to provide us an overview. I told him to stay close, since Spilling Moonbeams's invisibility web had its limitations, but that he could scout the magnolia garden when we reached it.

As we moved in, I found myself reflecting on how little the scrub demons could do. They were vicious brutes, equipped with natural weaponry, but not much more powerful than humans. Could Viss be right? Was this what demonkind was fated to become if she did not win us back into Origin?

Such thoughts made me doubt the wisdom of my choice to challenge her and that, in turn, made me quite uncomfortable.

We reached the walled magnolia garden without difficulty. Ba Wa flopped atop the wall and whispered the all clear. Then Spilling Moonbeams produced a strangely wrought key from her pocket.

"My father's crafting," she said. "It should open any lock we encounter."

It did, and we pushed the gate open just enough to slip through. When we were inside, Spilling Moonbeams relocked it. Our retreat would be by previously prepared spells.

I fingered the gun that Plum had provided me from her small arsenal. I would have preferred a sword, for they are silent and do not need reloading, but my armory had been buried in the rubble of my palace.

Plum carried the same gun that she had before. Li Piao bore the polished staff he had dedicated when he began his study of the Art. The three demons had their own resources.

In addition to her intangible assets, Spilling Moonbeams

bore with her a satchel that she had refused to explain. When I asked, she shared a conspiratorial grin with Plum.

The air was heavy with the rich, almost melonlike, perfume of the magnolias. There were several varieties, including the tall, somehow primitive trees whose shiny boat-shaped leaves and enormous flowers have become associated with plantations in the American South.

Ba Wa and Wong Pang scurried along in front, claws extended, yellow eyes shining. A kill, swift and silent, would prove their loyalty to me, and they knew it. My only concern was that they might attack too swiftly in their eagerness.

Apparently undetected, we made our way to the side door. I hadn't made this, but admired the fine crafting of the diamond-shaped stained-glass panel in the center even as I cursed it. The glass was opaque: pearly, sky-blue, violet, and cream. We could not see through it, but anyone within would see our shadows without.

"Ready yourselves," I whispered to the scrub demons. "Kill as silently as you can."

They growled something deep in their throats, reminding me of pit bulls or bulldogs. Ba Wa levitated just above the ground; Wong Pang crouched low, a runner on the mark.

Spilling Moonbeams touched her father's key to the lock. I heard the tumblers click, then a brass alarm bell clanged.

"Shit!" I hissed, but the scrub demons were away, even as the bell struck. I saw Spilling Moonbeams cast something from her hand, and the alarm bell stopped in mid-stroke.

Ba Wa went through the stained-glass pane; Wong Pang bashed into the door, bursting it open. What we saw when the door opened was quite ugly.

Two creatures resembling six-foot-long stag beetles clad in ornate copper armor lay flung on their backs. Six legs apiece flailed in death throes, massive scimitarlike mandibles snapped uselessly above their attackers. A variety of weapons was scattered on the wooden parquet floor.

The scrub demons' small size had served them well in this instance, for the guards had been designed to fight against larger opponents. Ba Wa had sliced open the top of his opponent's head; Wong Pang, always less given to finesse, had simply torn through its midsection, ripping apart the armored plates.

I heard Plum make a retching sound and sought to distract her.

"Clearly meant to be either bipedal or hexapedal," I murmured, putting an arm around her shoulders and urging her past the carnage. "Clever design, but our friends have found their weakness, don't you think?"

She managed a faint, "Oh, quite," and I felt her steel herself. Ahead, Spilling Moonbeams had taken point, with Li Piao directly behind her, telling her where to turn.

As he paused to check his bearings, the demoness glanced back and said apologetically, "I'm sorry about that. I never considered that the key wouldn't disarm alarms. Father made it since he was always misplacing some key or another at our house."

"We're inside," I said, smiling reassurance. "Now let's hope we make it out."

"Bell only banged couple times, boss," Ba Wa said, loping up beside me, still sticky with beetle juice. "Maybe nobody check too quick."

"Maybe," I said, but I wasn't hopeful. "Plum, you and I should be ready to shoot. Spilling Moonbeams—I leave you to your own devices, but remember, you have more essential things to do than fight."

She nodded, her demonform darkness within silver such a marked contrast to her doll-like human form that I wondered at her selection of such an innocuous human guise.

There was mystery in that lady, a mystery that at times fascinated me to distraction. I never remembered feeling this way before and credited it to the hormones coursing through the human male form I was bound within. I wondered if her father's offer remained open, wondered, too, what Spilling Moonbeams would think if I accepted it.

"You two," I continued, this to the scrub demons, "attack if the guns don't work. Otherwise, guard our retreat."

As Li Piao led us through the twists and turns the dragon bowl had taught him, I was aware of a side of Viss's taste I had known was there but had chosen in my arrogance to downplay. Many of the paintings dealt with battles rendered in exquisite—even sadistically—gory detail.

Antique weapons were lovingly displayed. I itched to take down one of the many swords we passed, but forbore. If they were functional, then they would have had alarms set on them; if they were flawed in some way—a weak tang or a cracked blade—then I would learn that only to my disadvantage.

We were quite deep into the rambling interior of the building when Li Piao gave the agreed-upon signal to indicate that we had reached our destination. Two fingers went up.

Only two guards then—perhaps no one had heard the aborted alarm or the breaking glass. Perhaps no one had found the dead guards. Perhaps, too, this was a trap.

Spilling Moonbeams made a throwing gesture toward our guns, and the tips of the barrels appeared to be cocooned in silk—a simple silencer, too contained to work on a person, but perfect for a gun or, as she had shown, an alarm. Plum and I crept forward and peered around a corner, keeping low as Li Piao directed.

Two guards of the stag-beetle type stood on their hindmost legs before a brass-bound door of formidable aspect. Plum was over her fright now, her hands steady as she aimed and fired. We both chose the center of the head for our targets, having had ample proof of its vulnerability, thanks to Ba Wa. I fired thrice, hitting each time within a few inches of the mark. Plum did the same and, from what I observed later, her shots were even closer.

This time she did not grow nauseated, and we hurried after Spilling Moonbeams and Li Piao. A sticky mass of whiteness showed that Spilling Moonbeams had silenced the alarm before touching her key to the lock. As the door swung open, I had reason to hope we might get away with this after all.

My bottles, bowls, platters, and cups stood as Li Piao had described, ranked on rising tiers of white marble with the smallest pieces in front. Li Piao motioned for me to stand in front of the lot, facing them. We had worked out a ritual the day before and he now began it.

"Seams bursting, overfilling, overburdened, overborne."

I lifted a *raku* teapot and cradled it between my hands, fingers overlapping its roundness. Despite my concentration, I heard Plum enter the room, Spilling Moonbeams with her. They crossed to opposite side of the marble tiers, where they could watch without being in the way. Doubtless, the scrub demons crouched somewhere out of sight, ready to launch themselves at any who approached.

"*Seeking surcease, easing release, 'afore bursting to piece*"—he drew a deep breath and continued—"*-es on the floor.*"

There were screams from the corridor without, shouts, the clashing of metal on stone, a dull thud that might have been a body falling onto the floor, a crash that almost certainly was a rack with a mail shirt displayed upon it being knocked over.

I heard Plum call something to Spilling Moonbeams, but I dutifully kept my attention centered on the teapot clasped between my hands.

Li Piao chanted more rapidly now. "*Recourse awaits you, from strain to abate you, 'tis not too late to . . .*"

He was cut off in mid-phrase when the point of a sword materialized at his throat. The holder of the sword materialized a moment later, elegant as always, his lower portion a swirling tornado of force, his upper body clad in antique but fully serviceable armor constructed in the Japanese style.

Four creatures made of wind and ice were with him. The foils lightly balanced in their hands had icicles for blades. Where a man would have kept heart or brain or something else vulnerable, they possessed only swirling fog. They moved, two to cover me, one to each of the ladies.

"I wouldn't recite any more of that chant, if I were you, old man," said Tuvoon the Smoke Ghost to Li Piao. "And the rest of you, stop what you're doing this instant."

"Why?" said the calmly defiant voice of Spilling Moonbeams.

I did not dare turn, but I thought I heard a rhythmic "chinking" sound. Apparently, the girls were moving the pots and bottles about on the marble shelves, although I couldn't spare enough attention from the matter at hand to guess why.

"Because," Tuvoon said, "if you don't, I'm going to spill this old man's blood on the floor. I'll deal with my revered mother's wrath when she gets in. Then I'll send my creatures after you."

"Viss isn't here?" I said, seeking to distract him.

"She is not," Tuvoon replied, "so you can't hope to expect any of her silly mercy. Now, are you women going to stop . . . Hey!"

He slashed out indignantly with his sword, but he was too late. Li Piao had vanished. Tuvoon moved toward me, but I held the teapot up as if I would smash it to the floor.

"You didn't bother to learn that he was a powerful wizard, did you?" I taunted. "Li Piao's out of your reach now. If you take another step toward me, I'll break this teapot."

"What's one teapot?" he sneered. I'd almost forgotten how much I disliked his sneer, but I fully remembered now. "We have the entire collection from your palace and more besides."

"But how much do you know about what you have?" I asked. "I, on the other hand, created each piece. You encountered things you didn't expect when you tried to take my bottle. Think carefully before you act."

Tuvoon was thinking, weighing the odds, and obviously finding them somewhat in his favor. My assessment pretty much matched his. I didn't know if Ba Wa and Wong Pang still lived, but I had to get the girls out of here. This wasn't chivalry. It was practicality. Spilling Moonbeams could conduct the campaign against Viss without me. The more I learned of Viss, the less I liked the idea of having her as Queen of Demons and Gods.

They say you can judge people by their pets. I think that, as far as you can take one of these analogies, this is true of children as well. Tuvoon's arrogant ruthlessness, his easy dissembling when it served his purposes, his cruel sense of humor, all revealed the values his mother had instilled in him.

A spoiled child may simply reveal indulgent parents, but a cruel child reveals parents who value nothing over their own interests.

"What do you want from me, Tuvoon?" I asked, for I had a sneaking suspicion that if his only purpose had been keeping me from looting the gallery he would have called in reinforcements and had me and my allies killed or marched off to the dungeons. (There were dungeons, too. I'd helped to design them, making them escape-proof without even a back door for myself. I'd never anticipated this parting of the ways, more the fool I.)

"Want?" He sheathed his sword, confident that his icy man-things kept the balance in his favor. "I want to finish our duel, Kai Wren. I want compensation for this!"

He ripped back the sleeve of his armor, shredding the cloth and wood in one easy motion. Beneath was a low, jagged cut that oozed small amounts of pus over incompletely healed flesh.

"You had to bring my spirit sword, Kai Wren. You had to play your dirty tricks. Mother stopped the duel before you could do more harm—curse her for a filthy whore—but this was enough."

"It was but a glancing cut!" I protested.

"But with a spirit sword." He cast a venomous glance at Spilling Moonbeams. "I'm certain my cousin has told you how she and I are inferior creatures—degenerated demons. It's true enough. I cannot heal as easily from such a wound."

"I didn't know . . ." I began.

"Don't make excuses, Lord Demon." He spat. "You *were* trying to kill me, and for what? To avenge a human! Or was it for the affront to your pride? Well, *my* pride has been affronted. I've been living with this aching arm for months. Nothing can heal it. Mother made me hide it, but now I have you."

"And you want to finish our duel," I said quickly. "Fine. Let Spilling Moonbeams and her friend go, then I will duel with you."

"Why should I release them?" He leered at Spilling Moonbeams. "Mother wants me to breed the bitch. Maybe I should do what Mommy wants. I could try the human, too. She's pretty enough, and a halfling or so will improve the race."

Spilling Moonbeams said coldly, "Fathered by you, the brat would be lucky to be a quarterling. Have you forgotten? Your mother still courts many of demonkind, seeking to gain support for her cause. If any learn of what you have done to me . . ."

"How should they learn? You're my prisoner."

"You forget, the human sorcerer has escaped. My father will learn from him where last I was. Besides, if your mother wins her war, you'll get me in the end. Your quarrel is with Kai Wren. Take his offer or—more wisely—let us all go and call it quits."

Tuvoon considered this, then he shook his head.

"No. I will need to account for the dead guards."

"Say you were asleep or away when it happened," I suggested.

"I can't," he said, almost blithely. "I can't lie to Mommy. She made certain of that long ago."

Viss certainly plays the angles, I thought morosely. My next speech showed nothing of my thoughts.

"I think you delay so that Viss will return and take this off your hands," I said contemptuously. "I think you're afraid to duel with me."

"I am not!"

"Then stop this idle chatter, supply me with a sword, and let's be about it. And while you're about it, you can bid the ladies good-bye."

Tuvoon looked confused. "Why should I?"

"Spilling Moonbeams has given you ample reason why you should release them," I said, setting down the teapot and beginning to stretch as I would before swordplay. "Besides, can you trust either of them not to interfere?"

"I'll call in more guards!"

"And trust them not to report to Viss? Don't be an idiot, Tuvoon. If she's ensorcelled her own son so he can't lie to her, she probably has the guards so thoroughly enchanted that they tell her their dreams!"

I unbuttoned my shirt and began peeling it off. As I did so, I concealed Plum's gun beneath a fold of the fabric. I hadn't had time to reload, but it still held a few rounds.

Spilling Moonbeams walked across to join Plum. The men of ice did not interfere with her, but I felt the cold tip of one of their blades against my back.

"We can get you out of here," she said urgently.

"Maybe," I said, "but maybe not. I think this is best. If I live, well . . . I know my way out, and I know where to find you."

Tuvoon motioned to one of his lackeys. The creature vanished, reappearing moments later holding two swords. One, I realized with a prickling along my spine, was my spirit sword, the same that I had believed broken and lost but that had been repaired by Seven Fingers at the behest of Night Bride, only to be stolen by Viss from the Armory of Truce. I recognized the other as the sword I kept here for use during lessons.

"Go then," Tuvoon said to his cousin, "and take your tame human with you. As you say, depending on how things work out, I may get you anyhow. Remember this then. I'll be dreaming on how to make it up to you."

His laugh cleansed my blood of all fear. I might die here, but I would do my best to stop him ere I did so.

Though I did not wish to seem to care overmuch about the ladies, I did glance over that way as I rose to my feet. There was something odd about the way they stood, about the array of goods on the marble shelves. In a moment, I realized what it was and flashed them an appreciative smile.

I plucked the sword meant for me from the guard of wind and ice and saluted them.

"Here's looking at you!" I said jauntily. "Now, Tuvoon, stop stalling!"

He unsheathed my spirit sword and cast the sheath to the floor. We needed no referee, for we well understood that this battle was to the death. Nor did we need any rules. His lunge at me was the signal to begin.

I backed away and he pursued, the tornado swirl of his lower body stirring up light particles of dust. Unwilling to be trapped within the narrow confines of the gallery room—or to see my captured artworks broken—I retreated into the hall. The two guards Plum and I had shot lay there, along with several of their fellows. As I had surmised, the rack holding the chain mail had fallen. I could not spare much attention, but I was heartened that among the blood and mess, I did not see the corpses of my scrub demons.

"Stand and fight, damn you!" shouted Tuvoon, pursuing.

I had no intention of doing so. Tuvoon had the advantage in size, strength, armor, and weapon. All I could do was choose position and hope to make him so furious that he forgot his skills. Otherwise, what edge I might have against him in skill (and I was not at all certain I did have that edge, given that he could have been holding back during our recent practice sessions) would be lost.

We crossed blades several times, and I praised the chance that had given me one of my own blades to use. Not having to guess at balance or weight told me just how hard I might press, just how far I might reach. Tuvoon was actually handicapped by his use of the spirit sword, for he had not practiced with it enough to know its limitations. Several times, he might have had me if he had chosen to use his own blade.

Still, he had four touches to my one, three of which had drawn blood. My single hit had been on his already wounded arm, confirming that he still favored it. As the duel progressed, I noticed a strange thing. Tuvoon was not going for the killing shots, nor even for those that would wound me severely. He was content to make any hit.

For a moment, I thought that he had forgotten that this was no practice session, no arena contest. Then I realized what he was doing. His spirit sword had hurt him severely when I had cut him. He assumed that mine would do the same to me. Not only did it not do so, I realized that the wounds did not hurt as severely as those that I had taken from that same blade during one long-ago contest.

This gave me an idea. I started appearing to flag, taking a defensive posture, leaving Tuvoon openings for those superficial cuts but keeping my vitals covered. The wounds I took hurt, but adrenaline masked much of the pain. Meanwhile, I worked closer and closer, looking for the moment when I could drop my defense and attack.

It came. I permitted Tuvoon to drive me back almost to my knees. While he pricked and sliced, I shifted my balance, came in under his guard, and brought my sword up, past the cone of swirling smoke that substituted for his legs, and through his vitals. He made a strangled sound, then, fury in his eyes, he shifted his hold on the spirit sword and stabbed through the hollow of my shoulder and down.

I felt a sick shudder as blade hit bone but retained enough mental clarity to begin the mystic rote that would pull me out of the bottle into the world of humans.

"You've won, Kai Wren," Tuvoon gasped, spitting blood as he glared up at me. "Finish me, but know that I've killed you, too."

I didn't wait for him to find out he was wrong. I just got the hell out of there.

Later, while I reclined on a mat on Plum's floor and let Spilling Moonbeams treat my multitude of wounds, I explained.

"Tuvoon thought that the spirit sword would damage me more severely than his usual blade, so he sacrificed his advantage for an illusory edge."

Spilling Moonbeams looked sharply at me, but there was fondness in her dark eyes as she scolded:

"Kai Wren, if you hadn't been so sorely hurt, I would withhold my help for that."

"What, the pun?" I looked as pathetic as I might. "I'm wounded!"

"Not that," she retorted, as the others groaned. "For taking such foolish risks."

"Not foolish at all," I said. "It enabled you and Plum to get away with the boodle, didn't it?"

"We might have anyhow," she said primly. "I made a fine argument for why Tuvoon should allow us to depart."

"But if he hadn't been furious at me and slavering for my blood, he might have taken a closer look at your satchel," I reminded her, "or at the shelves. Then he might have noticed that you two ladies had replaced some of my bottles with ordinary wine bottles. I'm hurt, by the way, that you thought such could stand in for my works of art."

"It worked, didn't it?" Spilling Moonbeams said dryly, sending a charge of her demon *chi* down into my worst wound—the deep one to the shoulder. "Tuvoon didn't notice."

"But you can be certain that Viss will," said Li Piao.

"Viss'll shit bricks," laughed Wong Pang. "Big ones with sharp, square corners!"

He and Ba Wa were feeling understandably pleased with themselves. Not only had they accounted for several of Viss's guards, they had stolen the small fortune in *shen* coins that one guard had in his purse. They had offered them to me, but I had only accepted enough to repay Spilling Moonbeams before returning the bulk.

"Kai Wren?" asked Plum, rather subdued. Her first experience with combat had clearly touched her deeply. "Did you know that the spirit sword couldn't hurt you before the duel began?"

She glanced at the myriad red stripes that marred my extremities and rephrased her question:

"That is, couldn't hurt you on a spiritual level?"

I wanted to say "yes" if only to stop Spilling Moonbeams from glowering at me. I didn't dare though. This was not a good time to start lying to allies.

"I didn't," I admitted, "but I gathered so rather quickly. Apparently, the spirit sword affects the same *chi* that makes us demons. When Viss and Tuvoon forced me to become human, they made me invulnerable to the sword's magical bind. Effectively, the spirit it is attuned to no longer exists."

I glanced over at the sword, which, cleaned carefully by Ba Wa, now resided on a coffee table. It had come away with me from Viss's bottle, embedded in my flesh.

"I'll make a gift of the sword to you," I offered, "to make up for the gun I left behind."

"That's quite a gift," Plum said, awed, "because when you are a demon again, that sword holds your life."

"Well," I answered, uncomfortably, "I do trust you."

Plum rose and picked up the sword rather cautiously, as if she thought it might attack of its own volition.

"The spirit sword is beautiful. I don't think I've ever seen a more lovely weapon. But although you may trust me, I don't trust others," Plum said firmly. "If you're really giving the sword to me, I'll have it destroyed."

Spilling Moonbeams, who had started glowering when I gave the sword to Plum, relaxed slightly at this sign of Plum's intelligence, and perhaps, too, at the compliment to her father's artistry. She stopped glowering at Plum (although she shifted me rather roughly so she could attend to some cuts on my lower arm).

To Plum, she said, "If you admire the sword for its beauty,

then I will introduce you to my father. He will make you a trade—the spirit sword for another of his making."

Plum shook her head. "The trade would have to be for a thoroughly nonfunctional spirit sword. I'm not letting this thing loose."

Spilling Moonbeams nodded approvingly. "You're right, there is a risk to letting it return to Kong Shyh Jieh. A broken spirit sword *can* be mended, as this one was once before. However, if anyone can destroy one beyond recovery, it would be Seven Fingers. He could melt it down in his crucibles, for example."

"We'll see," Plum promised. "After we've dealt with larger problems. How many bottles did we bring back with us?"

"Nine," replied Li Piao from where he had been sitting contemplating those selfsame bottles, "including Kai Wren's former residence."

"An auspicious number," said Spilling Moonbeams, "not to mention the maximum number my satchel could hold. Do you think they will do any good?"

Li Piao glanced at me. "I am somewhat out of my depth here. What do you think, Kai Wren?"

Glancing at Spilling Moonbeams for permission, I sat up to examine the collection of bottles.

"At the very least," I said, wanting to start with a compliment, "the theft has robbed Viss of nine possible conduits between Kong Shyh Jieh and Origin. That is something. Though she holds many other examples of my work, only the bottles have that property."

"But?" prompted Plum, sensing that good news was not to follow.

"Even if Li Piao drained the bottles completely," I continued, "a thing that would be difficult to do, for it would be tantamount to destroying them, these represent perhaps twenty percent of the items that Viss had present when she drew my life force from me."

"Twenty percent?" Li Piao asked. "I thought I saw more than forty-five pieces in your gallery."

"Very well," I replied, "even less than that—maybe ten percent."

"So," said Spilling Moonbeams, "there is no way that you will regain your full powers."

"I do not think so," I said, sorry to disappoint her. "However, there may be enough to work the transformation that will turn me from a human to a demon once more. Even if I am a weak demon, I will be one step closer to being myself."

"How," asked Li Piao, "shall we go about attempting this?"

I rose, walked about, testing the extent of Spilling Moonbeams's healing magic. As I paced and stretched, I considered.

"Let me have a full night to sleep," I said, "so that the work Spilling Moonbeams has done will reach its full effect. Then, after breakfast tomorrow, we may as well try the spell we designed for use in Viss's bottle."

"That spell was makeshift, meant to be worked where there would be a surplus of your *chi*," Li Piao protested. "Shouldn't we take the time to design something better?"

"I think not," I said. "Viss will not let this affront go without response. I don't know what form that response will take— it may simply mean that she steps up her timetable—but I don't wish to meet her response unprepared."

"Very well," the old man said, but I could tell that he was less than pleased.

Night passed and morning came. According to Ba Wa and Wong Pang, who had split the night watch, there was no sign of trouble. Spilling Moonbeams shifted into a body of dawnlight to scout the area and reported much the same. So, without further delay, we prepared for our ritual.

Clad in a saffron yellow sports shirt and khaki trousers, Li Piao consulted handwritten notes and gave directions to his granddaughter. Plum had donned the red-silk mandarin jacket and flowing silk skirt she frequently wore when working as a *feng shui* expert. Despite the dove gray top hat she wore as an incongruous contrast, she looked distant and professional.

A large, square, red-satin scarf was spread on the middle of the living-room floor. Around the perimeter of this were set the nine bottles that had been taken from Viss's domain. After some discussion, we had ruled out using the green-and-orange bottle and Li Piao's dragon bowl. Since neither of these had been used to draw off and then contain my *chi*, we feared that the process of draining off the surplus might damage or destroy them.

Next, Plum's *feng shui* equipment provided nine *ba-gua* mirrors. These mirrors, normally used in *feng shui* to redirect unfavorable *chi* flows, were positioned behind each bottle on the outside of the circle. Our hope was that they would direct the flow of the bottle's *chi* toward me.

After all of this was ready, I took my seat at the center of the circle on the red scarf. I wore a red tee shirt and shorts that Plum had purchased that morning. Li Piao had decorated these informal garments with freehand ink drawings of the Ram, the animal which according to the Chinese astrological system rules my year of birth.

Li Piao had chuckled when he learned this.

"It suits you, Kai Wren. Intelligent and artistic, but somewhat less canny in family matters than in those relating to money. Also, a bit morose and irresponsible, with a tendency toward misanthropy."

"I wonder what Viss is," Plum mused.

"A Tiger," Spilling Moonbeams said acidly. "I don't need to see her chart to know that!"

"I'm a Dog," Wong Pang said, eager to be part of the conversation. "Want to see?"

"Later," Plum said absently. "We need to concentrate on Kai Wren now."

The stupid little demon pouted, but seemed to forget his dismissal a few moments later in an argument with Ba Wa over who should light the joss sticks.

"Hold this," Li Piao demanded, thrusting a birdhouse gourd into my right hand and a bouquet of narcissus and willow into my left.

"Is this really necessary?" I asked, feeling rather silly. "In Viss's bottle, we were going to attempt this without any trappings at all."

"And I wasn't happy about it," Li Piao said bluntly. "I stayed up last night making preparations. Red is a lucky color. The Ram is your birth animal—I only wish I had the time and details to cast your full horoscope."

I breathed a silent thanks to whoever might be listening that he hadn't asked me for the details. My late mother had that horoscope cast when I was born, and one of my earliest lessons had been to memorize it. However, I didn't volunteer the information, not wanting further delay.

Unaware of my thoughts, Li Piao continued his fretful explanation:

"Gourds are emblematic of the body holding the spirit. Narcissus bring luck and success. As an added bonus, they can grow without any sustenance but water—that seemed auspicious to me, given that we are attempting to reunite you with a spirit that has been separated from its sustenance. Finally, willow is emblematic of the return of spring. It also wards off evil."

I swallowed further protests, seeing that my friend truly needed these crutches for him to believe that his magic would work. Perhaps the look of concern on Plum's face also forestalled me. I realized that the girl feared how her grandfather would react if he failed me.

"My knowledge of magic," I said humbly, "is of demon magic. You are the one who is educated in human magic, Li Piao. I will follow your directions."

This might have begun another round of worried explanation, but Ba Wa nearly knocked over a brass incense burner. As soon as it was righted, Li Piao motioned for everyone to take their places and began his incantation:

Seams bursting, overfilling, overburdened,
> *overborne.*
Seeking surcease, easing release,
> *'afore bursting to piece . . .*

As before, Li Piao drew a deep breath and continued,

-es on the floor.
Recourse awaits you,
>> *from strain to abate you,*
>>> *'tis not too late to*
>>>> *find release.*

Outward flowing,
*   to Kai Wren going,*
*   glowing with* chi.
Inward knowing, himself demon,
*   once and evermore.*

When the incantation commenced, I felt nothing. Then, as the words spilled out, I began to feel a burning against my skin.

"Again!" I urged.

Li Piao nodded, took a deep breath, and began again.

This time I was certain I felt something. A ruddy light emanated from the bottles, hit the mirrors, and focused on me. I held out my arms, hands up, palms out, and twisted at the waist so that I could face each bottle in the circle. Yet, as the chant finished, the *chi* had not yet centered on me.

"Again!" I said, half-plea, half-command, for I had heard the old man's voice falter on the final words and knew that the deceptively simple words were taking more from him than he would ever let on.

Yet, however punishing the ritual might be, I heard his quavering voice take up the third repetition. Plum's voice spoke with him, matching him word for word, cadence for cadence. This time, the ruddy light grew ruby red, coalesced into clear, narrow focused beams, one from each bottle. They rayed into me, each centering on a vital point.

Slipping slightly on the scarf, I struggled to my feet so that the *chi* might better penetrate all the salient points upon my body. There was a cry, one I hardly heard, as Ba Wa steadied a bottle that had started to topple. Then the chant was ending, the red light was dimming, and I opened my eyes (when had I closed them?) to see the others staring anxiously at me.

Li Piao leaned heavily against Plum, whose top hat was tilted to one side at an angle opposite to her slant-cut bangs. Ba Wa was sucking on an apparently burned thumb and forefinger.

"Did it work?" asked Spilling Moonbeams softly.

"I think so," I said, carefully stepping over the ring of bottles and to a chair. "My body . . . I'm . . ."

I swallowed hard, breathed deeply of air scented with jasmine and sandalwood, and tried again.

"Yes. I think so, but my system will need time to assimilate the *chi* before I can be certain just how much we have gained. Is everyone all right?"

Ba Wa stopped sucking on his fingers long enough to grin his pointy-toothed smile.

"Am good, boss. Just burned hand on bottle." He looked at the nasty blisters as proudly as if they had been war wounds—which they were in a way.

Li Piao nodded. "The casting was exhausting, but well worth the effort if it did indeed work. I could use a cup of tea, however, and something very sweet to eat—is there any plain *congee* and honey about?"

Plum took off her hat and set it carefully on a chair. She had regained her color almost as soon as the chanting ended.

"I don't think so, Grandfather, but I can get some easily enough. I'll run out and buy food for all of us."

I wanted to protest, but couldn't seem to shape the words. Spilling Moonbeams seemed to divine my concern.

"Don't go alone. We don't know who might be looking for us."

"Who could go with me?" Plum said reasonably. "Kai Wren and Grandfather are exhausted. You should stay to guard them. I can't very well take one of the little guys."

Ba Wa drew out his spittle-covered fingers and said mournfully, "Would go. Can't make disguise 'til this stops hurting."

Wong Pang bounced eagerly. "I can! Look!"

He made a complicated gesture and a moment later a small, extremely fluffy, black Pekingese dog stood where he had been, its curving tail wagging wildly. It grinned so that its round head seemed to split down the middle, revealing a pink tongue and lots of very white teeth.

Plum laughed. "There's my valiant protector! You look more like a bedroom slipper than a dog!"

The scrub demon whined. Plum looked seriously at it.

"Wong Pang, can you warn me if you see any of our enemies?"

The Pekingese barked sharply and wagged that ridiculously fluffy tail.

"Very well." Plum hunkered down and looked into the

round, slightly bulging brown eyes. "Three fast barks for trouble. If I ask you questions, bark once for 'yes,' twice for 'no.' Do you understand?"

Wong Pang barked once and wagged his tail. He really was much more attractive this way. Seeing him reminded me that as soon as my head cleared, I must turn my attention to the puzzle of what had been done to Shiriki and Chamballa.

Plum rigged a collar and leash from a belt and a length of gold cord.

"I'll be back within the hour," she promised. "You know where the tea and other stuff is."

Spilling Moonbeams nodded. "After you return, I need to go home and brief my father on these new developments."

"Good idea," Plum said. "I have a feeling that we're going to need allies very soon."

Lady and Peke departed, but I barely heard them. I had withdrawn in myself and was testing the channels opened by the influx of *chi*. The changes were subtle and did not affect my outward appearance at all, but fairly soon I was certain.

I was a demon once more.

XI

VISS IS THERE, her hair streaming black, her eyes coals of fire, beautiful and strong. Mounted upon the White Tiger, she charges up to me. I manage not to flinch.

"How's it going, Kai Wren?"

I look away from her, knowing what she is. My heart twists within my breast, a wrenching, aching thing. Demons cannot feel emotion—not as humans do. Why then do I love her so?

The breath of the tiger is hot against my face as the beast closes. Its eyes are huge ruddy garnets, slit with topaz. Reflected within them I see myself. I am what she has made me, a human with taunting memories of a demon's power.

"How are you, Kai Wren?" asks Viss of the Terrible Tongue.

"I'm all right." My voice sounds easy, strong. I am pleased.

"I'm glad to hear that. I was worried when I heard that you'd left the hospital. You've not been well, you know."

All I can see of Viss is one knee gripping firmly into the dense fur of the tiger's flank. It is a round knee, small and vulnerable. I know if I step back, I will see that she has become a child. I guess that's the way to enter the kingdom of heaven.

"Gee, Viss, I never knew you cared."

"I have always cared for you, Kai Wren, more than for anyone else."

It is within me to ask her about Tuvoon's father, about Po Shiang, about her son, to hear her tell me that she loves me more than any of them. She will say it, too. I know that.

Does saying it make it true?

I want this to be so.

"Where are you staying these days, Kai Wren? I'd really love to come and visit."

"I'm staying with friends."

"Friends?"

"Yes."

She chuckles. It's a friendly sound, so friendly that I laugh in return. Even the tiger laughs, and its whiskers tickle my face. Its breath is scented with honey.

"Well, Kai Wren, any friend of yours is a friend of mine. Give me the address, and I'll drop by in the morning."

It occurs to me to wonder where exactly are we. How are we having this conversation? I ask Viss this thing.

"You've strayed into a sideways realm," she says calmly. "I've been watching for you ever since you dropped by my house. I really regretted missing you then."

I remember that visit now, remember, too, that I had left Tuvoon in less than ideal condition when I had departed.

Awkwardly, I clear my throat.

"And Tuvoon?" ask I. "How is he?"

I step back away from the tiger so that I may see her, but the tiger matches me step for step so that my only vision is of its eyes, its fur, that one round knee.

"He's healing." Her voice sounds amused. "You should drop by and bring him some candy. He always did enjoy Earth candy. You are still on Earth, aren't you?"

Despite her friendly tone, I am feeling uneasy. Then a tantalizing notion strikes me. Perhaps Viss does love me best—especially if she is willing to overlook what I did to Tuvoon.

"I . . ."

A sharp rapping sound and a familiar voice distract me. I listen.

"Kai Wren? Kai Wren? Who are you talking to?"

I smile, recognizing the voice of Li Piao. I start to answer, but my voice feels thick and logy, clogged by sleep. Startled, I realize that I have been dreaming all along—an oddly vivid dream, for I can smell the acrid odor of tiger, the more subtle scent of Viss. I glance down at my feet and see that I am standing on a translucent surface not unlike scuffed Lucite.

Reaching out, I touch the tiger's nose. There, solid, but I can still hear the pounding and, more faintly, Li Piao calling.

"Viss?" I say. In my dream I speak easily.

"You were telling me whether you were still on Earth, Kai Wren," she prompts. "You were going to give me your address so that I can come to visit."

"But I'm asleep!"

"What of it?" she says reasonably. "Even demons dream. Did you not dream strange dreams after the slaying of Rabla-yu?"

"How did you know?"

"I sat by your side and held your hand, my darling," she answers with a light, amused laugh.

"I didn't know."

"You were pretty beat."

"Yeah."

I pat my pockets, but they are apparently empty.

"Damn!"

"What do you need?"

"I was going to write down the directions for you. They get pretty complicated."

"Tell me!" she urges. "I will remember."

I would have, too, right then, but there was a loud crashing sound, a sense of light, then strong, thin hands were shaking me.

"Kai Wren! Kai Wren! Wake up!"

Unwilling, I feel myself dragged from my dream, see the White Tiger raise an enormous paw, though whether to strike or to hold, I do not know. Instead, I found myself sitting up in my bed, Li Piao standing beside me, his hands still clutching the lapels of my pajamas.

"Are you awake?" he asked anxiously.

"I am," I admitted, "though I rather wish I wasn't. I was having a wonderful dream."

"What about?" Li Piao tried to keep an edge from his voice, but I could tell he desperately wanted to know.

I shrugged. "Viss, if you must know. She came to me, riding on a white tiger, proclaiming her love and, rather prosaically, asking if she could drop by to visit."

The old man looked worried but pleased.

"Then the dragon spoke correctly."

"The dragon?" I repeated, my head still fuddled with sleep.

"Old men rarely sleep soundly," Li Piao replied. "Too many aches and pains. I've been taking advantage of this to do some late-night scrying to search for the fu dogs. About ten minutes ago, the dragon rose from the bowl and demanded that I wake you. It said that you were in grave danger."

"I was asleep!" I say, but my indignation faded almost as quickly as it had arisen. "And I was about to give Viss an invitation."

"That would have rather ruined whatever protections we've managed to install," Li Piao said.

"Yes." I chewed the inside of my lower lip, then motioned for Li Piao to close the door so we could have some privacy. When he had done so I said, "I think I love her, Li Piao."

"Viss?" He sounded incredulous. "After all she has done to you?"

"After all that," I admitted. "It isn't rational."

"Love rarely is."

"She says that she loves me."

"Do you believe that?"

Looking into those wise, ancient eyes, I slowly shook my head. "No. I'd like to, but I don't think she does."

Li Piao surprised me. "She might, only after her fashion, and her fashion would be that of a demon, not a human. I do not claim to comprehend human women—I will not attempt to understand the loves of creatures such as you or Viss."

"So she might love me?"

"And still destroy you. The female praying mantis devours her mate even as they couple."

"True."

I found myself wondering what had happened to Tuvoon's father. Rumor had placed him dead in one of the wars, but I'd never really inquired. Viss seemed so absolute in herself and, to indulge in momentary honesty, I'd never really cared to think of her being intimate with another.

A scratching noise came from low on my door, firm and insistent. Li Piao rose and admitted Wong Pang, still a fat and fluffy Pekingese.

"You come late, guard dog," Li Piao chid.

Wong Pang whined apologetically. Then he directed his pop-eyed stare at me and yipped inquiry.

"I'm fine," I said. "Bad dreams."

He wagged his tail, then headed purposefully from the room, pausing to yip again as if ordering us to follow.

"He may need to be let out," Li Piao said. "Plum has promised to make slippers out of him if he wets on the carpet. If you're all right, I'll go let him out."

"I'll walk with you," I said, throwing back the covers and donning my robe. "I want to shake off that dream completely."

Wong Pang barked again, a little more loudly. Shushing him, reminding him to be considerate of Plum and Ba Wa, who presumably still slept, we followed him downstairs into the kitchen. Here he pawed on the door and, when it was opened, hurried importantly out. He waddled back inside almost immediately and for a moment I thought he had somehow duplicated himself.

A furry animal about his own size walked behind him. Like the Pekingese, it had long, thick fur, a curling tail held high over its back, and somewhat protuberant eyes. But these eyes were brilliant gold, and the fur was piebald orange and green in soft shades, rather like mixed sherbet. It was too young to have the thick curled mane or anything of its parents' size, but my restored demon sight knew it instantly for what it was.

"You must be of Shiriki and Chamballa's get!" I exclaimed. "Are they with you?"

The fu dog puppy turned its golden gaze on me and replied in a high-pitched yet rough-edged voice:

"No. I've lost my mama and papa, and the Walker is gone, too!"

Plum's sleepy voice called down the stairs, "What's going on?"

Li Piao, with Wong Pang circling his feet and barking excitedly, went to speak with her. This, of course, awoke Ba Wa, who drifted in from where he had been sleeping, levitating a foot or so above the floor rather than making the effort to walk. After a moment, our entire household assembled in the kitchen.

The puppy reacted to all the noise and strangeness by peeing on the linoleum. By the time I'd mopped that up, Li Piao had explained to the others what had happened, and Wong Pang had been told sternly to shut up and sit.

"But how did it get here?" asked Plum.

"And did anyone follow it?" added Li Piao.

This question brought Ba Wa out of his drowsiness.

"Deep shit, boss!" he said. "If we get found, we in it up to our noses!"

I nodded. "Take Wong Pang and patrol the house and grounds. Make certain you stay out of sight yourselves."

"Right, boss!"

Plum had knelt in front of the fu dog puppy and was holding out one hand for it to sniff.

"You said it talks?" she said to me.

"It did when it got here," I answered.

Plum scratched the puppy gently under the chin and was rewarded with a slight wagging of its tail.

"How'd you get here, pup?"

"Dunno," it answered, almost too softly to hear.

Plum didn't ask again, but continued her scratching, moving her hand onto the puppy's back.

"What's your name?"

"Fluffinella."

"That sounds like a girl's name. Are you a girl fu dog?"

"Uh-huh." The pup studied Plum, gold eyes unblinking. I thought I sensed a hint of magic. "What's your name, Lady?"

"Plum."

The plumed tail was beating faster now, the puppy's voice became more audible: "That's a pretty name."

"Thank you. So's Fluffinella. Now, your mom and dad are . . ."

"Shiriki and Chamballa."

"They didn't bring you here?"

The puppy's tail slowed, though it didn't stop completely. Fluffinella whimpered. "No."

"But how did you know where to find us?"

"The Walker told me. He showed me the door." The wagging stopped, the tail drooped. "I ran. Now the Walker is lost and may be eaten and I can't find my way back to my parents!"

She started whimpering in earnest now. Plum picked her up and cuddled her.

"There, there. It's all right now. You've found us."

I stood watching, hoping that Plum was right. What if the fu pup had been set to hunt us out? What if it was on the other side? Who was to say that Shiriki and Chamballa weren't working for the gods once more?

Li Piao glanced at me, his gaze seeming to indicate that he, too, shared some of my concerns. Then he went and opened the refrigerator.

"Are you hungry, Fluffinella?" he asked. "We have some sweet-and-sour chicken here, and there is always rice."

The puppy wriggled to be put down and hurried over to Li Piao, its sherbet-colored fur trailing like a mandarin's robe.

"I'm hungry! What's sweet-and-sour chicken? What's chicken? What's rice? Are they good?"

Li Piao scraped the leftovers onto a plate and set it on the floor.

"You tell us. If it isn't to your liking, we'll see what we can do."

While Fluffinella sampled, then set to her meal with the same enthusiastic daintiness I had noticed in the Pekingese, Li Piao came over and said softly:

"I'm going to get my dragon bowl. There's a very good chance that the pup doesn't know how to tell us where she came from or how she found you. However, the dragon may be able to help."

Plum said in even softer tones, "Can either of you tell if she is really what she says she is? Demons are shapechangers. Couldn't she be someone in disguise?"

I nodded. "She could, but she isn't. I have regained enough

demon sight to see her aura. It is quite like that of her parents. A shapeshifter would have to know her parents very well to forge that."

Plum nodded, relieved, but still holding on to a scrap of doubt. I found myself admiring her for her courage. Oh, she was no Viss, but she had a strength of her own, for she had cradled to her bosom what she knew might well be an enemy.

Fluffinella was finished with her meal now, her purple tongue questing to remove the traces of sweet-and-sour sauce from the fur around her mouth as she trotted over to join us.

"You are Lord Kai?" she asked me.

"I am."

She tilted her head to one side, studying me carefully.

"You don't look like I was told you look." She continued staring, and I felt the pricklings of what must be a juvenile version of the fu dog's powerful magic. "But you *do* look like him, too."

I hunkered down in front of her.

"I am he. I swear it on my long friendship with your parents. I've met with an accident of sorts."

This seemed to satisfy Fluffinella.

"My sire and dam," she said formally, the words sounding rehearsed, "do not care for their current residence. They wonder if you would help them to escape. If so, they will offer you their lifelong service."

"I would be delighted to help them," I answered, "even without their promise of service. However, I need to know where they are if I am to set them free."

I indicated where Li Piao had set up his scrying bowl.

"This man is named Li Piao, and he is a powerful human sorcerer. He may be able to help you show us the way by which you came here so that we can backtrack to your parents."

Fluffinella perked her ears and trotted over to Li Piao. She set her paws on his knee, and said:

"Pleased to meet you, Great Sorcerer."

He chuckled. "Li Piao will do. Now, let me set you on my lap so that you can see into the water. —No, no, don't drink it! —All I need you to do is tell us the story of how you came here. The dragon in the bowl . . . Do you see him?"

"Uh-huh."

"He will listen to your story and find the place from whence you came."

"I can try." The puppy sounded hesitant. "I was mostly scared—not watching carefully."

"Still, you saw more than you know," Li Piao said steadily. "The dragon will help us. Just start at the beginning."

"Okay." Fluffinella's voice was so soft I had to lean forward to hear her. "I was with my mom and dad when I heard a new voice."

The images that initially appeared in the bowl were not encouraging. Dark, oddly shadowed, full of moving columns and swishing curtains of some fabric, they confused rather than enlightened.

Then an enormous, hairy orange face filled the bowl.

"Mom told me to wait, but I followed her."

Li Piao grunted something and, one hand still steadying the puppy, made a few gestures over the bowl.

"Fine-tuning," he explained. "We were getting everything from precisely Fluffinella's point of view. I've asked the dragon to pull the perspective back and up."

Now we saw the curving walls of a room painted institutional green. The floor was tiled in the same pea-green shade. Against one wall there was a motley heap of old blankets. Upon closer examination, I realized that mingled in with the blankets were several sleeping fu dog puppies.

As Fluffinella continued her narration, we saw Shiriki and Chamballa walking away from the pups, Fluffinella trailing behind them. Their destination seemed to be a glowing spot in the wall.

Then, in my imagination, Fluffinella's narrative merged with the pictures:

"That looks like a gate taking form!" growled Shiriki. "Chamballa, stand ready. They aren't taking our pups without a fight!"

Chamballa growled her agreement.

The glowing spot burned red, then white about the edges. It was a gate of sorts, but a forced, not a natural one. Clearly, its maker was running into a great deal of resistance from the substance of the wall.

"I wonder if it's Lord Kai, found us at last," said Chamballa softly.

Shiriki answered, "Even if it's not, it would certainly be an odd way for Po Shiang or one of his lackeys to come inspect their prizes. Wouldn't they use the door?"

The waiting stretched on until an oval three feet high burned painfully blue-white against the sick green. Then a massive shadowy figure stepped through. Shiriki crouched, preparatory to springing. Chamballa stood as a barrier between any danger and her babies.

The shadow resolved into the centaurian figure of a young demon. His upper body was squat and muscular. His lower body was powerfully built: a cross between a bull and a lion, not horselike and effete after the fashion of centaurs of Western legend. A cascading mane of dark brown hair grew not only from his head but also down his spine to the small of his back.

The demon held up hands that might have been human but for their size and heavy claws.

"I am the Walker," he said. "A demon, not a god."

"Know you Kai Wren, he who is called Lord Demon?" asked Shiriki.

"I do," said the Walker. "He is friendly with my uncle, the demon called He of the Towers of Light. Although Kai Wren does not know it, I have sought you on my uncle's behalf."

Chamballa's flat nose sniffed the Walker's scent, though she remained between her puppies and the intruder.

"You speak the truth—at least as you know it. What is your plan?"

"My uncle has bartered for information and has learned where Kai Wren currently resides. He is on the Earth plane. Although keeping you hidden there might be awkward, I thought I would take you to him."

"What of his bottle?" asked Shiriki.

"It is not in his possession."

"And your uncle's residence?"

The Walker looked hesitant. "He did not give me permission to bring you there."

Whatever the fu dogs might next have asked was interrupted by a sharp click.

"Someone is unlocking the door," said Chamballa, moving to interpose her pony-sized body between the door and the Walker's entry point, effectively hiding the oval gate from easy detection.

"Come away with me!" the Walker urged.

"Not without our pups," replied Shiriki, moving to rouse the still-sleeping ones. "What the gods plan for them I would not wish on a dog."

"Hurry!"

Shiriki then noticed Fluffinella.

"Go with the demon, girl," he ordered. "We'll be right behind."

The pup obeyed, running as quickly as her short puppy legs could carry her. Since Fluffinella had not been paying any attention to what came next, the dragon bowl could not show what she had seen, but she faithfully reported the fragments of conversation she had heard as she bounded toward the oval gate.

". . . only a few more seconds," from Chamballa. "Weapons . . ."

"Get out of here, demon!" commanded Shiriki.

"But . . ."

There was more to the Walker's speech, but Fluffinella only heard it as a confused babble. Her attention was on getting through the oval gate, but it was too high for her. Then hands grasped her and she was through, rolling tail over nose, the Walker sensed as a presence behind her.

"Mom?"

"Run, pup, run!" shouted the Walker. "I'll catch up after I close this gate!"

So she ran. Her entire life had been restricted to the pea-green walls of that one room, so she did not know how very odd was the place in which she found herself. Those of us watching most certainly did.

The ground was deep purple, with a sheen like rumpled satin. The surface was somewhat slick, and her infant claws often could not find purchase, betraying her to slide uncontrolled, rebounding off white or pink pillowlike lumps that might have been shrubs, for they smelled lightly of roses or lavender. Farther in there were massy, rounded hills in various colors (many dark blue or black) that she climbed, her claws sinking into the soft surface and so granting her better purchase.

It was tiring going, like walking on fine, deep sand, though the surface was not at all granular. She kept climbing, adrenaline giving her strength beyond her weeks. Behind her she could hear the ferocious howls of her parents, the pinging of something striking a hard surface, the fainter yaps and yells of her littermates.

Then the ground began to vibrate rhythmically, and she tumbled down the slope she had just laboriously climbed. A firm hand smelling of the Walker lifted her up. At first, he held her suspended by her ruff, then clasped her to his chest, never ceasing to run. Over his shoulder, she could see the oval portal. It was blocked with something dark, but a red seam was burning around the edges.

"I think they're following us," she yipped.

"They are," gasped the Walker. He was more skilled than she at finding solid footing, often leaping from rounded hill to hill, but the going was far from easy. "I had hoped to take the longer, safer route, but we may need the shortcut through Hanger. It's dangerous."

"So are the gods," said Fluffinella. She knew this from her parents' stories, from the gods' own behavior.

"True." The Walker chuckled. "Then I will find the Hanger Gate."

He did. This was not like the oval portal, a rough cut opening, but more like a proper door: rectangular and reinforced with wooden beams. The Walker paused before it to look at Fluffinella.

"I'd like to be able to use both of my hands. If I put you on my back, can you grab hold of my mane?"

"I think so."

Now Fluffinella's vision as portrayed by the dragon bowl was nearly completely taken up by the Walker's thick brown hair. Li Piao muttered commands to the dragon, but had to apologize.

"I can't get a clearer view. The dragon says there is no wider perspective to draw upon."

"Tell it to do the best it can and let Fluffinella tell on," I ordered. "We still don't know what happened to the Walker."

The pup looked longingly at the scrying bowl.

"Can I have something to drink? Sweet-and-sour chicken and rice makes me thirsty. So does talking."

We stopped for refreshments for everyone before Fluffinella continued her account.

When the Walker passed through the gate, Fluffinella felt several soft things dragging over her. Then they were through and the Walker carefully shut the door and dropped a metal bar into place.

As he did so, Fluffinella became immediately aware that the scents had changed. The pleasant, rather floral, perfumes of the first plane had given way to dusty, metallic scents, strong enough to penetrate through the odor of the Walker's sweat.

"Hold tight," the Walker said. "I'm going to run hard and hope to leave them behind. They may not be able to perceive the Hanger Gate. Not everyone can, but if the gods turn out the dogs, being far ahead is our only hope. The Hangers don't like invaders."

Fluffinella knew that by dogs the Walker meant fu dogs—not her parents, but the gods' own fu dogs. She hadn't seen them. Shiriki had, recently, though Fluffinella was somewhat confused about the circumstances of the meeting—and he had spoken scornfully of them to Chamballa.

"They have our nose and the general appearance," he had said, "even something of the magic, but they are poor things compared to *our* generation and those that sired us. They do have something on us, though—size and teeth. The bitches they brought me to were my size and half again."

Chamballa had shushed him then, but Fluffinella had often heard Shiriki grumble about the gods' dogs to himself.

The Walker carried her through the Hanger plane for so long that Fluffinella's jaws began to ache and her nose to throb from frequent bumps into his muscular back. Her few glimpses of the plane did not encourage her to look more. It was a drab place: black and white and steel gray.

After a while, the Walker spoke, his breathing easier now and his gait steady. He reached around, grabbed Fluffinella, and carried her in his arms again.

"In case we get separated, I'm going to tell you how to get to Kai Wren. My uncle told me that fu dogs were bred to perceive and locate gates. What do you see over there—at the farthest reach of the horizon?"

"A ball," she said promptly.

"Good show!" he exclaimed. "You are sharp!"

Fluffinella wagged her tail.

"Now, to find Kai Wren, you need to get to that ball or one like it. They're scattered throughout this plane. Most people need to hunt for them, but you . . ."

He shook his head in admiration.

"When you get to the ball, check to see if it's mostly blue and green—more blue than green, in fact. Can you read?"

"I'm only a few weeks old!" the puppy protested.

"Sorry." He went on painstakingly to describe how to recognize the North American continent, then how to find California, and, finally, how to locate San Francisco. When he was certain that she had that, he told her:

"When you've found the place, press down on the ball with your paw. You may need to press hard, since you're so little. When a thin beam of white light appears, roll the ball so that San Francisco is directly under that light. Press again. When the light turns yellow, you'll see a door. Go through it. After that, trust your nose. There can't be many demons in San Francisco. Will you know one by scent?"

"Uh-huh. They smell like you."

"Do we really smell that much different from gods?"

"Oh, yes!"

The Walker mused on this for a moment, never stopping his steady canter. Then he laboriously described me—both as demon and in my usual human form. Then he made Fluffinella memorize the message we had already been given. All of this was done while loping through a flatland that resembled a nearly monochrome Cubist painting.

The ball—which I recognized as being similar to the mapping globes I used on the transit plane—was growing more distinct when they heard the first low howls.

"Fu dogs!" said the Walker. "Shit! Now the Hangers will be alerted."

He'd hardly finished speaking when there was a harsh, metallic clanking. Fluffinella glanced over his shoulder and saw something angular and metallic materializing from a thick slab of gray. Then the Walker had her by the scruff of her neck.

"I'm going to delay it," he said. "There's no reasoning with a Hanger. You run to the ball and do what I told you. Go through the door as fast as you can."

He slowed and set her on the ground, wheeling to face the menace clanking up behind them.

"I'll follow!" he promised. "Now go!"

And she did. There were confused images of the Walker battering with a quarterstaff at something larger than him by half, though far less solid. The baying of the fu dogs grew louder, too, interspersed with snarls and the reports of weapons.

And Fluffinella ran. She operated the gate (not without some fumbling), and hurried through the door that materialized just as a pair of shaggy blue-and-umber monstrosities came shambling up the hill.

To the eye, they were just barely recognizable as fu dogs. Their fangs were like those of a saber-toothed tiger, and they were at least the size of a horse, but chunky, like a bear. Yet, Fluffinella's nose told her that they were fu dogs—and that they were her enemies.

After she fled through the gate, Fluffinella remembered how the Walker had closed the door to the Hanger plane and pressed her head against the door. It slid shut easily. When she inspected her surroundings, she found herself in an alley intersecting Grant Street in Chinatown. The night was dark and somewhat foggy. Although sobbing with exhaustion and terror, she put her nose to the ground and started tracking. She persisted until she reached Plum's house.

There, Wong Pang sensed her and came outside. Despite

his peculiar odor, she thought him some strange fu pup, and gladly followed him into the house.

"And that's all," she finished. "Is that enough for the dragon?"

Li Piao communed with the bowl's resident spirit. "The dragon thinks so. Some parts are sketchy and . . . Kai Wren, the dragon seems puzzled by the pup's perceptions. It says they are abnormally sharp."

"They are," I agreed. "I've never seen anything like them. If I'd realized how easily fu dogs can track across planes, I'd have tried some experiments with Shiriki and Chamballa."

"It makes sense," Plum said. "If they were bred to protect the gods' temples, they would need to be able to follow their prey across the planes."

"Yes," I said, reaching to pat Fluffinella. "The globe she used also puzzled me. I've never seen one like it. Was it natural to that plane or did the Walker create it?"

"Or," Li Piao added, "did the fu dog's own power make a mapping globe more effective?"

"That's a possibility," I admitted. "Well, in addition to a log of Fluffinella's route, I think we have a good idea why Po Shiang wanted Shiriki and Chamballa."

Plum frowned at me. "Not in front of the puppy!"

Fluffinella looked at her. "My mom said that, too. Why?"

"Because," Plum said, coloring, "it isn't very nice."

"Oh."

"Who do you think told He of the Towers of Light where I am?" I asked, withholding suspicions of my own.

"Either Spilling Moonbeams or her father," Plum answered immediately, "but since no trouble has come from that, I think we can assume that they're still on your side."

I nodded. "And judging from the dream I had last night, Viss is worried."

"What dream?" asked Plum.

I gave a quick summary, leaving out my romantic speculations. Those were private, but I wondered if she caught some of the tone anyhow, for she looked at me and frowned.

"I wonder how much longer we're safe here?" she asked.

"If the gods' fu dogs track Fluffinella, or the Walker is questioned, we might have visitors any moment. I'd hate to put my neighbors in jeopardy."

"Good point," said Li Piao, "and I know just where we can go."

He gestured toward the living room, where the bottles we had taken from Viss stood ranked on a coffee table. The dawnlight was just filtering through the blinds, making the glass resemble liquid gems.

"Tell us, Kai Wren, are any of those fit for habitation?"

We chose the green-and-orange bottle for several reasons, not the least of which was that since it had not been in Viss's possession, even briefly, she could not have set any traps or tracers within it. The bottle itself we hid beneath a layer of towels in Plum's upstairs-bathroom linen closet.

As I stowed the remaining bottles in a box at the back of Plum's pantry closet, I wondered about the various sages who resided in some of them. I hoped that their extended meditations had not been too greatly disturbed by recent events. I would need to check on them when this was over—assuming I survived.

The interior of the green-and-orange bottle was the basic landscape template I use when I'm concentrating on other things: a couple of mountains with attendant valleys and hills, a river or two to supply fresh water and to generate a bit of native *chi*, basic plants and critters. Maybe fifty acres in all, nothing like the universes I've stored in some bottles.

"What does this bottle do?" asked Plum after I had shown them all how to enter and exit, and we had set up housekeeping in a generic valley. "I mean, it's very pretty, but it doesn't seem to reflect one hundred and twenty years of work."

"Oh?" I said, cocking an eyebrow at her. "I didn't know you knew so much about creating magical bottles."

She colored, but held her ground. "It's nowhere near as elaborate as your other bottle."

"And how do you know that my home didn't take me even longer to create?" I asked, then I relented. "You're right. The major magic in this one is not related to its interior decor. It's something else entirely."

I had all of their attention now. Even Wong Pang stopped begging hopefully for scraps from the table.

"It will grant me wishes," I said softly. "Three to be precise."

"Three wishes?" Li Piao repeated. "For anything?"

"Within reason," I said. "I couldn't end the universe or raise the dead or suchlike. Nor can it inspire a permanent change of heart in a person."

"But we could wish that Viss had never been!" said Plum eagerly.

I held up a warning finger. "Consider the ramifications of that wish. If Viss had never been, what other things never would have happened?"

"Oh." Plum thought some more. "Oh. I see what you mean. Those three wishes aren't going to provide an easy answer, are they?"

"No," I agreed. "But they will be a valuable tool. Now, the first thing we should do is rescue Shiriki and Chamballa—and their pups," I added quickly, seeing Fluffinella's anxious look.

"Wish 'em here," suggested Ba Wa.

"I'd hate to waste a wish on something we can do ourselves," I said. "Besides, we need to find the Walker—or at least learn what happened to him. We can hunt for him when we rescue the others."

"Can't just wish for him, too?" asked Ba Wa sadly.

"Not a good idea," I said. "We don't know where he is or if he's still alive. Besides, we're going to need those three wishes for bigger things. If you're afraid, you can stay behind."

Ba Wa looked as if he didn't think that was a bad idea at all, and I did not press him. Scrub demons were not known for either their courage or their reliability, and he had been behaving far beyond the limits of his type.

"I assume that we will backtrack Fluffinella's route to find Shiriki and Chamballa," stated Li Piao. "Can you make a gate through the wall like the Walker did?"

"I think so," I answered, wishing I could be that certain. "Fluffinella will go with me. She has a remarkable gift for traversing the planes."

"You're not going with just a puppy to protect you!" objected Plum. "I'll come with you."

"My good lady"—I sighed—"what could you do to help? This is not a matter in which knowledge of *feng shui* would be of use."

"Still," she persisted stubbornly, "you shouldn't go alone. You're not up to your full strength. Look at the trouble the Walker got into out there."

"I will go with Kai Wren," Li Piao assured his granddaughter. "I do have magic—quite a bit more than I know how to employ. And perhaps Spilling Moonbeams can be recruited to assist us."

Plum might not like *that* idea at all, but she couldn't help but admit that a demoness—even one of the unsubstantial younger generation—would be a great help.

"You and the scrub can remain here in the bottle and hold the fort," I said. "If my dream held any truth, Viss is not waiting quietly for us to act. She's searching for us, even as we speak."

Ba Wa looked as if he was regretting his desire to stay behind, but Wong Pang bounced and barked sharply, clearly stating his desire to remain with Plum.

"Are you willing to stay here alone?" I asked Plum. "It could be dangerous."

"Especially if Viss finds us," she said, nodding. "I'll stay. I hate the idea of her getting ahold of the one place we know is safe."

I smiled approvingly. "If you need something to distract you from the prospect of an invasion by Viss, you could remodel the landscape's *feng shui*—design it so that it will aid in our defense, perhaps."

"I could do that," Plum answered, growing somewhat more cheerful, "especially if Ba Wa and Wong Pang use their magic to move the heavier items for me."

"Can't move mountains!" Ba Wa protested.

"I won't need you to do that," she assured him with a smile, "just a few rivers."

So it was decided. When contacted via Ba Wa, Spilling Moonbeams proved amenable. Within twelve hours of Fluffinella's arrival, we set out to rescue Shiriki and Chamballa.

XII

WITH A SWORD borrowed from Seven Fingers concealed within sidewise space and some magic once more at my call, I felt more myself as we departed the Bottle of Wishes for the travel plane.

I knew well this confidence was foolish. I was far reduced from the demon who had some months before destroyed four scrub demons with barely an effort, far weaker than the arrogant creature who had swaggered about making inquiries and missing the forest for the trees. But I did feel good, and some of my confidence spilled over to my companions.

Li Piao had conjured the spirit of the dragon bowl (a new trick and one I had not needed to teach him) and it flew beside him, sometimes resting on his shoulder and whispering in his ear. Spilling Moonbeams bore a long, slender, polished piece of wood. It resembled a staff, but I would have wagered what magic I still possessed that it concealed as many secrets as did one of my bottles. Fluffinella trotted in front, stumbling occasionally over her own paws. Her footing might have been less than sure, but she led us directly to one of those complex spheres.

I did not see it at first, but when in response to my query, she touched it with her nose, I could just perceive it. My ego was comforted in that Spilling Moonbeams also had to struggle to see it; but, with a joint effort, we brought it forth from whatever had shrouded it from sight.

This sphere was shaded mostly black and gray, with occasional seas of white. I spun it under my fingers.

"Fluffinella, can you tell us where you entered the Hanger Plane?"

"I can try."

While I slowly spun the globe, she set her nose to the sphere and sniffed enthusiastically.

"There!" she said, indicating a triad of dark cubes. "That's the place."

I had started to press down on the sphere to activate it when Spilling Moonbeams said:

"I wonder if we could go directly to that other plane—the one you told me the Walker had found was tangential to Origin."

"We might," I said, "but there are a few problems with that course."

"Oh?"

I had the impression of eyebrows arching within the shadows of her face and hastened to explain.

"One, we need to find the Walker, and he was last seen on the Hanger Plane. Two, I don't know how large that tangential plane is. We could wander for a long time before finding something that Fluffinella recognized. She has a better chance at tracking from the Hanger Plane."

Spilling Moonbeams twirled her staff. "But can't the dragon spirit guide us?"

Li Piao shook his head. "It is only a manifestation of a scrying bowl—an automation of a map."

The dragon hissed, indignant.

"At least in regard to this," Li Piao clarified. "I'm afraid it knows no more than the fu pup. Its greatest virtue is that it cannot become confused in what it does know. Is there a particular reason that you do not wish to retrace her steps?"

Silver framing darkness nodded.

"Yes. Wouldn't the gods be wise to await us? Couldn't we be walking into an ambush?"

"We might," I said firmly, "but we cannot be certain that they believe anyone is coming. The gods would be wiser to center their forces on Shiriki and Chamballa rather than scattering them hither and yon. I don't know enough about these Hangers even to guess what they will do."

Spilling Moonbeams relented then, but I could tell that she was still very nervous.

Not wishing to delay any longer, I pressed down on the globe and activated the gate. After we had hurried through, I shut the way behind us. Fluffinella immediately began snuffling the ground, while Li Piao sent the dragon ahead to mark the way.

"I smell the Walker," Fluffinella reported when we were a few hundred paces from the gate, her rough-edged voice very soft. "The scent is faint, though."

"Keep sniffing," I said. "We will keep watch."

We strode on, listening for the metallic clanking that would herald the approach of the Hangers, all three of us too seasoned to jump at shadows, yet jittery with alertness. Our route took us across an area divided into rectangular channels walled off from each other by smooth, flat partitions. The partitions were not terribly high, so the effect was rather like being giants walking over a maze meant for mice.

In the distance, we could see what might have been a forest of wiry, leafless trees. Beyond the forest was something towering and black: a mountain range made from jumbled cubes. When a breeze blew, it rattled through the skinny trees, carrying with it a fine dust that made my eyes gritty and my nose run.

I longed to shift into another shape, but I did not want to waste my limited *chi* on something so incidental, so I bore the discomfort and hoped that the dust was not interfering with Fluffinella's sense of smell.

After a time, she halted and, bidding us to wait, quested about, her flat face touching the ground. At last, she looked up.

"The Walker's scent goes that way," she said, indicating the forest to our right.

"The way to the gate is this direction," chirped the dragon spirit, darting ahead.

"I know," Fluffinella said, "but the Walker went this way."

"Of his own accord?" I asked.

"The Hanger smell overlies his," she said. "I don't know."

"Can you scry?" I asked Li Piao.

"I can try," he said, "but as I have never met the Walker . . ."

Several minutes later, he looked up from the bowl and shook his head regretfully.

"It is as I feared. Fluffinella's impressions are not strong enough for me to use. Also, I have the feeling that this place is not conducive to my magic."

Spilling Moonbeams nodded. "Yes. The *chi* is bound into the forms that surround us. It would be difficult to do much magic here."

"So," I said, while Li Piao poured the contents of his scrying bowl back into a flask, "do we go straight or follow the Walker's scent?"

"Follow the scent," said Li Piao.

Fluffinella panted agreement; even Spilling Moonbeams agreed with only minimal hesitation.

"His uncle values him," she said, glancing about nervously, "but let us hasten. This place makes me very nervous. I feel as if we are being watched."

We went away from the gate then, avoiding passing beneath the wiry trees for as long as we could without going too far from the route dictated by Fluffinella's keen nose. There were no fallen leaves beneath the trees, just a smooth, flat, metallic surface, devoid even of the mazelike markings. Since the ground rose slightly as we penetrated more deeply into the forest, our feet soon began to slide.

I longed for claws, but settled for stepping carefully and trusting the rubber soles of my hiking shoes. Eventually, I had to carry Fluffinella, periodically setting her down to ensure that we were still on course. A sound ominously like thunder rumbled in the direction of the Cubist mountains.

Li Piao gave an unconvincing grin. "I guess we're perfectly safe since we're standing under a whole forest of lightning rods."

"I wish that was the case," I said, "but the ground could conduct, and I fear we will be in trouble then—especially if we complete a circuit."

"And where are the Hangers?" fretted Spilling Moonbeams. "We've been here for hours, and they haven't found us."

"When the Walker fled here with Fluffinella, the Hangers did not emerge until the howls of the fu dogs alerted them to intruders," I said with a confidence I did not feel. "Perhaps we have been too stealthy and they have not yet detected us."

"Perhaps," she said, but she did not sound reassured.

I thought her nervousness odd. She was a demon, possessed of a demon's powers, but in many ways she was more timid than the merely human Plum. Was this because she was more attuned to the dangers we faced? Or was it because she had been told for much of her life that she was somehow a diminished demon, whereas Plum was not only a competent human, but a specialized sorceress as well?

I put such mysteries from me and was preparing to set Fluffinella down to check the scent once more when a stray motion caught my eye. Looking up, I found what we were seeking.

The Walker was suspended in the boughs of one of the wiry trees. His six limbs were contorted at uncomfortable angles from his centaurian torso and held firmly in place by cable-thick loops of "branch." Other cables twined around his waist, his barrel, and his throat. So restrained, he could not speak, but his large brown eyes blinked rapidly. It was this fluttering of his eyelids that had caught my attention.

Lightning flashed again, and this time I was certain that I felt the slight prickling of an electric charge.

"Don't anyone cry out," I said, "but if you look into the boughs of the large tree ahead and slightly to the left, you will see the Walker."

My companions did as they were bid, and I heard two suppressed gasps and a smothered yip.

"How do we get him down?" asked Fluffinella quietly.

"I am open to suggestions," I admitted. The situation did not look good. The Walker was firmly imprisoned, and I felt certain that any effort to free him would alert the Hangers. It also might end his life—I didn't like how that one cable in particular was wrapped snugly about his neck.

Moreover, an electrical storm was moving in. Sparks jolted from the tree trunks. I had no doubt that in the midst of the storm there was to be a flurry of lightning bolts as well. That they might be directed at us seemed quite plausible. There were no safe places and the maze plain was a long way below.

But what if . . .

An idea so twisted that it seemed quite possible occurred to me then. I whispered to my companions:

"At my word, I want all of you to climb the Walker's tree."

"Why?" asked Li Piao.

"Just do it!" I said. "We don't have much time before the storm strikes in full."

Fluffinella whined in fear. "But I can't climb!"

"Don't worry," I assured her, already heading toward the tree. "I've got you."

The trunk of the tree was as smooth as a section of pipe, but I boosted Li Piao up, handing Fluffinella to him. Spilling Moonbeams hovered beside me and, when I was ready, gave me a boost. Then she flew up into the branches.

As soon as the tree felt us, there was a powerful rippling in its boughs. Small branches wriggled and hooked our clothing. Larger branches flexed slowly, apparently trying to coil about us as they had about the Walker.

They met with immediate difficulty. There were too many of us to be effectively entrapped, especially as all but the smallest branches moved in ponderous slow motion.

Spilling Moonbeams quickly grasped the situation and used her insubstantial form to complicate matters for the tree. Making an arm or a leg solid, she would leave it that way only long enough for a branch to grab her. When the branch was set, she would mist into light and shadow once more. The rest of us could not do as much to confuse our would-be captor, but we struggled and climbed, keeping in constant motion, ruining our clothing and enduring myriad gashes from the sharp tendrils.

As the tree attempted to capture us, it was forced to loosen its hold on the Walker. He freed one arm first and used it to tear at the cable around his throat. Then he gasped:

"The Hangers will come! Flee while you can!"

"As soon as the storm is over," I said, pushing a cable off of my leg and watching it coil over itself before beginning to reach for Fluffinella. "Quickly, tell me, am I right in assuming that the Hangers put you here?"

"Yes." The Walker looked puzzled at my query. "I fought as best I could, but they captured me and brought me to this place."

"Good. Have you been here through a storm?"

The Walker's face paled at the memory. "I have."

"Then we should be safe here for the duration of this one." I lifted Fluffinella away from the cable and climbed a few feet out of its reach. "I took a gamble that they would not have imprisoned you in a place where you would be killed."

"Quite a gamble," the Walker said. "What if this was the first storm since I'd been here?"

I shrugged as best I could. "Then we would all have died."

"We would have anyway," called Li Piao. He had made his way to a relatively stable place where two thick limbs met near the main trunk of the tree. "Look at that storm!"

It was even more impressive than I had imagined. Jagged bolts of lightning in retina-searing shades of gold, green, and blue plunged from the massed clouds. Sometimes they struck the taller trees. These then gouted forth smaller, but no less lethal, bolts from limbs and branch tips. Sparks glittered along the trunks.

When the bolts struck the ground, the metallic surface below liquefied. The molten metal swirled along the polished surface surrounding it, joining with other streamlets, sometimes becoming raging streams that ran with electricity as well as metal.

How does it become polished again? I wondered, even as I basked in relief that my guess had been correct. Had we chosen to flee into the plains below, most of us would be dead. Even Spilling Moonbeams would have found escape difficult.

Deafened by the thunder cracks that accompanied each lightning bolt, I did not notice when the storm began to abate.

Li Piao's gestures directed my attention to where the Cubist mountains were becoming visible behind parting clouds.

"Can we get down now?" Fluffinella asked, when the last sparks faded some fifteen minutes later. She was trembling, and my shirt and trousers were downed with the green-and-orange fur she had shed in her panic. "I've got to pee."

I glanced at the Walker. With Spilling Moonbeams's assistance he had worked free of the branches, but they were coiling after him again. His size made evasion difficult, but he was still a demon and brought his enormous strength to bear in order to dissuade them.

"Wait," he said, pushing back a singularly stubborn branch. "There is more to come. Can you hear the wind?"

Now that he drew it to our attention, even my numbed hearing caught the rumbling howl that was building in the direction of the mountains.

"It will reach here in about thirty seconds," the Walker said. "Grab on to something and hold on tight."

"The tree will get us again!" protested Fluffinella.

"The wind doesn't last long, but . . ."

The words were literally blown out of his mouth. Despite his warning, it was all I could do to keep a firm hold on both the fu pup and the tree limb. My eyes screwed shut of their own volition—my ears would have done the same if I had possessed the spare *chi*. Tiny granules cut into my exposed skin, abraded the many cuts caused by the tree's tendrils. I felt, rather than heard, Fluffinella's terrified howl.

Then, just as I thought I could bear it no longer, the wind died. When I could force my eyes open once more, I saw that the metal ground below had been polished smooth. Not a trace of the many spillways and channels that had marked it remained.

The Walker kicked away the branches that had been restraining him and floated to the ground. He held up his arms.

"Toss me Fluffinella," he called. And then, as I did so, he smiled. "And thanks for coming to rescue me!"

The Walker told us the rest of his story as we slipped and slid down to the plains, angling our route to where the dragon spirit assured us the gate awaited.

"There isn't much you don't know," he said. "I turned back to give Fluffinella a chance to escape. The Hangers got me. They're frightfully hard to fight. Their bodies are like the trees—not given to mass, but incredibly dexterous. I've never had any luck going after them with an edged weapon, and it's hard to batter them. What works best is magic, but they have the *chi* tied up in some odd way . . ."

He shrugged. "So they got me."

"Did the fu dogs help them?" I asked. "The ones the gods sent after you?"

"No," he replied. "I saw a contingent of Hangers go after the two at the Earth Gate. No fu dogs got hung in the tree with me, so I don't know what happened to them."

He glanced at Fluffinella, reluctant to discuss the details in her hearing. I could easily guess the options: escape, capture, or death. The last seemed most probable.

Li Piao conferred with the dragon, who was once more resting upon his shoulder.

"We don't have far to go," he said. "We should see the gate soon. The dragon says the only reason we haven't already is that its frame blends into the surrounding surface."

Fluffinella, still cradled in the Walker's arms, licking her wounds, craned her neck to look.

"I can see it," she said, apparently puzzled by our blindness. "Another ball. This one is lots of different colors, blended together in round blotches."

"We won't make it there without being discovered by the Hangers," the Walker said with morose certainty. "They put me in that tree for some obscure purpose of their own. I must believe that they know I have escaped."

"You're awfully gloomy," said Spilling Moonbeams pertly. She was walking with us, partly substantial, conserving her *chi* in case of danger. "We rescued you, didn't we? Why shouldn't we get out of here, too?"

"Because this is the Hangers' plane," the Walker said, "and they're very good at defending it."

I was about to suggest that he lope ahead with Fluffinella and open the gate when there was an ominous clanking and tinging: metal on metal. Then, from the broken ground in front of us, the Hangers rose.

Or perhaps I should say *The* Hanger rose, for my first impression was not of many creatures, but of one great monster made from intertwining segments of wire. The average section was about as big around as my index finger, but there were others twice or three times as thick. These, on closer inspection, proved to be several cables twisted together.

The Hanger elongated, becoming a steel-mesh barrier fifteen feet high and at least three times as wide. Its segments were roughly triangular, but too small for any of us except possibly Fluffinella and the insubstantial demoness to pass through.

The creature had taken advantage of the terrain, picking a spot where the maze walls rose higher than usual. We could go around it, but we could not go over. Even as I started to double back, I heard more ringing of metal on metal and a second grouping began to emerge from behind us. We were well and fitly trapped. I had no doubt that given time the segments would merge overhead. Then . . .

Would they care to capture us, given that we had helped the Walker to escape, or would they just figure we were a bad bet? I really didn't want to wait to find out.

"Out of here!" I ordered Spilling Moonbeams. "You, too, Walker. You can't help us from here."

Demons do not cultivate foolish nobility. We lost all of that tendency early in our wars. The two fled as I had commanded, taking the fu pup with them.

"Any ideas?" I said to Li Piao, as casually as I could. "You're the one with the power."

The old man looked back and forth between the two converging Hanger clusters.

"I've tried flying out, but something keeps forcing me down!"

The triangular segments of Hanger within the barrier were now moving up and down, irresistibly reminding me of moving mouths. They might be toothless, but I had no doubt that they could crush and rend. Curved claws were emerging at the joints.

Capturing us did not seem to be what the creatures had in mind. Above the sound of the barrier closing, a clattering noise told me that the Walker and Spilling Moonbeams were having troubles of their own.

"Oh, for a pair of wire cutters!" Li Piao said mournfully.

"Conjure some then!" I said.

"I don't know how!"

There wasn't time to instruct him properly. Instead, I grasped his temples.

"Put your hands in front of you," I ordered, "and visualize what it is that you want. Be as precise as possible. I don't have much *chi*, but . . ."

"Wire cutters," Li Piao muttered, "big ones, like bolt cutters, long handles, hard steel."

While he muttered, I merged my limited *chi* with his much greater store. It helped that his *chi* was related to my *chi*, for his great powers had been activated by the charge I had given him back when I was still his healer. Our joined *chi* took direction from me, shape from him. I heard his triumphant cry as the desired cutters manifested in his thin hands.

They were just what he had requested, complete with insulated handles, padded in rubber foam. He clipped the cutters around the nearest section of Hanger and pushed down hard. The wirelike surface resisted for a moment, then gave with a cry like a broken guitar string.

"Got it!" Li Piao shouted.

"Go for the thicker parts," I said. "We need to cut the joints. I'll help push."

He aimed the cutters, and I put my strong hands on the handles just above his wrinkled and age-gnarled ones.

"Press down!" I ordered.

We did. The doubled cable tried to wrest free, tried to uncoil, but we sliced it apart. A few more cuts and we had made a hole big enough for us to slip through. As we ran out of the culvert, my arm supported a heavily panting Li Piao. Conjuring can be hard work, even for a powerful natural magician.

Behind us, I could hear the rattling as the damaged Hanger barrier reoriented on us. Fortunately, at least for the moment, it was blocking its fellow.

Meanwhile, Fluffinella had reached the gate sphere and was in the process of activating it. Spilling Moonbeams guarded her, dodging in and out of the grasp of small, hook-headed Hangers who defied logic and gravity to flap around her like weird bats. The Walker stood a few yards away, dealing with another such cluster. Shiny blue ichor ran from numerous slashes in his pelt.

"Hangers!" said Li Piao, his tone incredulous. "They're Hangers!"

"I know," I said, hoping the strain had not broken the old man's mind. "Can you use the cutters to help Spilling Moonbeams? I think I can use my sword to snag some of the rest. We only need a few more minutes, and we're through."

"I can," the old man said.

We beat back the flying Hangers as best we could. The cut ones lost the ability to fly. The ones I snagged on my sword chewed the blade up something fierce. Anything less than Seven Fingers's steel would have been rendered useless. I found that I could sling a snagged Hanger at one of its flying fellows, causing them both to tangle and crash.

Yet for all our valor, we were near to being overwhelmed when we heard Fluffinella's high-pitched bark:

"It's open! Hurry!"

Retreating side by side with the Walker, I caught glimpses of Spilling Moonbeams and Li Piao doing the same. We stumbled through the opening in the air, and stumbled again on the soft ground on the other side.

Four-legged, the Walker kept his footing, slamming the gate shut behind us and dropping the bar. On this side, the gate looked like a door, and I was too weary to ask questions. Someday, I would ask the Walker for his theories about the appearances of gates, but not just then.

For now, my main concern was that the gods would have set someone to watch this gate, but Li Piao's dragon reported the area was clear. Fluffinella sniffed the air, sneezing at the floral scents that perfumed it, and confirmed the dragon's report.

"They were Hangers!" Li Piao said indignantly as soon as he had caught his breath.

The Walker studied him, obviously wondering what insane creature I had found to aid me.

"Of course they were Hangers," he said. "What else would they be, demons?"

"No, I don't mean that," said Li Piao. "I mean they were hangers—metal clothes hangers, just like the ones I put my shirts on."

He paused and considered: "Well, not just like. The ones at home have never tried to attack me. Where are we now, the land of lost socks?"

"Precisely," said the Walker. "I had heard the legend and . . ."

"Wait!" protested Li Piao. "I don't understand."

"The legend," repeated the Walker, glancing at me. "The legend that missing socks turn into wire clothes hangers—this is the reason why you always have too many hangers and too few socks. For that to be true, there had to be some continuity between the planes. Everyone knows that drawers and cabinets often have access to other dimensions."

"They do?" asked Li Piao, glancing at me for reassurance.

The Walker added soothingly, "It's true. That's why things you are certain you put securely away get lost or end up trans-ferred to another place entirely."

"I've never studied the theory," I said, "but I did encounter it in my work on bottles."

The old man held his head. "I think I've been through too much. The lightnings must have fried my brain. Where in all truth are we?"

"This is the Sock Plane," explained the Walker patiently. "It is contiguous with the plane we call Origin, although, naturally, the two planes do not intersect. That's why the gods had no guards here when I passed through before. Like the Hanger Plane, its *chi* is bound up in its own nature, so it is not an inviting place for our kind."

"Right. Just as you say, my good demon." Li Piao held up his hand. "I don't think I want to know."

I decided the time had come for introductions.

"Valiant Walker," said I, my tone at its most conciliatory, "most of you know each other . . ."

"That is so," said the Walker. "I am pleased to see Spilling Moonbeams again."

"And I you," came her soft voice from the shadowed face.

The Walker patted the fu pup. "And I am delighted that Fluffinella made her escape. I wondered if I was dangling in that tree all for nothing."

The fu pup replied by licking his face.

I then said, "But I do not believe that you have met my friend, Li Piao. He is a human, a sorcerer, and a master of kites."

The Walker bent his head in a slight bow. "I am honored and grateful."

"And this humble one is pleased to make the acquaintance of the Walker Between Planes," Li Piao replied, "and begs that he forgive this one his ignorance and incredulity."

"There is nothing to forgive," the Walker said, "now that I know you are human. Our learnings are different. Had I studied your aura, I would have known. The fault is mine."

I hastened to interrupt before the next exchange of apologies and compliments could begin.

"The tangential point between Origin and this plane cannot be far," I said, "if we understood Fluffinella correctly."

"It isn't," the Walker said. "However, I lack the tools with which I pinpointed it last time. The Hangers left me with little but my life."

"I can smell the way," yapped Fluffinella. "The odor is strong—gods and fu dogs both!"

"If everyone is rested," I said, "then we should go on as quickly as possible."

We did this, laboring across the soft surface. Li Piao looked bemused as we rounded mounds of balled socks, hiked across unmatched socks, slipped over fine woven silk stockings or labored over the broken ground of coarse weave. The colors were brilliant and vivid, patterned occasionally in argyles or prints.

"Have we become small," Li Piao asked me, "or have the socks become large?"

"Neither, really," said I, "just as you do not shrink to enter my bottle, so we do not change to come here. We merely enter into the Tao of the place."

"If you say so," he said, but he did not cease looking puzzled.

The place where the plane came closest to Origin proved to

be—at least as perceived from this side—a heap of oversized, mateless tube socks.

"Li Piao," the Walker said, "could you assist Spilling Moonbeams and me to pinpoint the best point to cut our gate?"

The two younger demons had been talking softly as we progressed, and I surmised that Spilling Moonbeams had told the Walker of my mishaps. It felt odd not to be consulted on a magical matter, but I had to admit that they were correct in not doing so. I covered my feelings by drawing my much-chewed-upon sword from sidewise space and standing guard. We had not yet encountered anything dangerous, but that was no excuse to get lax.

Li Piao unwrapped the dragon bowl and, calling its wandering spirit back into residence, poured in water. Over this, he spun a piece of old Chinese cash through whose square center hole he had tied a silken cord.

"To the right of where you are standing, Walker," he said. "No, a bit more to the left. Up a few inches. That's good. Now, to the left just a touch more. Put your thumb there. That point is the same one through which you passed last time you were here."

"Good!"

Spilling Moonbeams lifted Fluffinella so that her round golden eyes were level with the Walker's thumb.

"What do you see there, Fluffinella?"

"A thumb?"

"Anything else?"

"Just the socks."

The demoness set the dog down. "Well, that's not too good. The gods have sealed the Walker's portal."

"Can you make another?" I asked, not ceasing in my restless scanning of the colorful hills. I was certain I had seen motion, but there was no need to call alarm prematurely.

"I can," he said, "but the Hangers have taken my tools and my personal *chi* is low. I'll need help."

Spilling Moonbeams said, "I have *chi* stored in my staff, but no skill in making gates."

"And I," Li Piao said, as if he was still uncertain about making such declarations, "am apparently quite powerful—

though I have about as much knowledge of how to use my powers as would a child."

"Gather round, then," the Walker said. "I've made a study of gates, natural and otherwise. What do you see out there, Kai Wren?"

"Movement," I answered, "something amorphous. Do you know what dwells here?"

"Socks, as far as I know," he answered, "and some odd bits of lingerie. Still, this plane is full of holes . . ."

("Socks would be," I heard Li Piao mutter.)

". . . And anything might wander in."

"I'll keep watching," I promised, for I knew well that a magical operation such as was contemplated might attract anything hungry for *chi.*

Twice more I saw something move, something larger than me, soft gray in color and covered with dense fuzz. It did not venture closer than the second range of hills, so I did not attack, but I did not doubt that it was building its courage.

"We have a door," called the Walker triumphantly, then, "Shit! They've moved the dogs!"

"We might have expected that," I said, backing toward my companions so as not to lose sight of whatever lurked out beyond the hills. "And they will have been alerted by the opening of this gate."

"We cannot waste *chi* to open another gate," Spilling Moonbeams said decisively. "Fluffinella, sniff out your family for us!"

She lifted the pup through the gate and stepped after. With those two committed, there was little we could do but follow and hope that this was the best course of action. I came through last, seeing that we were in the same pea-green room I had glimpsed through Fluffinella's vision.

"Walker, can you bar the gate, but leave it open for our retreat?"

"Easily," he said. "Taste the *chi* here!"

Indeed, even I could do so. It flowed into me, replenishing what I had exhausted on this journey and even a bit beyond. I could see from the brightening auras of my companions that the effect was universal.

"No wonder the gods are reluctant to share this plane!"

said Spilling Moonbeams. Her silvery hair snapped sparks as if tousled by an eldritch wind. "And no wonder Viss wants to conquer it!"

"Can someone open the door for me?" whined Fluffinella. "My family went this way."

Spilling Moonbeams made a casual gesture with her staff, and the lock popped open. She smiled, the shadowy curves of her features more solidly visible in black and dusky blue. The door swung open, and the puppy pelted through before I could order caution.

Cursing, I ran after, sword in hand. I realized that my comrades were doubtless drunk from tapping into this wellspring of *chi*. Even Li Piao was running along as if he had eaten the Peach of Immortality, his feet a good six inches above the ground. Only I retained some judgment, doubtless because even with the additional *chi*, my partially restored demon nature was less potent than what I was accustomed to.

I sprang into the air and glided after, not really flying, more like a boy pushing a scooter. In this fashion I drew even with Fluffinella.

"Take care," I cautioned her. "The gods will not relinquish your parents easily."

The others sobered enough to heed, but their eyes still sparkled as if they were on holiday. The Walker was tossing a ball of raw *chi* from hand to hand; Spilling Moonbeams had gathered hoops of tiny stars about her staff and was spinning them like the rings around a planet.

Fluffinella wagged her tail. "They're ahead. All of them and more."

The wagging ceased as she realized what that "more" must be.

"Any other scents?" I asked. "Gods? Guards?"

"I can't be sure," she admitted. "The air is thick with an awful god smell."

"Right," I said. "Walker and Spilling Moonbeams, hold back a moment. Li Piao, send the dragon spirit to scout."

The dragon reported the corridor was empty right up to where it opened into a large garden.

"A kennel," it clarified, "with giant fu dogs roaming about

loose. Shiriki is in one cage; Chamballa and their pups are in another."

"No wonder Po Shiang didn't worry too much about guards," I said, motioning for us to start that way and thinking of the massive creatures that had chased Fluffinella. "I don't suppose any of you know of a secret weakness of fu dogs?"

Heads shook all around.

"You're the expert," Spilling Moonbeams said, "unless— Fluffinella?"

The pup's tail drooped so that the feathery ends dragged behind.

"I don't know anything."

"Then we'll improvise," I said. "Remember. We're not here to fight a war. We're here to fetch Fluffinella's family."

"But how to distract the fu dogs?" I heard Li Piao say, then his old eyes twinkled. His wrinkled hands gathered *chi*, then kneaded it as I might clay. When it had solidified some, he shaped it into a quadrupedal form.

"A cat!" he said proudly. "Do fu dogs chase cats?"

If Fluffinella's bristling mane and baby growl were any indication, they did indeed. Quickly, we shaped a few more. I found that if someone gathered the *chi* for me, I could work it more skillfully than any of the others.

"You are good at that," said Spilling Moonbeams as she tossed me a glowing lump.

"Years of practice," I said depreciatingly, as a seventh cat rapidly took form.

"I think we have enough," yapped Fluffinella, interrupting our fun. "Some of the dogs are getting our scent."

"We don't want to be trapped in this corridor," the Walker agreed. He produced a couple of mesh bags from loosely woven *chi*. "Put the cats in the bags. Spilling Moonbeams and I will handle delivery."

"And when the way is clear we'll get the cages open," I added.

The Walker and Spilling Moonbeams rushed down the corridor, lifting into flight as soon as they were outdoors. A cacophony of barking told us that the cats were out of the bags.

"Come on!" I said, gesturing, for nothing less than a shout would have carried over the sudden din.

We ran. The kennel area reminded me somewhat of Origin Park in Kong Shyh Jieh. Bright outpourings of the five elements conducted *chi* into shapes vaguely like fountains. We ran over bars of primary colors, feeling them break and blend under our feet. I suspected that had I been born here, I would have known how to recognize the equivalents of flora and fauna. As it was, I was like a primitive confronted with a painting but seeing only blotches of color.

In the midst of this visual and mystical cacophony were creatures only too recognizable. Whatever the gods had done to the fu dogs in the thousand years since the last Demon War, I did not think it an improvement.

Shiriki and Chamballa had an elegance about them despite their obvious powers. These creatures were strength without elegance. They also were apparently far less intelligent, for they chased after the *chi* cats with single-minded attention. Those who spotted us became confused. Swooping above, Spilling Moonbeams and the Walker diverted these with a tossed fireball or a sarcastic meow.

I knelt by Shiriki's cage to inspect the lock.

"At last, Lord Kai," he said, not quite reproachfully. "We never gave up hope."

"Good," I said, thinking of the times that I had. "I'll have you out of here in a jiff."

"I want Po Shiang's blood," the dog growled.

"You may have to stand in line," I said, snapping the lock open. "Come on."

Li Piao had opened the other cage, and Chamballa and the pups spilled out. As they milled about my feet, there seemed to be dozens.

"How many are there?" I asked, leading the way to the corridor while Li Piao sent his dragon to retrieve the two younger demons.

"Eight," said Chamballa complacently, turning from sniffing noses with her spouse. "All healthy and bright."

"Only eight?" I said, certain I saw more.

"They multi-manifest," Shiriki said, herding a pup back into line. "It's a defense mechanism."

Pleased to learn that my recent trials had not driven me insane, I sent Li Piao to lead the way back to where we had made our gate. Then I devoted myself to herding fu pups. I was relieved that I could still recognize Fluffinella among her similarly colored siblings.

"Don't let me lose anyone," I told her.

"Right, Lord Kai!" she barked with a self-important wag of her tail.

We met no interference in the long corridors, a thing I tried to convince myself was due to the presence of Shiriki and Chamballa. Spilling Moonbeams and the Walker caught up with us just as we were funneling pups around the last bend. The two young demons were laughing, heady from excess *chi* and success.

"The gods' dogs are locked in their kennel," reported Spilling Moonbeams, "and the Walker has sealed the door tight as a drum."

"Good," I said. I would have said more, but a commotion from the front of the pack attracted my attention. A moment later, Fluffinella skidded to a halt in front of me.

"Lord Demon! Li Piao needs you right away!"

I started running, darting around the fu pups.

"Why?" I asked.

"There are some people . . ."

The pup didn't get a chance to finish before I skidded to a halt beside Li Piao. Fu Xian and Ken Zhao, Po Shiang's human lackeys, waited in the pea-green kennel room; they stood between us and our gate. The demon gambler Devor was with them.

"Long time no see, Lord Demon," he said.

Devor still looked like a human conception of a fallen angel, with his sweeping swan's wings and golden skin, but the slanting silver eyes were no longer expressionless. They looked worried, and no wonder. He and his pals were outmatched. One demon and two human sorcerers were nothing against my team—even without the fu dogs to tip the balance.

"Hello, Devor," said I, sparing a nod for each of the other two. "You don't think you're going to stop us, do you?"

He surprised me.

"No. That's what we're supposed to do, but we're not even going to try. Instead, we have shielded this room from outside observation. We want to trade you some information for a favor."

"Oh? Show me evidence of your good faith. Get out of the way, so we can start moving pups."

With the barest flutter of his wings, Devor did so. The humans were less graceful but equally prompt.

"Move 'em out, Shiriki," I ordered. "Now, Devor. What do you have for me?"

Ken Zhao looked apprehensive. "Don't tell him anything until we have his promise, Devor."

Devor gave me a demon to demon grin. "Sure, Kenny."

"What do you want?" I asked.

"We're taking a risk, meeting you like this," Devor said. "We want you to cover for us."

"Oh?"

"Make it look convincing that we tried to hold you back. Knock the humans out. Whatever it takes. Then, if you beat Viss and Po Shiang, assure the folks back home that we were on your side all along."

"You're staying here?"

Devor nodded. "There are complications. Our servitude cannot be severed just on our say-so. Were we to depart now, the consequences would be painful—if not fatal."

Chamballa was rounding up a confused and overexcited pup, so I turned to Li Piao.

"You heard what the demon wants. Can you and Spilling Moonbeams create a bomb? Make it so that either the Walker or I can detonate it. I want him to pass through last since he's the best at sealing gates."

The old gentleman nodded, a wicked twinkle in his eyes.

"Consider it done, Lord Demon."

I returned my attention to Devor.

"Now. Give me the dope. And fast."

The noble head bowed in acknowledgment.

"Kai Wren, you may have the impression that Viss and Po Shiang have solid backing for their plot. That's far from true. Viss has managed to charm and intimidate enough demons so that she does have a following, but my impression is that most of them would love an excuse to back out."

I didn't ask why they couldn't. Demons are like humans in possessing a herd instinct. Combine that with the fact that the first couple of rebels would be shredded to set an example for the rest, and Viss had a convincing argument against backsliding.

Devor went on: "Po Shiang's position is worse. Most of the major gods are happy with the status quo. They don't want the demons here and they don't share his lust for our real estate. His real backing is with the younger set, the ones who think a war will make their reputations."

I nodded. Ever since I had tasted the *chi* of Origin, I had wondered what the gods had to gain by taking Kong Shyh Jieh.

Fu Xian cut in somewhat morosely: "That's why Po Shiang needed our magical support, but he's put us on the fringes since he got the dogs. I don't think he'll need us at all once the coup is complete."

"We might even be," Ken Zhao added, "something of an embarrassment."

"And you, Devor?" I looked at the demon gambler.

He shrugged, shedding a stray pinion. "They've been using me. I didn't care at first—it kept me in *imbue*. But some masochistic streak has kept me from reacquiring the habit, and the longer my head is clear, the less I like the situation."

"So you've turned traitor."

"I prefer to think of it as reassessing the odds."

The last pup was out. Li Piao was tossing an interesting blob of multicolored *chi* from hand to hand; doubtless it contained something that would trash the room without quite killing the three who would remain behind.

"This is interesting," I said, "but not quite enough. If you don't want Viss to learn of your betrayal, tell me one thing more."

"What?" Devor's eyes narrowed into slits.

"I want to know Po Shiang's god name."

"But I don't know it," he protested.

Ken Zhao shook his head, his eyes widening with terror as he imagined Po Shiang learning of their treachery.

"Well, then," I said, motioning to my companions to pass through the gate. "We'll move on."

"I . . ." Fu Xian swallowed hard. "I may know it. I learned *a* name early in our association. It may be his. Will that be enough?"

I nodded. Spilling Moonbeams was through the gate. Li Piao had tossed his blob of preprogrammed *chi* to the Walker before stepping through the oval.

Cautiously, for spoken names can attract attention, Fu Xian conjured a pen and paper, and wrote: "Belcazzi."

I swallowed hard, filled with a rush of fear and horror that rapidly became something like delight.

Nodding to the Walker that this was sufficient, I took the paper and tucked it into my pocket. It seemed to whisper to me from the darkness.

Belcazzi.

Behind me, as I stepped through the gate, I heard the rumble of the *chi* bomb exploding.

Vibrations raced through my frame, my sight blurred. Again I was temporarily deafened, but through all that happened, I remained centered. At last, I knew my enemy's name. I knew the one who had corrupted my beloved Viss with his cordial of ambition and *chi*. I knew him, and he would die.

Belcazzi.

XIII

BELCAZZI.

I dwelled upon that name throughout all the long journey to our most recently established refuge, chewed over memories a millennium and more old as I ran with the pack of fu dogs across the planes.

We had been enemies, he and I, for he had been squire to Chaholdrudan and had taken his master's death most personally. The Demon War had ended, however, before that enmity came to a terminal resolution. With the Truce, I believed it over forever. Seems that all the Bad Old Things had not ended then, as I had naively believed.

If the others thought me silent, they also respected that silence. I might have lost much of my power, but I was still Kai Wren, Lord Demon, Godslayer. That reputation meant much to them. Thinking of Belcazzi, I wondered at the enemies those words had won for me.

I wondered, and I felt a sudden surge of pride, for I knew that however I had sought to deny it, I deserved those titles.

But Belcazzi!

It was no wonder I had not recognized him during my brief meetings with Po Shiang. Po Shiang was a tall, thin aesthete. Belcazzi manifested most commonly as a powerfully built creature somewhat like a minotaur all of brass and iron, with curving horns like scimitar blades and just as sharp. Despite this solid exterior, the pale eyes in that bovine head were shrewd and, as our demon troops had learned to their dismay, his tactical sense was anything but plodding.

Habitual shapes mean much to us who can choose our form. Belcazzi's shape during the Demon Wars proclaimed that he would batter through all that stood in his way.

What was I to make of his mandarin guise? Perhaps nothing. He might have chosen it to impress his human recruits. In that case, it held no message for his foes. However, we demons have lived alongside humanity long enough to respect the mandarins, for their training and guile permitted them to survive when emperors fell.

Those ways have vanished now, along with the emperors and their courts. A system more modern reigns where once even the least peasants knew that they lived in the center of the world, beneath the eye of Heaven. Yet the Red Army's new symbols have not won demon hearts—even as they have not won the real heart of China. We still answer to the potency of old things.

Po Shiang—Belcazzi as I now knew him to be—had donned scholar's garb. Did he seek to conceal the warrior he was, or was this a new self gestated in the thousand years since last we warred?

I mulled and I mused. Even as I did those things I knew that I was yet seeking to avoid doing what I must if I were to win this war that had been given unto me. To do that, I must remember, and when I remembered I would know that for a thousand years and more I had been a dupe.

In this state of mind, I was almost relieved to return home to a battle.

Shiriki scented the trouble first, even as the Walker was rigging one of his remarkable spheres to provide a bridge to carry the fu pups into the green-and-orange bottle.

"Trouble, Lord Kai," the great green dog said to me. "I smell gods and demons."

I did not doubt him. "How many?"

Shiriki turned his head where the Walker was keying his bridge and took a deep sniff.

"More than four."

"Of each?"

"Yes."

That was not good. On our side, we had three demons, one human sorcerer, and a mess of fu dogs. I ruled out Shiriki and Chamballa as combatants right away. They would be busy enough keeping their pups out of danger. I also could not count on Plum and the two scrub demons. Quite likely they were already dead.

"Walker," I said, "don't activate the bridge yet. There has been a new development."

I gave a quick briefing. When I was finished, Chamballa spoke: "I agree with Shiriki, but I can add more. Among the demons is Tuvoon. Po Shiang is not among the gods."

"And Viss?" I couldn't decide if what I felt was hope or dread.

"Not her," Chamballa said firmly.

"Do you recognize any other scents?" asked Spilling Moonbeams.

"Just Tuvoon."

"Good work, Chamballa," I said. "Now, this is my plan. The four of us will scout ahead. If Plum or the others need rescuing, we'll do it. Otherwise, the first order of business is staying alive. If that means abandoning the bottle, we will."

"But the wishes!" protested Li Piao.

"Our enemies don't know of them," I assured him. "Nor can they use them. We have other places we can hide. I'd rather use one of them."

"How do you think they got in?" the Walker asked.

I shrugged. "Viss was searching for me. She may have found Plum's house and searched all the bottles. She may have used some bit of god magic. You remember how much *chi* the gods have to burn. How Tuvoon got there isn't important for now."

I laughed bitterly. "Maybe Tuvoon has come to join our side."

"Do you really think that?" asked Spilling Moonbeams.

I remembered the Smoke Ghost's arrogance, how I had defeated him in a duel he thought a foregone conclusion.

"No," I answered honestly, "but we cannot completely disregard the possibility. I would never have believed that Devor would help us either."

The adult fu dogs protested that one or the other should accompany us, but I was adamant.

"We went through a lot to set you free. I'm not taking any chances with you now. If we don't make it, go to either Seven Fingers or He of the Towers of Light. Or flee now to some other plane. There's no reason for you to hang around."

Shiriki looked offended. "There is plenty of reason, Lord Kai."

Fluffinella wanted to go with us as well, but fortunately her parents quashed that. No doubt she would be formidable in time, but for now she would be just one more person to protect.

Without the fu pups, we did not need to enter the bottle via anything as obvious as the Walker's gate. Instead, I guided us in through a back entry I had kept secret until then. We emerged into thick forest and made our way as stealthily as possible to where we had made our camp.

Even a quick glance showed that Plum had not delayed in reconstructing the area's *feng shui*. A couple of large boulders had been positioned more advantageously, and the bed of a large stream had been diverted a dozen or so feet to the south. There were also a few rocks scattered apparently at random and a rather oddly angled fallen tree.

But a quick glance was all that any of us were taking. Looking down from our concealed position, I quickly dismissed any faint hopes that Tuvoon and his party had come to talk truce. They had made themselves right at home in our camp.

Four of Tuvoon's stag-beetle guards were standing watch about the fringes. The long-barreled weapons they held so easily in their upper hands did not appear to be theronic rifles, a thing for which I was deeply grateful. I wondered if Viss had refused to trust her son with the weapons.

Tuvoon himself stood in the center of the guarded perimeter accompanied by five creatures that I assumed were gods. This merry band was occupied with something they had suspended from a sturdy sapling. It swung back and forth as Tuvoon poked it with the tip of one of his guard's spears. I heard a faint squeal and realized that what was hanging there was the scrub demon Ba Wa.

My sense of irony noted immediately that the first time I had encountered Ba Wa he had been engaged in much the same game with the body of Oliver O'Keefe. This time, however, there were a few differences. For one, Ba Wa was still alive. For another, he was working for me.

Li Piao started to rush to the rescue, but I restrained him with a light touch to his arm. The Walker and Spilling Moonbeams, being demons, of course, felt no such surge of pity.

"Don't," I said. "That's what they want."

"But they don't know we're here," he protested.

"It tells us that someone is—someone they want to provoke. I would guess that Plum escaped, and they don't dare go after her."

"Why?" said Spilling Moonbeams. "She's just a human."

I felt a flash of annoyance. This was no time for silly female rivalry.

"Because she is a wizard in her own right," I said sharply, "and I'd guess that she has attuned the bottle's *chi* to her use."

The Walker had been studying the layout below. "Yes. She must have. That fallen tree has smashed one of the demon guards. It's still alive, but Tuvoon mustn't want to spare the resources to free it since it's useless to him now."

"It's a wonder the other guards don't mutiny," said Li Piao.

"They don't dare," I said. "Tuvoon is their master."

Our discussion was interrupted by a deep, rumbling sound from the hills above the camp. This slope was covered with rocks, and now those rocks were beginning to roll.

"She's awakened the dragon!" I gasped admiringly.

And the dragon emerged. It was less magnificent than the Lung Shan of my residential bottle, but then, it was younger. Scales the precise shade of lapis lazuli absorbed the sunlight so that the sinuous body glowed. Its teeth were sapphire, and its eyes the darkest shade of violet. I had been in a blue mood when I designed it, I suppose.

The blue dragon of the mountain caught the air currents and swam aloft. I thought I saw something small and black rise to meet it. Li Piao confirmed my guess.

"That's Wong Pang. Why is he still a Pekingese?"

I shrugged. "Who can figure the ways of the scrub? Plum must be down there in the vicinity from which Wong Pang came. If we're quick about it, we can get to her while the dragon keeps Tuvoon and his goons occupied."

"Let Spilling Moonbeams and me join in the fight," the Walker suggested. "We can turn ourselves invisible and what harm we cause will be credited to the dragon. In that way, we will not alert the enemy to our presence."

"Good idea," I said, "but I cannot help you. Even with our sojourn in Origin, I have little more power than a scrub."

Spilling Moonbeams had already begun to fade from sight. I heard her voice croon softly:

"Tuvoon . . ."

The name was a curse, and I recalled how Tuvoon would have taken this beautiful and dangerous creature as if she were nothing but a vessel to bear him young.

"Be careful," I said, "and free Ba Wa if you can."

The Walker nodded. Then he, too, faded from sight.

"Will they be safe?" asked Li Piao. "Can't demons and gods see invisible forms?"

"If they care to search for them," I answered. "Let us hope that these do not. Come, we don't have much time to find Plum."

During our conversation, I had kept my eye on the black, furry blot that was Wong Pang. When it landed after giving the dragon whatever message it bore, I had noted where.

We kept to the cover of the forest, Li Piao and I. I had power enough to carry the wizard when a ravine interrupted the most direct route. He concentrated on making us not so much invisible as uninteresting. As long as he maintained his spell, all but the most disciplined observers would dismiss us as things they expected to see—something no more important than a rock or tree.

In this way we rounded the meadow, crossed the rocky escarpment from which Plum had drawn this *lung shan*, and entered another stretch of forested land. As we traveled, I spared what attention I could for the battle below.

Tuvoon's demon guards were firing their rifles at the dragon, but it was taking little harm from their fire. No wonder. In the vicinity of its own terrain, a mountain dragon is a fearsome thing, a living embodiment of the area's *chi*. Although possessed of fangs and claws, its greatest power lay in its ability to command the ground itself.

I felt the first rumbles of the budding earthquake and lofted Li Piao into the air. Unattuned to the bottle, those below had no such warning.

What had been a pleasant meadow rippled like a bedspread being shaken by an attentive housemaid. The ground lifted, rippled, shook once more, and rippled flat. Flowers and grass were mostly undisturbed, but trees toppled, including the one from which Ba Wa hung.

Tuvoon launched into the air with the aplomb one would expect from Viss's son, but two of his godly companions were less prepared.

One, a chubby monstrosity with a tusked boar's head, was pinned beneath several trees. The other, a purple octopoidal thing that recalled a large beach ball possessed of a ring of bright yellow eyes and many legs, attempted to jet above the falling debris and only succeeded in becoming entangled within the limbs of a slowly falling tree.

I saw the Walker's role in both of these mishaps, but their victims did not. Tuvoon guffawed rudely at his allies' distress, his attention on the dragon. No doubt he thought fighting it good sport to divert him while he awaited my return.

"My sword is iron, Dragon!" he called as he flew into the air.

Chinese dragons are notoriously afraid of iron, but never would I have left any creature of mine so obviously vulnerable. Spilling Moonbeams did not know this, of course. She caused a rain to fall that ate Tuvoon's blade into rust in his grasp. Her shrill laughter blended with the shriek of the winds upon which the dragon swam.

The dragon spat fire, which Tuvoon parried with his armored forearm. Then their battle was joined, the dragon's coils hiding from my view the finer details. I knew, however, how I had crafted my lapis dragon, and knew also that Spilling Moonbeams's vindictive magic would play its part.

Meanwhile, Tuvoon's guards were prevented from assisting their master (had they wished to do so) by a plague of hornets that swarmed from the wood. The three gods who were not occupied with freeing themselves from the suddenly animate limbs of the fallen trees found themselves confronted by small tornadoes of mist and sand.

Li Piao and I located Plum before the battle ended. Although clad in the same artfully torn jeans and tee shirt in which she had made her escape from the Earth plane, she wore her sorceress's aspect. Never more had I seen evidence that her top hat and elaborate costumes were mere props, for with nothing more than a pocket mirror and a few pieces of raw quartz crystal she was involved in awakening the spirit of the *lung shui*, the water dragon who inhabited the closest stream.

She had marked out the appropriate trigrams from the I-Ching with dark red lipstick. Wong Pang, faithfully on guard, was the first to see our coming.

The fluffy black tail wagged welcome, but he did not yap or otherwise disturb Plum's conjurations. I did this thing, clearing my throat so as not to startle her—a bad thing with a sorcerer of any type.

"Plum?"

She looked up, and I absently noticed that her artistically cut hair could use a combing and that she had a smudge of dirt on her nose. Her hands, however, held the pattern of her spell and I could see the crystalline chain of water *chi* which connected her to the *lung shui*.

"Kai Wren?" she said.

"Let drop your spell," I answered, "and recall the lapis *lung shan*. We are here."

Her gaze sought and found Li Piao, who gave her an approving nod.

"Grandfather!" The single word held both relief and joy.

Then she looked to me once more. "If I drop the spell, will you promise to save Ba Wa?"

"It is already done," I said, gesturing. The Walker had poured healing *chi* into Ba Wa, and the scrub demon had burst his bonds and was scampering to cover beneath the aegis of a cloud of mist. "Withdraw the lapis dragon. I don't want him harmed. Li Piao, can you contact the Walker and Spilling Moonbeams?"

"I can," he replied, pulling out his scrying bowl. "What should I tell them?"

"That they should withdraw from the field. We'll never win in a direct attack, but I have something in mind."

Li Piao cocked a brow at me, but did not ask. "I'll pass on the word, Lord Demon."

For her part, Plum touched the chain that linked her to the water dragon. I heard her command it to lie still and await further orders. Then she tossed the prettiest of the quartz crystals into the water as a gift.

"I promised the *lung shan* pearls," she said. "It wasn't interested in anything else."

"A connoisseur," I said, amused. "I hadn't known that about him, but I will make good your promise."

She relaxed some and began recalling the lapis dragon.

Waiting for my *lung shan* to get clear, I studied the situation as it stood. The Walker had done his work well, as had Spilling Moonbeams. Three of the five gods were neutralized along with Tuvoon's stag-beetle guards. Still, Tuvoon and two of his deific allies remained free, and the others could be freed. I must act now if I hoped to take advantage of what the others had gained.

"Wait here," I commanded, and plummeted like an arrow to where a brace of Tuvoon's guard were battering away the last of the hornets. What I did next would gain me no honor on a human battlefield, nor, indeed, on many others, but it was necessary and fitting.

Drawing my sword from sidewise space, I plunged it where the first guard's *chi* glowed brightest. It was a killing blow, unfairly given. As when I had slain the god Rabla-yu, I tasted the dying demon's energies in the air about me. I sucked them into myself, temporarily restoring my depleted resources. Then I twisted free my blade and did the same to his companion.

I wished I could have so slain one of the gods, but killing a god isn't that easy. That's why they give titles for doing it.

The energies so gained would not last long, but they were enough to restore what I had lost since departing Origin and perhaps a bit beyond. Tuvoon had located me now, so I dared not drain another guard. Instead I scooped up one guard's rifle and aimed it at Tuvoon.

"Hello, Tuvoon. Nice of you to drop by."

His cruel smile did nothing to improve his battered appearance.

"Kai Wren. I won't call you Lord Demon, for you have barely more power than a scrub demon. Still, that was a nice trick you pulled during our last meeting. My mother was not pleased with me."

"So she sent you out to find me?"

"No. I came on my own initiative."

"Oh. She didn't think she could trust you to get it right, huh?"

That hit home.

"She was busy," he said curtly. "And I had my own score to settle."

"How'd you find me?" I asked, buying time for the others to withdraw from the field. Ba Wa had done so, but the Walker and Spilling Moonbeams continued to hover, still invisible. I could tell that they weren't going to heed my orders.

"Wenobee"—he indicated the purple octopus with a toss of his head—"tracked down your most recent lair on Earth. Then we searched the bottles. You didn't hide this one very well."

"You brought a god to Earth," I said, tut-tutting slightly. "Doesn't that violate the last treaty? Wasn't the agreement made that the Earth plane was to remain exclusively demon property?"

"Those treaties don't matter anymore," Tuvoon said brusquely. "My mother is now the law—she and Po Shiang."

"Smoke Ghost," said Wenobee, his voice thick and glottal, "why do you parley with this weak thing? Kill it or capture it and let us be gone."

I grinned at the god.

"He's afraid to," I said conversationally. "I've beaten him twice before. He's scared I'll do it again."

Tuvoon nearly solidified, he was so angry.

"I am not afraid!"

"So, come and get me."

He motioned to the others to cordon off my escape. I yawned and ran my free hand through my hair.

"Can't do it alone, Tuvoon? Got to bring on the gods, too? While you're at it, why not call for Mommy?"

Savagely, he growled, "Back, all of you. I'll take him alone."

"Is that wise?" queried another of the gods, a vaguely human-formed being that appeared to be woven from panels of multi-colored light. "He is the Godslayer."

"Shut up, Moxabanshy!" Tuvoon replied. "If you're scared to tackle him, I'm certainly not!"

Then he sprang at me, his lower body a swirl of smoke and glittering particles of dust. He didn't even draw a weapon, but the talons growing from his hands were easily the equal of most short blades—and he had ten of them.

And I?

I leveled the rifle that I had held all this time and pulled the trigger. The weapon had a fully automatic setting and I let the clip empty. It might not have been a theronic rifle, but it was loaded for demon—for me, in fact.

Solid bolts of pure energy vomited forth. They burned light-ning bolts into my retina and made the air rumble like distant thunder at their passage. When the clip was empty, Tuvoon the Smoke Ghost lay mere inches from my feet—that's how fast he had been moving when he leapt at me. His chest was a ruin; his gut as well. Below that, his smoke was dissipating. Only his face remained untouched, twisted with wrath and pain.

"Who's next?" I said, facing the gods and scooping up an-other rifle. "Want to see what else the Godslayer can do?"

Moxabanshy glanced at his comrades, then at Tuvoon. For a moment, I thought he was actually going to attack. One of my allies must have thought so too, for unsummoned by me a bolt of purest blue came forth from the sky. I heard a howling in the distance, the baying of some multiheaded monster.

"Well?" I said. "Who's next?"

Wenobee gulped air from below, rather like a jellyfish.

"I was only here to help Tuvoon."

"Then get out. I have no quarrel with you—yet."

He vanished, taking with him the guy with the boar's head.

I'd gotten into a better position, one where the Walker or Spilling Moonbeams might be able to cover me. I had no doubt about my chances taking on a god alone—even one of these punks. Still, I would if they forced me, and they seemed to know it.

Moxabanshy strolled over to inspect Tuvoon's corpse, then he glanced at me.

"I don't think I want to play just now," he said, then he glanced where the two remaining gods hovered indecisively. "Skywamish, Zvichy, pick up this mess."

Moxabanshy grinned at me. "I can think of an easier way to get you killed, Kai Wren, far easier than dealing with you and with those I sense around us."

Skywamish and Zvichy vanished, holding Tuvoon's body between them.

"I think we'll show Tuvoon's doting mother what you've done to her little boy."

Moxabanshy laughed unkindly then, and dissolved in a puff of evil-smelling, sickly yellow smoke.

When I was certain he was gone, I looked where my companions had gathered. Wong Pang growled at the remaining stag-beetle demons, but the fight had gone out of them. They could have been held by a child, much less by a particularly valiant Pekingese.

"I don't think Viss is going to be very happy," I said. "I don't think she's going to be happy at all."

Later, I popped out into Plum's house and gathered up my bottles. Typically cocky, Tuvoon had left them where he had found them. I was carefully wrapping all but two in dishcloths borrowed from the kitchen and setting them in a storage box when I felt a change in the air.

"Hello, Plum," I said without turning.

"How did you know it was me?"

"The bottle told me."

"Of course. I should have known."

She crossed to stand beside me. "I came back to get a few things. Are you almost done?"

"Almost. I took some of your sweaters out of this box, so I could use it."

"That's fine. What are you going to do?"

"Hide all but the green-and-orange one and this cut-crystal one."

"And how are you going to do that?"

"Nosy, aren't you?"

"Well"—she cocked an eyebrow at me—"last time you hid a bottle, my house got ransacked by gods and demons."

"Fair enough. I'm going to drop this box in the ocean. Moving water tends to mask scrying. Then we're going to move our temporary headquarters into this bottle." I pointed to the crystal one. "I picked it because it can contain the green-and-orange one."

"Anyone living in there?"

"No. A very old Buddhist sage did for a couple of hundred years. Then he got tired of seeking solitary enlightenment and moved into another bottle with a traditional Taoist. They've been contentedly debating finer points of religious philosophy since."

"Oh."

Plum was still looking at me. I found I rather liked it.

"And why did you come back?"

"I wanted to get some more ammo for my gun. Grandfather's dragon says the odds of us getting into a fight are pretty good."

"Oh."

I felt vaguely disappointed—about her motives, not about the prospect of a fight. I'd been rather figuring on a fight. My disappointment bothered me. I didn't really want to like Plum too much. Spilling Moonbeams was a much more appropriate partner, and the political advantages of being allied to her father could not be overlooked. I especially didn't dare spurn her in favor of a mere human.

"Better get your stuff then," I said brusquely. "I'll be ready to go in a few minutes."

"Right."

She departed, and I could hear her rummaging around somewhere upstairs. When she came down, she had a satchel in one hand and her top hat in another.

"Might as well have the trims," she said. "They help me concentrate."

"Good. Can you squeeze those two bottles in at the top of your bag?"

She tried and did, giving the green-and-orange bottle a curious glance. "It seems odd to think of Grandfather and the rest inside there."

"They're not, precisely."

"I know." She raised her dark gaze from the bottle and met my eyes with what looked like guilt. "Kai Wren?"

"Yes?"

"Your spirit sword . . ."

"Yes?" I felt a twinge of anxiety, knowing what she must be about to say.

"It's gone. I'd hidden it under the bed in my room. It's not there now."

I didn't ask if she was sure. I knew she was telling the truth. I also knew where that sword must be.

"Tuvoon didn't use it when we fought," I said, "and you know what that means."

Plum nodded, pain mixing with the guilt in her eyes.

"Viss has it," she said so softly that I could hardly hear.

"Yes. Tuvoon must have given it to her as a way to make reparations for his letting us escape with the bottles. I wouldn't be surprised if he had been searching for it when he found your house. He must have sent the sword to Viss, then come after us himself."

"You don't seem very worried."

"I am concerned," I admitted. "However, thanks to your discovery, we now know that the damned sword is in enemy hands once more."

"I'm very sorry," she said.

"You didn't know they'd come after it. I was the fool." I frowned. "Again."

I didn't like where that train of thought was leading, so I straightened my shoulders, gave her a smile, and said briskly:

"Would you take the other handle on the storage chest?"

"How heavy is it?" she asked, setting her hat on her head.

"It's not very heavy. However, I'm going to attempt to transfer us into the traveling plane. With my currently reduced power it's easier for me to move both of us and the gear if we're in physical contact."

A flurry of emotions crossed her face. I don't care what the cliché says. An Oriental is not always inscrutable—especially when she's a woman and she's mad at you.

"Why don't you just put me back into the bottle!" she said angrily.

"I thought . . . I mean, I supposed . . ."

I stopped, took a deep breath, and tried again. "I had thought you could accompany me. It's an interesting trip."

She didn't look completely mollified, but some of the anger was muted.

"And I'm to hold one end of this plastic box?"

Light began to dawn.

"Unless you would do me the honor of permitting this humble one to hold on to your ever-so-delicate hand."

"Don't overdo it," she said severely, but she held out her free hand.

I took it. There was a funny fluttering in my chest. I hoped sincerely I wasn't blushing and had a terrible feeling that I was. There was only one thing I could do, and I did it.

I got us out of there.

Once in the traveling plane, I regained my composure. Plum watched with interest when I consulted a globe.

"That looks like what the Walker used."

"It's related," I explained, "but his are better. This is just a map."

"You have it turned to England."

She leaned closer, and I could smell her perfume. Jasmine.

"No," she said, drawing back, "Ireland. I thought you were just going to dump the box in the ocean?"

"I am, but I'm going to hedge our bets a bit. I'll drop it in waters ruled by the Irish sidhe. They've made clear they don't want to get involved in our wars. That should mean they'll keep out anyone who comes poking around."

"Clever!"

"Thanks."

The journey to the Irish Sea took longer than it would have if I possessed my full powers, but with Plum's slender hand tucked in mine it ended far too quickly for me. I leaned out of the traveling plane just long enough to drop the box into the water.

"Good luck," I said, as it vanished beneath the crest of a wave.

"I hope it doesn't wash ashore," Plum said when this was done.

"It shouldn't. I've instructed the bottles to become unreasonably heavy. The chest should stay in this general vicinity."

"Good." Plum withdrew her hand from mine. "Now what?"

"Into the crystal bottle with you, Lady. Take the wishing bottle with you. I'll bring our friends in a nonce."

"And what are you going to do with the crystal bottle?"

"I thought I'd have the Walker stow it on the Sock Plane."

She laughed, having been regaled at length by her grandfather with tales of that improbable place.

"That's a good idea. Who can ever find anything in a sock drawer!"

Even the fu dogs chose to join us in our new hideout.

Now, I sat in front of a fire in a cozy stone cottage. The interior of the crystal bottle had been devoted to a fairy tale of winter. The key word was "fairy tale." Therefore, the weather was cold but not unpleasant, just perfect for sitting by a blazing fire sipping tea or hot chocolate.

I was having tea. Several others had chosen the chocolate, so the air was redolent with sweetness and spice and damp dog. Unlike the green-and-orange bottle, which I had barely finished before my troubles commenced, this bottle was an older project, well-appointed with all those luxuries that make living pleasant.

The Buddhist sage who had resided here had followed the middle path and thus did not believe in excessive deprivation. After his departure, I had restocked and commanded the servitors to keep things fresh.

My companions were near drowsing when I spoke:

"I believe that I have been less than honest with myself about the development of events, for when I study myself and how I have lived my life these past centuries, I see contradictions that I cannot resolve."

Li Piao stirred and blinked himself awake.

"What do you mean?"

"I mean that I find myself a demon who believed that demons were solitary when there was ample evidence to the contrary—even within my own knowledge. I simply chose to ignore the contradiction."

"Contradiction?" asked Spilling Moonbeams. She had again taken on her China doll shape and looked quite lovely in a robe of jade-green silk.

"You reside with your father and a host of servants. He has apprentices and customers that you both visit with as well. Devor had quite a mob of cronies. Even the Walker—who has often explored in solitude—has friends and relations he visits. Yet I lived alone but for my creations and one human."

"That is odd, now that I know you better," Spilling Moonbeams agreed. "We all believed you a recluse by choice and did not invade your privacy."

"Yes, by choice," I said, "but whose choice? I am beginning to suspect that it was not my own."

"Viss?" suggested the Walker.

"Perhaps," I agreed. "Most likely. There are other contradictions within my behavior as well. I was a warrior—a great one. Then, after my greatest battle, I became a hermit and practically a pacifist."

"We think you tired of kicking ass," Ba Wa said. "What do big shot Godslayer got to prove?"

"Yes, I can see how you would think that," I said, smiling a bit at his choice of words, "but I never recall making that choice. I just stopped fighting. I retired to my bottle and started making bottle after bottle—with an occasional interlude to make a bowl or cup. Though I shared a few, sold a few more, *why* did I keep doing it?"

"A search for perfection?" suggested Spilling Moonbeams, who, as an artist herself, might be said to know the impulses.

"Perhaps," I said, "or perhaps someone who already owned such a bottle was looking ahead to a day when she might need many more."

"Viss, again," commented the Walker.

"And why," I continued, "am I so susceptible to emotions that demons usually cannot feel? Viss herself stated that I loved Oliver O'Keefe like a brother. I did. Why? When my own sister died in long-ago battles I don't recall feeling so grieved and bereft. I accepted the loss of my parents as the way of things, yet if Li Piao should die, I would mourn as if he were my own grandfather."

Li Piao looked only a bit surprised at this confession. Perhaps humans recognize affection more easily than demons because they feel it so easily.

"Could it be that your solitary existence made you more prone to affection?" he suggested.

"I don't think so," I said. "I suspect ensorcellment. When I was changed human, I felt as a human. What if something was changed within me long ago so that I would love as a human even while functioning as a demon?"

"But why?" protested Spilling Moonbeams, vaguely disgusted by my admissions. No wonder. As I had often discussed with Viss and Tuvoon, demons feel hate more easily than love. We have loyalties and codes, but we view love as a weakness peculiar to humanity.

"Why?" I answered. "I think to make me vulnerable to manipulation. Look what loving has done to me! I have risked my life and property to avenge Oliver O'Keefe—not out of indignation that my rights were trespassed upon, but out of love! Look what my love for Viss has done to me! I have been twisted this way and that, ignored advice and warnings, and been dispossessed of almost all I value."

I was shouting now. Chamballa looked up from where she

was dozing with the fu pups, Fluffinella nursing sleepily from the bottom of her paw.

"A bit quieter, Lord Kai, if you please."

"Sorry."

Plum said hesitantly, "Then you love Viss?"

"I did, once," I said honestly. "Now that I know it to be a delusion of sorts, I'm not quite certain what I feel for her. Hate. I think."

"Oh."

The Walker broke the long silence that followed.

"Your theories are interesting, Kai Wren, but is there any way to prove them?"

"Li Piao might be able to do so," I said. "If he can scry into my past. There will be spells set to block it but . . ."

"But I am getting very good at this," the old man said, "and if you will add a drop or two of your blood to my usual mixture of water and oil, I think it can be done."

He worked for half an hour before he got the answers we wanted. There were spells set to block him, but he got past them. Even then the images were patchy and vague. Still, they were enough to confirm what I had guessed.

Viss, with the help of Belcazzi, had neutralized me, then given me a compulsion to create as many bottles as I could. They had been planning even then, but there had been no rush; there had been too many details to get just right. Why worry about speed when you are nearly immortal and detail work may mean the difference between success and failure?

When I was turned human their control spell had become uncoiled since it had been linked to my demon *chi*—to my soul. We also learned something I had not even suspected. I had not found Shiriki and Chamballa by accident. They had been sent to gain entry to my home and to keep an eye on me.

Viss and Po Shiang hadn't figured on the fu dogs' changing sides.

"They were cruel to us, Lord Kai," said Shiriki simply. "They left us starved and homeless. They compelled us to serve one we believed an anathema to all creation."

"Thanks," I muttered.

"You," Chamballa continued, "gave us home and food and

freedom. Our only sorrow was that away from Origin we could not breed. And when we were permitted to return, the gods perverted even that."

She licked the closest of the drowsing pups in apology.

"You didn't want pups?" asked Plum.

"We did," said Shiriki, "but not born as slaves and breeding stock for gods. We wanted them to live as Lord Kai let us live— as companions and friends."

"They stole us," Chamballa said, "because we would not let them into the bottle to harm you. Po Shiang knew old ways to compel us, and these he used in addition to chloroform, but he learned quickly enough that he must keep us prisoner or we would flee."

I felt immensely honored.

"You'll have a home with me once this madness is ended," I promised.

"We know," Shiriki said.

I realized everyone was staring at me, even Wong Pang, who had, till that point, been sound asleep on the hearth rug at Plum's feet.

"What's wrong?" I asked, and my own voice sounded strange to my ears.

Without a word, Plum handed me one of her ubiquitous *feng shui* mirrors. I looked into it and froze—a demon's face looked back at me, blue of skin, with black patches about the eyes. I realized that I was taller, that a hand with talons curled about my teacup.

I was myself again, with my demon *chi* coiled hot in my belly.

"The last of the spell is broken," said Li Piao, and I knew as I would not have a moment before that he was channeling the dragon from the bowl. "As long as you were ignorant of its existence, the spell supplied an impediment to keep you from reclaiming yourself."

"I am reborn," I announced, "and ready to go after those who have used me these thousand years."

The Walker smiled fiercely. "Let's get in touch with my uncle and Spilling Moonbeams's father. It's time we learned what's been going on back home."

XIV

WE WENT AFTER the gods at dawn, backed by the forces of He of the Towers of Light and Seven Fingers. We'd planned our move carefully, choosing a time when Viss was due at a meeting with some holdouts to her cause. The meeting was being held in her bottle, and I planned to keep her from interfering with us by the simple expedient of sealing all means of entry and egress from her bottle once the meeting commenced.

She might not even know what I had done, but if she did, she was going to be rather angry.

"Oh, why can't we just leave her in there?" said Spilling Moonbeams wistfully as I set the seal in place. Viss had not bothered to protect the mausoleum beyond routine wards, so certain was she of her power.

"It would be a violation of her civil rights," responded Seven Fingers.

Although I had turned invisible for the journey, he had escorted me there since his presence would not be questioned and would shield me to some extent. Spilling Moonbeams had come with him as a matter of course—or perhaps of privilege. He of the Towers of Light and the Walker had taken the rest of our group via a roundabout route to where we knew Belcazzi had his headquarters.

"As if Viss hadn't violated Kai Wren's rights!" Spilling Moonbeams exclaimed indignantly.

Seven Fingers's tone became parental and admonitory.

"Laws do not exist only until the other side breaks them. They exist *despite* the other side's behavior. The alternative is chaos or worse."

"Worse?"

"A situation where the strongest make the rules—rules that are only to their advantage and are meant solely to entrench their position."

Spilling Moonbeams might have her full share of arrogance, might be the favored child of a powerful demon, might know herself beautiful beyond belief, but she was not such a fool as to forget that Viss had numbered her among those inferior.

"I wonder what place I would have in Viss's new order," she said thoughtfully.

"Tuvoon the Smoke Ghost's bride most certainly," Seven Fingers said. "With him slain . . . That would be an interesting question. She might ostracize you for not taking her son's part."

"As if my only value was to breed!" Spilling Moonbeams said angrily. "You'd think that Viss could see farther than that."

"Mothers have their blind spots," Seven Fingers said mildly.

"As do fathers?" She smiled at him. "When we were in Origin, Father, I felt such power—the *chi* was unlimited. No wonder Viss wants access to that place."

"Unlimited *chi* may not be the asset that it would seem," replied the smith, "but I would like to see the reproductive problem solved."

I spoke for the first time in this exchange, for although I had been busy, I also had been enjoying the byplay of these two.

"I have some thoughts on how to solve the problem," I said, setting the bottle back into its niche in the mausoleum, but though they questioned me, I refused to say more.

"First, let us deal with the gods. If we fail there, the rest is moot."

"True," said Seven Fingers somberly, and we made our way from that place to another.

There are conduits between Origin and Kong Shyh Jieh, and these have been contested points many times in our history. After the last Demon War, these points were sealed and locked with rituals that required cooperation on both sides to open them. This truce had held a thousand years and, indeed, had not yet been officially violated.

Belcazzi and Viss had gotten around this difficulty by crafting summoning rituals that would carry a single individual back and forth. They were expensive and exhausting—thus the desire for my bottles—but they did work. Since Belcazzi could not cross back and forth at will, he had established a headquarters. There were few places on Kong Shyh Jieh where his presence would not be instantly detected. The most logical of these—and the one he had chosen—was within Origin Park.

Using a deific version of our *shen* coins, Belcazzi had transported sufficient *chi* from Origin to permit him swiftly to construct a subsurface lair. It was well disguised, but working with He of the Towers of Light, Li Piao had pinpointed it within a matter of hours.

"It lies beneath the Speaker's Rostrum," HE told us. "A good choice, for it obviates the need to build a concealing structure. Since the Rostrum is also the site of a great many gatherings—concerts, dramatic performances, and the like—any movement of troops or gear could be done under that guise and no one would be the wiser."

"Is that where Viss has stored the weapons she stole from the Armory of Truce?" I asked.

"Yes."

"On Kong Shyh Jieh?"

"Yes."

"Wouldn't someone have noticed the unauthorized traffic?" asked Plum.

HE smiled at her. "Demons are like humans in that if somebody moves about with sufficient confidence and importance, we assume that they must know what they are doing."

Plum nodded. "You're very like us, aren't you?"

"And very unlike," HE said, "as you will most certainly learn."

While we were sealing Viss's bottle, HE had been directing the erection of a barrier around the park. Our purpose was simple. We had established that all the gods on Kong Shyh Jieh were in that place at this time. We did not want them to flee. Also, we did not desire that any other participants join us, for we could not be certain on whose side they would fight.

Superficially, Origin Park is quite like Origin, but although filled with abundant *chi*, it lacks the heady superabundance that we had encountered on Origin itself. This was to our advantage. The gods would be working with fewer resources than they were accustomed, while we would have more. Yet that more would not be sufficient to play havoc with our thoughts and judgment.

Or so I hoped. So many of our tactics were based on hope and supposition. In reality, we were badly outclassed. Even with the forces Seven Fingers and He of the Towers of Light had brought, we were no match for gods.

As a result of Viss's spell, I had never built a personal army, so my forces were limited—all my servitors were tied to their bottles and bowls. What I could gather here consisted of two humans, two fu dogs (Shiriki and Chamballa had insisted on coming, but had agreed to leave the pups behind), and a band of scrub demons recruited by Ba Wa. I was uncertain what to count Wong Pang, since he adamantly refused to be anything other than a fluffy, black Pekingese.

Our situation did not look good. We had been unable to ascertain exactly whom Belcazzi had at his disposal, for any detailed scrying would alert his defenses. For the same reason, we had not been able to tell exactly where the stolen weapons were hidden. Cursory scrying had not revealed them. We dared not do more.

Thus, when all barriers were in place and the troops were arrayed, I called out in stentorian tones:

"Belcazzi! Come forth. Your hour of reckoning is at hand."

Histrionic, I know, but circumstances rather demanded such words.

Nor did Belcazzi disappoint. Shaped as a minotaur with a

head of steel and horns of needle-tipped bronze, he appeared on the Rostrum.

The Rostrum is a simple structure, an oval lozenge of polished stone four feet high, the edges decorated with bas-relief sculptures depicting great events in the history of Kong Shyh Jieh. There's a frieze devoted to my slaying of Chaholdrudan and there had been talk of adding one depicting the slaying of Rabla-yu.

Storage areas and such are underneath, dug beneath the ground and accessed by tall doors at the base of sloping ramps. The doors are big enough to admit large pieces of stage scenery and would certainly have admitted Belcazzi, but he eschewed them to appear before us in a thunderous wash of fire and smoke.

That set the tone. A moment later, smaller explosions heralded the appearance of other gods. I recognized Moxabanshy, Wenobee, Zvichy, Skywamish, and the guy with the boar's head. There were at least a dozen of the monster fu dogs along with a horde of things that resembled sheep with acid dripping from their writhing wool and six-inch fangs.

There was no discussion, no negotiation. All knew that the point for such was past. So, without even a word of command, Belcazzi charged directly at me.

I fired a full clip from a rifle Seven Fingers had given me—hit, too, but there was no effect beyond making Belcazzi laugh as if he'd been tickled.

"You'll need to do better than that, Kai Wren," he bellowed.

I tried, pulling my sword from sidewise space while commanding his right hoof to turn to stone. It grayed a little, but he gave it an irritated shake and came on.

As I waited for him to close, I fired off spell after spell: Fire Fall, Water-in-the-Lung, North Windstorm, Pale Lightning. He shook them all off, though the water spell made him cough.

I saw him try a spell, too. Something in an ominous shade of lime green formed at his fingertips, then dissipated. I rejoiced, for I knew that Plum was doing her job.

She and HE had worked out a process by which she could use her *feng shui* manipulations to render ineffective the dreadful *chi*-sapping green fire of the gods. If the gods could use that, the battle would be over before we had a chance. But now I had proof that she could negate it and, hidden as she was beneath a caul of unnoticeability, the faithful Wong Pang guarding her, she should be able to continue negating it.

Belcazzi reached me, but he could not use his horns as long as I kept him outside the reach of my blade. He wasn't all bullheadedness, though; his work as Po Shiang proved that. With an annoyed gesture, he flicked a theronic rifle out of nothingness and stepped back to take aim. Needless to say, I didn't wait around.

Instead, I launched myself into the air, coming down behind him, and scoring a broad slice in his hide. My blade broke in the process, but I had been prepared for that and pulled another out as he was turning. His shot went wild, destroying a section of the Rostrum and taking one of the acid sheep along with it.

I cleared out again, jumping over a fallen scrub demon and noting with a gladness that surprised me that it was not Ba Wa.

The gods had not broken out the theronic weapons in any force yet, probably conserving them against the planned coup in their homeland. Still, one or two were in evidence, and I silently hoped that the Walker would be able to carry out his own mission of locating the cache and sealing it.

Continuing to dodge the shots that Belcazzi sent after me, I caught sight of Devor in the company of Po Shiang's two human dupes. The three lay half-buried in a pile of bodies, but when I glanced at their auras I saw that they still lived. Badly wounded, then, or feigning death in the hope of surviving the battle and then claiming alliance with the winning side. Quite a gamble, I thought, for not all the fighting was person to person. They could easily be slain by a stray spell or weapon burst.

As Belcazzi closed once more, I glimpsed Chamballa tangled fang and claw with a monster fu dog, of Spilling Moonbeams shedding a cold hard light into the eyes of Moxabanshy, of Ba Wa coiled within the tentacles of Wenobee. I had no chance to interfere, no time to help, for Belcazzi was upon me once more.

He'd grown an extra set of hands and was using one set to ready the theronic rifle while he worked a spell with the other. I tangled the rifle with a glob of Contracting Spider Silk, but that left me vulnerable to the Comet of Ill Omen he targeted on me. It hit me squarely in the left shoulder, leaving a bad burn and knocking me on my ass. That turned out to be lucky, because my head wasn't there when one of the acid sheep took a chomp at it.

I rolled out of the way and, while flying clear, assessed our situation. I'd thought we were at least holding our own, but now that I could see I realized the truth.

We were losing, and it was imperative that we win. There was but one choice, and I made it without regret or delay.

Touching the green-and-orange bottle with the hand that did not wield my sword, I spoke the strange and awful keyword that would trigger the wishing aspect of the bottle. When I felt the bottle acknowledge my command, I said aloud, but not with any great volume:

"I wish that all the gods and their minions, including Belcazzi and his followers, be barred from this plane now and henceforth, this barring to be absolute and without end, to revoke any previous or future invitations or summons, and to last until I, Kai Wren, the one known as Lord Demon, Godslayer, and the Bottlemaker, do so revoke it. So I wish it, and so it shall be."

And so it was.

The gods vanished in an eyeblink, in mid-swing, slash, or shot. The monstrous fu dogs vanished as well, but Shiriki and Chamballa remained, proving beyond a doubt that they were no longer under the gods' control.

There were many cries of surprise and shock, accompanied by not a few of delight and relief when this happened. Li Piao ceased hurling lightning bolts and looked at me.

"What . . ." Then he saw where my hand rested upon the green-and-orange bottle, and he understood. "You used a wish to send them away."

"We were losing," I answered simply, not just to him, but to them all. "There was no choice. My only regret is that to some it will seem like a coward's solution. Belcazzi was a foe who deserved more."

He of the Towers of Light grunted. "Seemed like an intelligent solution to me. I wonder that you waited so long to employ it."

"My resources are limited," I said, "and I entertained a hope that we could win without using them."

"Did you wish Viss away, too?" asked Plum eagerly.

I shook my head. "Viss of the Terrible Tongue is a demon problem. We must deal with her by our own laws."

"But she has been trying to break those laws!" the human protested, unaware that she echoed Spilling Moonbeams's words of maybe an hour—was it only that long?—ago.

"There is no law against trying to become absolute ruler," corrected He of the Towers of Light, "if you can convince the rest of us to follow."

Plum shrugged and straightened her top hat.

"Demons! Sometimes I think I'll never understand you."

"I anticipated that you would say something like that," said HE, and she colored.

I interrupted, though I was greatly amused by this exchange.

"My seal upon Viss's bottle will not last forever. I suggest that we send summons to all of demonkind to gather here in Origin Park and witness our resolution."

Ba Wa leapt forward. He was smeared with ichor in a curious shade of purplish gray, but otherwise seemed hale.

"I do it, Lord Demon! I fetch 'em all here, slick as shit!"

"Then the job is yours, Ba Wa. Enlist some of your fellows to help you. I will pay in *shen* coin."

The scrub demon nodded and vanished.

"Good," said Seven Fingers. "I will go to the mausoleum and bring Viss's bottle here."

"It is warded against removal," I warned him.

The massive demon smiled. "Then I will bring the mausoleum as well, if I must."

He departed, Spilling Moonbeams with him.

"And what would you have the rest of us do, Kai Wren?" asked HE.

"Succor the wounded, gather the dead for burial." I looked at the ruined walls about me, at the gaping holes torn by theronic rifle bolts, at the pools of blood and ichor. "And clean up this mess. It looks like a charnel house."

"It has been," said HE simply, "and I fear it shall be again."

*   *   *

We cleaned, but we did not repair, for it was essential that evidence of the battle remain. The corpses of the few slain gods puddled into goo after I made my wish, but the corpses of the demons remained. These we displayed upon platforms that HE constructed from light and afterthought.

Assisted by a half dozen scrub demons, Plum did some quick relandscaping. Now all who entered the park must pass close to where the dead were displayed and the *feng shui* of the park itself emanated sorrow and regret.

In answer to the messages that Ba Wa sent out, demons filed into Origin Park at the Hour of the Rooster. Some arrived in clusters, some in twos or threes, some alone, but all looked upon our dead, all gathered in the natural amphitheater facing the Rostrum.

I read their reactions in the subtle shading of their auras: curious, nervous, excited, angry, afraid, horrified.

I cannot say for certain whether all the residents of the demon realm not currently entrapped within Viss's bottle were there, but to me, the focus of all their attention, it seemed to be so.

Lord Swizzlediz stood in the midst of a crowd of admirers and hangers-on. Stormmiller stood alone and watchful. Night Bride's multiple eyes gleamed with fanaticism and Icecap's with nothing at all. A band of scrub demons milled about, some wailing loudly for their slain kindred, others holding their silence but radiating a curious pride that so many of their number were among those to die in a battle with gods.

Many shapes, many sizes, many colors, demonkind gathered and turned their vari-shaped faces to study me. From where I stood on the Rostrum, letting them look upon me and make their conjectures, I heard mutterings from the crowd and knew that until that moment many had thought me dead, others gone mad, still others committed to Viss's cause.

When HE signaled that the last latecomers were straggling in, I began my speech. Simply, eloquently, I summarized the events that had brought us to that point. I gestured to the mute testimony of recent battle on the Rostrum and its environs. I reminded them of Viss and her plans, told them of her alliance with Belcazzi.

There's an advantage to orating for demons, if you're telling the truth. Too many of us have tricks or devices that enable us to tell honesty from falsehood. They don't protect against misleading emphasis—that's how Viss managed—but they do spare one from tedious accusations.

I finished by saying:

"There is no question that Viss must be dealt with. The only question is how we shall do so. Many of you were content to follow her. Perhaps many of you are still so prepared. If so, I shall step down and let you call her queen, although I shall never do so."

From the crowd a voice called out: "I suppose you want us to follow *you* now!"

I shook my head. "No. Not at all. However, no matter what this assembly decides, I have my own score to settle with Viss. If I do so with your support, all the better. I have no real desire to spend the next hundred years cleaning up vendettas."

"Viss offered us Origin and the chance that the next demon children would be as strong as our most powerful ancestors," called someone else (Pigeon Eyes, I thought). "What do you have to offer?"

"I offer," I said without a pause, "to remake the essential *chi* of the Demon Realm so that no more degenerate children are born. Moreover, I offer to do so in such a fashion that these children will be as resourceful as any demon who has ever lived—whether born before the Exile or after."

I had their attention now.

"I have the power," I said, "to remake the Demon Realm so that it would precisely duplicate the Origin plane, but I do not desire to do so."

A tumult arose at these words—some accusing me of exaggerating, some of bragging, some simply demanding clarification. These last I chose to answer.

"I have spent the last one hundred and twenty years constructing three wishes of almost absolute power. I will employ one to restructure the *chi* of the Demon Realm. My reason for not extending the wish to give us equivalent *chi* to Origin is twofold.

"The first reason is simple. I do not know what the ramifications would be for the universe at large. That much *chi* must come from somewhere. The questions we must consider are where and what it will mean to us. Unless you are willing to wait a hundred years while I do the research to answer these questions, I do not think such a wish would be prudent."

Relative silence met this declaration. We all knew how difficult was the task that had faced those first Exiles. No one but the most foolish of the scrub demons believed that Kong Shyh Jieh could become as Origin without cost—perhaps a terrible one.

"My second reason," I continued, "is that I believe that demons since the Exile have become a different people—a people who are more resourceful, more creative, even more intelligent than those who were exiled from Origin."

I glanced at He of the Towers of Light, one of the few remaining of those Exiles, but far from disagreeing with me, he was nodding in agreement.

"I have visited Origin," I went on, "albeit briefly. The wash of energy was so powerful that I could hardly think straight. Moreover, we have evidence in the actions of the gods themselves. They have done little since our peoples separated. We have furnished a barren plane, created a new and multifaceted culture, learned to interact with humans and the native spirits of the Earth. The abundant *chi* of Origin is a curse—a trough that fattens pigs. We all know that the only thing a fattened pig is good for is slaughter.

"Therefore, while I will use a wish to make over the essential *chi* of the Demon Realm so that our unborn children will no longer suffer, I will not do any more. The wish will be made before I face Viss, so that the benefits you accrue will not be contingent on my winning—only on your permitting me to face Viss in single combat.

"Consider my offer. Discuss it among yourselves. At the beginning of the Hour of the Dog, I will ask you to vote. A vote of 'Yes' accepts my offer and permits me to deal with Viss on my own and with no vendettas to follow. A vote of 'No' will reject my offer now and for all time. I still will deal with Viss . . . and also with any who care to trouble me."

Without answering any of the questions that were shouted at me, I turned my back and descended into the caverns beneath the Rostrum. He of the Towers of Light and Seven Fingers had agreed to deal with the inevitable chaos. I was content with this. They were wise and respected. Moreover, they knew I would not compromise and so would make no compromises in my name.

"How did it go?" asked Plum. She and her grandfather had chosen to remain beneath the Rostrum and watch the proceedings within the dragon bowl.

"You know as well as I," was my answer. "I think they will support me. A few radicals, eager to make their names, will come after me someday. If I survive Viss, I'll be in good odor to deal with them."

"And your reputation," said the Walker, shimmering in through a wall, "will go up another notch or two."

"True," I said, "though I have yet to see what good that reputation does me."

I spent most of the period of debate resting and meditating. However the vote turned out, I would be fighting Viss soon. For that, I needed a cool head.

Fifteen minutes into the Hour of the Dog, Spilling Moonbeams appeared.

"The vote is taken, Lord Demon," she said, kowtowing before I could stop her. "By a three-quarters majority, the demons have agreed to accept your gift and to let you settle matters with Viss—if you can."

I grinned wryly at her. "There is that, isn't there?"

"There is," she said solemnly. "The reasons of the quarter who did not vote for you varied—at least as debate revealed. Some felt you were niggardly with how you would employ the wish. They would have you wish the Demon Realm to hold the power of Origin and leave the consequences to others."

"Tough!" said I.

"Others had relatives in conference with Viss or truly desired her as queen. These may be your enemies someday."

"I'll deal with that as need arises," I said. "Maybe I'll pay

Ba Wa to drop rocks on their heads. My worry now is Viss. Is the barrier in place?"

"It is," she said. "It walls off two-thirds of the Rostrum top as an arena. Once you enter, you will be sealed in place."

I looked over at the bottle I had made for my beloved teacher, Viss of the Terrible Tongue. Did she know yet that it was her prison? I suspected so.

"Then let us go. There is no need for us to wait. I will make the wish, then I will fight."

"You'll have quite an audience," the Walker predicted, "most of whom will be framing speeches to explain to Viss how they were really on her side all along."

"I know," I said. "Let's be about it."

The Hour of the Dog was half over before I had finished speaking to the assembled demons and making my wish. Then I privately thanked those who had supported me without question: Ba Wa, Wong Pang, He of the Towers of Light, Seven Fingers, Spilling Moonbeams, the Walker, and, of course, Plum and Li Piao. With their good wishes in my ears, I strode through the barrier in the center of the arena.

Using lore known to none but me, I lifted the seal on the bottle, lifted it to permit only one egress. I could not force her out, but she did not disappoint me. As soon as the way was clear, Viss of the Terrible Tongue streamed forth in a fury of red steam and took solid form upon the Rostrum.

She wore the shape that I had least resistance to, the lovely young woman with eyes of dark power and a body of lithe strength. By this, I knew that she had learned—whether through divination or natural cunning—who was her enemy. Therefore, I wasted little breath on speeches.

"Viss, you have wronged me. Our people have agreed to let us settle this between ourselves without interference. Surrender to me now and accept banishment to some plane from where you will never return, or fight me. Only by my death will you win your freedom."

She surveyed the crowd, seeing no doubt many who had cheered her every statement just the day before. The gaze she cast upon them was contemptuous, but the one she turned to me was filled with sorrow.

"You killed my son, Kai Wren."

"Yes."

"You banished my allies."

"Yes."

"Why? You were always the favorite of my pupils."

"Maybe so, but I have no wish to be your lapdog."

"A pity. Were you less proud, someday you might have been my king."

"Is that intended to tempt me?"

"No. We are past that. I was just stating the truth."

Then, without warning or declaration, as I had known she would, yet even so, almost missed, Viss drew my spirit sword from sidewise space and lunged at me.

I dodged. I could do little else. Unlike my duel with Tuvoon, now that I had resumed my full *chi* the blade had power to slay me if Viss landed a solid hit. I might permit her a nick or a light slash, but nothing more.

My weapon was by no means as potent. Seven Fingers had once forged a spirit sword attuned to Viss, but it had been stolen along with the other weapons from Truce. Even as I dodged her thrust, I wondered if the vulnerability that her spirit sword offered might have been one of the main reasons Viss orchestrated that raid.

I would never be able to ask, for when this fight was over one or the other of us would be dead.

Knowing that my skill with a sword could not equal hers, I concluded that I must resort to magic. This was a risky choice, for Viss's honor was such that she would not introduce magic against a weaker opponent, but once it was introduced she possessed more than a few tricks of her own—though I was the greater in the Art.

Coming up from the floor after dodging her second strike, I raised my blade to parry a third. Simultaneously, I fanned my fingers, coating the surface of the Rostrum with a substance both slick and sticky.

Viss lunged. Viss slipped. I dared hope that she might fall as her right leg overextended. Faintly, I was aware of the roars of the crowd, but my entire universe was centered in that moment, so centered that I was only faintly aware of my own arm bringing around my blade to parry—or to attack—as need demanded.

With a contemptuous snort, Viss aborted her lunge and leapt into the air. When she came down again, her feet were clawed like those of a harpy. My faint hopes that the sticky surface would restrain her vanished as she continued her attack—apparently, she had counteracted that, too.

Not bothering to banish my first spell, I tried another gambit. I shifted my shape until I resembled Tuvoon the Smoke Ghost. I had hoped she would balk at attacking her dead son; I was wrong. If anything, her attack became more ferocious. Since I possessed Tuvoon's appearance, but not his facility with a body of smoke, I must needs swiftly relinquish this form and return to one more familiar.

During all of this, I had kept pressing with my blade as much as possible, but Viss parried my attacks as if they were nothing. Increasingly, I was held to defense, and even that was weakening.

Viss drew first blood from my forearm, a slight wound in normal circumstances, but the spirit sword traced a burning trail that transformed each blood drop to acid. She drew second blood as well, a short cut that bounced off my rib. If it hadn't, the blade would have punctured my lung.

I spared some *chi* to give myself an armored carapace and greaves on calves and thighs, only then realizing how severely the two wounds from the spirit sword were draining my *chi*. If I did not defeat Viss soon, she could switch to pure defense while my life's energy drained drop by bloody drop.

Frantically, fearing that the tactic would have as little effect, I generated a flurry of attacks as I had against the god Belcazzi.

I bombarded Viss with firestorms and lightning bolts, sent a miniature tornado to twist her from her feet and a hail shower to batter her. As I lunged and was parried, parried and beat past her guard to land a thin slice along her hip, I, too, suffered from the attacks, but less than did my opponent.

However, she did not lack her own power. With a single adamant gesture, she canceled my magics.

I might have cast more, but hail adhering to the substance of my earliest spell had cobbled the arena floor with ice. Simultaneously, we launched into the air. I grew wings, but Viss had the power to ride the air currents without them.

Her next attack sent a shower of my wing feathers to the floor. I summoned winter's cold to diminish the air's thermal currents, and we both sank downward. When we were scant inches from the ice-covered floor, I essayed a powerful beat of my wings and surged forward.

With my blade I parried her attacks, even as I shifted shape, lengthening my arms until my free hand could wrap around her delicate human throat. I squeezed, while I pressed her back onto the ice where she could not get purchase for a return thrust with that deadly spirit sword.

Harpy talons raked against my armor. Breath coming short, Viss shifted shapes, seeking to escape my grasp: a piteous child, a venomous serpent, a tiger, a flea. I shifted the shape of my hand, accommodating each change, preserving some *chi* to counter her increasingly creative forms, some of which sought to slay me, others to fool me into letting go. She became a horse, a dragon, a goldfish, a chunk of sharp obsidian, a bit of slime, a thorn-covered vine, a stinging wasp.

To each I held, though I was torn and bloodied, and every muscle in my body cried that death would certainly be preferable to such continued punishment. And with every moment, I grew weaker.

Viss had let the spirit sword fall in her initial panic, for a snake or a flea cannot hold a weapon. She realized her error now and groped after it, but though I straddled her and strangled her, I had not forgotten that deadly blade. My free hand still pinned it to the ice and at my will the ice was taking it, encasing it, enclosing it in solid glass.

Screaming in terrible rage, Viss lifted both of us from the ice on a fountain of fire, dragging me into the air by the hand that I would not release from her throat. She knew the spirit sword was lost to her. My hold on her throat was unrelenting, but I could not quite break her neck. My sword arm was free now, so I brought my blade into play once more.

She lacked a sword, but parried with an arm covered in

iron. I struck sparks, sometimes I drew blood. From memory of our many lessons, I recalled what she had taught me and turned it against her. Yet, I doubted that this would be enough.

Then, suddenly, we fell back onto the arena floor. The hail had melted beneath Viss's fire, but the prison I had conjured still held the spirit sword in its glassy embrace. Aching in every limb, I believed this fall one more trick of Viss's, until I saw her aura and knew the truth. She was beaten, her *chi* depleted, her body exhausted, her weapon taken.

She had lapsed at last into the form in which she had entered the arena, but the young woman was no longer beautiful, even to my eyes. Her skin was gray with fatigue and her eyes bloodshot, red, and filled with pain. From those eyes, she looked up at me and her bruised mouth spoke:

"Kill me, Kai Wren. If you ever loved me, kill me here and now. Tuvoon is gone. My dreams are as dust. I do not care to live."

"And if I refuse?"

"I cannot suicide. It is against my nature. You will have condemned me to a life I can no longer bear."

I looked out into the milling crowd of demons beyond the barrier. Ugly expressions were plentiful, and ugly thoughts, too. Viss had insulted and manipulated them all. They might have forgiven her for that, but she had failed them as well. For that there could be no forgiveness.

"There might be others who would be happy to grant you your death if I refuse."

Viss of the Terrible Tongue looked out at the throng and spat contemptuously. Her spittle was pink with blood. Her breathing came only with pain.

"Them? Would you prefer to have me die at their hands when I might have at yours?"

"I might."

"But you said that you loved me!"

She looked so genuinely puzzled that I was vividly reminded that Viss was a demon—capable of hatred, but not love, at least as humans knew it. She truly believed that my admission of love gave her power over me, and she sought to use that power to force me to do her bidding. In this way, even in defeat she would have her victory. Not such a small thing for a demoness who had been ranked among the most dangerous of our kind.

"I did love you."

"Then do this last office for me, Kai Wren. Kill me! Why did you enter this arena if not to kill me?"

"You left me no choice, Viss. If I did not confront you, then you would have continued to hunt me, and innocent people would have been hurt."

"You do not deem yourself innocent?"

"No," I answered bitterly. "I have been a fool. You and Belcazzi used me, and I was too stupid to see."

The emotion that filled those bloody eyes was not pity, but it was as close to it as a demon could come.

"Kai Wren, we made certain that you would be too stupid to see. How can you blame yourself for that?"

"I do. That's all."

She smiled and shook her head, once again the teacher I had known and trusted.

"Don't blame yourself, Kai Wren. Don't. You are free now of the compulsions we laid upon you. Make what you will of your life."

I studied her, nodded, then lifted my blade and took her head as neatly and cleanly as she herself had taught me. Viss had a moment's warning, for none better knew my style, but she did not protest, did not offer any defense. I killed her as she had asked, my final gift to one whom I had sincerely, and with most undemonlike intensity, loved.

XV

IT WAS OVER. Viss of the Terrible Tongue lay dead at my feet. Beyond the barrier, a crowd cheered me, as crowds always cheer the victor. In their cries I heard fear, ambition, greed, and perhaps some relief, but no real joy. Demons don't know joy, just as they don't know love.

Seven Fingers was waving for me to come and acknowledge the crowd. I recalled the last time someone had insisted that I give the crowd its due. I'd just killed the god Rabla-yu. Then the one insisting had been Viss. Now there was no one I cared to obey in that fashion.

I looked at Seven Fingers and shook my head. Then I vanished.

I brought myself into being within the blue bottle that was my home. Back in the Demon Realm, evening was rapidly becoming night, but here the sun was high, a permanent noon.

Rebuilding was under way. There was a sky above, the sound of waves in the distance. The battle scars in the vegetation were healing. I could sense the darting, delighted presences of the invisible servitors as they greeted me.

My palace was still in ruins, of course, and the Lung Shan no longer dwelled beneath the mountains I had created to evoke a Taoist painting. My ogres and milkweed fairies were gone as well, along with nearly every living creature in that self-enclosed ecology.

There was much for me to do, but my contemplation of where to begin was interrupted by a fearsome howling deep within the mist-shrouded peaks. Two deep howls and a chorus of howls more shrill. I looked in that direction and smiled.

Breaking through the clouds was a streak of jade green and one of cinnabar orange. In their wake, like sparks trailing a meteor, came smaller streaks in sherbety mixtures of orange and green. The fu dogs were coming home, and my heart lifted.

I crossed the fields to greet them, meeting them in a field bright with flowers suddenly burst into bloom.

"Welcome," I said, bending to pat Fluffinella, who had set small, muddy paws against my leg.

"Thank you, Lord Kai," answered Shiriki. "Can we take up residence in the Lung Shan's old cave once more?"

"In his old one and his newer," I said. "The Lung Shan was slain by the forces of Viss."

Chamballa turned upon me a gaze that motherhood had made far too wise. "But certainly you plan on reawakening the dragons of the mountains and the waters, Lord Kai!"

"I hadn't thought about it," I said, not quite truthfully for I *had* asked the servitors to preserve the Lung Shan's bones. The truth was I doubted that any could replace my old friends. "Do you think I should?"

"You must!" she said indignantly. "The *feng shui* of the bottle cannot thrive without the dragons."

"True," I said, amused. "Have you been talking with Plum?"

"A little," she said, "but fu dogs understand *feng shui*."

"What else do you understand, I wonder?" I said.

"You never asked." Chamballa chuckled. "And I will never tell. You'll simply need to learn by observation."

"I see." I knew that she was offering a puzzle to awaken a spirit made curiously dry and uninterested by the events of the day.

"Lord Kai," said Shiriki, "you'll want to be getting clean and to start preparing for guests."

"Guests?" I said, a mite indignantly. "I invited no one. Who is coming here?"

Fluffinella began, "Ba Wa and Wong Pang . . ."

"And Plum and Li Piao," interrupted another, yapping shrilly to be heard over her sister's voice.

"And Seven Fingers, Spilling Moonbeams, He of the Towers of Light, the Walker . . ."

The chorus of puppy barks stopped and round golden glances met each other as the pups reviewed their list.

"That's all," said Fluffinella.

"That's quite enough!" I said sharply. "Especially since I did not invite a one."

"They wanted to speak with you," Chamballa explained, "and tell you of the aftermath of the battle."

"There were decisions that had to be made," Shiriki continued, "such as what to do with Devor and his human allies, and whether to return the stolen weapons to the Armory of Truce."

"Let others decide," I growled. "I have done my part."

Chamballa gave me another of those too-discerning looks.

"If you do not care to speak with your friends, then they can visit our family."

I bit back a protest. I had told the fu dogs to consider my bottle their home. I couldn't well do that and then refuse to let them have guests. A bit ill-temperedly, I bowed to the inevitable.

"Take a bath, Lord Kai," Chamballa advised. "You'll feel more civilized when the blood is off and your wounds have begun to mend."

Grumpily, I acceded, walking to the waterside where my sailboat was berthed. Unbidden servitors brought me soap and towels and clothing retrieved from the ruin. They'd even found my hat with the red feather, miraculously intact.

I scrubbed and used *chi* to mend my wounds, until only those from the spirit sword remained. They would need to heal in their own time. As I cleaned myself and dressed in bright colors, my spirits rose. I found myself anticipating visitors.

When they arrived, I entertained them on the beach. I had

no silken cushions or fine carpets, but the sand was purest white and clusters of bamboo along the shoreline offered shade. I didn't need to worry about refreshments, for HE and Seven Fingers brought enough for even the greedy fu pups.

A moment of awkwardness—quite understandable, given what I had done an hour or so before—was broken when Wong Pang went pelting down the beach, chasing his own shadow in the sea foam. The fu pups followed behind, and we all watched, laughing to heal the soul.

"Ba Wa, is Wong Pang ever going to change back?" I asked.

"Don't guess so, boss," the scrub demon said, helping himself to sticky rice balls from one of the hampers. "He like being a dog—or he too stupid to change back."

"I don't see why he should," Plum said. "If he wants to, he can come home with me. He may be a stupid demon, but he's a smart dog."

"Ask him." Ba Wa grinned a pointy-toothed grin. "I bet he go with you."

Seated cross-legged in the sand, Li Piao had made a simple diamond kite out of food wrappings and thin strips of bamboo. I noted with amusement that he had carefully set the dragon bowl in the sand and offered its resident spirit something to eat.

"Do you have any string, Kai Wren?" he asked. "It seems far too great a time since I flew a kite."

I started to shake my head regretfully "no" when Seven Fingers reached into a pocket and produced a ball of thin twine.

"Here," he said, handing it to the old man. Then, his voice oddly gruff, he turned to me. "Lord Demon, if I could have a moment of your time in private."

"Of course," I said. "We can walk inland."

We did this thing, and Seven Fingers kept his silence until even the barking of the puppies faded into the distance.

"Lord Demon," he said formally, "do you recall how once I intimated that my daughter might be available if you wanted her for your bride?"

I recalled what he had said when we dined at the Conventicle and nodded. "Yes. She seemed quite interested, too."

"I . . ." The hulking, three-eyed swordsmith bit into his lower lip, looking for all the world more like a nervous boy than a powerful demon. "I regret to say that she is no longer available."

"Oh?" I cocked an eyebrow at him, wondering at the curious lightness of spirit I felt. "You have contracted another marriage?"

"More correctly, *she* has contracted one, without my consent, even though she knows my feelings on such matters."

"Demons are not ancient Chinese," I said, "and Spilling Moonbeams has her rights. Do you disapprove of the demon she has chosen?"

"No," he answered honestly, "I do not. He is a powerful demon and his house is among the best. She wants to marry the Walker."

"His house *is* good," I said, "and HE agrees?"

"Yes."

"Why has she changed her mind?" I asked. "Is it because I never offered and the Walker did?"

"That is part of it. The other part is . . ." Again Seven Fingers chewed his lip. "The other part is that she says you are too human for her tastes."

"Too human?"

"Yes."

"The human-style emotions?"

"The love, particularly. Spilling Moonbeams views it as a great weakness."

"Ah. It is, I suppose. She doesn't love the Walker, of course."

"No!"

"But she wants to make a contract with him."

"Yes. She likes his company, his courage, his point of view. She also thinks that his urge to travel will make certain that she is the primary authority in their home. After being second in prominence in my home, I believe she is eager to stretch her boundaries."

"Then it sounds like a good match."

"You will not sue for breach of contract?"

"We never made one," I said, "only discussed it in the most general fashion. I will give them my best wishes. Perhaps they might like a bottle as a gift. I have a lot on my hands just now."

"I am certain. They would be honored to have a bottle."

"It would need to be a sort of long-term lease, I'm afraid. I don't think I'll be selling any more. I learned my lesson from Viss. I'll keep track of them all now."

"They will understand the wisdom of a lease."

"Very good. Now, shall we rejoin the party?"

"Let's."

When we returned, Seven Fingers excused himself to find the Walker and Spilling Moonbeams, who had gone for a stroll beneath the waves. Li Piao and He of the Towers of Light were down the beach a ways, flying the kite. The dogs were romping farther down the shore. Only Plum remained.

She was sitting with her top hat beside her in the sand, looking out over the ocean, but for all her apparent absorption, she knew at once when I came up.

"How are you doing?" she asked.

"Fine." I sighed. "It has been a day, though."

"Did you hear about the Walker and Spilling Moonbeams?"

"Yes."

"And?"

"And I think that it's nice. They suit each other."

"You're not hurt?"

"Oh, maybe my pride, just a little. It's not easy to have a demoness go from idolizing and adoring you to wanting to marry someone else. Still, I think it's the best choice. She's right about me."

"What about you?"

"I've become too human."

Plum looked at me, seeing a creature eight feet tall with deep blue skin, talons, claws, and fangs. She began to laugh.

"You!" Then she quieted. "Maybe Spilling Moonbeams is right. Appearance isn't what makes a person. I should know that. My clients prefer when I dress a bit outré. They take comfort from my top hat, the way I wear my hair, my clothing. Never mind that I could analyze the *feng shui* of their property just as well if I was wearing gym shorts and a tee shirt."

"So would you be more comfortable with me if I looked like this?" I shifted shape to the human form I used most often.

"Well, it's easier to think of you as 'human' then."

We sat there for a while, watching the gulls and sandpipers.

"Plum, can I ask you a question?"

"I reserve the right not to answer," she said.

"Can I hire you to help with the *feng shui* here?" I asked.

She looked offended. "You don't need to hire me! I would consider it a privilege."

"I'd hire you anyway," I said. "When I've retrieved my bottles, I'll have wealth and resources to spare."

"True."

"Tell me, do you think me still at all human?" I asked after a pause. "I wonder if I lost the capacity to experience emotion when the spell was broken."

She studied me. "How did you feel when you slew Viss?"

"Terrible," I answered honestly, "yet it needed to be done."

"Viss asked you to kill her," Plum said. "I heard her."

"That, too."

"Is that why you did it?"

"Yes."

"Because you loved her once?"

"Yes."

"Did you hate her at the end?"

"No."

"Even after everything she did to you?"

"No. I hated some of the things she had done. I hated the death of Oliver O'Keefe and of the denizens of my bottle, but I don't think I hated Viss."

Plum turned to face me. "Then you're human in your loving, but you might be something else in that she didn't make you hate her. I would have hated her if she had done that to me."

"But I'm at least somewhat human?" I prompted.

"Yes."

"Human enough for you to consider marrying me?"

Her brown eyes went wide with surprise and disbelief.

"You can't mean that! I've heard how demons speak of humans. I'm not one of you."

"Nor am I, any longer."

She still didn't answer, so I continued, explaining myself to me as much as to her.

"For the last thousand years, I've lived with emotions that demons don't usually feel. My closest friends in recent centuries have been human—Ollie and your grandfather. I've been lonely. I know that now, but I wouldn't be content with a demoness. I might love her, but she would never be able to love me."

An "Oh," from Plum, very soft, but nothing more. I forged on.

"So I'm asking you. You are an outsider in the human world—your magic makes you so, just as my emotions separate me from demons."

"But I'll age and die in just a few years, as you see it."

"I offered Li Piao the Peach of Immortality."

"You did!"

"He refused, said he wanted to live out his life as a human, to finish growing old."

"I can hear him saying that," she said, looking to where the kite flew, a spot of red and white against the blue sky. "He's like that. Look at him, flying a kite when he has magic enough to fly himself."

"You don't need to make his decision, Plum. I don't despair of getting Li Piao to change his mind someday. He's had many strange experiences these past few weeks. They may have altered his point of view."

"True."

We sat in silence for a long while, listening to the cries of the birds and the barking of the dogs.

"Do you love me, Kai Wren?" she said after a time.

In answer, I touched her face, turned it so that I could look into those deep brown eyes. Within me, love was still tangled up with the discovery that it made one vulnerable. Could I make myself vulnerable to this human-born sorceress?

Looking at her, I played across the tablet of my mind scenes of her courage, her steadiness, her patience, her humor.

"I think I could. How about you, me?"

"It's possible," she said with a grin, "but I'd never considered the thought. I need to get used to it."

"I see," I said. I frowned. "I guess you aren't going to throw yourself into my arms, weeping with gratitude for my proposal."

"Sorry. Why don't we try dating?" she offered. "Get to know each other better first. Immortality is a big offer. You shouldn't hand it out lightly."

"I'm not!"

"Well, then"—she patted my leg comfortingly—"try to see things from my point of view. I don't want to make the wrong decision. You've given me two tremendous offers, immortal life . . . Does that come with youth and health?"

"It does," I assured her. "No Tithonus here."

"And you've offered me marriage," she finished. "Two amazing, astonishing, impossible things. Let me think."

"My wounded pride!" I exclaimed theatrically. "My fate must be to be spurned by beautiful women!"

"I'm not spurning you," she said, exasperated. "I'm just thinking."

"I know." I laughed, daring to enfold her in my arms. "I know. Can I buy you a pizza this Saturday night? Tony's on at Pizza Heaven."

"Sure," she said, leaning her head against my shoulder.

"And we could go visit the sages who live in the other bottles. I've been concerned about them."

"I'll need to check my schedule," she said, "but that could be fun."

Thinking of other things we could do, other wonders we could explore, I tightened my hold on her. Somehow, I knew I would never want to let her go.

The telling thing was that I knew that I would never hold too tightly, for such is the mystery of love.